carrington cove: book one

SOMEWHERE YOU *belong*

HARLOW JAMES

Copyright © 2024 by Harlow James

All rights reserved.

No part of this publication may be reproduced, distributed, or transmitted in any form or by any means, including photocopying, recording, or other electronic or mechanical methods, without the prior written permission of the publisher, except as permitted by U.S. copyright law. For permission requests, contact [include publisher/author contact info].

The story, all names, characters, and incidents portrayed in this production are fictitious. No identification with actual persons (living or deceased), places, buildings, and products is intended or should be inferred.

Book Cover by Abigail Davies

Editing by Jenny Ayers (Swift Red Pen)

ISBN: 9798325373770

Contents

Dedication	V
Epigraph	VI
Content Warning	VII
Prologue	1
1. Chapter 1	4
2. Chapter 2	12
3. Chapter 3	24
4. Chapter 4	39
5. Chapter 5	51
6. Chapter 6	68
7. Chapter 7	81
8. Chapter 8	101
9. Chapter 9	114
10. Chapter 10	130
11. Chapter 11	147
12. Chapter 12	155
13. Chapter 13	173

14.	Chapter 14	181
15.	Chapter 15	196
16.	Chapter 16	228
17.	Chapter 17	255
18.	Chapter 18	268
19.	Chapter 19	284
20.	Chapter 20	305
21.	Chapter 21	319
22.	Chapter 22	337
	Also By Harlow James	350
	Acknowledgements	353
	Connect with Harlow James	355

To anyone who has ever felt lost.

Figuring out who you are is the best way to find out where you belong.

Get to know yourself: who you are on the inside, what matters to you in your relationships, and what you want out of your life.

I promise, it's the best work you'll ever do.

True belonging never asks us to change who we are.

True belonging requires us to be who we are.

Brene Brown

Content Warning

Somewhere You Belong involves heavy military themes including flashbacks to war scenes, mentions of death, and suicidal thoughts. If any of those subjects are triggering to you, please proceed with caution.

Prologue

1991

My body sways in my seat as the Humvee bumps slowly along the dirt road, making its way toward our camp. The sweltering summer heat presses in on us through the windows.

I turn to the journalist sitting next to me and ask, "Where are you from?"

"Virginia." He smiles proudly.

"And I take it this is your wife?"

The woman in question leans across her husband to shake my hand. "Yes. Nice to meet you, soldier."

"You can call me Sheppard, ma'am," I reply, intercepting her small palm in mine and then readjusting myself in my seat, holding my gun to my chest. "So what brought you two over here?"

The man huffs out a laugh. "We're here to capture the human side of this conflict. It's one thing to report on strategies and politics, but we want to tell the stories of the people affect, the soldiers on the ground." I nod in acknowledgement. "I can understand that. There are many untold stories in times like these."

"I'm still very nervous though," the wife chimes in. "And we're so far away from our daughter."

"How old is she?"

"Two." She reaches into her pocket and extracts a Polaroid picture. Eyes so full of happiness stare back at me, the beautiful little girl with two blonde pigtails holding a stuffed duck in her hands standing proudly for the picture.

"She's beautiful," I reply as the woman brings the photo back to her lap, her eyes locked onto it. "Who is she with while you're gone?"

"A good friend of mine from college and her husband," the woman answers, fondly trailing her finger over the picture. "Our parents live too far away to watch her, and truth be told, aren't that involved as far as grandparents go."

The vehicle continues to roll along the rugged and uneven roads, forcing us to rock with the movements.

"Do you have children?" The woman asks me.

"Yes, I do, ma'am."

"It's hard to leave them, but sometimes we have to make that choice."

"I understand that more than you know."

Commotion outside of my window catches my attention and puts my senses on high alert as a man begins to approach the vehicle, his arms flailing high above his head, screaming something in the native language that I can't quite make out. He looks panicked, fear stricken, and desperate.

"Reddington, stop the vehicle," I order the soldier driving the car.

"We're not supposed to stop, sir."

"I'm ordering you to stop."

The vehicle slowly rolls until the tires are firmly planted in place, and I watch as the civilian freezes about thirty feet away. As I step out of the vehicle, a sense of dread crawls up my spine with each step I take toward him. But before I can even speak, he reaches behind his back and grabs a small device.

The deafening sounds of the explosion hit me before anything else registers. And then there's the overpowering stench of gasoline mixed with the musky scent of dirt, a smell that is unmistakable—and unforgettable.

Clouds of dust and debris are all I can see when I first open my eyes and try to blink away the disorientation of what just happened, along with the ringing in my ears. I struggle to grasp how much time has passed since the man activated his device, and then every one of my senses comes alive as the shock subsides and reality crashes in.

"Fuck!" I scream, rolling onto my side on the ground, frantically looking for the two journalists and Reddington, the driver.

What the fuck happened?

And that's when I see it to my right—what's left of the Humvee, what's left of the husband and wife and my fellow soldier. And there, next to me on the ground, perfectly intact except for its singed edges, lies the Polaroid. The little girl with blonde pigtails and soulful eyes stares back at me, her life forever changed.

And it's all my fault.

Chapter One

Willow

Present Day

"Katrina, did Fletcher ever call back?" I call to my assistant as I shuffle through the papers on my desk, searching for a Post-it note she may have left me, but I know the bright pink paper would be sticking out if there were one among the sea of white.

"No," Katrina says as she strides through the door of my office, landing right on the other side of my desk. But I don't look up at her as I pick up the other stack of papers to my right, eager to review the latest marketing campaign submitted for approval from one of my teams.

Marshall Advertising is my pride and joy, the company I started from the ground up when I left the University of Nevada and traveled back to Washington, D.C. in hopes of making a name for myself in our nation's capital.

And I have.

Just three years ago, my company hit the multimillion-dollar mark.

As owner and CEO, I make it my mission to be involved in every aspect of the business while keeping it very separate from my personal life. Separating emotions from my work means I can make tough decisions and still sleep at night. And taking ownership of what I've created means I'm in control, the way I like to be—*the way I need to be*.

"Um, Willow…" Katrina quietly starts, pulling my eyes up to her. She's chewing on her bottom lip as she clutches her iPad to her chest.

"What's wrong?"

"There was…a *situation* this morning during one of the meetings with our remote team." Her eyes widen as she speaks.

We have several employees that work remotely since they live in other parts of the country, but very rarely are there any issues. In fact, hiring remote staff has allowed us to double the number of accounts we can represent. It was a smart business decision, but the look on her face has me questioning if that's still true.

"What kind of situation?" I ask hesitantly as I drop the pen and papers from my hands to give her my full attention.

"Well, I think I'd rather just let you watch the video." With a shaky hand, she hands me the iPad and then steps away from my desk, as if the video in question might reach through the screen and grab her.

With a pinch in my brow and a slightly accelerated heart rate, I press play on the recording from the Zoom call and watch, waiting for something to catch me off guard.

And boy, does it ever.

"Is that…"

"Yes." She pauses. "That's a penis, Willow."

On one of the small screens in the video, a man stands up, showcasing his rather proud and rock-hard erection with semen leaking from the tip as if he just finished making himself "happy" during the meeting. And if I'm being honest, it doesn't look like his dick was camera-ready.

But then, as the rest of the employees notice the inappropriate display of his manhood, the supervisor, Francis, freaks out and begins yelling, clicking around frantically in an attempt to minimize the offender's window, but ends up pinning his screen, so the entire view of the call is of his dick.

"Oh. My. God," I say, channeling my inner Janice from *Friends*.

Katrina's lips fold in as I look up at her. "Yeah."

"Holy hell." I shake my head, unable to look away from the chaos going on in the Zoom call. "I don't even know what to say."

"Francis has already handled it and terminated the employee, but I figured you'd prefer to be in the loop."

I shut the iPad off and set it on my desk, heaving out a sigh. "I appreciate that, although, I'm pretty sure I would have been happier never having seen that in the first place."

Katrina stifles her laugh. "Agreed."

"Anything else? Maybe a surprise nip slip on a client call? Did someone shit their pants during a pitch?" My words drip with sarcasm. How can I not be a little on edge after an unsolicited, face-to-face encounter with an employee's penis at nine in the morning?

"Nothing as bad as that. Your meeting at eleven got pushed until one. Fletcher hasn't returned your call yet, but I plan on sending a follow-up email when I get back to my desk. And this came for you." She pulls an envelope from under her arm, swapping it with the iPad that's now sitting on my desk.

I glance at the address written on the envelope.

From the law offices of Timothy McDonald, Carrington Cove, North Carolina.

"Looks like junk mail. I don't recognize this name or place." I try to hand it back to Katrina, but she doesn't move to take it.

"The courier said you might say that, but he assured me it is meant for you, Willow Marshall. He even confirmed your age before leaving it."

My age? What the heck?

My eyes scan over the writing once more as I run my thumb over the crisp, white envelope. "Well, okay then."

"I'll be at my desk if you need anything." Katrina leaves my office as my mind begins to spin with questions.

With absolutely no idea who this could be from, I run my finger under the seal, breaking it open to extract the paper folded up inside. I momentarily debate if I should be more cautious, especially given my public status. But my gut tells me if someone wanted to sabotage me, they wouldn't do it with a hand-addressed envelope.

As I take in the words on the paper, utter shock slams into me as my heart rate climbs. My eyes race across each line and it suddenly feels hard to breathe, my mind spinning as flashes of memories infiltrate my mind.

I never imagined a piece of my past would come hurtling into my present.

But it has.

And it's calling me to Carrington Cove.

***

"I'm sorry. You're headed where?" Shauna, my best friend, asks for clarification as I continue to cruise down the highway, well more than halfway into my drive. When I called the law office to clarify the intent of the letter, the attorney explained that all matters were best discussed in person, so here I am, driving to this town I've never heard of.

"North Carolina."

"And you said it's for some inheritance?"

"That's what the letter said. I don't even know who this man is, Shauna, but he said he knew my parents. Am I crazy for driving down there? What if it's a scam?"

Given the magnitude of my company's success, I've grown wary of people wanting to get close to me for the wrong reasons. And a long-lost friend of my parents sounds like the perfect con to back me into a corner, especially since they died when I was two and there's hardly anyone left who knew them. I have no other family except for Mandy and Jason, my godparents who took custody of me per my parents' will.

But Mandy, who practically raised me on her own after she and Jason divorced, never mentioned the man behind this letter. I figured I would wait until I knew more before asking her about it. No sense in stirring up old memories for nothing. Besides, Shauna is the first sounding board I turn to when I need to talk, and I know she'll tell me what I need to hear.

We met at UNLV and bonded quickly over our love of sarcasm and shared disinterest in dating. My focus was on my degree to kick-start my business, while she navigated a breakup with her high school boyfriend. From then on, it was us against the world—well, until she ended her engagement last fall and returned to Newberry Springs to reconcile with her high school sweetheart, Forrest. Now, she's happily expecting their son.

"You said you confirmed the law firm is legitimate, right? So the letter most likely is too, Willow. They wouldn't risk their reputation on a scam."

That right there. There's the logical perspective that I needed.

"That's true."

"And it could be some sort of mix-up, but if there's a connection to your parents, you owe it to yourself to find out."

Shauna is the only person I've ever been honest with about how losing my parents has affected me. I might not have been old enough to remember them, but that loss has haunted me and left a giant hole in my chest I've never quite filled. Add on a lack of a stable family unit and less than stellar luck in dating throughout my life, and it just became easier to shut off my feelings about my past than try to deal with them.

But with every mile I drive, it feels like someone is widening that hole, digging roughly into the hard surface I've built to cover old wounds as the anticipation of what awaits me intensifies.

"I know. I just…I don't have time for this. Business is so crazy. The holiday season is coming and there are so many accounts we have pitches and campaigns to get ready for. Oh! And you won't believe what happened the other day."

"Well, you have time and so do I waiting for this baby to come out, so spill all the details."

I spend the next several minutes recounting the morning wake-up call of a dick on screen three days ago.

"Do you think he was jacking off during the meeting, then?" she asks through her laugh.

"I mean, that's what it looked like. Perhaps the dog food campaign they were working on really got him fired up and horny?" Shauna cackles as I switch lanes. "But if stuff like that is happening, it just goes to show that the last thing I should be doing right now is following a wild-goose chase."

"First of all, you can't control when a man decides to whip out his dick, Willow. That's beyond the scope of running a company, and I think any other CEO would agree."

The corner of my mouth lifts. "Fair point."

"And secondly, you and I both know that you're a workaholic, and you take on so much more than you need to in your role."

"That's a matter of opinion."

"No, it's a fact. You could delegate way more than you do." Shauna lets out a big sigh as I consider her perspective, not liking how it makes me feel. "Look, I know you have all sorts of questions right now, but you won't have any answers until you meet with the attorney tomorrow. So, figure out the details and make decisions then. But please, Willow, at least enjoy the change of scenery. When's the last time you took a day off?"

I start thinking back, searching desperately for a date to give her.

"Your lack of a response is your answer. It's been too freaking long."

Sighing, I flip my blinker on and move into the lane on my right. "Fine. You're right. I just hate not having all the information."

"Oh, I'm aware. You're the biggest control freak I know. But believe me, sometimes when life throws you a curve ball, it can turn out to be for the best. Look at me and Forrest."

"I'm pretty sure you ran into Forrest again two weeks before you were about to marry another man, and then you ended up leaving that man at the altar. How is that not disastrous?"

She laughs, but replies, "You're right. It was disastrous at first. But then it led me back to the man I never stopped loving and in a few weeks, we're going to be parents. I'd say that's pretty serendipitous, wouldn't you?"

"Yeah, I guess," I murmur in agreement, knowing that I've never seen my best friend so happy. I'm just not feeling particularly agreeable at the moment.

"Always the optimist." She pauses and then says, "Just breathe, Willow."

I let out the breath I was holding. "How did you know I needed that reminder?"

"Because that's what you do when you're stressed. I'm sorry I can't be there with you, but it's going to be okay."

"And what if it's not?"

"Then you'll tackle whatever comes your way. Because you're Willow fucking Marshall and that's what you do. You're a survivor."

"Thank you," I mutter as I feel the sting of tears. But I fight them down and focus on the road.

Shauna lets out a yawn. "I'm always here. However, I am exhausted so I'm going to let you go so I can take a nap."

"Fine. I guess you can go and continue growing my nephew."

"Thanks for your permission. Text me when you get there safely."

"I will. I still have a while to go, though."

"Enjoy the ride, Willow. I have a feeling you're in for one hell of one."

Why is it that at this moment, I get that feeling in my gut too?

Chapter Two

Dallas

"You gonna stand there and stare at her all night, or are you actually going to do some work?"

Penn, my younger brother, pushes himself off the bar and shoves me as he walks past. "I wasn't fucking staring at anything."

"Yeah, just keep telling yourself that," I mutter as I wipe the counter down.

"Fucker," he grumbles as he pushes through the door that leads to the back of the bar, leaving me out here all by myself.

Luckily, it's not very busy yet, which gives us a little bit of time to stock the front before the rush begins, and plenty of time for me to give my brother shit for his unrequited crush.

Astrid comes over, brushing her bangs from her eyes with her forearm. "Everything okay, Dallas? What's wrong with Penn?"

"What's *not* wrong with Penn?"

She rolls her eyes. "I swear you two fight more than you get along."

"Mostly."

She sets her tray down on the counter and moves to the computer to input an order. "We still have fish and chips, right?"

"Yeah, plenty. Harold made quite the catch this morning, so we should be good for a few days at least." Harold is a long-time Carrington Cove resident that brings in fresh fish for all of the local businesses, especially mine. And his luck today means more money in both of our pockets.

She nods. "Perfect."

My eyes carry over Catch & Release, my bar and restaurant that has been prospering over the past four years, the windows in the front of the establishment offering a breathtaking view of the cove that is our town's namesake, which draws in tourists from the beginning of spring through the end of fall.

After leaving the Marines and returning home twelve years later, I wanted something that I could pour my heart and soul into, a place that would keep me busy and leave me with little time to think since my mind loves to torment me if left to its own devices.

Bill, the former owner, was looking to sell and retire around that time, so I jumped on the opportunity. I had no idea how to run a restaurant or bar, but I picked it up quickly and have kept this place thriving since I took over. Although an established clientele and the booming tourism in Carrington Cove definitely helps too.

Catch & Release is the quintessential coastal bar, everything inside decorated in a nautical theme—fishnets hanging from the walls with starfish and seashells scattered throughout, old anchors mounted to the walls' wooden slats, and navy-blue booths and padded chairs at each of the dark wooden tables. Steel lamps hang above each table and the bar is edged in the same steel, lining the surface made of reclaimed wood.

It's rustic and familiar, perfectly capturing the essence of our town in the décor and the hospitality we offer, an experience that keeps people coming back for more.

Penn returns from the back of the restaurant a few minutes later, carrying cases of beer and liquor.

"Is Dallas giving you shit again?" Astrid asks when she returns from her table, leaning against the bar as she smiles at my younger brother.

Penn just stares at her, much like he does any time the woman is in his view. I'm sure even a kindergartener could pick up on his crush. Thankfully, he finds his voice quickly. "When is he not?" he grunts as he moves around her.

Astrid shakes her head at us and then steps to the soda fountain to fill drinks. "You two are so much alike sometimes that it's frightening." She pushes glasses against the metal triggers as soda fills each one up.

"I take offense to that," I counter, slapping my rag on the bar.

"Yeah, so do I," Penn adds.

Astrid glares at us over her shoulder. "I do not have time to referee you two today. I have money to make, and you're both in my way." She stands in front of us, a tray full of beverages filled and waiting to be delivered, her eyebrow arched as she waits for us to move.

It's a look I've also seen our mother give us a time or two and Astrid nails it flawlessly.

Penn and I part and let her by.

"Her children must be downright terrified of her," I say jokingly.

"She's a good mom," Penn replies under his breath, restocking the bar.

I slap my hand on his shoulder. "Hey, I don't have time for you to mope tonight, all right? We have that reservation of twenty people coming in for a birthday party, and we're down a server. Sally called out."

Penn shoves me off. "I'm not moping."

"Ha. Okay." I decide to drop it. There's no use in poking that bear anymore, or he won't be any use to me at the bar tonight.

It's a Friday night and that always means business will be good. Between people coming in for the fresh fish and chips special, celebrating the end of another work week with a drink or two, or tourists arriving for the weekend, there will be no slowing down until the bar shuts down in the wee hours of the morning.

It's nights like this that make me grateful I live above the restaurant in the small apartment the previous owner built when he bought the building. It's perfect for a single guy like me and makes the commute to and from work a breeze. However, sometimes I feel like I never leave this building, but hopefully that will change soon.

Buying a house is in my future plans—I'm just waiting for the right hand to be dealt my way.

By the time seven o'clock hits, the bar is swamped. There's a line of customers around the building, a waitlist a mile long, and the kitchen is pumping out food as fast as the cooks can. My bartenders and servers are running a flipping marathon with a smile on their face, and I am filling in wherever I'm needed.

"How's it going, gentlemen?" I set three beers on the round table in the corner, where Harold, Baron, and Thompson are seated in their usual spot as the hostess fills the empty booth beside them that I just cleaned. These three men have probably lived in Carrington Cove as long as the town has been established, except for the time they spent serving as Marines, that is.

"Be careful who you're calling gentlemen, Dallas. I'm about to kick their asses in darts, and that means things are about to get ugly." Baron tips his glass in my direction before taking a sip of his beer.

"This one." Harold juts his thumb over at Baron. "Always counting his chickens before they hatch. Everyone knows I'm the reigning champ."

"Ha! Let me get a few more beers in you and then we'll see who's winning," Thompson interjects, partaking in their usual shit talking before they take control of the dart board in the corner of the bar area.

Even before I took over ownership of the place, these three have spent every Friday night at Catch & Release challenging each other in darts. And since I don't want to start a fight, I decide to keep the fact to myself that Harold is, in fact, the one who wins the most.

"Well, the night is young boys, and anything can happen, right?" I say as I stand back, placing my hands on my hips.

"When are you gonna play with us one of these nights, Dallas?" Baron asks.

"When you three can stay out past ten."

They all cackle as I walk away, back to managing the increasing number of people filling the room while making sure the kitchen is staying on top of the influx of orders.

Regulars fill the tables, nodding hellos as I pass by. I recognize many veterans I've met over the years, whom I offer a discount—a courtesy I give to anyone for their service to our country since I know personally what that sacrifice is like.

Anyone unfamiliar is assumed to be a tourist or someone from a town nearby, but the chatter and laughter ringing out sends a wave of pride through me. It's a satisfying feeling, knowing my place brings joy to others.

It's rare to have these moments, where everything feels right and the world is still spinning as it should. So much has happened recently and throughout the years that the axis feels off-kilter more often than not, but nights like this help me feel like my world is slowly returning to normal, or as close to normal as it can get.

Just before nine o'clock, I find myself behind the bar helping fill drink orders. I'm grateful for YouTube videos to add to my non-existent bartending skills, but between Penn, Tabitha, and me, we manage to fulfill any drink order that comes our way. My brother has worked a few nights here with me ever since I bought the place, but he had prior experience tending bar while I was deployed. During the day, though, he works at the hardware store and is known as the residential handyman around our little town. He truly is a jack-of-all-trades, and I'm grateful for his help.

I flick my eyes in the direction of the door, the waiting area still packed with people, and that's when my eyes land on a woman that certainly isn't from around here, her tall stature and poised presence sticking out like a sore thumb.

She wears a white silk blouse and a black pencil skirt that hugs shapely curves. Her blonde hair is slicked back into a low bun that rests right at the base of her neck, and her pursed, plump lips are painted a cherry red, intoxicating and forbidden.

Any woman I've ever seen wearing red lipstick usually wears it for one of two reasons. One, because she's feeling sexy and is ready for attention or a little danger—or two, she wears it as a shield, letting everyone know that she's impenetrable and in need of no one else.

She's the one in control.

Her eyes scour the room, assessing the crowd with a slight curl to her lips as if the establishment is beneath her. Then her gaze locks onto the last empty seat at the bar, one that was just vacated moments ago, and the click of her heels rings out as she sways her hips with each step in my direction.

I spin around, not wanting to be caught staring at the woman—by her or anyone else. That's all I need is for Penn to see me before he starts giving me the same shit I give him.

Plus, the last thing I need right now is trouble, and that's exactly what this woman exudes—trouble with a capital T.

I make myself busy for a few minutes, helping other customers and moving down the bar before finally standing right before the mystery woman. Sliding a cardboard coaster across the surface of the bar in front of her, I wait for her to acknowledge me before I speak. But she's entranced in her phone.

"Dirty martini, three olives," she says without meeting my gaze, her fingers continuing to tap the keys on her screen. Studying her, I wait a few moments to see if she'll finally meet my eyes. But after one long-ass minute, I finally give up and speak to her instead.

"Was there a *please* behind that order?"

That catches her attention. Brown eyes like pools of melted milk chocolate swirled with caramel lift and stare back into mine. And that's when I feel like someone just slapped me across the face with a brick.

Shit, she's stunning up close.

"I'm sorry?" she asks, tilting her head at me, a perplexed look on her face.

Trying to fight against the way she just paralyzed me, I reply, "I heard your order, but didn't hear a please after it."

One of her brows arches painfully high on her forehead, but her lips curl into a grin. "Are you allowed to speak to me like that?"

"You bet your ass I am." Resting my forearms on the bar, I lean over it slightly.

Her eyes narrow on me now as she slides her tongue across her teeth, her lips still closed. "Can I have a dirty martini with three olives, *please*?" she grates, clearly irritated with the challenge I dished out. But I don't care who you think you are or where you're from, manners go a long fucking way.

"There's the magic word." I dip my chin and say, "Coming right up." I push off the bar and reach to the side, gathering a glass to make her drink, fighting the urge to look up at her again. But I can feel her watching me, tracking each one of my movements as if I might try to poison her after our exchange. When I'm done, I slide the drink across the bar to her. "Here you go."

"*Thank you*," she punctuates her reply as she takes a sip of her drink, smacking her lips in approval, and then moves her gaze back to her phone, ignoring me once more.

Irritation runs through me, so I take the opportunity to check on other customers, even move to the kitchen to make sure the cooks have everything they need and refill their cups with ice water. It gets hot as hell back there, so I try to keep them as comfortable as possible.

Back out in the front of the restaurant, I make sure to keep my distance from the woman that captivated me when I have no idea why. Everything about her screams red flag.

But she also got your blood pumping, didn't she, Dallas?

My eyes drift over to her casually as I stand behind the bar again, taking note that her drink is empty. Reminding myself that she's still a customer, I inhale deeply and then make my way over to where she's sitting. "Care for another?"

She bites her lip, staring at her drink, and then up at me—the movement so calculated it almost makes me think that she's flirting with me. But then she speaks. "Are you going to make me say *please* again?"

The corner of my mouth tips up this time, in response to her wit. "Of course. Manners are important, ma'am."

"Ma'am?" She scoffs. "Yup. I'm definitely not in the city anymore."

A city girl, huh? I wonder which one. Raleigh? Atlanta?

Why do you care, Dallas? Just make her a god damn drink.

Before I can fire off a witty reply, she sighs. "Well, I guess I can't argue with an appreciation for manners. I'll have another, *please*. It will help take the edge off this long-ass day."

As I pour the gin and reach for the olives again, I take a moment to appreciate the fact that she cussed, revealing a little crack in the shield she wears.

Personally, I love a woman that can use profanity and not feel ashamed about it. I think it shows confidence in who they are and how they communicate. It shows authority too.

My mouth starts moving without permission. "You don't seem like you want to be here."

She huffs, flipping her phone upside down. "Not at all, actually."

"And you don't seem like you're from around here either."

"Nope." She pops the p.

I study her as I slide her drink across the bar. "Then what brings you to Carrington Cove? Most people are either from here or they're on vacation. Clearly, you're neither."

She swirls the liquid around in her drink, reaching for the stick of olives, placing it in her mouth before drawing it back out with one less olive attached. She locks her eyes with mine as I watch her chew, trying not to get lost in the visions my mind is conjuring of what else those red lips could be used for.

Finally she sighs. "You don't need to do this."

"Do what?"

"That small-town thing where you attempt to strike up a conversation to be polite. No offense, but I have no intention of being here long enough to establish some sort of repertoire with the townsfolk."

She darts her eyes around the room. "I'm here on business. Shouldn't be here more than a few days, I imagine. Just need to tie up a few loose ends."

"I see."

She takes another drink from her martini. "And believe me, this is the last place I thought I'd ever end up."

Crossing my arms over my chest, I stand against the bar, growing more curious about this woman, even though my brain is telling me to walk away.

But I'm a man—when do we ever listen willingly to our brains?

"And why is that? Carrington Cove is a great place."

"Ha. Yes, well, to someone like you, I guess that makes sense."

My head rears back on my neck. "Someone like me?"

She nods. "You have local handyman-bartender vibes written all over you," she says, waving her hand at me.

"More like restaurant and bar owner. My brother is the bartender and handyman."

"Well, good for you, and your brother, but I don't belong here." She brings her glass to her lips, draining her drink dry right before my eyes. I watch her throat bob up and down as she takes back the martini with minimal effort. As she sets the glass on the bar, she moves to stand, unsteady on her feet.

"You shouldn't be driving." I nearly reach out to steady her but catch myself.

"I'm fine," she says as she clears her throat, pasting on a smile.

"You're swaying in your Manolos."

"They're Louboutins, and they were not made for these uneven wooden floors," she retorts. "But I'm impressed you know designer shoes."

"Well, I figure the price of the shoe should match the pretention you exude," I reply, feeling myself grow more irritated with this woman by the second.

Who does she think she is waltzing into my town and sneering down at me, or anyone else for that matter?

"You have a lot of nerve judging me when you don't know the first thing about me." With a purse of her lips, she tosses a fifty-dollar bill on the counter and then reaches for her purse. "That should cover two martinis."

"More like four. That's too much."

"Keep the change. Consider it a large tip." She tosses her gaze around the room. "And perhaps you can use the extra money to buy yourself some manners as well." With a lift of her purse, she spins on her heels and walks away from me, and I hate that I'm watching her ass as she does.

Who the fuck is that woman?

It doesn't matter. She was just another tourist passing through. Don't let her get to you, Dallas.

"Who was that?" Penn asks, coming up beside me, mimicking my own thoughts as we both watch her walk out the door and down the sidewalk, the dark sky providing a backdrop that she clearly stands out against.

"Someone too good for our little town apparently."

Penn narrows his eyes at me. "What happened?"

"Nothing," I mutter, attempting to shake off the interaction with her. "I'm going to go into my office for a while. You think you can hold down the fort?"

He nods. "You got it."

I pat him on the back. "Don't stare at Astrid too much though, okay? I don't want a harassment suit to deal with."

Penn shoves my shoulder. "Fuck off."

Chuckling to myself, I push through the double doors and walk down the hallway that leads to my office. As I take a seat in my chair, I begin gathering paperwork with the intent to get some work done, but all I can see is *her*—the blonde from out of town, the stuck-up suit that clearly thought she was better than all of us here.

It's not the first time someone like that has come through our small town, and I'm sure it won't be the last. But I hate that no matter how hard I try, our conversation—albeit a brief one—won't leave my mind.

And neither does the image of her ass in that skirt and heels as she walked away from me.

Chapter Three

Willow

"Sleep. You need sleep and tomorrow this should all be over, Willow." The stressful breath that leaves my lips as I exit the small-town bar I stumbled upon when I arrived in Carrington Cove a little less than an hour ago has me feeling unsure about being here all over again.

And the owner—all broody and judgmental from the moment he laid eyes on me—he's the exact kind of person I want to avoid while I'm here.

One of the things I like about living in the city is the fact that people don't give a rat's ass about who you are or what you're doing. Everyone is too busy with their own lives, their own to-do lists and priorities, to be bothered about what's going on in the lives of others.

But in small towns like Carrington Cove, people make it their business to know *your* business, and that is not something I want to flirt with while I'm here, especially if those people look anything like that man, someone I *definitely* wanted to flirt with.

I've watched enough Hallmark movies to know what to avoid in a small town, and the man in question was wearing a freaking flannel.

That's like red flag number one!

It's not as if I've never seen a good-looking man before. I mean, I live in the capital of our country. They're everywhere—dressed in custom tailored suits, clutching briefcases like they hold all their power, smirking over cups of gourmet coffee, and eye-fucking you as you walk down the street in your heels and pencil skirt. Until they find out you're the owner of a multimillion-dollar business, and they only see you as a threat to their manhood.

Speaking of manhood, the image of that restaurant owner pops back into my mind for the fifth time since I left his bar, including the noticeable bulge in his jeans, indicating the size of his own manhood.

Jesus, Willow. Get a grip.

Ogling the citizens of this town while I'm here is definitely not on *my* to-do list, so I do my best to block out our brief interaction, start my car, and pull out of the parking space I found down the small one-way street near the building. I just needed a drink to take the edge off after the six-hour drive from Washington, D.C., and the eerie feeling I got as I crossed into the town limits—like this place held secrets and feelings, both of which I've been avoiding most of my life.

Turns out two drinks still wasn't enough to keep those feelings at bay.

After receiving that letter, let's just say unresolved feelings are all I've been able to focus on for the past few days—feelings a woman like me doesn't have time for.

I make my way down the two-lane road that winds along the coast, passing by small shops and businesses nestled tightly together along the boardwalk while the cove that offers the town's namesake glistens under the moonlight.

Part of me wonders what it would have been like to grow up in a place like this, where everyone knows your name, life is a lot slower, and people born here rarely ever leave.

Would my life be different if I grew up here?

The sign for the Carrington Cove Inn comes into view on my right just another mile up the road, so I take the exit and then pull into one of the empty parking spaces left in the lot. For a small inn, this place sure seems to be popular.

"Good evening." The cheery gray-haired woman behind the counter greets me as soon as I step inside.

"Hello. I have a reservation." I reach into my purse for my wallet.

"Okay, great. Can I have your name, please?"

"Willow Marshall," I reply, pulling out my credit card as the woman clicks away on the keyboard.

"I'm Dolly," she offers with a smile before glancing back at the screen. "Ah, yes. There you are. Good thing you called ahead. We're booked solid for the weekend."

"It did look like the lot was full out there."

"Tourists. Our little town depends on them for survival."

"Well, I'm not here for a vacation, that's for sure," I mutter under my breath.

The woman narrows her eyes at me, but a smile remains on her face. "You're not from around here, are you?"

"What gave me away?" I grin, appreciating how friendly this woman is compared to the bar owner from earlier.

Her eyes dance up and down my body. "Business attire, a purse that costs more than my mortgage probably…"

I decide not to give her a response to that remark because I'm pretty sure the answer is a resounding yes.

"What brings you to town then?"

I hand her my credit card and she finishes checking me in. "Just tying up some loose ends," I reply.

"Loose ends? Sounds messy."

"Messier than I need it to be or have time for." I flash her a tight-lipped smile as I take my card back from her. "So what room am I in?"

"104. It's the fourth room down that hallway to your right."

"Perfect. I'm guessing there's no room service in a little place like this, huh?" I'm partially teasing, but the other part of me is becoming increasingly aware that I'm not in the big city anymore and that means certain amenities I'm used to will be few and far between.

The woman winces through her smile. "No, dear."

"Didn't think so. Thank you, though." I hold up my silver key—not an electronic keycard like most modern-day establishments—and then turn toward the front door of the small lobby that smells of stale carpet and ocean air.

"We do have fresh muffins and coffee for our guests in the morning, though!" she calls after me. "Think of it as a continental breakfast, if you will."

"Good to know. Thank you." I tell her over my shoulder before I head for my car. I grab my suitcase from the trunk and stop to take in my surroundings. The vast, dark sky is a breathtaking expanse of twinkling stars.

Stars—gosh, when's the last time I saw actual stars, or even bothered to look up at them?

I shake off the thought and the twinge of sadness that resonates in my chest and wheel my suitcase to the door of my room, inserting the key in the lock, and jiggling it around a little before it finally turns and the door creaks open.

Oh my God. This is where I'm going to die.

As I take in my surroundings, all I can picture is the scene of movie where a woman stays alone in a cheap motel and answers the door when someone knocks, only to be kidnapped and murdered just for the main character to search for her body throughout the rest of the movie.

"This was a mistake," I mutter to myself as I close the door and lock it behind me, walking further into the room. The bedspread is made of rough cotton in a classic paisley fabric of reds, blues, and greens. The walls are a dark beige, and I can't tell if that's the color they were painted, or that color is a product of salty ocean air and age.

The bed is centered on the wall to my right, with a nightstand on each side complete with bedside lamps, and a red cushioned chair in the corner under the window. The room has one of those AC units under the window with the vents that blow up into the curtains, and on the wall to my left is a small tv stand and a box television that looks like it escaped from the '80s and is still surviving.

"I'm definitely not in D.C. anymore."

Once I'm changed, showered, and my teeth are brushed, I open my laptop, respond to emails that came in during my drive down here, and make sure my schedule is clear for tomorrow.

When I'm done, I lie in bed staring at the ceiling, thinking back over the last few weeks—how I ended up here in the first place, how this meeting tomorrow might go, and the letter that started it all.

And as I drift off to sleep, those familiar images come back to my mind—a woman with blonde hair like my own, a man whose smile I swear I can still remember, and the other memories I allow my brain to conjure up every once in a while—the ones I would have had if my parents hadn't died.

***

"There's not a Starbucks around here?" I ask Dolly when I make it down to the lobby, ready for the meeting I came all the way down here for.

She shakes her head. "Nope. Carrington Cove residents shut that idea down before it even made it to the town council."

"How did that happen?"

Dolly flashes me a knowing grin. "You'd be surprised what a group of strong-willed people are able to accomplish when they set their mind to something."

I try not to react, but instead swallow hard. "Noted."

"Anyway, that coffee on the table is the best you're going to get in town. Keely delivers it fresh every morning. She owns Keely's Caffeine Kick, the coffee shop on the boardwalk."

"Charming." I spin around to see a stack of Styrofoam cups and black plastic lids next to two insulated coffee dispensers, along with a basket of muffins complete with a red and white checkered cloth lining the inside.

"And the muffins are made fresh each morning by Greg and Jenny over at Sunrise Bakery."

"Well, okay then." I move to the table and help myself to the goodies as I feel the heat of Dolly's stare on my back.

"So what are you up to today?"

"I have a meeting," I mutter as I fill my cup to the brim with coffee.

"With whom?"

"Timothy MacDonald."

"The attorney?" There's a note of surprise in Dolly's voice.

I twist to see her eyebrows reaching her hairline. "Is there another one?"

"No. Just odd for an out-of-towner to be meeting with Tim."

"Well, like I said, I'm here on business."

Dolly hums in thought. "Well, you best get along. Traffic will start to back up along the parkway at this hour—tourists headed toward the beach and all that."

"Good to know. Thank you for the coffee and muffin," I say, and the memory of the bar owner chastising me about my manners pops up. But I don't have time to go down that road right now.

"Happy to oblige. Have a good day, Willow."

With one last smile in her direction, I hustle out of the lobby and back down to my car. Once I'm settled, a loud growl from my stomach reminds me I should probably eat, so I break off the muffin's crumble topping and plop it in my mouth.

"Holy crap," I mumble around the bite, letting the sugar and fresh blueberries swirl around in my mouth. That is, by far, the best blueberry muffin I've ever had.

I guess there is one perk about this place after all.

Once I finish chewing, I carefully take a sip from the coffee that is still steaming hot. And when the liquid hits my tongue—smooth and not too bitter—I let out a moan.

Okay, make that two perks.

Now I can see why a Starbucks isn't needed here.

"What kind of caffeine crack is this?" I take another sip, surrendering to some of the best coffee I've ever tasted before I start the car and pull out of the parking lot, following the signs to get back on the parkway.

And Dolly was right. It's stop and go traffic for miles, which feels like an eternity as I slowly roll along the coast.

But I take the opportunity to stare out at the water when traffic's stopped. Might as well.

In the distance, white reflections of light gleam off the dark-blue water. As my eyes veer closer to the shore, the blue lightens into patches of light turquoise. Green brush and grass pop up along the coast too, giving way to white sandy beaches and kids running around near the water, full of energy and laughter.

A deep breath of relief hits me all at once.

I can't remember the last time I saw the ocean, or felt the cool, salty water against my skin. I can't remember the last time I took a few days off from work either.

Running a company means your personal life often takes a backseat since you're more wrapped up in the lives of your clients and employees. And being one of the best in your field definitely means you don't get much of a break. I'm constantly grinding, pushing myself and my company to be the best because my job is my life.

It's the one thing that no one can take away from me.

But this trip is rattling the solid foundation I've built my life on, a realization that hit me hard as I fought sleep the night before.

When I arrive at Timothy MacDonald's office with five minutes to spare, I flip down the visor to check my appearance once more. Every hair is in place, swept back into my signature low bun. My lips are painted a deep rose color today and the black, square-neck dress I chose is professional and appropriate, given the circumstances.

"I'm here to see Timothy MacDonald," I say to the receptionist as I step into the office and up to her desk.

The woman, who can't be much older than me, stares up at my face over the rim of her round, black framed glasses. From what I can tell between last night and this morning, this town probably doesn't get many people dressed like me waltzing around here.

"And what is your name?" she asks with a slight southern drawl.

"Willow Marshall."

She flicks her eyes at me one more time with an assessing stare, and then clicks through the page on her computer screen. "Ah, yes. I see you here. If you want to take a seat, I'll let Mr. MacDonald know you're here."

"Okay. Thank you." I say as she stands and steps down a narrow hallway.

A few moments later, a balding man in a blue plaid shirt and khaki pants walks into the reception area.

"Thank you, Mable," he says to the receptionist as she returns to her desk.

"Of course, Mr. MacDonald."

He turns to face me, and his eyebrows rise as he takes in my dress. "Well, hello there."

"Hello." I stand to greet him, extending my hand. "Willow Marshall."

And then his eyes widen in recognition. "Well, what a pleasure it is to meet you in person, Miss Marshall. Please, follow me."

He takes a seat behind a cluttered desk as we enter his office, file folders stacked high and papers strewn about. In a rush, he clears a few stacks to the side and pulls a file from the stack, slapping it on his desk.

"I have to say, you are not what I was expecting." He rests his hands over his bulging belly.

"How so?"

"Well, when Mr. Sheppard made this decision, he always spoke of you as this little girl." He shakes his head and then chuckles. "I guess that *was* a long time ago. But in my mind, I guess I still pictured you as that little girl with pigtails."

"No pigtails for me these days, sir." A twinge of sadness grips my chest, but I unclench the hold it has on my heart and push it away.

He laughs louder this time. "I understand." I watch him take out a few papers from the folder, turning them to face me so I can read them. I lean over the desk, placing my hands on the surface as I peer down at the words on the paper. "Well, let's get down to it. Obviously, you've already read the letter since you're sitting here before me." I nod. "So, let's take a look at what you've inherited."

"I don't need anything from this man, Mr. MacDonald." I shake my head, feeling my nerves build with uncertainty the longer I sit here. "I don't even know him."

"Willow," he says, reaching over and placing his hand on mine, the gesture so foreign that I instantly retreat, pulling my hand back. "I'm sorry, dear. I'm not trying to be overbearing..."

"Just tell me why I'm here, please," I say over the lump in my throat, growing more anxious the longer I sit here in limbo.

"Mr. Sheppard, upon his death, wished to leave you with something." He pulls a paper from the stack and places it closer to me. "This is the deed to his house."

"What?" I gasp as my heart begins to hammer harder.

"The property sits right along the coast. It's isolated and a very sought-after piece of land."

"I—I don't understand." My eyes continue to scan the paper as my brain scrambles to absorb the words Mr. McDonald just uttered.

"Now the house needs some work," he says, leaning back in his chair and placing his hands on his belly again, intertwining his fingers and completely disregarding my response. "But I have to tell you, I think it's worth the investment. Even if you don't keep it, fixing it up and selling it will get you top dollar in this real estate market."

I slink back in the chair, my jaw dropping slightly. "He left *me* a house? Why?"

Mr. MacDonald nods. "He did. Brand new appliances have been installed per another stipulation upon his death. The electricity, gas, and water have also been activated. I have no idea what else is inside, but if you'd like to take a look, I have time to take you there." He pulls a key from a small envelope and places it in front of me.

"I..."

"I know you must have many questions, but you read the letter, dear." He tilts his head to the side, smiling softly at me.

And then the words from the letter replay in my mind.

And a fresh new wave of anger mixed with guilt comes crashing down on me.

***

"See? The bones are good." Timothy—he insisted we be on a first name basis as we left his office—leads me deeper into the home that has seen better days as he knocks on a wall that separates the kitchen from the living room. And as soon as the sound rings out, all I can think about is how that wall would look better with a hole cut out so you can see through the two rooms. Layers of dirt cake the floors and counters, and sheets cover old furniture in the open space. I honestly feel like I'm walking through a haunted house, even if it does have a beautiful view of the ocean rather than a forbidden forest.

"Um, sure," I respond, taking it all in.

"It originally belonged to Mr. Sheppard's grandparents. He loved this house, but it couldn't accommodate his growing family, so he just held on to it. It's been empty for years."

I turn to see him watching me as I stand in the center of the room. "I just...I'm still having a hard time wrapping my head around this."

"Understandable." He shrugs. "But my job was just to draw up the paperwork so his wishes were carried out. Beyond that, I'm afraid I can't offer much."

I nod, thinking back to the letter that started this entire adventure. And that's putting it optimistically—because right now, I feel like I'm living in a nightmare. What I hoped would be a quick, easy trip down to Carrington Cove and back in a weekend after learning of a random inheritance, has now turned into property ownership and a multitude of decisions to make.

Spinning around to take it all in, I decide I should probably get the full scope of what I'm working with. "Can I see the rest of it?"

"Of course." Timothy leads me up the staircase to three bedrooms—a master that has a balcony with a beautiful view of the ocean and two small bedrooms that would be perfect for an office or kid's room. The master bedroom is smaller than the one in my penthouse back in D.C., but it's also more welcoming.

The house is definitely not big enough for a large family, though, as Timothy pointed out, but it is enough for someone like me—unattached and kid free.

"So, what do you think?"

I shake my head, still perplexed by all of this. "I honestly don't know what to think, Timothy. This is the last thing I expected. My life is back in D.C."

"This could be a nice vacation home, somewhere to retreat to in the summer when you want to get out of the city," he suggests.

"With all due respect, Timothy, this is the first trip I've taken out of D.C. in eight years. I'm not exactly the vacationing type."

He tsks. "That's no good, Willow. You have to take a break from life every once in a while. Soak up the sun, bask in the breeze, visit somewhere you've never been," he says fondly, waving his arm around.

"Some place like Carrington Cove?" I ask sarcastically.

He nods, his smile growing. "Exactly. There's a reason people visit our town, travel far and wide for this kind of peace."

I scoff. "Does anyone ever truly find peace in their lives, Timothy?"

The way he narrows his eyes at me makes me think he can see right through me. "I think it's perfectly attainable, Willow. And perhaps you can find some while you're here." He moves toward the front door, turning his back to me. "I left the key on the counter for you."

"So that's it?" I call after him, desperation filling my voice.

He's just going to leave me here?

"The house is yours now. I did my part. Mr. Sheppard told me what his last wishes were, so I made them happen. I'm glad you're here, though, and I'm honored I could be a part of this story. But my role is done."

And I guess that's all I'm getting out of him. My eyes veer around the space. "And what if I want to sell it?"

"Pam over at Cove Real Estate can help you." He gives a mock salute and walks out the door. I'm normally comfortable being alone, but standing in this empty, strange house with all my unanswered questions magnifies the solitude somehow.

Standing in place, I survey the house once more, looking directly out the front windows toward the sandy shore just a few feet away.

I have no idea what to do with this.

A house? What in God's name was this man thinking? And if he had a family, why wouldn't he leave it to them?

Guilt overwhelms me, making each breath I fight to take burn my lungs.

This can't be happening.

How is this part of my past popping up right now?

Within seconds, I find myself numbly walking out of the house, pausing at the top of the staircase that leads down to the beach desperate for oxygen to fill my lungs as emotions barrel into me all at once.

As the salty ocean air whips against my face, I struggle to decide what I'm going to do.

I feel helpless, drowning in emotions and memories, flashes of a life I could have had if not for this man and his connection to my parents.

Reaching up, I yank on the neckline of my dress that feels like it's suffocating me the longer I stand here in view of the house that just flipped my world upside down.

I must be a sight for sore eyes, ever the professional businesswoman, standing on the porch of a beach house looking as if the world is ending.

I stick out like a sore thumb, an outsider if there ever was one.

I don't belong here.

This isn't where my life fits.

But do you even know where *you fit, Willow?*

That's always been part of the problem, hasn't it?

Before my thoughts spiral any further, I kick off my heels, pull my hair free from my bun, shaking out the strands, and then I make my way down the steps of the house and across the sand toward the water. I let my feet carry me faster, outpacing the whirlwind of thoughts trying to piece this puzzle together—running from the problems, the emotions, the decisions I have to make.

My arms hang limp beside my body, my legs ache as I step off-balance on the sand, but I just keep going, inching closer to the ocean that is calling to me right now.

I could run into that water and drown, and no one would know the difference. I could disappear and take all this mental chaos with me.

But I slow down as I approach the water's edge, watching the waves slide up the sand and kiss the tips of my toes. A stark reminder that leaving this earth isn't really what I want, even though everything feels so heavy right now that irrational thoughts crowd my mind.

The water is cold and frigid—mirroring how I often feel inside. But being here and absorbing what just happened makes me feel like a volcano is about to erupt.

And then I crumble, falling to my hands and knees as the sand digs into my skin. The simple task of breathing, of existing, suddenly feels monumental.

My lungs constrict and I gasp for breath, leaning back with my legs folded beneath me. I stare off at the water and let a few tears spring free, each one underscoring the deep sense of loneliness this place has brought to the surface.

I remain there on the beach for an unknown length of time, gazing off into the distance across the ocean in contemplation—until my soul hardens again, until my mind buries the anger and resentment six feet under, and I push myself back up on my feet. As I've done so many times before, ready to weather yet another storm life has thrown at me, refusing to let it sweep me away.

Chapter Four

Willow

"Where are the muffins?" I ask, spinning around to face Dolly when I spot the empty basket.

"The early bird gets the worm, Willow."

A huff of disappointment leaves my lips. "You just ruined my morning, Dolly." Although, with the last twenty-four hours I've been through, another obstacle like this doesn't surprise me.

She holds her hands up jokingly. "Don't shoot the messenger. We only order a fixed amount each day, and once they're gone, they're gone."

"Well, can I get them somewhere else?"

She grins in my direction. "Seems someone really liked the muffins."

"Well, I mean...they were okay," I reply, even though inside I feel like I'm having a mini panic attack and all the joy I was anticipating with that first bite has been robbed from me.

Is it sad to admit that the only thing that got me out of bed this morning was knowing I would get to eat one of those muffins again?

"Just okay?" she teases.

I roll my eyes. "Fine. It was the *best* blueberry muffin I've ever tasted and I need another, Dolly. Like right now."

She chuckles and reaches under the counter for something, handing me a bright yellow business card for the Sunshine Bakery. "This is where you can get one if that is what your heart truly desires."

"It does. Thank you." I reach for my coffee cup and move to leave, but her voice stops me in my tracks.

"What are you up to today?"

Ah, the million-dollar question that I don't even really know the answer to.

Yesterday, after I picked myself up off the beach, I walked back to the house—*my house*—and started assessing the place for what all needed to be done. I know that selling the property is probably in my best interest, but it needs to be cleaned and brought up to code before I can do that. I need it inspected by someone who knows what they're looking for, since that is something I don't have *any* expertise in.

The real question I'm lacking an answer to is, why do I care?

I could pay someone to take care of this for me. I could have been on my way back to D.C. an hour after I picked myself up off the sand, but one thing stopped me—Mr. Sheppard.

So, after a quick Google search, I found the one hardware store in town and plan to stop by to talk to someone today to see if they can recommend a contractor. I know I can get cleaning supplies from there as well, so I figured it was the best place to get the ball rolling so I can get back to my life—my life that is growing increasingly more stressful the longer I'm away from my business.

Katrina and I spoke on the phone this morning, but I feel helpless being so far away. I know she's got things handled back at the office, and we've pushed my appointments to next week, but now I have to decide what to do about this house and how that's going to affect my schedule.

I snap back to the present, remembering Dolly had asked me a question. "Just out to run a few errands," I reply.

"Are you staying past tomorrow?" she asks, knowing my reservation only extends through tonight. At least Katrina knew that I could be gone through Monday due to the uncertainty of this trip, and now I'm glad that I took that extra time. However, I need to decide how much longer I'm going to stay, and if I'll stay in the house instead of the inn. Perhaps after someone looks at it and confirms it's safe, that's where I'll sleep. After I get a bed, that is. I ordered one online last night—just in case—and Timothy graciously agreed to let me have it delivered to his office.

"I'm not sure yet. Can I let you know this afternoon?"

"Of course." Dolly smiles and then takes a sip of her coffee casually. "I'll be here, as always."

"Thank you, Dolly."

With a parting smile, I head out to my car and then plug in the address for the Sunshine Bakery.

Priorities, Willow. Muffins, then house.

In five short minutes, I'm driving down a small street lined with shops that look like something out of a movie set, the glistening water of the cove as the backdrop. Signs for small businesses hang from the eaves of the joined shops, and sidewalks are littered with people. Park benches are evenly spaced out among tall lampposts and potted planters. It's exactly what you would imagine finding in a small tourist town, or on the set of a Hallmark movie.

Honestly, I always wondered if places like this existed in real life.

I find a parking spot along the street very close to the bakery, and then speed-walk to the door.

As soon as I step inside, sugary, buttery goodness hits my nostrils, instantly making me salivate. And then I see them—those little blueberry mounds of heaven sitting on a shelf in the display case, just waiting for me to devour them.

I swear, I'm not normally this passionate about baked goods, but these muffins are making me act out of character.

Hell, I feel like this entire town is.

"Good morning." A cheery voice pulls my eyes from the display case to the owner of the voice, a woman that looks vaguely familiar.

"Hello. Can I get a half-dozen of the blueberry muffins, please?"

"Absolutely." The woman moves with an elegance as she pops open a box and starts loading my breakfast inside. I'm not going to eat all six today, obviously, but I know I'll at least have some for tomorrow and the day after, just in case. "Anything else I can get for you?"

"No. That will be it."

The woman moves to the register, so I meet her there. "That will be ten dollars."

I hand her my card. "Thank you. I'm not proud to say I nearly had a panic attack this morning when I missed out on these at the inn."

"Oh, you're staying at the inn?"

"Yeah, just for a few days."

"Vacation?"

"More like attending to some business," I reply as she hands me a receipt to sign, feeling like a broken record each time I answer that question.

"What kind of business would bring you to Carrington Cove?"

"The kind I wish I could avoid," I answer honestly.

"Well, at least you're getting a little vacation out of the deal. And some fantastic blueberry muffins." She hands me a copy of my receipt and then the box.

I tap my finger on the top of the box. "No, this is a problem. I live six hours away and now that I've tasted these little bites of heaven, I'm not ashamed to say I might have to come back a few times a month just for more of these. Or pay for a very expensive delivery."

The woman laughs. "You wouldn't be the first to say that. And a lot of folks say the same thing about the fish and chips at Catch & Release."

And then it clicks as I snap my fingers in recognition. "You work there too, don't you?"

"Yeah, a couple days a week."

"I was thinking you looked familiar. I was in there Friday night."

She wipes her hand on her apron before extending it toward me. "Well, nice to meet you. I'm Astrid."

"Willow," I reply as I shake her hand.

"That's a lovely name. Fits someone who'd travel six hours for our muffins." She laughs through her reply.

I smile. "Thanks. They're worth it."

I know I shouldn't be conversing with this woman right now, but something about her is so genuine and honest, you can't help but want to talk to her. And friends of the female variety are few and far between in my line of work *and* my life.

But you're not looking for friends, Willow. You're not staying, remember?

"Well, I hope we see you around again. The muffins won't be going anywhere, but we do run out fast," Astrid says as I adjust the box in my arms.

"Yeah, tell Dolly to order more from now on, will you?"

Astrid laughs. "I'll pass along the message." She waves as I walk out the door and get hit with a gust of salty air.

Once I deposit my muffins in the car and shove one in my mouth as fast as I can, I head for the hardware store, my mood significantly improved after satisfying my craving.

Walking into this place is like stepping into another world. I have no idea what I'm looking for or where anything is, so I grab a shopping cart and just start pushing it up and down the aisles. Luckily, I find the cleaning supplies rather quickly, so I grab a broom, mop, rags, and about every cleaning liquid I can think of.

I may be able to afford to pay someone to clean my penthouse for me now, but I was raised to know how to clean a toilet and mop a floor. Hard work builds character, something my godmother, Mandy, always made sure I never forgot.

I'm completely entranced by the cleaning supplies, deliberating my choice as a sudden voice behind me makes me jump out of my skin.

"Are you finding everything you need?"

Spinning around, I lock eyes with a man that towers over me by at least eight inches. I'm five-foot seven, but this guy makes me feel tiny.

"Jesus. You scared me." My hand falls to my chest where my heart is pounding erratically.

He chuckles and then brushes a hand through his short, dark-brown hair. "I'm sorry. That wasn't my intention."

"I think I just lost five years of my life."

"Let's hope not." He grins down at me again. "So did you need any help, or are you okay?" His eyes drop to my basket full of household cleaning supplies.

"Well, yes and no. I found what I needed here, but I actually need to know where I could find someone to come take a look at a house for me."

That has his eyebrows lifting. "Well, I could help you with that, actually." He reaches his hand out. "The name's Penn, and I'm kind of the resident handyman around here."

This guy looks familiar too, but at this point, I'm thinking maybe this town is so small that it only takes five people to run the whole thing. *How can I have already seen all of these people?*

"Willow." I shake his hand quickly.

"New to town, Willow?"

"Not exactly... I won't be here long."

Something along the lines of recognition passes through his eyes, but he shakes it off. "So where is this house?"

"It's on Bayshore Drive."

His eyes widen. "Oh."

"Oh?" His response makes my hackles rise.

"Well, there's only one house on Bayshore Drive whose owner I'm not familiar with, so I'm guessing I know which one it is."

"Yeah, well, you're looking at the new owner."

The corner of his mouth tips up, like he's secretly happy he's met me. "Well, this is just perfect." He chuckles.

"What is?"

Shaking his head, he says, "Nothing. Anyway, you need someone to take a look at it, huh?"

"Yeah. It's been empty for years and I need to know what kind of work it needs so I can put in on the market."

"Wait. Didn't you just buy it?"

I bite my lip, fighting with myself over whether to divulge too much because my gut is telling me I should watch what I say. These people don't need to know everything. Hell, I still haven't processed it all. And the more I talk, the more they will.

Hopefully, this little project won't take too long, and I can be on my merry way back to D.C. in a week or so, leaving behind this little obstacle and returning back to my life the way I like it—minus the blueberry muffins, of course.

"Not exactly."

"I don't understand…"

I cut him off. "I don't need you to. I just need your expertise. Do you think you can handle that?"

His head retracts a bit on his neck. "Well, that's my job, so yeah. I can handle it."

"Good. So, when can you come by?"

His eyes move around the store as he thinks. "How about tomorrow morning? I can be there by eight."

"Perfect. Thank you."

We exchange contact information, and then I follow him to the register to pay for my supplies. A display of refrigerator magnets right next to the register catches my attention, but I quickly turn away, knowing I don't need anything that trivial, something that will only remind me of what brought me here in the first place.

"You want one?" Penn slides his eyes to the display and then back to mine.

"No. I'm good."

"Ah, come on. Everyone should take a little piece of Carrington Cove with them when they leave."

Actually, Penn, this place is taking pieces of me and making me feel more incomplete than I already did. I don't need any reminders.

"I don't have a need for it. I'm here to settle things, not collect souvenirs."

He grimaces at me but drops it and finishes ringing up the last few items.

In true gentlemanly fashion, he helps me out to my car, loading the items into the trunk. "Nice car," he says admiringly.

"Thank you."

"We don't see many Teslas around here."

"I imagine not."

Penn raises an eyebrow, a spark of amusement in his eyes as he steps back and shuts my trunk. "Well, I guess I'll see you tomorrow?"

"Yes. Bring your toolbelt, or whatever else it is you need, please."

That comment makes him smile. "I'll be ready."

"Thank you again...for *all* of your help."

"Oh, I haven't done anything yet, Willow."

"Yes, but I can already tell that you'll be able to help me get out of here quicker than I would on my own."

He crosses his arms over his chest. "Why are you in such a hurry to leave?"

"Because there's nothing for me here," I mutter, and then catch myself. Walking around to the driver's side of my car, I effectively end the conversation and prepare to drive off as Penn watches me from the sidewalk.

But the way he studies me has me feeling even more uneasy. All I need is for him to help me fix the house and then I can move on. I'm not looking for friends or for anyone's opinion. All I want is to get back to my life. To what I know.

When I arrive at the house, I park in the back on the gravel driveway and begin unloading the bags from my trunk, placing them all on the kitchen counter. Once everything's inside, I start to unpack the sponges, buckets, and bottles of bleach and Lysol that I know will be put to good use.

But as I empty the last bag, a magnet falls to the counter.

I pick up the ceramic anchor, the deep brown paint to mimic wood on the symbol standing out against the dark blue and white lettering in the name of the little town. It's so trivial, useless and unnecessary to a person like me, but nonetheless, I find myself walking over to the fridge and placing the magnet in the top righthand corner. I stand back, studying the trinket that makes the house feel more like a home.

But this isn't home.

Could it be though, Willow?

Shaking off the convoluted thought and the feelings accompanying it, I realize I forgot my purse in my car, so I head back out to fetch it. With only a few steps out of the door, I hear a noise so foreign to me it has me pausing in my footsteps. But then it stops, so I wearily continue down the path to my car.

"What the hell?" I twist my head toward the sound just as it rings out again, but this time there's no missing the source of the noise. "Oh my God!"

"HONK!"

A goose emerges from the bushes by my car, light gray all over except for its black neck and white spots around its eyes. It stands there, turning its head so that it can see me before opening its black bill and honking at me again. Fear kicks in, and before I can think otherwise, I turn back around, forgetting my purse entirely.

As fast as my legs will carry me, I sprint back toward the house as the goose continues to honk at me, closing the distance between us faster than I expected.

"Son of a bitch!" I twist to see the bird waddling after me, honking such jarring and drawn-out calls that I almost run into the side of the house. I sidestep to avoid the collision and race up the steps that put me on the wraparound porch leading to the front door.

Another honk rings out, and then I notice that the goose has a friend that's joined in on the chase, forcing me to hustle even faster as my hand lands on the doorknob. But as I twist the knob, the door won't budge.

"Come on!" I shout at no one but myself, throwing my body weight against the door, having no luck. My eyes dart over to the side of the house just as the two geese come around the corner, honking at me still. "Oh my God! Get away! Go! Shoo!" I kick my foot in their direction as I continue to wrestle with the door.

I take back my earlier assumption about the Inn.

This is how I'm going to die.

I can see the article headline now: *Death by Geese. Willow Marshall, multimillion-dollar advertising mogul, died tragically by goose attack. All they could identify her by were her teeth. Those birds tore her to pieces.*

Sweat drips down the side of my face as I push against the door with every ounce of strength I can muster. I make the mistake of looking back and see the geese beginning to climb the steps, determination in their beady little eyes.

They're contemplating my murder, I just know it.

I can't go out like this.

Finally, after one final shove of my shoulder against the door, it creaks open and I dart inside, slamming it shut behind me and locking it—safe at last from the feathered assassins.

"Shit." I lean against the door with my back to it, closing my eyes while I fight to get my breathing under control. "Get a new doorknob and some WD-40," I mutter out loud, reminding myself to add it to the to-do list while I stand there, waiting for my heart rate to return to normal.

And as I do, I realize that killer geese are yet another reason why I need to handle this situation as fast as possible and get as far away from Carrington Cove as quickly as I can.

Chapter Five

Dallas

Cruising to my parents' house on a Sunday afternoon in my '68 Mustang convertible always puts me at ease. Being able to drive this car between deployments was something I looked forward to when I got the chance to come home, and now that the weather is warmer, it means I get to drive it a little more until the winter months hit.

Classic rock blares through the stereo as I pull into the driveway of the home I grew up in and shift my car in park, turning the key in the ignition and cutting the engine.

"Do you have to blare your music loud enough for the whole town to hear?" My little sister, Hazel, stands on the front porch with her hands on her hips, glaring in my direction.

"It wouldn't do anyone harm to appreciate music in its finest form."

She rolls her eyes and then steps toward me as I stand from the car and shut the driver's side door, intercepting her hug as we meet each other in the middle.

"I feel like it's been forever since I've seen you," she mumbles in my ear as I lean down, squeezing tightly before we let each other go.

"It's because it has been a while, Hazelnut. How are you? How's business?"

"Social media has been both a blessing and a curse." We walk up the pathway to the front door, sliding inside the house together.

"Staying busy, I take it?"

"So busy I need to hire a new photographer and a social media manager. I can't keep up with the demand on my own."

My little sister by nine years owns her own photography business and studio right on the boardwalk in town. She's been wildly successful since she started over a year ago, and I couldn't be prouder of her. Tourists have been a huge source of income wanting family photo shoots during their stay in Carrington Cove, and the locals support her as well.

"That's good. Just find someone you can trust."

"Easier said than done."

"Is that my favorite son?" My mother comes around the corner from the kitchen, wiping her hands on a dish towel.

"I don't know. What day of the week is it and what have Penn and Parker done to piss you off?"

"I haven't done shit," Penn says as he walks into the room from the hallway.

"And Parker isn't here to defend himself yet, so the jury's still out on that," Hazel adds.

My mother rolls her eyes much like my sister does all the time—*wonder where she gets that from*—and then pulls me in for a hug. "Shut up and hug your mother."

I wrap my arms around my mom, holding her close for as long as she can stand. I worry about her constantly, especially now that Dad isn't around. During Dad's final year, I made it my responsibility to make sure that *she* was cared for and aspects of her life were running smoothly. Mowing the grass, fixing anything that broke, running errands while she took Dad to the doctor's office—I did what I could so she didn't feel alone.

But I still don't feel like I did enough. She lost her husband.

There's nothing I could have done to prevent that.

"How are you?" I whisper in her ear as I feel her squeeze me harder.

"I'm okay." When we part, I can see the sadness in her eyes that she's trying to hide behind her smile.

"Sorry I'm late," Parker announces as he walks through the door with his medical bag in hand, pushing up his glasses along the bridge of his nose. "Mrs. Hansen's dog had puppies, so I had to make an emergency house call."

My brother Parker is the town veterinarian, a classic hometown celebrity since almost everyone has a pet of some variety in our town. He's the sibling that always managed to stay out of trouble and could do no wrong. But it's not like he hasn't dealt with shit in his life, too.

We all have.

"Saving Carrington Cove one animal at a time?" Hazel teases as Parker lets out an exasperated sigh.

"You're not late, Parker. Come here." My mother moves to my brother as Penn and I make our way into the kitchen.

"Is Brian on duty tonight at the bar?" Penn asks as he sits on a stool at the counter.

I nod as I reach for two beers in the fridge, passing one across the granite counter toward him. "Yeah. Who else would be?"

"I was just asking. No need to get testy."

"I'm not. I just hate when you ask questions you already know the answer to," I fire back, not sure where the animosity is coming from.

But the truth is, I've been on edge all week, ever since that blonde came into my restaurant.

Not even jerking off twice a day has made me feel less irritated.

It's because you're picturing those red lips when you do.

"Damn. You sound like you need to get laid," Penn mutters as he takes a sip from his beer bottle.

"I could say the same about you, Penn." The glare he gives me could cut glass, but luckily our mom breaks up what's brewing between us.

"What are you two fighting about already?" mom asks as she steps back in the kitchen, forcing us to part and move around to the other side of the island so we're out of her way.

Penn and I argue like most brothers do, but of my three siblings, he's the one I'm closest to. I guess that's to be expected when you're only fourteen months apart.

"Not fighting," Penn replies, still scowling at me from the across the island.

"Well, I don't want to listen to it tonight. I have all four of my children together, and I want us all to get along."

"You don't have to worry about me," Hazel interjects, grabbing a Coke from the fridge and popping the top.

"Yes, the princess can never do anything wrong," Parker chides as he reaches for his own beer from the fridge, sitting on the stool next to Penn.

Hazel is both the only girl and the baby of the family, so we're used to her getting away with bloody murder and never getting blamed for anything. I'm pretty sure she had the best relationship with both of our parents, too. Lord knows Dad and I had our issues.

My mother laughs. "All of you took turns being the troublemaker. You boys were just out of the house when it was your sister's turn."

She shakes her head in amusement. "I never knew raising a teenage girl would be harder than raising three teenage boys."

Penn and I snicker as Hazel drops her jaw. "You act like I was a hellion or something!"

"You sure weren't innocent, Hazel," Mom says while eyeing my sister over the stove, tucking her shoulder-length black hair behind her ear. "And if you want your little indiscretions to be kept between us, I suggest you drop it," she warns.

"Oh, no. I think we need to know what little Miss Hazel was up to while we were all too busy to pay attention." I smirk before taking another drink. Hazel shoots me a daggered glance.

"Now, now. That's enough. Boys, set the table, please. And Hazel, get over here and help me finish dinner."

The three of us settle into the same routine we used to have when we were kids—I'm responsible for place settings and plates, Penn grabs glasses of water for everyone, and Parker grabs the condiments from the fridge.

When my mother and Hazel bring over the casserole dish and bowl of salad, we all settle in and start eating.

It feels right being here all together, even though a huge part of our family is missing. But I don't want to be the one to point it out. In all honesty, I don't think anyone needs to. We all feel it.

It's just easier to let it remain the elephant in the room than bring it up and risk us slipping into dark moods.

Nevertheless, my eyes drift over to the empty chair at the head of the table, faintly hearing all of the criticism that would be directed my way if he were here. I hate that my mind goes there, but it does. Sometimes the bad moments are more prevalent in our minds than a dozen good ones.

Forcing out those stifled thoughts, we eat our dinner while catching up on each other's lives. And when we finish eating, I grab another beer and step out onto the back deck of the house to catch the sunset. I hear Penn follow closely behind me.

"I need to come over here and trim those branches," Penn declares as he and I stand along the railing of the deck, staring at the overgrown trees in the yard while Parker and Hazel help my mom clean up inside.

"Yeah. I should probably cut the grass out front too."

"I know Mom's capable of handling stuff on her own, but I don't want her to feel like she *has* to, especially with Dad gone. I want her to know we're here for her, you know?"

I nod. "I feel the same way."

"I can't believe it's been six months already."

Mentally, I knew the significance of today's date, but again, I didn't want to bring it up. And every time I think about the last conversations I had with my dad, anger steeps in my gut. "I know. It still doesn't seem real, even though we knew it was coming."

"I'm not sure death is any easier even if you know to expect it or not." He sighs, and for a moment, I remember his own experiences with death that still affect his life. I love my brother, I do. But damn, the man lives way too far in the past while his future is slipping away.

Much like my own, but I'll be the last one to admit it.

"All we can do is make sure we take care of her and don't let her feel like she's all alone."

"I agree," Penn says, sighing into the air around us. "But I feel like it's not enough."

"Seems like nothing ever is," I add, knowing those words apply to many aspects of my life, ones I can't do anything about now even if I tried.

"So, I got a job for tomorrow." His change of topic is welcome.

"Yeah? Doing what?"

"The renovations for the house on Bayshore Drive."

That detail makes my ears perk up. "Really?"

"Yeah. Seems like the new owner's looking to fix it up and sell it."

"Fuck." In the years since I left the Marines, there's only been one house in Carrington Cove I've had my eye on buying, and it's the very one Penn's talking about.

Growing up here, I used to walk by that house all the time, wondering what it looked like inside, envisioning myself living there when I was older. And about six years ago when I knew my time in the service was coming to an end, I decided to look into the house since it'd always been vacant. Turns out it was tied up in a trust with an obscure name, and the owner asked not to be contacted about selling.

I was disappointed, especially because I knew if I'd just had the chance to talk to the owner, I probably could have convinced them to sell. Instead, I've been biding my time, ready to make my move if the opportunity arises.

And my brother freaking knew about this and didn't tell me.

"Did you at least tell them I'm interested in the house?"

He scoffs. "No."

"Why not?"

"Because I don't think the owner is going to want to sell it to you."

"Why not?"

He grins mischievously, and I instantly want to punch him in the face. "Just a hunch."

Narrowing my eyes at him, I consider his response. "What aren't you telling me?"

With a pat on my shoulder, he begins to walk away. "Just think of this as payback for all of the shit you give me about Astrid."

"Penn!" I call after him before he gets too far.

"Yeah?"

"Brandon's been gone for four years. It's okay for you and Astrid to move forward."

His head hangs as soon as I remind him of why he doesn't act on his feelings for her. "Believe me, I know how long it's been, Dallas. And that's exactly why things have to stay the way they are." Then he heads back inside, and I'm left standing there turning over his words in my mind.

I've never felt so stuck in my life. And sounds like I'm not the only one. Hell, I bet all of my siblings also feel stuck in the rotation of this earth. Life has held us in place for the past year, and I'm not sure how to move on.

For me, buying the Bayshore house could be the key. Twelve years in the service has shaped me into a man that doesn't give up, but life outside of that structure is far too unsettling sometimes. There's a reason why so many vets have a difficult time adjusting to civilian life.

But I was hellbent on not letting that be me.

And even though I heard Penn's warning, it only makes me more curious about the new owner of the house that I want more than anything—the house that will help solidify for me that all of my sacrifice and hard work were worth it.

Plus, I think Penn is full of shit. I'm a charming, friendly guy with a commanding presence I know how to use when I need to. I bet I could talk to the owner and convince them to sell the house to me, save their money and let me do the renovations myself, or have Penn help me if he needs the work. So basically, everybody wins.

Pleased with my newfound determination, I go back inside the house and the spend the rest of the night with my family, absorbing the moments when we all get to be together because they are becoming fewer and farther between, even though the wheels are spinning in my head, formulating my plan to get the house I've always wanted, once and for all.

***

The next day, I go through the Monday morning delivery at the restaurant, checking in every item and helping Trent, one of my employees, put things away. By mid-afternoon, the cooks arrive to begin prepping food for the dinner service. We open at four Monday through Thursday, and at eleven on the weekends since tourists start rolling in as soon as Friday hits.

By the time the cooks arrive, I leave Brian, my other manager, in charge and fire up my Mustang, heading to speak with the owner of the Bayshore house since time is of the essence.

Penn mentioned the owner would be there today, though he didn't specify when. If they're there still, maybe he can help persuade the new owner to give me a chance to take the house and all its problems off their hands.

As I cruise down the road with the top down, I contemplate all the reasons I could give to help convince the owner.

First off, I have the money for a hefty down payment. Second, as a successful business owner, qualifying for the loan won't be an issue. Third, it's so much more than just a house to me. It's a piece of home; a familiar and comforting presence throughout my life. I figure a little bit of my backstory can't hurt.

But if none of that works, then I'll resort to extreme measures.

I'll fucking beg.

As I pull up to the house, I spot a Tesla parked in the driveway—definitely not a local. If someone in town had bought one, it would've been the talk of the town.

The obvious wealth doesn't bode well for me and my cause, but I owe it to myself to at least try.

The slam of my car door reverberates, along with the crunch of the gravel underfoot as I make my way to the front of the house. As I come around the bend, the sight of the ocean stops me dead in my tracks. Damn, I forgot how beautiful this is. It's been months since I've been by, but just seeing this view—the potential view from my own my front yard—makes me more determined to turn my dream into a reality.

With renewed purpose, I trek through the sand along the bushes that line the sides of the property and separate it from the neighbors. But nothing could have prepared me for the sight I encounter as I come around the front of the house.

A woman is walking backward up the front porch steps, waving an umbrella in front of her as she yells at a gaggle of geese. Nearly ten of them are gathered just a few feet from her, honking obnoxiously in protest as she wields the umbrella like a weapon to fend them off.

"Go! Get!" she yells, but there's something familiar about that voice that makes me pause. And the longer I watch her, the stronger the sense of déjà vu becomes.

"Back up!" She lunges forward as the geese squawk and jump backward, only to move forward again once she runs to the door, keeping the umbrella behind her as a shield.

Once I snap of my daze, I figure I might as well lend a hand. As amusing as the sight is, she seems genuinely scared. "Need some help?"

Her head snaps up, and when our eyes lock, my stomach plummets.

It's her—the blonde from the bar.

She still looks uptight, although the gaggle of geese might be partly to blame.

"You!" she spits out, disdain lacing her words.

"Me?" I retort with just as much conviction. "What the hell are you doing here?"

She twists and lunges toward the geese with the umbrella again, huffing in frustration. "Well, currently I'm trying to get inside my house, but as you can see, these geese seem to have an agenda of making my life a living hell."

My house.

Did I just hear her correctly?

"This is *your* house?"

"Jesus Christ! Get away!" She rushes the geese as their honking rings out and they scurry away from the house. She smiles triumphantly, but in a flash, she rushes toward her door again and struggles with the knob. "Stupid doorknob."

"Fuck," I mutter for a multitude of reasons before my feet carry me toward her, slapping her hand out of the way and then pushing the door open with brute force.

"Oh my God." She runs inside the house and moves to slam the door in my face, but I stop it with my hand before she can.

"No, thank you."

She glares at me through the crack in the door. "Again with the manners?"

"Well, I did just help you escape the geese and get your door open."

"I didn't ask for your help," she fires back, glaring at me through the crack in the door.

"Then perhaps I'll just keep the secret to getting rid of them to myself." I cross my arms over my chest, knowing I actually have no clue how to deter the geese. But hell, it can't be that hard.

"You know how to get rid of them?"

"When you live around them for most of your life, you pick up a few tricks." I shrug, feigning confidence.

She hesitates, considering my offer as our eyes lock through the gap in the door. Just then, the honking grows closer. I twist around to see the geese have gathered and are hellbent on trying to make their way up the steps again.

"Are you going to leave me out here to fend for myself?" I ask as I turn back to her.

"Why are you even here?" She narrows the gap in the door even further.

Panic builds in my chest as I see the opportunity I came here for slipping away. This might be my only shot at asking her directly about the house. Despite this woman being rude and clearly out of her element, I can't miss this chance to discuss my proposition.

"I wanted to talk to you about something."

"Me?"

"HONK!" The geese call grows louder as I spin my head back and forth between her and the birds.

"Can we talk inside, please?" The pleading in my voice is not something I'm proud of, but truth be told, I'm getting a little concerned about the determination of these fucking geese.

She huffs loudly, but then quickly pulls open the door. "Hurry up!"

I scurry inside just as she slams the door behind me, locking it for good measure. "I swear, those birds are predatory."

"Nah. They're probably just hungry, or not used to seeing someone here," I say just as my eyes take in the entirety of the woman standing before me, and I allow myself to do so blatantly.

She's not as dressed up as she was the other night, but even though she traded the heels for flats, she still looks all business. Black polyester capris cover her long legs that I still remember vividly from Friday night, and a lavender blouse covers her torso. Her hair is back in the same bun as before, pulling her face tight and adding to her cold demeanor even more as her brown eyes stare at me.

But her lips—they're bare this time, the softest pink that makes me lock onto them for an unknown length of time. I see them move, but don't register the words coming out of them.

"Hello?" she says, fanning one of her hands in front of my face.

Shaking my head, I pull myself together. "Sorry. What did you say?"

"I said what are you doing here?"

"Oh. Well, I guess I could ask the same of you..."

What the hell are you doing, Dallas?

You should be buttering this woman up instead of acting like an ass.

She crosses her arms over her chest and pops her hip out to the side. "That's none of your concern."

"Maybe not, but Carrington Cove *is*. And you made it pretty damn clear this little town is the last place you want to be. So what's changed?"

She scowls and says, "Oh, my opinion hasn't changed. But circumstances have, and it looks like I'm stuck dealing with this town and its rabid geese much longer than expected."

"First of all, geese can't get rabies. And secondly, what circumstances?" I shove my hands in my pockets, struggling to contain my frustration. I'm pretty sure I already know the answer, given the timing of her arrival and what my brother told me yesterday.

"It looks like I've inherited a project," she grates out, her eyes flashing with irritation. And, somehow, I find myself admiring her spitfire energy and the purse in her lips from irritation.

Stop looking at her lips, Dallas.

I shake my head and focus on making my case. "Well, what if I told you I could take this project off your hands?"

She twists toward me so fast, I think her head might spin off her neck. "What?"

"This house. That's the project, right?"

"Yes…" she draws out hesitantly.

"I want it." Crossing my arms over my chest, I widen my legs and stand my ground.

Her eyes bug out before a smirk flickers across her lips. "*You* want this house?"

"I do. And it's clear that *you* don't. So, if you sell it to me, it's a win-win."

"I can't just hand it over to you. It needs a lot of work." She waves a hand behind her.

"Well, you're in luck. I will take it as is and fix it up myself. I'll even pay more than it's worth. If you sell it to me now, you can get back to your big city life that much sooner."

She furrows her brow at me. "Why are you so set on *this* house?"

I let out a heavy sigh and answer honestly. "Because it's been my dream for years. And despite your disdain for this town, this is *my* home and this house is where I've wanted to live as long as I can remember. I have the money for a down payment. It's just a matter of drawing up paperwork for the loan and it'll be done. I just…" My words trail off as I search for the right words, but this woman's face stays cold as stone.

I don't see a glimmer of hope in those eyes, or in her stance—firm and unwavering. I feel like I laid my cards on the table too quickly. The silence stretches between us, thick with anticipation.

Then, cutting the tension sharply, she simply says, "No."

Just like that, she smashes my dreams. My hands fall to my sides, like a toddler ready to throw a tantrum. "What? Why?"

She stays silent as we hold a stare-off. "Because you didn't say *please*," she replies, her smirk erupting into a full blown, clearly-pleased-with-herself smile.

With a heavy sigh, I roll my eyes and give the woman what she wants. "*Please* sell this house to me."

She laughs, shaking her head. "Still no."

My patience snaps. "Why the fuck not?"

"It was *given* to me," she says, letting out a harsh breath and shaking her head. "And even though I do plan on selling it eventually, I'm not in the position to make that decision yet."

Fuck.

No wonder the previous owner never wanted to speak with me. This house wasn't just a piece of property; it was a gift for this woman. Now the obscure name of the trust makes sense.

But I'm not giving up hope.

"You can't be serious about wanting to fix this place up on your own. Do you have even the faintest clue how to do that?" My eyes dart around us, looking at the bones of the house and all of the potential here—potential that she could screw up by making the wrong decision or damage further with the wrong vision. My blood is boiling with frustration the longer this conversation drags on.

She narrows her eyes at me. "Again, that's not any of your concern. And a word of advice?"

My head pops up at her tone. "Huh?"

"The next time you want to ask for a favor, try not insulting the person beforehand." She pops her hip out again, arching a brow at me this time.

"You're one to talk, lady. You came into *my* restaurant with a stick up your ass, acting like you were too good for this place."

Definitely not going to win brownie points with those words, Dallas.

Her gaze turns fiery. "Excuse me?"

"I'm just trying to help you out, despite the fact that you and I see things very differently, we come from completely different walks of life, and under that cold exterior, you clearly don't have a heart."

Her eyes blaze with anger now. "You don't even know me!"

"I know you don't belong here," I say, and I'm surprised by the way she jolts as if I'd delivered a physical blow.

Her lips press into a thin line as we stare at one another, but she finally clears her throat and walks to the door, holding it open for me. "I think you should go."

"Gladly," I mutter. "This was clearly a waste of time."

"No. It wasn't." I turn to face her as I step out of the house. "Now I know who I *won't* be selling this house to when it's finished."

Fuck. "Well, maybe I'll make sure everyone in town knows not to trust the seller," I counter, feeling immaturity take over. Something about this woman makes me feel like a teenager, itching for a fight.

"Good luck with that." She flashes me a tight-lipped smile as I walk out the door, and then slams it in my face as soon as I turn to have the last word.

"Fuck," I mutter as I move away from the door, feeling her eyes on me through the windows as I walk around the porch and head back to my car, pissed off that I let this woman get under my skin yet again.

"HONK!" Behind me, geese start to gather and follow me down the gravel driveway. But hell, at this point, let them attack me on her property.

Maybe I'll sue. Maybe I'll use it as leverage. Because come hell or high water, I'll find some way to get that woman to give up this house.

And find a way to get her lips out of my mind.

Chapter Six

Willow

"Ugh! Who does that guy think he is?" My arms are shaking with the anger racing through my body and my breathing is harsh.

How dare that man come into *my* house, demand I sell it to him, and *then* insult me when I don't give in.

Funny how all of a sudden you're willingly claiming the house as yours, isn't it, Willow?

I growl in frustration and head back up the stairs to continue setting up the things I bought for the bathroom since it looks like I'm going to be staying here for a while after all—a decision I made just a few hours ago after Penn left and I realized I wanted to be here to oversee the renovations.

Knowing the best way to process the developments today is venting with my best friend, I call Shauna and place her on speakerphone as I begin opening the bags of items for the bathroom, taking out my raging frustration on the plastic.

"I haven't heard from you in a few days. I was starting to think you'd been swept off your feet by a charming local carpenter. Or given up corporate life to start teaching yoga to retirees. Or maybe you'd started renovating a quaint but rundown—"

"Ha-ha. Very funny." I say, cutting her off before she can throw any more clichés at me.

"I thought so. Well, what's the update on the house?"

Naturally, I called her the second I gathered myself the other day and updated her on the mysterious inheritance that brought me here.

"I found a handyman to check out the house today. His name is Penn."

"Oh, that's kinda rugged. Is he hot?"

"Um… He's tall."

"Nice. Are you planning on climbing him like a tree?"

"Not why I called, Shauna. Can we focus, please?"

She chuckles. "Sorry. I just thought maybe you could kill two birds with one stone and get laid while you're down there, too."

I laugh. "He's not the one I would want if that were the case."

Her excitement is palpable, even from miles away. "So you're saying there *is* a man that you want to get it on with?"

"Yes. I mean, no." I slap my hand to my forehead. "We're getting off topic."

"Sorry. Please continue, but you'd better tell me about the man that has you all flustered."

"There's no man."

"Sure…" she draws out.

"Back to the house," I say, tearing open the plastic on the pale blue shower curtain I chose for the bathroom. "So, Penn showed up today, we did a walk-through, and he determined that most of the issues are cosmetic. However, he insisted the roof be redone and advised that I replace the water heater. It's working for the time being, but given the age of the house, it would probably have to be replaced upon selling it anyway. He checked the foundation, electrical, and the air conditioner and heater, advising I get them serviced, but also asked if there was anything I'd like to change structurally. I really want to put a cut-out in the wall separating the kitchen from the living room to open up the space, and then the more we spoke about things to fix or change, the more energized I got about watching everything come together."

"You sound invested."

"I can't remember the last time I got excited about something like this, Shauna," I reply honestly. "Probably when I started Marshall Advertising and worked my ass off to make it what it is today. But it's been years since anything new has happened, and even though that's typically how I like things, a part of me also knows this isn't permanent. My goal is still the same—fix the place up, sell it, and return to my life as I know it. But, I figured I could at least stay here for the time being and maybe enjoy the change of scenery…"

Just saying it out loud makes the situation more real by the minute. But my heart likes the sound of this idea the more I entertain it.

Be careful, Willow. You sound like you just might enjoy yourself.

The house needs work, obviously, but it's all manageable. Deep down, I guess I resonate with it—like me, it's a little worn down, with flaws I'm not sure can ever be completely mended. With some effort, though, both the house and I can find ways to mask these scars, even if they never fully disappear.

This is my way of trying to make up for my mistakes.

The words from the letter that started all of this cross my mind as I thread the hooks through the holes in the curtain and situate it on the shower rod.

Despite being here against my wishes, something about this place is stirring up a feeling in my chest that I can't name and, oddly, the same feeling pops up every time the man from the restaurant is near.

It's a complicated mix of being cautious yet curious, wanting yet holding back, and annoyed but somehow still intrigued.

Still, the fact remains, that man is just *another* distraction, and that's the last thing I need to pile on the already chaotic mess that is my life right now.

"That's a huge decision, Willow. What about your company?" Shauna asks, bringing me back to the conversation.

"I'm going to still be involved, obviously, working remotely until the house is done. Katrina and I will figure out how to manage everything, but—"

"I'm proud of you, you know," Shauna says, cutting off my thought.

"Why do you say that?"

"Because I know going down there wasn't easy for you, and now you're facing this head-on instead of running away."

"I don't run away from things," I argue, feeling immediately defensive, but it's probably because I know deep down that Shauna is right.

"Willow, you know I love you, but let's not rewrite history. You weren't sure about going down there in the first place, and as soon as you called me the other day, I was convinced you'd throw money at this and run. But you're not. And that's huge." She pauses, and then lowers her voice. "I really think you need this, babe. You need an adventure. You need to do something out of your comfort zone for once."

I stare at the shower wall, one half of the curtain hung up, the other still in my hands. "Part of me agrees with you, Shauna. But hell...I'm questioning if I'm being responsible about it. In the past week, I've dealt with a penis palooza within my company, inherited a house from a random stranger that knew my parents, fought off a gaggle of rabid geese, and then the sexy bar owner that acted like I didn't belong in his town came over just a few minutes ago and asked me to sell this house to him."

"Geese can't get r—" she starts before I cut her off.

"I know, I know! It's an expression," I huff.

"Well, we're coming back to the geese, but you really caught my attention with sexy bar owner. Now we're getting somewhere." Shauna laughs and I roll my eyes. "Spill, Willow. I knew there had to be another reason for this call."

Sighing, I muster up the resolve to admit the main source of my frustration. "I stopped into his restaurant to have a couple drinks the first night I got here, and he lectured me about my manners."

Shauna laughs. "I like him already."

I scoff. For someone who acts like the chief of the manners police, he sure didn't make any effort to make me feel welcome. At all. It's ironic, given that his restaurant and all of Carrington Cove thrive on tourism. And the way he demanded I give him this house. Truth be told—a part of me was ready to hand him the keys the second the words left his lips, just to rid myself of the hassle. It would certainly be the easiest option. But like I said, once Penn and I started talking about the house and what needed to be done, my heart lurched with want—the desire to do it myself.

And now, knowing he wants the house so badly only makes me want to hold onto it that much more. Maybe Mr. Manners needs to earn it. And maybe he needs to stop being so damn attractive that I'm contemplating entirely unethical ways in which he could earn it.

So what if he's tall and muscular, and his neatly trimmed beard is so tempting that I had to fight the need to reach out and stroke it?

So what if his jeans hugged his sculpted ass, indicating his clear dedication to his body?

And so what if the way he pursed his lips in frustration makes me wonder what those lips would feel like against my skin?

I'm just horny, haven't been tended to by something other than my hand or a vibrator in very long time. And using him to scratch that itch just isn't a smart idea.

"No. He was rude, grumpy, and way too hot for his own good," I say, setting Shauna straight.

"Oh, then he's definitely the one you need to sleep with."

I shake my head. "Um, did you not hear me before when I said he wants to buy this house?"

"I did, and what I'm confused about is why that's a bad thing. It's perfect. Have some good hate sex while you're down there, fix up the house, and then voila! You already have a buyer when you're ready to sell." I hear her rap her knuckles against a table. "What's the problem?"

Sighing, I say, "I don't need another distraction or obstacle right now, Shauna."

"Yeah, that's where I think you're wrong. A good distraction is exactly what you need. Your life is about to be very different for the next few months, so I say you jump in with both feet, and that includes getting down and dirty with a handsome bar owner."

I close my eyes and groan. "Why can't you just be on my side for once?"

"Because your side is boring."

"God, he's so hot, Shauna," I mutter softly, like saying the words is physically causing me pain.

She clicks her tongue. "We've established that. So, what's he look like?"

I slump as I take a seat on the edge of the shower, picturing him standing on my front porch and in my living room just now. "Tall, broad, jet-black hair and a trim beard on the kind of jaw you want to lick. And his forearms…" I hum in approval.

"I love forearms," she moans enthusiastically. "I think they're one of the most underrated body parts on a man. Forrest's make me feral."

"Agreed. I swear, I could lick his and I think I'd have an orgasm just from that alone." We share a hearty laugh. "But he acted so self-righteous that my attraction was flipped off as fast as you flick a light switch. Don't get me wrong, it took a lot of balls to make me that offer, I'll give him that. But the look on his face when I told him I wouldn't sell the house to him because he didn't say *please* made me more than *pleased* with myself."

Shauna laughs. "Well, now you know what he wants, so I say you use that to your advantage."

"I don't know." I shake my head, staring at the wall in front of me. "I want to screw him and punch him in his pretty face at the same time. That can't be a good sign."

"Maybe, maybe not. But it *is* a sign that you'll be facing some choices in the next few months, Willow, and maybe even a few that will benefit your vagina." We share a laugh again. "But the real question is, are you willing to choose what you really *want*, not just what you think is safe?"

I wish I could give her an answer.

***

"Don't stress." Katrina rests her hands on my shoulders as we stand in my office back at Marshall Advertising.

"Easier said than done."

"Willow, I'm telling you. Everything will be fine. Natalie is more than capable of managing things while you're gone."

Natalie is my VP of marketing, and she was one of the best employees I hired when I started my agency. She started at the bottom and worked her way up, holding as much pride in the company as I do.

"I know, and it's not like I won't be involved still. It's just hard…"

"To give up control?" Katrina finishes for me as I roll my eyes. She flashes me a reassuring smile. "I know, but you deserve this. You've never taken a vacation."

"That's not true. I took some time for both of Shauna's weddings," I counter.

"That was like four days total and you were still glued to your phone the entire time. This time, I swear, I'm only going to contact you if it's absolutely necessary." She holds her hand up like she's making a pledge to me.

My skin nearly breaks out in hives. But my assistant is right. If I'm going to do this, I need to take advantage of the trip. Relaxing is going to be difficult, but I will make an effort to let my mind rest.

Easier said than done, obviously.

My shoulders finally drop a bit. "I appreciate you. I hope you know that."

Katrina smiles. "I know you do. And when you're back, I'm going to take *my* hard-earned vacation."

Chuckling, I say, "You've got it."

With one final hug, I leave my office and make the rounds through the building, making sure to speak to each one of my employees before I leave. One thing I pride myself on is the culture I've created with my staff. I make it a point that they know I'm not just their boss, but their mentor, the person behind the name on the door and the one who is invested the most in our success—success that doesn't happen without their hard work.

When I finally exit the building, I settle into my car and start the drive back to Carrington Cove, my brimming suitcases situated in the back of my Tesla, along with my patience, as I sit in Friday traffic for hours.

But as soon as the lights of Carrington Cove fill my windshield, I roll down the window and breathe in the salty sea air from the driver's seat.

Just one inhale has my shoulders relaxing and my lungs expanding in comfort, a detail that I choose not to acknowledge, or I'll freak myself out again. Earlier this week as I made arrangements with my company for my extended absence and let my apartment building supervisor know I'd be gone for a few months, anxiety bloomed in my body when I realized that a part of me was apprehensive to return to the beach house.

Not just because the sooner I did, the sooner the work could be completed.

No.

It was the idea that the sunrise and sunsets over the ocean were waiting for me on the balcony of the master bedroom.

It was the idea that I could fulfill my craving for blueberry muffins from the Sunshine Bakery and coffee from Keely's.

And it was this new feeling, wondering about what would happen at the end of this trip, that had me itching to drive back on Friday evening, feeling completely different upon my return than I did the first time I came down here a week ago.

***

Walking into Catch & Release, I inhale the smell of fried food and burgers. I figured I might as well start this trip off with another martini, even if the bartender was far from welcoming. At least he could pour one hell of a drink.

The same stool I sat on last week is free, so I sashay over in my heels and navy A-line dress, taking a seat as a familiar face flies past me.

"Hey! I know you." Astrid points a finger at me as she hurries by.

A smile instantly graces my lips. "And I know *you*."

"What are you doing here? I thought you were only in town for a few days last week." She drops a serving tray on the counter and stands before me a second later, brushing her hair from her face.

Sighing, I say, "Well, it seems I have to stick around for just a little while longer."

Her head tilts to the side. "How come?"

"Hey, Willow." Penn slides up behind Astrid, reaching underneath the bar for a few glasses before I can answer her.

"You know Willow?" Astrid turns to him, a pinch in her brow.

Penn nods. "She owns the Bayshore House now. I'm helping her with the renovations."

Her eyes widen in recognition and a knowing smile follows. "Well, isn't that convenient?"

Penn chuckles. "It sure is."

"Standing room only tonight, and here you two are, just standing. I could use some help out here."

That voice.

I don't even have to look in that direction to know who it belongs to.

"Calm your nuts, Dallas," Astrid fires back as she rolls her eyes and grabs her tray again. "I was just saying hello to my friend here." She gestures in my direction, which has his gaze drifting my way.

And when it locks onto mine, the same rage from Monday comes barreling back into me, followed by an inconvenient spark of lust.

Dallas—so that's the man's name. He stares at me with narrowed eyes, clad in a black polo shirt and dark-wash jeans. His beard is trimmed to perfection, his hair freshly cut as well, and his eyes are dark and menacing as they stare down at me, brimming with frustration and annoyance at my presence.

Well, the feeling is mutual pal, even though my vagina apparently hasn't received that message.

"Dude. You look fucking psycho right now." Penn shoves Dallas's shoulder before he places two margaritas on Astrid's tray. "This is Willow by the way," he says, motioning toward me.

"Oh, we've met."

Penn chuckles and Astrid hides a snort as my eyes bounce between the three of them.

"Oh yes. Dallas, it's *such* a pleasure, as always," I reply sarcastically.

Penn full-blown laughs this time, shaking his head as he moves around Dallas and reaches for a dish towel from a bucket. "Shit, brother. She's got your number already."

"Wait. This man is your *brother*?" I say, a little too loudly.

"Is that a problem?" Dallas asks, crossing his arms over his chest, drawing attention to the muscles in his upper body and the veins in his forearms. The man should be a walking advertisement for arm porn, and I hate that I'm thinking about that right now.

I clear my throat and lean back in my seat, flicking my finger back and forth between them. "Oh, not at all. I just don't understand how you two could be related."

Astrid throws her head back in laughter. "Oh, just hang around here a while longer, and you'll realize just how alike these two are." She pats the bar in front of me. "It was good to see you, Willow. Will

I be seeing you in the morning?" She winks at me, so I'm sure she's referring to the bakery.

"Oh, definitely. I need my fix."

With a nod and a smile, she takes off to deliver her drinks, leaving me with the Beast and his brother.

Penn turns his attention back to me. "What can I make for you?"

"I'll have a…"

"Martini with three olives," Dallas finishes for me, shoving his brother out of the way. "I've got it. Go help out Brian."

Penn smirks in my direction, shaking his head at his brother before walking away. Dallas lowers his gaze to the bar well as he begins making my drink.

"I don't know if I trust you to make my drink after what happened on Monday," I quip as he moves with ease in front of me.

"Contrary to what you might think of me, poisoning my customers isn't part of my business model." he replies dryly, skewering three olives and dropping them into the glass before sliding it along the bar toward me.

"Thank you."

The corner of his mouth tips up as he crosses his arms again. "You're welcome. Looks like you've found your manners."

I scoff, reaching for my drink. "Oh, I've always had manners. I just reserve them for people who are deserving."

His smile grows and his stare becomes more intense. "Well then, I'll take those words as a compliment." I fight the urge to roll my eyes as he clears his throat. "So, I take it you're back in town for a while?"

Squinting at him, I take a sip of my martini. *Damn. Of course it's perfect.* "I am."

"Then I guess we'll be seeing a lot more of each other, won't we?" One of his dark eyebrows arches.

"Not if I can help it," I tease, more playfully than I intended. But there is something about verbally sparring with this guy that is making my heart flutter. And the longer I talk to him, the more I get to stare at his stupid face, those stupid lips, and that stupid beard that are making me feel stupid inside.

This is not good.

"Well, then I guess you won't be needing my help with the geese after all." The snark in his voice brings me back to the present.

Fuck. The damn birds. I've forgotten all about them. "Ummm…"

"No. It's probably best this way, right? You don't trust me. Who knows if I would be giving you accurate information anyway?" Unfortunately, a small growl climbs up my throat and Dallas catches it, laughing at the sound. He taps the bar in front of me before saying, "Good luck, Willow. You're going to need it." And then he walks off, leaving me to stare at his beautiful backside as he does.

Not wanting to get caught, I shift my focus around the bar, watching Astrid wait tables, Penn help clear dishes, and other employees smile and assist other customers as I fight with my own willpower not to strangle Dallas and the notion that maybe part of me is happy to be back more than I care to admit.

There's a familiarity here, a sense of community that, before this trip, scared the living shit out of me.

But maybe it's not the worst thing in the world to be in a place where people know you by name, remember your favorite drink, and are eager to help make you feel at home. As long as you can make sure to separate business from much needed pleasure—the kind I feel a man like Dallas could definitely deliver.

Chapter Seven

Willow

Standing on the balcony of my bedroom sipping a cup of coffee as I stare out at the ocean on a Monday morning *almost* makes up for the fact that I have to jump on a call later this morning.

Working remotely will definitely be an adjustment for me, but when this is the view you get to wake up to, I guess the sacrifice is worth it.

A feeling of peace washes over me as I stand here, such a contrast to the anxiety I felt the first time I stepped into this house. But like Shauna said, I need to treat this as an adventure. Keep an open mind and do something out of the ordinary.

So that's what I'm going to do.

I drop my head down to look for a place to sit on the balcony, even though I know there isn't one. Looks like there's one more item to add to my mile-long to-do list—get a chair.

After I finish my coffee, I hop in the shower, make myself look presentable, and then log in to my call a few minutes early, ready to sync up with Katrina. When I'm satisfied with the plan we've laid out for the week, I end the meeting and decide my schedule is light enough today that I can knock off a few things for this house as well.

As I make my way into town to look for some furniture, I make a pit stop at the bakery to see if they have any muffins left. It's almost noon, but there's no harm in trying. Plus, I kind of want to see if Astrid is there. I need her input on something else too.

"Well, looky here. You're awfully late!" she calls out as soon as the bell rings above the door.

"Yeah, I had a conference call this morning. I know it's a long shot but…" My eyes drift to the display case, where I see nothing but a muffin-shaped void. My heart instantly deflates. "I guess the early bird also catches the muffin."

Astrid flashes me a knowing smile and then reaches behind her for a box, popping the lid open and revealing a dozen muffins. "Call it intuition, but I set these aside for you this morning, just in case."

My jaw drops in shock, and appreciation. "Oh my God. I swear, I think I might cry."

She just laughs and moves to the register, taking her time since the place is empty.

"Thank you so much, Astrid."

She waves it off as I hand her my card. "Don't mention it. In a town this small, you learn to look out for your neighbors. The little things mean the most sometimes."

And her words resonate with me. "Yeah. That's true."

When's the last time someone did something thoughtful like that for me that wasn't related to my job? Better yet, when's the last time I did that for someone else?

"Well, Willow, since you'll be sticking around for a bit longer, I'd like to know more about you. Like what kind of work you do that allows for such flexibility." She slides my card and the receipt across the counter for me to sign.

If it were anyone else pushing me for information, I'd have my guard up in a flash. But there is something about Astrid that makes me want to open up, at least a little. Still, I think I'll keep my millionaire status to myself. People tend to look at you differently when they see dollar signs. "I work in advertising. Basically, people pay me a lot of money to help them make a lot of money."

Her eyebrows shoot up. "That's so awesome! But it sounds stressful."

"It can be, but I'm good at it." I slide my card back in my wallet and then drop it in my purse. "What about you? Working two jobs sounds stressful too."

Her shoulders drop and the change has me on high alert, worried I might have offended her. "It is, but that's life as a single mom."

"Two jobs *and* you're a mom?"

Her smile returns with my question as she fishes her phone out of her pocket. "Yeah. This is my son, Bentley. He's eleven. And my daughter, Lilly. She's seven." The look of pride on her face is laced with a subtle twinge of pain as she points at the picture on the screen. "They're with my mom right now since school is out for the summer. But on my day off, we're planning a family beach day." Her eyes light up at that.

"That sounds like a good day."

God, I can't remember the last time I laid out in the sun on the beach.

Then her entire body perks up. "You should come with us!"

"Oh, I don't know. I have to—"

"Nonsense!" she says, cutting me off. "It would be fun. It might even help you fall in love with Carrington Cove a little more."

Uneasiness rests in my gut, but part of it is because deep down, I do want to go. "I'll think about it." She nods. But then another question pops into my mind. "If it's not too personal, may I ask about their father?" I ask timidly.

Her eyes instantly drop to the counter in front of her and my pulse picks up. "He, uh…he passed away."

This is why I don't usually ask questions. You never know what kind of nerve you might hit. "Oh, Astrid. I'm so sorry."

She waves me off, sniffling before standing up tall again and plastering a smile on her face once more. "Thank you. He was a Marine. We always knew the risks, but that doesn't make it any easier." I swallow hard, not sure if I should offer up my own loss, but she doesn't give me a chance. "Thank God for Penn, though. He's been a huge help since Brandon died."

"Penn?"

"Yeah. He and Brandon were best friends. We all kind of grew up together. And when Brandon died, Penn made sure I never felt alone, that me and the kids were taken care of. Anytime anything goes wrong with the house or with life in general, he's there or my older brother, Grady, steps in."

I can feel my heart slow down, thinking about how lucky she is to have people like Penn and her brother around to support her. "Well, Penn seems like a good guy. And I know he's handy since he'll be helping out with my renovations."

Astrid's smile could light up the room. "Penn is the best."

"A far cry from Dallas, it seems," I add, shifting the conversation to the person I'm itching to know more about.

Astrid chuckles. "Actually, like I said Friday night, those two are more alike than different."

I scoff. "I find that hard to believe, no offense."

"Oh, you're just lucky enough to have seen Dallas's asshole side before you get to see the good guy he is underneath."

I arch a brow at her, skeptical. "I'm not so sure with everything he's shown me. Did you know that he wants to buy my house?"

"The Bayshore house?" I nod. "Oh yeah, Dallas has wanted that place since we were in high school." I instantly recall him saying that the other day, but he never explained it further.

"Why?"

"Hello? Have you seen the view from that house?" she asks.

And that has me chuckling. "Um, yes. It's stunning. And I plan on enjoying it while I renovate it. Even though Dallas offered to take it as is and do the renovations himself."

She turns to face me head on. "Really?"

"And I told him no."

Astrid chuckles. "Well, that explains some of the animosity between the two of you then."

"He was acting like an ass, and I don't know..." I shake my head.

Astrid eyes me suspiciously, a small smile forming on her lips. "Well, there's still time for you to change your mind about the house...and him."

There is. There's time for me to change my mind about a lot of things.

"Willow?" she asks, pulling me from my thoughts.

"Yeah?"

She leans over the counter, resting on her forearms. "Dallas really is a good guy, underneath all of that surly attitude, of course. His brother is too. Hell, most of the people you find in this town are good people. He's got his issues, just like anyone else, but don't write him off just yet. You probably caught him off guard. It's been a long time since I've seen him look at woman the way he looks at you..."

"What?" I bark out through a laugh. "I think you've got it all wrong, Astrid. The man acts like he can barely stand the sight of me."

She just hums. "I know what I saw." But then she changes the subject. "Obviously though, because you own the house that he wants, he's going to throw a fit about it. I mean, the old owner of that house wouldn't even meet with him when he offered to buy the place…"

Yeah, because he was saving it for me.

"I've known his family for more than half my life, and I've worked for him for the past four years. I think if you two sat down and talked, you might be able to reach an agreement."

"I'm—I'm not even sure what I want to do with the house yet, Astrid." I blow out a harsh breath, my stomach feeling uneasy again. "I had no idea I would be inheriting the place. It all happened so fast, and now I have to make all of these decisions…"

She places her hand on mine this time. "I get it. Believe me. Life can change in an instant," she says as her voice begins to crack. "But time helps put things into perspective. Just keep an open mind when it comes to Dallas. And maybe Penn can give you some insight into his brother as well."

"Those boys sure are attractive, aren't they?" I whisper, shocking myself at my candid words. But let's be honest—my attraction toward the man is clouding my judgment and making this far more complicated than it already is.

Astrid laughs as she stands up again. "Oh, yes they are. And their other brother is too."

"There's another brother?"

She nods. "Yup. Parker. He's the vet here in town."

"Wow."

"And they have a little sister, Hazel."

My eyes bug out. "I couldn't imagine having that many siblings."

"Only child?" she asks.

"Yeah."

"Where are you from?"

"Virginia. But I've lived in D.C. for the past eight years."

"Big city life is very different from life in Carrington Cove."

I scoff. "You're telling me."

"Well, enjoy this place while you're here then and don't be a stranger. If you ever need someone to talk to, I'm here." She squeezes my hand again before I reach for the box of muffins. "And I'll try to keep some muffins put aside for you."

"I appreciate that, Astrid. A lot. Thank you."

Ugh, my chest feels all warm and fuzzy right now.

Am I developing feelings for this town?

Or just the woman in front of me that has offered me friendship with no strings attached?

"Anytime. And hey, let me get your number while you're here. I'm not letting you out of this beach trip." With a cunning smile, she pulls her phone back out of her pocket as I rattle off my number to her. "I'm gonna text you so you have mine too."

I feel my phone vibrate in my purse. "Okay. Thank you."

"Have a good day! And good luck with the house!" she calls after me as I wave with my free hand and make my way out to my car, ready to find a few things I can work on to fill in the time between work and when Penn is scheduled to swing by the house later.

And maybe I can push Penn to give me more insight into his brother, too.

***

I drag my chosen chair in its bulky cardboard box up to the register, stopping every few feet to catch my breath. Of course the one I liked the most was also the biggest. It's not like this tiny hardware store had much to choose from anyway, but, seeing as the only other place to buy furniture around here is the dollar store, I figured I'd have better odds here.

I was also hoping to run into Penn since I had a few questions for him, but he's nowhere to be found. Instead, the older woman behind the counter watches me with a mixture of curiosity and amusement, not bothering to assist.

"Having some trouble?" It's more a statement of the obvious than an actual question. When I only grunt in response, she asks, "What's a little thing like you doing with a chair that size anyway?"

"It's for my new house," I huff out as I continue to drag the box with what little upper body strength I possess.

"New in town, huh?" she prompts as she leans on the counter, her interest clearly piqued.

"I am. And I just need to pay for this chair and get it home, okay?" *This damn chair better be worth all of this trouble.*

"Good choice." A voice to my right pulls my attention, and the person it belongs to holds it for a moment before I realize I'm staring.

Dallas.

"That's the one I had my eye on for the balcony," he says.

The thump of my heart has me taking a moment to gather my thoughts. "Um, yeah, that's what I was planning."

"Gotta have somewhere to sit to watch the sunrise and sunset, right?" He walks over to me and takes the cardboard behemoth from my hands, lifting it with ease and walking around me toward the register.

"I had that!" I call out as he walks away from me, carrying the box like it's as light as a feather.

"Just say thank you, Willow," he says over his shoulder as I sigh in defeat.

"Thank you," I mutter, trailing him as the employee watches us both now with her eyes bugged out.

"Mrs. Hansen." Dallas nods at the woman as he leans the box against the counter. "How are the puppies doing?"

Her face lights up for the first time since I've walked in here, and her eyes finally focus on something other than me. "Oh, they are perfect. Such a rambunctious little bunch. Your brother came by yesterday to check on them."

"Sounds like Parker is doing his job, then."

"All of you boys are responsible and loyal to a fault. Your daddy would be proud of y'all."

I watch Dallas's face fall, but he simply clears his throat and nods. "Thank you."

"Such a shame the cancer took him so young." She shakes her head as she holds up a handheld scanner to the box.

I try to make it look like I'm not paying attention, but she is doing a better job of offering up information about this man than Astrid did earlier today.

His dad died from cancer? Well, that presents some intriguing insight.

Seems we actually have something in common.

"Yes. It is." He flicks his eyes over to mine. "I think Willow here needs to pay so she can get going, right?"

"Oh. Yes. Go ahead and insert your card into the machine, dear." Her voice has taken on a much lighter tone as I break my stare with Dallas and pay for my item.

"Thank you." She hands me the receipt just as Dallas turns to face me.

"So how did you plan on getting this thing back to your house?"

"Uh, I have a car." I point out the window to my Tesla.

He shakes his head, his smile full of amusement and cockiness. "Like this is going to fit in that."

"Yes, it will," I say with determination. "I can slide this into the backseat, no problem."

He arches a brow. "Is that so?"

"Oh, absolutely. Don't underestimate me, *Dallas*."

"Well, this I can't wait to see, *Willow*." The low grumble of his voice makes me wonder what my name would sound like coming off of his lips while his head is between my legs, and the thought has me tripping over the box in front of me as soon as I try to step around it.

"Whoa." Dallas reaches out to prevent me from falling forward. "Easy, Goose."

"Goose?" I ask incredulously when I find my footing again.

He smirks, and suddenly I want to slap that smirk off his face. "Yeah, seemed more fitting than 'Tiger.'"

"Ha. Ha." I fake a laugh, straighten my blouse, and then make my way out to my car, assuming that Dallas is going to carry the box out for me. Luckily, when I look back over my shoulder, he's following with the box in his arms.

We arrive at the rear passenger door, and after I unlock it and set my purse inside, I attempt to lift the box and turn it so it will fit through the doorway. I twist and turn the box, trying various angles and approaches to make it fit. Despite my efforts, including pushing, pulling, and a bit of seat adjustment, the box refuses to comply, stubbornly remaining a few frustrating inches too big.

"Ugh. Stupid box." I let it fall onto the asphalt beneath me just as Dallas's laugh rings out.

"Damn. I want to say I told you so, but that was just too damn easy. Thank you for the entertainment though."

"That's not necessary," I huff, glaring at him over my shoulder. "Damn it." Irritation bubbles inside of me, more so because I have him as an audience to my monumental fail than the new problem I now have to solve.

He sighs and the sound of him scratching his chin through his beard draws my eyes back to his face.

Damn. That beard will be the death of me.

"Look. I have a little time before I have to be at the restaurant, and lucky for you, I drove my truck today. I can take it to the house for you."

I cross my arms and eye him skeptically. "And why would you do that? Newsflash, but you and I don't exactly get along."

He smiles. "That's a matter of opinion." His gaze moves down my entire body before focusing back on my face. And the way he's assessing me right now has my body temperature rising to levels I don't think are healthy. "But to answer your question, sometimes people just do nice things to be nice, Willow. It's one of the charms of living in a small town."

"But how do I know that you're not offering so that you can get me alone and murder me, make it look like I was crushed by this box in a freak accident, and then jump on the house the second I'm dead?"

He stares at me, blinking slowly before bursting into laughter. "Oh fuck. That's good."

"Excuse me?"

"You're a piece of work, Goose."

"Stop calling me that," I seethe through clenched teeth.

He huffs out a laugh again while shaking his head. "Nope. Can't do it. Especially now that I know it gets under your skin."

I throw my hands up. "God, you're a child."

"And you need my help. So what's it going to be, Willow?" He mimics my stance, crossing his arms and putting those strong, sinewed forearms on display, taunting me.

Silence rests between us as I debate my options, which are pretty cut and dry at this point—i.e., I have none.

"Fine. If you could bring the box over, I would appreciate it."

"Happy to. All you have to do is say the magic word."

My mouth drops open slightly. "What?"

"Oh, come on, Goose." He taps his temple mockingly, leaning toward me and narrowing his eyes. "Think really hard."

I squint back at him, hoping I'll suddenly shoot lasers from my eyes and he'll turn to dust right in front of me. Sadly, this isn't a sci-fi romance. Wait, this isn't a romance at all, which makes that thought perplexing.

"*Please*," I grate out, and his smile builds to an unworldly degree.

"Attagirl." With a wink in my direction, he bends down, hoists the box over his head, and walks just a few feet to a black truck, depositing the box in the bed of it. "I'll see you there."

He turns toward his driver side door and hops inside, leaving me standing by my car, confused by the anger and desire mixing inside of me right now.

How can you want to punch someone in the face but want to ride that face at the same time?

Let me just add the undeniable attraction I feel for him to my long list of things to deal with that doesn't seem to get any shorter as the days go by.

***

"Can you take it up the stairs, *please*?" I ask Dallas as he carries the box through the front door. Luckily, the geese are not around to make this delivery any more difficult.

"I'm impressed. You said please without me having to remind you."

"Dear lord, what have I done to deserve this," I mutter, closing the door behind him and watching his jean-clad legs carry the box up my stairs, putting his round ass on display.

Reluctantly, I follow his lead and find him in the middle of my room, staring out at the ocean through the sliding glass door.

"Damn. This view is even better than I imagined," he says, his voice low and full of awe.

Taken aback, I drop my tone to match his. "You've never been in here?"

He shakes his head slowly. "Nope. I wanted to, but never got the opportunity. I've looked through the windows on the first floor each time I'd come by, but never stepped foot inside until the other day when I came to talk to you." His eyes are still focused on the view in front of him.

"Are you telling me I'll have to watch out for you spying on me now?"

He twists to face me, crossing his arms over his chest yet again. I don't know if he does it to put off a commanding presence, or because he knows how good it makes his entire upper body look.

His lips turn up on one side. "Guess you'll just have to wait and find out, won't you?"

"You're not helping your case right now, Dallas," I tease, stepping around him to break our eye contact and to get my heart to slow the furious pace at which it's pumping. "Now, if you'll excuse me, I have a chair to put together."

"Do you even have tools?"

Defeat pulls my shoulders down as I pinch the bridge of my nose and close my eyes. "No."

"So how are you planning on putting this together?"

"Through telepathy?" I wince, turning around to face him.

He laughs. "Right. You know, I happen to have a few tools in my truck. I could…help you…if you want." His offer isn't solid, more like unsure, waiting on my reaction.

But I feel like there must be an ulterior motive because this man can't possibly just be that nice, especially given our interactions so far. "You don't have to help me, Dallas. I can figure this out."

He steps forward, closing the distance between us, forcing me to lean my head back so I can meet his eyes. Sweat mixed with the spice of his deodorant or cologne has me drawing in a deep breath, soaking in his smell.

Damn. He smells good—like a man that isn't afraid to get his hands dirty.

And you don't find a lot of those where I live.

"Contrary to what you think you know about me, I help those in need." His voice is solid now. "It's ingrained in me. Twelve years in the Marines will do that to you. And despite our irritation-fueled conversations so far, a part of me is hoping that you'll change your mind about the house if you see I'm not a complete asshole."

"At least you're being honest."

I watch his eyes dip down to my lips briefly, but then he takes a step back and shoves his hands in his pockets. "I'm always honest, Willow. And that goes for my offer. I can put the chair together for you…if you want. Or I can leave. It's your call."

With no other options, I accept his offer. It definitely has nothing to do with the way his ass looks in those jeans. "That would be nice. Thank you."

With a quick nod, he heads downstairs and I hear the door open and shut. For some reason unbeknownst to me, I run into my bathroom to check my appearance. Smoothing down any flyaway hairs from my bun, I spritz hairspray over my head and then put some clear gloss over my lips.

Everything seems to be put in place on the outside, but inside? I'm squirming. My heart is racing. My body is humming with nerves at the thought of being around this man for a significant length of time.

Who knew that lust and hate could feel so very similar?

I *can't* like him. I *can't* want him. Getting involved with someone to that degree—especially a man who has openly admitted he's being nice to me because he wants me to sell him my house—is *not* a rational decision. But I know damn well that Shauna would approve. She'd push me into him and hope my face falls on his penis.

Sighing out loud and muttering to myself about what an idiot I am, I completely miss the sound of Dallas coming back up the stairs.

"Talking to yourself?"

I spin on my heels, clutching my hand to my chest with surprise. "Jesus Christ. Warn a person, will you? Did you pick up that skill from your brother?"

"I thought that's what I was doing." He steps further into the room and wields a pocket knife from his jeans as he sets a bag of tools down on the carpet. "And when did Penn scare you?"

Slicing open the cardboard, he extracts the pieces of the rocking chair from the box as I take a seat on the edge of my bed, grateful I had one delivered while I was back in D.C. "At the hardware store last week."

"So how long are you staying?" Dallas asks as he gets comfortable on the floor and starts reading the instructions.

For a man to do such a thing—I'm impressed.

"Two months as of right now. Potentially three. Your brother seems to think that will be enough time."

He nods. "With a new roof, flooring, fixtures…that sounds about right."

"How did you—" I stop talking once I realize he probably spoke with him. "He told you?"

He nods again. "Yup. I was curious in case I could convince you to let me take the place off your hands."

An uncomfortable silence falls between us. I've already made it clear to him that I don't plan on selling right now. But each time he brings it up, it makes me more uneasy.

"So you've lived here your entire life?" I ask, changing the subject while I watch his forearms flex each time he tightens a screw, assembling yet another piece of the chair.

"Except for my time in the Marines, yes."

"The Marines, huh? That must have been interesting."

He scoffs. "Interesting is one way of putting it."

"Why do you say that?"

Shaking his head, he grabs another tool and keeps putting pieces together. "War isn't interesting, Willow. It's violent. Risky. There are days when you don't know if the sunrise will be the last one you ever see." His words falter, but I hang on to each one of them as they dredge up emotions I've been fighting to keep at bay.

I wonder if my parents ever thought the same thing while they were overseas.

"I take it you were in Iraq then?"

"Afghanistan, mostly." He searches on the floor around him before finally looking up at me. And his eyes are darker somehow, but with pain laced in the edges of his irises. "Can you hand me the hammer in my bag, please?"

I stand from the bed and reach down, shuffling through his bag before locating the hammer and handing it to him. But when I look up, I see his eyes trained on my chest, the sliver of my boobs displayed through the opening of the neckline that fell when I bent over.

He clears his throat, realizing he's been caught as I settle back down on the bed.

"Well, you must have made your family proud by serving your country. It's a noble thing to do."

He scoffs, shaking his head as he hammers a rod in place. "Not all parents support such a decision."

"What do you—"

"So where are *you* from, Willow?" he asks, changing the subject and cutting me off. The question lingers in my brain, but his next words are full of sarcasm and divert my attention. "I obviously know it's not here. We've pinpointed that detail the first night we met." His cocky grin is back along with my urge to twist his nipple.

"Virginia originally. Washington, D.C. for the last eight years."

"And what do you do there?"

Ah, the burning question I find myself hating to answer the longer I'm here. "I work in advertising," I reply, stretching the truth a bit.

"Impressive. Do you enjoy it?"

"I'm good at it."

He glares up at me. "That's not what I asked."

"Yes. I enjoy it," I reply, but something about my tone doesn't settle well with either of us.

"I don't believe you."

"What do you want me to say? I make good money. I live a good life." He shakes his head at me. "What?"

"Nothing."

"What happened to you'll always be honest with me?"

That draws his attention back to me, determination in his eyes and voice. "Fine. You want the truth?" I raise my brow at him. "You don't sound happy. In fact, the first night I met you all I could see was a woman who was unhappy, unfulfilled, and lost." My heart is pounding. "But what do I know?"

Standing from the bed, I walk toward the window, needing to look anywhere but at him.

How could he get all of that from that brief interaction? From a moment when two strangers simply exchanged a few words, and not nice ones at that?

For someone who prides myself on being closed off and holding my emotions close to the vest, this man sure dialed me in within moments of meeting me.

"You're not entirely wrong, but I don't want to talk about it. Okay?"

"Consider it dropped." I hear him shifting against the ground, and when I turn around, I see the makings of the chair standing before me. "Just a few more pieces."

"I'll be downstairs." I walk past him, needing space, needing to reset my frame of mind.

Having this man in my house is making me question too many things. And I know that's what I came here to do—work through my shit, get some space from the life I've been living for the past twelve years. I just didn't anticipate a complete stranger calling me out on it.

Ten minutes later, Dallas comes down the stairs with his tool bag in hand. "All done. I put it outside for you. It looks good out there."

"Thank you." I force down the lump in my throat and then we stand there, staring at each other.

"You know, Carrington Cove is a good place to get lost in, Willow." His words are soft, but the meaning behind them is not. His brow pinches and then his hand moves toward me, inching closer to my face before he catches himself and retracts it. Breaking our stare, his eyes shift to the ground. "I guess I'll see you around…"

Nerves race through me, but all I can manage to say is, "More like stalk me, right?" Thankfully, he lightly smiles at that.

"Sure, Willow. Whatever you say." He pauses before he grabs the doorknob. "Just do me a favor?"

"What's that?"

He points down at the floors. "Don't rip up the hardwood. It just needs a good polish. The original wood is part of what makes this house special."

I tilt my head at him, fighting a smile. "That was the plan. Contrary to what you might think, I'm not going to completely rip the house apart. It's too special to do that."

"At least you have half a brain in there."

I roll my eyes playfully. "There you go insulting me again."

His head drops, eyes closing. "Fuck, Willow. I didn't mean it like that."

I hold my palm up. "I'm just kidding, Dallas. But good to know you at least have half a heart in *there*." I move forward to poke his chest jokingly, but that proves to be a big mistake.

Solid muscle barely gives way under the press of my finger against his pec. And getting close to him again allows me to see deeper into those dark chocolate pools of sadness and spite he has for eyes.

I may be dealing with some issues, but it seems to me that Dallas is probably battling his own, too. And as much as I enjoy sparring with the man, perhaps it would serve me best to remember that every person we cross is fighting battles we know nothing about.

"Have a good rest of your day, Willow," he finally says, a crack in his voice, retreating from our close proximity and moving for the door again.

"You too. And thanks again for your help. There's one problem gone off a long list of others."

"I'm sure you'll solve them soon enough." And with those parting words, he opens and shuts the door behind him, leaving me trailing him with my eyes through the windows on the side of the house until I can no longer see him.

And my heart lurches at the reality of being alone once again.

Chapter Eight

Dallas

"Get down!" I can barely hear my voice over the cacophony of noise surrounding me. Bullets fly through the air, dust clouds penetrate the sky, and more yelling and screaming ring out as I take cover behind the wall in front of me.

But that's when I see them—a woman, gripping her child, crying in the corner of the alley.

She's basically a sitting duck.

"You need to get out of here!" I call out to her. But all she does is shake her head, continuing to cry and hold her baby. "Run!"

I vaguely hear one of my other men say something to me, but my focus is shot—it's locked and loaded on this woman.

Disregarding the imminent threat around us, I move toward her, knowing that if I at least help her find cover, she has a chance to survive. Twenty feet seems like one-hundred yards as I crouch down, attempting to avoid being shot myself as chaos swirls around us. And I can sense how close I am to victory, how narrow of a distance there is between saving *two innocent lives to make up for the ones I've taken with far too many bullets to count.*

Within an arm's reach, I close in on the woman just as a bullet pierces her neck.

"No! Fuck!"

Slamming down to the ground, I wait out the rain of gunfire filling the alley.

And then I feel it—a sharp, searing pain as a bullet slices through my side. The physical pain is excruciating, yet it pales in comparison to the searing guilt and heartache that flood in.

My vision goes blurry, the dust and red haze around me making it hard to see.

But I'll never stop seeing her—the woman in front of me, gasping for air as she holds her baby—fighting for her life as I curse the circumstances and choices of my own.

Only this time, her face is different as I look up at her for one last glance—it's the face of a woman who has taken up more space in my mind lately than I care to admit.

It's Willow.

***

"Fuck," I grumble as my eyes snap open and I stare up at the ceiling, my heart beating erratically from the dream that I haven't had in months. It always pops up when I least expect it, but I've heard that's par for the course after serving in a war for years, and something my therapist has helped me through as well.

With a groan, I roll out of bed and brace my forearms on my knees, closing my eyes but still seeing the woman's face staring back at me, life draining from her eyes—*Willow's eyes.*

That same feeling filters through my veins, feeling the need to save this woman despite knowing it's a lost cause, holding me captive as my body remains frozen in place.

But saving a different woman than the mother who haunts my dreams?

That hasn't happened before.

It must be because I can't get her off my mind. Her smart mouth, her fierceness, her *body.*

I'm a thirty-four-year-old man, so I'm not a virgin—let's be honest about that. But between my time in the service and coming home to build a business, the last thing on my mind has been pursuing a woman, or a relationship of any kind. I dated in high school, and casually hooked up with women while in the service—but none of them ever captivated me.

Not like Willow has.

And Willow isn't just *any* woman—she's the woman who owns the house that I want, a woman that is so far from the type I see around my small hometown every day that it's fucking with my head.

But maybe that's the draw?

I see pain in her eyes, the same pain I fight to hide in the moments when memories and loss threaten to overtake me.

I see determination and independence, which is so damn sexy I find my thoughts drifting to what she tastes like while kissing her senselessly just to shut her up.

But like I told her, I also see someone who is lost, searching for something—and what that is, I'm not entirely sure yet.

What bothers me, though, is that I fucking care—because deep down I know I'm still a little lost too.

I want to know what she's searching for, and I want to help her.

"Damn it." Lunging from the bed, I make peace with the fact that I won't be getting any more sleep tonight, glancing at my alarm clock that reads three in the morning. Sounds about right. That's usually the time when my brain overtakes my body's ability to shut off, and since I can't usually fall back asleep, I accept the fact that my nightly rest is over.

I look in the mirror above my dresser, focusing on the scar below my ribs where that bullet hit me, running my fingers over the warped skin, wondering if the internal pain will ever decrease as much as the physical has.

Scars can serve as reminders on the outside.

But the internal ones no one can see?

I wonder if those ever heal, or we just learn to deal with them.

Lord knows I have plenty of those too.

Putting on a pair of running shorts and a zip-up jacket, I lace up my shoes and then head outside for a run to clear my mind and tamp down the adrenaline running through me.

Even though it's still dark outside, I've never worried about running here alone with nothing but a few streetlights and the moon illuminating the dark sky. Like I told Willow, there are perks to living in a small town, and this is one of them for me.

Willow.

I wonder if she's awake, if our interactions are running through her mind as much as they are for me. I've caught her staring at me more than once since she came back into town, so I'm fairly certain that this attraction I feel isn't one-sided. But with her, there's no telling.

Her fiery spirit is addictive. She has me yearning to see what she'll say next. But even throughout our conversation yesterday, I could tell that she uses her snark as a defense mechanism. And maybe I can see that because I do the same thing.

After I kill four miles beneath my sneakers, I return to the bar just as the sun is cresting over the horizon on the water, lighting up the sky in soft yellows and oranges, making the water appear more turquoise at this time of day.

And I hate at that moment that I'm wondering if Willow is watching the sunrise too—sitting in the chair that I built for her, rocking with a cup of coffee in her hands, absorbing any sort of peace that the sight before me is offering, hoping she finds some too.

***

"Mom?" I softly shut the door behind me, balancing the cups of coffee I picked up on the way over here.

Call me a momma's boy, but sometimes just getting a hug from her and some of her hard-earned wisdom can help calm the demons inside.

I've always been closer to my mom than my dad, for reasons that she tried to stay out of. But once Dad died, that overprotective need to keep her safe and free from worry multiplied. She's all I have left, the one person who I've always felt supported me no matter what and cheered me on despite the risky decisions I've made.

I wish there was more I could do for her, to show her how much I appreciate her and love her, but there's nothing I can do to take away her grief—just like there's nothing I can do to let go of the resentment I still harbor toward my father.

Setting down the cups of coffee on the kitchen counter, I peek outside to see if maybe she's watering her garden. The woman has the greenest thumb I know of, so much so that other residents of our town will seek her out for gardening tips. But the yard remains empty, eerily quiet at this time of day.

A soft cry pulls my attention down the hallway and kicks up my heartrate in the process. I slowly push open the door to my parents' bedroom, not sure what to expect to see on the other side of the door.

But the image I find is not one I'll soon forget.

Curled up in a ball on the bedroom floor, my mother clutches one of my father's shirts to her chest, tears streaming down her cheeks. Her eyes are closed tightly as she hiccups between sobs, holding onto one of the last lifelines she has to my dad. A piece of paper rests on the floor beside her.

The grief pouring out of her takes hold of my heart and pulls me toward her instantaneously.

"Mom?" I question softly, not wanting to startle her.

But my effort was in vain.

She shoots up from the floor, wiping under her eyes as I slowly walk toward her and crouch down to her level. "Dallas? What—what are you doing here?"

"I just wanted to see you. I brought you coffee." Gently, I pull her into my chest, sliding down to sit on the floor beside her bed. I wrap my arms around her and lean back against the bedframe, inhaling deeply. "Are you okay?"

"No," she says through a sniffle, shutting her eyes again as she clutches the shirt in her hands tightly. "No I'm not. And I don't want you to see me like this."

"Mom." I press a kiss to her temple as moisture builds in my eyes.

Fuck, it's been months since I've cried, but the sight of my mother completely broken is something my emotions just can't ignore. "It's okay to be upset."

"I was fine this morning, feeling like today was going to be a good day. And then I started opening the mail from yesterday, and I broke." She reaches forward to pick up the piece of paper, bringing it closer to my face. And as I take in the words, my heart plummets.

"The veterans' dinner."

She nods, her face scrunching up in agony. "This is the first year he won't be there for this." Inhaling deeply, she shutters as she exhales. "I'm trying to be strong, like he wanted, like I need to be for you kids. But sometimes…" she trails off, shaking her head as fresh tears stream down her face.

"No one expects you to be strong all the time, Mom." I pull her in closer as she rests her head on my shoulder. "You lost your husband. We lost our father. We have every right to be angry and sad."

"I know. I just miss him so much."

"I miss him too," I say, even though I can feel my heart twist in my chest as I do. My relationship with my father was complicated, but of course I miss him. Of course I live with regrets that no matter what I did, no matter how many times I was deployed, and no matter how much I'd changed with each return, it never seemed to be enough to earn his respect.

He never wanted me to dedicate my life to the Marines, and what irks me the most is that he never gave me a good enough reason why.

"I don't know how I'm supposed to go to the dinner without him. I know they'll probably say something about him, and I don't want to break apart in front of everyone."

"Well, we'll all be there to support you. Dad would want us there to honor a cause that was so important to him."

Even if he never honored my choice.

"I know." She sighs, melting into me more. "Even though I never wanted you to see me like this, I'm glad you're here, Dallas."

"Me too, Mom. I love you." I press a kiss to the top of her head, holding her close to me. "I wish I could take your pain away."

"Sometimes I wish that too, but grief is just love with nowhere to go, Dallas. That's a feeling that is both a blessing and a curse."

This is what happens when you love someone and they leave—either physically or emotionally. Pain that can borderline on intolerable rests deep in your soul and threatens to stay until you can't possibly fathom existing without it.

I feel my mother's pain because I have my own that haunts me too—the loss of my father, the loss of my fellow soldiers, and that mother—the one I couldn't save.

"I had that dream again," I say, breaking the silence that had settled while I gave my mother time to collect herself.

Her sigh has her relaxing in my arms more. "I'm sorry. Dreams can be devilish little suckers."

"Yeah. But…it was different this time, too."

"How so?"

"The woman's face wasn't hers. It was…someone else."

"Who?"

"I'm not sure," I lie, not wanting to bring up my mixed feelings about the new girl in town with my mom right now, feelings I know I shouldn't be entertaining at all.

"Well, sometimes our minds will play tricks on us, make us think one thing when there's really an entirely different meaning behind it."

I huff. "Yeah. Sounds about right."

"Is that why you came over here? Because you had a bad dream?" she teases, pushing herself from my shoulder so I can see her face now.

The lilt in her voice makes me grin. "Maybe."

She smiles, and fuck if the sight doesn't make me feel ten feet tall. After seeing her moments ago, cradled on the floor, the bright white of her teeth is bringing a sense of comfort.

On our hardest days, it's important to remember that we survived every single one that came before it.

"Good to know that my motherly powers are still intact." She pulls me in for a hug. "I love you, son."

"I love you too, Mom. We'll get through this. I promise."

***

"Hey." Penn walks through the front door of the restaurant just after two, sweaty and covered in dust.

"Hey," I reply. "What have you been up to?"

"I was over at Willow's house, starting on some of the demolition."

Just the mention of her name has my pulse spiking. I've lasted a few hours without letting her cross my mind, but work can only serve as a distraction for so long. "Is that so? What are you starting with?"

"Ripping out the shower in the downstairs bathroom. Since it's something she won't use, we thought we'd start there first. I want to do as much on the inside as I can while I wait for the materials for the roof." He moves around me, reaching for a glass and filling it with water, draining the entire thing in one long drink.

"Sounds like a good idea." I'm not sure what else to say that won't make it seem like I'm fishing for information, but part of me wants to know everything I can about the house—or about *her*.

Penn flicks his eyes over to me, reading my mind. "Just ask whatever it is you want to ask, Dallas."

Crossing my arms over my chest, I strengthen my stance. "I can't believe you're helping her." *Okay, that's not what I planned on saying, but apparently my mouth took over my brain.*

The smirk he flashes has me itching to put him in a headlock. "Why not? It's good money. Surely you can't fault me for wanting to be able to pay my bills."

"I'm not. But it's *her*, and it's *that* house."

"Does it matter? Or is your problem more about the fact that you want to fuck her, and not that she's living in the place that you've already claimed as your own?"

I shake my head at him, clenching my jaw. "You're a dick, and you have no idea what you're talking about."

"No, I believe you've claimed that role with the way you've treated the woman since she got here." After she left the bar last Friday night, I told Penn briefly about our interactions thus far, but he doesn't know about what happened yesterday with the chair. "And contrary to what you remember from grade school, being a dick to a girl is not an acceptable way to tell her that you like her."

"You've got it all wrong, Penn." I slap the towel down on the bar and then move to walk away from him.

"Not so fun to be ridiculed about your crush, is it?" he calls after me, stopping me in my steps.

I spin to face him once more, striding back up to him, poking a finger at his chest. "This isn't the same thing. I barely know this woman, and the situation is completely different."

He straightens his spine, locking his eyes with mine. "No, it's complicated, and so is the shit between Astrid and me. So maybe you'll finally leave it alone because now you know what it feels like."

I sigh, pinching the bridge of my nose, taking a step back. "I don't want to fucking fight with you today, all right? I slept like shit and I'm just...frustrated, with a lot of things. And I went and saw Mom today."

He softens his stance instantly. "Is she all right?"

"Yeah. She'll be okay, but she was crying, man. The invitation to the veterans' dinner came in the mail."

"Jesus." He runs a hand through his hair. "Is she going?"

"I think so. I think we all should, actually. It would mean a lot to her, and to Dad."

He nods. "Yeah, I agree."

"I just hate seeing her like this, you know? She's alone, and it fucking kills me."

Penn stares off to the side. "Same. I don't know what's worse sometimes—loving someone and losing them, or never letting people in and dying alone anyway."

Fuck. I hate that my brother's words hit me so hard.

The older I get, the more I wonder if I'll ever settle down or have a family. I always envisioned that being the end goal, but as each day passes, that vision gets blurrier. It's hard to accomplish something like that when you live a life of solitude.

By your own choice, Dallas.

"Since when did you become philosophical?"

The corner of his mouth lifts, easing the seriousness of the conversation slightly. "I don't know. It's just been on my mind a lot lately."

An image of Willow standing in front of me with her hand on her hip flashes in my mind. "Well, whatever is meant to be will be, right?"

"You sound like Mom," he says with a grin. "Why don't you just try to talk Willow about the house again, Dallas?" he asks, shifting the subject back to where we started.

"It's pointless. I got a flat-out no."

He shrugs. "Maybe because you were acting like an ass to her every time you crossed paths."

"I wasn't…"

"Uh, yeah, you were. But maybe making things right with Willow will help your cause."

"What makes you think I need to make things right?"

"She kept bringing you up today, asking questions about why you act the way you do. I think she was trying to be casual about it, but I saw right through her."

"And what did you say to her?"

"I said she should ask you herself. She didn't like that reply very much." He grins.

"I built her a chair yesterday," I admit, which has his eyes bugging out.

"Oh, shit. How did that happen?" I relay the details of our encounter, which only makes him smile more. "That's a good start to smoothing things over, I guess."

"I'm not sure that it's enough."

"Look, Dallas. You act like a dick most of the time, but that's not who you really are. And if you want any hope of this woman selling this house to you eventually, you need to kiss her ass—both figuratively and literally, if you want to."

I shove his shoulder. "Shut up."

"Seriously, though. Why don't you come over and help me a few days with stuff, let her see that you're not a bad guy and you care about the work being done right. Not that I can't handle it, but you get what I mean."

"Yeah, I hear you. And truth is, I wouldn't trust anyone but you to work on that house."

His mouth drops open as he slams his palm to his chest, mockingly. "A compliment? From you? You must not be feeling well," he chides.

"Don't make me fire you."

As my mind whirls with ideas, something sparks, and Penn sees it on my face.

"Uh oh. Does the look on your face mean the light bulb finally clicked on in your brain?"

I nod and flip him the bird at the same time. "Yup. If this woman wants her ass kissed, then that's exactly what I'm going to do."

"Just use protection," he mutters as he walks away.

But I don't give him the satisfaction of a response. I've got work to do.

Chapter Nine

Willow

Yet another morning where the sight of the sun rising from my balcony is making the thought of leaving this place behind even harder to imagine.

I bring my cup of coffee to my lips, blowing steam off the top before taking a sip and smacking my lips in approval. I've never been much of a morning person, but waking up to this every day is quickly changing that.

Folding my feet underneath me, I take a seat in the rocking chair now perched on my balcony thanks to Dallas.

Unfortunately, sleep has evaded me lately as my mind and body have been stirring with thoughts of that man, the man that is just as good-looking as he is infuriating.

I wish I didn't care to know more about him. I wish he didn't pop up at the most inopportune times. And I wish his little act of kindness of putting this chair together didn't make me want to lower my defenses just a tad.

But it does.

And I'm still struggling with why.

As the waves crash up onto the beach, I watch a flock of seagulls fly overhead, a few of them landing in the sand in front of my house. And as I watch them, my eyes catch sight of something that has me standing up from my chair, entirely perplexed in an instant.

"What the hell?"

I march through the sliding door, down the stairs, and out the front door as fast as my feet will carry me, walking right up to the figure that has my jaw dropping open instantly.

"You've got to be shitting me."

Astonished laughter escapes my lips as I stare at the scarecrow standing in front of the house. I mean, I guess you could classify it as a scarecrow, so we'll go with that description.

But the goal of *this* scarecrow is to deter geese.

Placed strategically in the ground on a rather substantial stake is a painted figure that resembles a woman with her blonde hair in a bun sitting low on her neck. A straw hat covers her head, and dark blue coveralls adorn her body. In one hand is a martini glass, and in the other is a sign that says, *No geese, PLEASE!* I laugh at the emphasis on "please."

There's only one person who could have come up with this, giving me yet another reason not to truly hate him—although I'm not sure my mind or body ever really got that message to begin with.

***

"Thank you again for inviting me." I turn toward Astrid, who is busy slathering her son with sunscreen while I watch her daughter play at the shoreline, where the water kisses the sand.

"Of course. I'm glad you came. After you left, I worried whether the invite was too forward." She shakes her head. "I forget that we barely know each other, so I may have come off a little too friendly and overenthusiastic at the idea of making a friend."

I smile, understanding completely. "I understand that, but honestly, you're the first person I've met here that hasn't made me feel like an outsider, so I appreciate you being so forward. Lord knows I wouldn't have been."

Astrid chuckles. "Well that makes me feel a little bit better."

"Am I done?" Her son, Bentley, whines as she releases him.

"I still need to get your face."

"Ugh!" He rolls his eyes and I fight to hold back my smile. "You know I'm old enough to do this on my own, right?"

"Yes, but you won't be as thorough as I will, and trust me, you'll thank me later in life when you don't have melanoma. Or wrinkles." She applies zinc under his eyes so he looks like a lifeguard and ushers him off.

"Did you rub it all in?" he shouts as he runs off toward the water.

"Totally!" she calls after him, and then takes a seat back in her chair next to mine, waving her hand to the side. "He'll never know."

"Ruthless. I love it."

She laughs and then takes a sip from her drink. "Anyway, how are things going with the house?"

"The list that I made is deceptively short considering the amount of work that needs to be done. But Penn has completely stripped the downstairs bathroom and will start restoring it this weekend. Then we're going to paint, restore the hardwood floors, replace light fixtures and outlets, refinish the kitchen cabinets, and the last thing is to replace the roof."

She nods in understanding. "That's quite the list, but if there is anyone who can accomplish it, it's him. He'll probably be there after the soccer game on Saturday then."

"Soccer game?"

"Yeah. He and Dallas coach Bentley's soccer team."

Seriously? The man coaches his employee/friend's son's soccer team?

How am I supposed to keep him at arm's length when I learn these new pieces of information about him that don't make him sound like a neanderthal?

"He did mention he wouldn't be able to come by until Saturday afternoon, so I guess that makes sense now."

"Yeah. It means a lot that those two give up some of their time to coach the team. Ever since Brandon died, I know Bentley has felt like he's missing out on things that his dad should be here for. Brandon used to coach him when he was home—not on deployment, I mean."

I nod in understanding, but I can sense Astrid becoming emotional as her thoughts turn to Brandon. "Hey, we don't have to talk about it," I say as I reach out and place my hand on her arm on instinct.

Astrid stares at the ocean. "It's okay. It's just crazy how sometimes I feel at peace about it, and others it takes me by surprise and overwhelms me. It must be because the veterans' dinner is coming up."

"Veterans' dinner?"

She nods. "Carrington Cove has a dinner every year to honor those that have served or are still serving in the military. Since we're so close to the Marine base, Camp Lejeune, many veterans live here or come here for treatment after returning from deployment. Brandon and I used to go to the dinner together every year." Her eyes cast right as we watch the kids ride waves into the shore on their boogie boards. "I didn't go the first year after he died. But then when I went the next year, Penn stayed by my side the entire time." She sighs at the memory.

The demanding part of me that always seeks answers wants to know more about their dynamic. But the part of me who is trying to make a friend here accepts defeat for now and decides not to push.

She clears her throat and then she twists rapidly in her seat, her eyes widening as she stares at me. "What if *you* came with me this year?"

"Me?" I ask, pointing to my chest.

"Yes! It will be fun! We get to dress up, have a few drinks. There won't be any kids," she mumbles out the side of her mouth. "Penn will probably be tied to his mom this year, so I'll need a friend."

I can't help but grin at her candidness. But then trepidation sinks in. "I don't know, Astrid. I don't know anyone really. I feel like everyone will wonder why I even came. I'll stick out like a sore thumb."

"No, I think it will do the opposite. Help people in town see that you're getting involved and supporting the community."

"But I don't live here, Astrid..."

"Hate to break it to you, *friend*," she teases, "but you own a home in Carrington Cove now. That means you *are* a member of this community, at least until your house is ready to sell. So why not see everything we have to offer? I mean, I know the veterans' dinner isn't a Vegas night out, and to be frank, it will probably be a little depressing at times. But it's important to the people here, and I think it would mean a lot to them if you were there."

I mull over her points, still unsure as uneasiness rests in my stomach. "Can I think about it?"

Her shoulders deflate, but she smiles at me. "Of course."

"When is it, by the way?"

"Two weeks from now."

"Okay."

"Mom!" Lilly runs up to us, her hands cupped as she holds something inside. "Look at all of these shells that Bentley and I found!"

"Those are beautiful, baby. And so many purple ones! Put them in the bag." Astrid lifts a plastic bag from the wagon she used to carry all of her stuff onto the beach, popping open the seal and holding it open so her daughter can gently place the shells inside. "We'll add them to the vase when we get home."

"I'm going to go find more!" Lilly shouts as she races back toward the water.

"We have a vase in their bathroom full of purple seashells they've found over the years. It was Brandon's idea, something fun that they would do together whenever we came to the beach. He told them the purple ones were rare treasures, little pieces of the ocean's magic." She pauses and then laughs lowly. "Really, we just didn't want to bring the whole beach home with us every time we came. I don't know what I'm going to do when that thing is full."

I reach for her hand, knowing that even though our losses are different, Astrid's grief and the underlying grief I hold onto are still very similar—a pain that comes in unpredictable waves just like the ocean before us. Sometimes it's calm, and memories gently wash over you, leaving you with a sense of peace and comfort. But then, out of nowhere, a wave of sorrow crashes over you, so powerful it knocks you off your feet and leaves you reeling.

I squeeze her hand in silent understanding. "You'll just buy a bigger vase."

***

After my beach day with Astrid and a few more days of working from my house, I decide to venture out on Saturday, reminding myself that it's not good to be alone all the time. Funny thing is, that's exactly how I preferred to be before I came here. But like many aspects of my life recently…things change.

I stop by Keely's, treating myself to one of her gourmet coffees that puts Starbucks to shame, and then find a cute little breakfast spot to enjoy a hot meal by the water. It's a bold summer day at the end of August, so the temperature is quickly rising.

And even though a part of me knows better, somehow, I find myself driving around town looking for a park where soccer games are being played. It doesn't take me long to locate a sports complex that is filled with cars and people, whistles echoing in the background and bursts of cheering grab my attention as I step out of my car and head toward the fields.

I don't know why I'm here.

Well, that's not entirely true. It turns out that curiosity is a powerful drug, and after my conversation with Astrid on the beach, I convinced myself that knowledge is power. If Dallas won't show me this side of himself, perhaps I just need to discover it on my own. Plus, I need to thank him for the scarecrow, especially since I can already tell that it's working. It stopped the geese in their tracks this morning when they attempted to ambush me as I left.

But I'm still riding the denial train as I walk along the grass.

I'm not here because the man intrigues me.

It's not because every time we're near each other my blood hums through my veins with electricity.

And it's not because the man has been starring in one too many dirty dreams of mine that remind me how long it's been since I've enjoyed the touch of a man.

Nope. It has nothing to do with of any of that.

"Yes! Go toward the goal!"

Shouting to my right has my head spinning in that direction with recognition. I find Astrid jumping up and down as a young boy dribbles the ball toward the goal.

"Pass, Bentley!" Penn yells just before Astrid's son sends the ball across the field to the one of his teammates. The other player moves past a defender and then passes it back to Bentley, who perfectly kicks the ball past the goalie and into the net.

"Yes! That's what I'm talking about!"

My eyes shift in the direction of that voice, landing on Dallas with a proud smile on his face. His eyes are covered by aviator sunglasses, his head by a backward ball cap, and his broad chest by a lime green t-shirt that matches the team jerseys. It's then that I notice the word *COACH* on his back and on Penn's shirt as well.

"That's right, boys. Let's do it again!" Penn and Dallas share a small conversation after encouraging their players, and then the game picks back up.

I find a spot right next to Astrid, who's seated in a folding chair and texting someone on her phone, oblivious to my approach. "That was a beautiful goal."

Wide eyes peer up at me before her smile goes just as big. "Oh my gosh! What are you doing here?" Launching from her seat, she pulls me into a hug.

"I was just in the neighborhood. Thought I'd stop by and cheer on Bentley."

She narrows her eyes at me. "Sure," she drags out. "It has nothing to do with me telling you who else would be here today."

I roll my eyes at her. "Whatever you say. What's the score?" I ask, changing the subject.

"Three to one now. It's been a nail-biter."

"How much time is left?"

"I'm not sure. Probably ten minutes or so. They just started the fourth quarter."

"Then I'd better stick around to congratulate them if they win."

"Yeah. Okay." She nudges me with her shoulder with a knowing grin on her lips, and then we focus back on the field where the game grows even more intense as the other team scores a goal, making the score three to two.

***

"That was insane." My hands rest over my racing heart. "How do you do that every week?"

"I feel like each game I watch takes another year off my life," Astrid jokes, and we share a laugh.

"Mom! We won!" Bentley races over to her, slamming into her side.

"I know, honey. I was watching. Congratulations! You guys did amazing." She kisses the top of his head.

"They did, didn't they?" Dallas walks over, pride etched into every line of his face. "If they keep playing like that, they'll be going to the championship tournament, no doubt."

"We will. We're unstoppable," Bentley states confidently.

"No, you guys work hard and as a team. But no one is unstoppable," Dallas corrects him. "Come on, bud. We need to shake hands with the other team still." He casts his eyes to me, offers me a curt nod, and then walks away.

Bentley runs after him as they display sportsmanship that warms my heart. I never played sports growing up, but I can appreciate the fact that Dallas and Penn are teaching these boys to be gracious winners. That speaks very highly of them both.

After one of the parents hands out snacks to the boys and Dallas and Penn talk to the team for a few more minutes, Bentley runs back over to Astrid and me. Lilly jumps from her spot on the grass where she was playing with one of the siblings of another boy and hugs her brother.

"Good job, B."

"Thanks, Lilly."

"You did great, Bentley. I was very impressed," I say, smiling down at him.

He flashes me a genuine smile. "Thanks, Willow. I didn't know you'd be here today."

"Neither did I," a familiar voice interjects.

I look up to see Dallas striding toward us, a backpack slung over his shoulder and a clipboard in his hand. When he stops in front of me and takes off his sunglasses, I'm immediately captivated by those intense dark eyes. The longer I look into them, the more hypnotized I become—and no matter how hard I try, I can't look away.

God, he looks more mouthwatering each time I see him.

And a backward hat? Why is that so freaking hot?

"Well, it was a spur of the moment kind of thing. I was in the neighborhood." I shrug, trying to act aloof.

"Out exploring the town?" Dallas asks, continuing to hold my gaze.

"Something like that."

Astrid grins as she looks between us, but then ushers her kids to the side. "We're going to get going, but thanks for coming, Willow. See you soon?"

"Yeah. I'll text you."

Astrid walks away, leaving me and Dallas alone.

"You two seem to be getting awfully friendly," he says, shifting in his stance while he shoves the clipboard under his arm.

"Is that a problem?"

He shakes his head. "Not at all. Astrid is exactly the type of person you want in your corner."

"Well, I happen to think so too." I tuck a strand of hair behind my ear that's escaped my ponytail. "She's been extremely kind and welcoming, something I'm not used to around here," I say in a teasing tone.

"Well, maybe some people didn't give you the best first impression, but they're trying to correct their mistakes."

I squint up at him. "Are you speaking about yourself in the third person right now?"

He smirks. "Maybe."

"Well then, I guess this would be a good time to say thank you for the scarecrow, especially if that was your attempt at apologizing. Although, I think it would have been even scarier if you had put *your* face on it instead of mine."

His grin is infectious. "I don't know. Those geese were after me just as much as they were after you. I think my face would only attract them more."

"Are you saying I'm attractive?"

"No. I'm saying I am." He's teasing me, I know it. But part of me really is curious if he's attracted to me or not.

God, I hate that I really want to know the answer to that question.

I roll my eyes at him instead. "Lord, you're so full of yourself."

"I'm full of a lot of things…"

"What do we have here?" Penn comes by, gripping the shoulders of a young boy in front of him and side-stepping him to move closer to us.

"Willow was in the neighborhood and just happened to show up at our game," Dallas replies before I can.

"Huh. That's convenient." Penn plays dumb, his eyes bouncing back and forth between the two of us. "Well, I'm going to go home and grab my tools, and then I'll be by your house in little while, right, Willow?"

I shift my gaze over to him. "Yes. Thank you. I think I might try to paint today while you're working downstairs."

"Sounds good." Penn walks away with the boy, leaving us alone once more.

I clear my throat, intent on following through with why I came here in the first place. "As I was saying, thank you for the scarecrow. I think it's helping."

"How so?"

"Well, they wouldn't walk past it this morning when I was leaving. It was like it put off an invisible forcefield, blocking their path."

"It actually is covered in a repellent that helps deter them as, although I think it's the sign that really does the trick." He taps his temple and winks. "I told you, Willow. Manners go a long way."

I shake my head at him, fighting my smile. "Gosh, that must be it. But seriously," I pause, drawing a deep breath before uttering, "*thank you*. It was a...pleasant surprise. And I'm sorry too, for how I acted before."

Leaning forward slightly, his hands shoved in his pockets now, our eyes lock as I catch a whiff of his scent—sandalwood mixed with sweat. "You're welcome, and I accept." I bite my lip, not sure of where to go from here, but luckily Dallas speaks next. "We should probably get going. Where are you parked?"

"Over there." I point to the lot adjacent to the field.

"Me too. Come on"—he nods in that direction—"I'll walk with you."

We walk toward the parking lot side by side, stealing glances at each other as we go.

"So painting today, huh?" he asks, replacing his sunglasses on his face again.

"Yeah. Big plans. Although I actually have some experience with that, so at least I'm not afraid of messing it up too badly."

"What room?"

"The master."

Dallas grumbles. "I hate painting. My hand always ends up looking like The Claw."

"From *Liar, Liar*?"

He nods. "Yup. I bet Jim Carrey painted for hours so he could make his hand look like that."

Laughing, I say, "It definitely takes a toll on your body if you do it for too long."

He nods again but keeps his eyes forward. "What color are you thinking?"

"Bright yellow," I answer without hesitation, curious to see what his reaction will be. Honestly, I'm not opposed to the color, but I have a feeling Dallas might have an opinion about the choice.

His lips turn up in disgust. "Yellow? Are you insa—" He stops himself and tries again. "I mean, why such a... vibrant color?"

"I think it's cheery, will make even the grumpiest person feel happier." My smile peeks through my words and Dallas catches it.

"You're joking, aren't you?"

Chuckling under my breath, I reply, "Yes. I just wanted to see how'd you react."

"Well, if you didn't read that correctly, it was utter disgust."

"I mean, I don't have anything against yellow, but I feel like a light gray is more neutral, and it entices buyers. You can decorate in pretty much any color scheme with gray walls."

"I agree. That's a smart choice. Especially to *this* buyer." He points his thumb at his chest.

I squint at him, chuckling. "Subtle."

We arrive at my car moments later, which just happens to be right next to his, a classic car that is enticingly sexy and something that I can totally see Dallas driving.

"Do you have anything else planned today?" I ask him without thinking. For a second, I wish I could take my question back, but Dallas doesn't read too much into it.

"It's Saturday, so I'll be at the restaurant. Saturdays are always busy."

"Right."

"You should come by for dinner."

"I'm not sure. It probably depends on how I feel after all the painting." *But does that mean he wants me to come by?*

For a second, Dallas almost looks disappointed by my answer. "Makes sense." His eyes dart out over the park, and then back to me. "Well, this was a surprise, Willow, but I'm glad you came by."

"Me too. Astrid told me that you and Penn coach Bentley's team, and I guess I just had to see it for myself." With a shrug of my shoulders, I unlock my car with the key fob.

"So you weren't just wandering around town then?"

Damn it. "Yes, and no. I also wanted to thank you for the scarecrow, so I figured this was the perfect opportunity to do that and see you in action, doing something noble instead of just sneaking onto people's property in the middle of the night and putting up polite signs."

"It was actually the early hours of the morning," he corrects me, grinning from ear to ear.

"Where did you get it by the way?"

"Judy's Knick Knacks. It's on the boardwalk near my sister's photography studio."

The mention of his other siblings rings a bell. "Oh. I haven't been to visit that area yet."

"You should. The view alone is amazing, but so are the businesses. Judy can make almost anything and she takes custom orders. I put a rush on it, but she followed my instructions to the letter." He smirks as he unlocks the door to his car and puts his bag and clipboard inside.

He catches me admiring the car for a moment before I bring my gaze back to him. "I can tell you were very specific about details."

"I needed it to be perfect."

"It was scarily accurate, that's for sure." A thought pops into my head. "You own a business, help out your brother, sneak around town in the early morning hours to deliver gifts, and coach soccer." I shake my head at him. "How do you manage it all? And why do you do it?"

His gaze is steady. "I like helping people. With the soccer thing, it's more than just them needing a coach. A lot of those boys have parents in the service, so they're not here. Or, they lost a parent like Bentley did. So Penn and I help out because no matter how old you are, you need a positive role model in your life, and Marines always stick together."

My insides melt. "That's pretty incredible of you, Dallas."

"And I have amazing employees who keep my business running smoothly, so that's not as demanding as you might think." He reaches up and scratches his chin through the scruff that's grown out. "Maybe it's the oldest brother in me, but I take pride in taking care of people.

I feel like everyone needs someone they can depend on in life, Willow. Don't you agree?"

A resounding *yes* is on my lips, but the truth is, I've only been able to depend on two people besides myself, so I'm not sure that I'm qualified to answer. Instead, I offer, "I think the people in your life are lucky to have you."

Dallas's lips spread into a soft smile. "Thank you. Well, I hope Penn gets some work done for you today. I need to get to the restaurant to prepare for the evening rush."

"Oh yeah. Sure. Good luck with that," I manage to say, stumbling through my reply. I'm not sure how to leave things, or that I want to leave at all. The last ten minutes have been eye-opening, revealing glimpses of a man I'm only just beginning to understand beyond the surface, to the parts that truly matter.

"Thanks. I'll—I'll see you around?"

"Um, yeah. I'll be here." I give him an awkward wave and then move to get in my car as he does the same, the sound of his motor firing up and vibrating behind me, igniting awareness in my entire body. When I sit in the driver's seat of my car and look out my window, I catch a glimpse of him backing up, his hand draped casually over the wheel as he spins it then shifts into drive and presses on the gas, not so much as casting another look in my direction.

But I look at *him*, admiring the sight of the man driving his car that only adds to his allure, leaving me a pile of mush before I realize I'm still sitting in this parking lot and I haven't moved at all.

"Jesus." I slap a hand to my forehead and then prepare to drive home, knowing I have more than enough work to keep me busy and hopefully keep my mind off Dallas for a few hours.

Except there's not much else to do while painting except think, and forgetting about Dallas is much easier said than done.

Chapter Ten

Willow

"Who on earth could that be?"

The next day, I hear the doorbell ring from downstairs as I'm getting ready for work in the master bathroom. I'm finishing my makeup before I hop on a conference call with my firm. These Zoom calls have taught me the critical importance of decent makeup and strategic lighting—without them, I'd resemble a troll that has crawled out from under a bridge.

I finish the last coat of my mascara and then cinch the tie around the waist of my white silk robe, hoping maybe it was just a package being dropped off on the doorstep. Online shopping has been a godsend for finding products that the stores in this small town don't carry. It's given me a much broader selection of choices when it comes to home décor and essentials as well, compared to the hardware store that I seem to know like the back of my hand now.

As I tread lightly down the stairs, I cast my eyes over my home that looks fairly put-together considering the construction going on around me.

My home.

The more I utter those words out loud and to myself, the more that reality sets in.

Living in an apartment for most of my adult life and then moving into a house has made me realize that the walls I've called home in D.C. don't hold as much sentiment as this house does in even one square inch. These walls have character, the floor holds secrets, and the windows offer breathtaking views of the ocean just a few hundred feet away.

The desired feeling of belonging and finding roots is starting to take shape, which only adds to the conundrum I've found myself in—my desire to sell this place dwindling with each project Penn and I complete on the house, turning it into a place I could actually see myself living in.

I push my hair from my face, knowing that by now the person that rang the doorbell has to be long gone, so I pull open the door—with my new, non-sticking doorknob installed just yesterday—expecting to see a box on the porch.

And there is a box.

But it's in Dallas's hands.

"Dallas?" I gasp, clutching at the neck of my robe, cursing the fact that the instant I see him my nipples get hard, which are glaringly easy to detect through the thin silk.

I see his eyes widen, drop down to my offending chest, and then glance back up just as fast, clearing his throat as he finds his words and averts his eyes. "Good morning."

"Uh, good morning. What are you doing here?" My grip on my robe grows tighter.

"I, um, came by to give you something." He stares at me as I wait for him to continue, but it takes us both a minute to process what's going on here.

"Okay?"

He finally blinks. "Can I come in?"

"Um." I glance down at my robe, feeling borderline naked the longer I stand here.

"It will just take a minute."

"Sure." I open the door wide, allowing his large frame to walk through, watching him wander toward the kitchen where he deposits the box on the counter.

"I was cleaning out a closet at the bar and found this box of painting stuff." He motions toward the cardboard as I step closer, still holding my robe together. Cool air hits the underside of my thighs while I make sure to keep my back to him so he doesn't get a show. The only thing I have on under this flimsy piece of fabric is a light pink thong.

"Okay..."

"It's from when we remodeled the place last year. There are brushes, brand new paint rollers, and gloves. I think there's half a can of navy blue paint in there too, which is probably still good." He finally meets my eyes. "I don't know. I just figured you could probably use this more than I can."

"Oh." The racing beat of my heart is both from surprise and skepticism. He came all the way out here to bring me painting supplies—basic things, really, that I can easily grab from the store. It's thoughtful, sure, but why go to the effort?

"It's the little things that mean the most sometimes."

Astrid's words from weeks ago jump back into my mind, and one of the walls I built up toward this man slowly crumbles as we stand there.

"Thank you. That was—this was really thoughtful of you."

He waves his hand dismissively, trying to play off my gratitude. "It's nothing. Hell, I wrestled with myself about even bringing it by. But I just thought…"

Without contemplation, I step around the counter and gently lay my hand on his chest, letting my robe go in the process but holding his stare. "I appreciate it. No one has ever done anything like this for me before."

I watch his throat bob as he swallows roughly. "No one has brought you painting supplies?"

I grin, shaking my head slowly. "Nope. And no one has brought me a scarecrow before, or built me a rocking chair either."

His gaze holds me captive as his response comes out low and gruff. "Well, I'm glad I got to be the first then."

We stand there, our eyes bouncing back and forth between each other, deciphering the air around us and feeling the ground beneath us shift all at the same time.

What the hell is going on here?

We're being nice to each other. He's showing me that he listens when I speak, he's not as bad of a guy as I initially thought, and…

And why am I desperate to kiss him right now?

I feel my lips fall open as I suck in a breath, desperate for oxygen to pull me out of this haze. And when I do, I watch Dallas's eyes drop to my mouth, studying my lips before dipping lower to the opening of my robe which I'm sure is parted enough at this moment to give him a perfect view of my cleavage.

"Your hair is down," he whispers, moving his hand to my hip as I pull in a sharp breath again.

"Yeah."

"You never wear it down."

"I—I was going to put it in a bun."

"Don't." One word. One command, and my body relents to his order instantly.

"Okay."

Dallas's face moves only an inch closer to mine as he leans forward, and I swear the world stops spinning while I anticipate his next move.

Is he going to kiss me?

Are those full lips I've been admiring way too much going to press against mine?

Will I finally know what that beard is going to feel like against my skin?

Inch by inch he moves closer until I swear a spark fires between us…

And my phone rings.

We both jump apart as we're jolted back to reality. I smooth my hair from my face as I move away from him and his eyes widen, processing what almost happened.

"Uh…" I clear my throat "I need to get that. And I have a call…"

Glancing behind me at the clock on the microwave, I note the time and curse the fact that I need to log in to my meeting in less than ten minutes.

"No, yeah. I understand. Shit, I'm sorry I bothered you." He turns to walk away, running a hand through his hair and nearly runs into the couch while he finds hit footing.

I follow him to the door, not wanting to leave things like this—not wanting him to leave at all.

What the hell is that about?

And were we seriously about to kiss?

"It was no bother. Thank you again, Dallas. I mean it."

"No problem, Willow. Hope your call goes well." As he shuts the door behind him, the ringing from my phone continues to echo from upstairs. Cursing the timing of it all, I huff up the stairs to my room, answering the phone without trying to sound angry and frustrated, and finish getting ready for work.

And as I log in to my meeting, I fight my subconscious for the next hour with trying not to think about what would have happened if Dallas would have kissed me. And if maybe I should wear my hair down more often.

***

"I can't believe you convinced me to come here," I whisper, leaning over the counter so Astrid can hear me.

"You needed to come out. You can't hide in that house of yours and be scared of seeing Dallas after your little *almost* kiss." She waves her hand at me while she fills up her tray with drinks.

"I knew I shouldn't have told you about that," I grate out, slinking back in my chair and taking a large sip from my martini as she smirks at me from her side of the counter.

It's been five days since Dallas showed up on my front doorstep and, like the strong, independent woman I am, I've been avoiding him ever since. After our *almost* kiss and his front-row seat to my nipples beneath thin silk, I felt like keeping some space from him would help remind myself that no matter how badly I want to know what he's like in bed, no good can come from crossing that line.

If only my libido would get the message.

"But you did. And now it's my job as your friend to torture you about it."

"I'm not sure that's how friendship is supposed to work."

"That's how good friendships work," she counters, depositing two fishbowl margaritas on her tray. "We support each other, talk about our feelings, and then give each other shit when the other one is acting like a chicken."

"I am *not* acting like a chicken."

"Who's acting like a chicken?" Dallas's question pulls both of our attention to where he stands behind the bar, wiping his hands on a dishtowel.

"No one," I answer before Astrid can get another word in. My eyes dance appreciatively down his torso and the denim that encases his thick thighs, but then I return them to his face as quickly as I can before he notices.

"Hey, Dallas. Willow's drink is almost empty. Why don't you give her a refill?" Astrid suggests as she lifts up her tray and waltzes off, leaving the two of us alone.

And despite my desire to ebb my growing attraction toward him by staying away, the second he stands directly in front of me, my entire body comes alive.

Guess five days with no contact wasn't long enough.

"You ready for a refill?" Dallas asks as he clears a few empty glasses from the bar.

"Uh, sure. Thanks."

"No problem. You must have been busy this week. Haven't seen you out and about much…"

Did he notice I was avoiding going out in public so we wouldn't run into each other?

Or more importantly, was he looking for me?

"Oh, yeah. I've been busy."

Leaning over the bar, his face comes within inches of mine. "Busy avoiding me?"

"No," I lie.

The lift of his lips tells me he knows that. But then his face falls serious again, and he reaches out to tuck a strand of my hair behind my ear.

God. Why is he touching me and why don't I want him to stop?

"You don't have to hide from me, Goose."

"I—I wasn't."

"I'm not so sure about that. In fact, I feel like you hide an awful lot from the whole world."

My stomach twists in knots. I feel like he can see right through me, see the scars I keep hidden on the inside, see the pain that is resting right underneath the surface—pain that was buried deep until I traveled to this little town and started thinking about all the "what ifs."

"I told you. I was busy," I manage to croak out.

"Busy doing what?"

"Working."

"And..." he draws out, waiting for me to continue.

"Uh, and working, Dallas."

He eyes me skeptically as he stands again. "You're telling me that all you did this week was work?"

The way the words leave his lips makes me feel as if I have some infectious disease or something. The truth of the matter is that I was actually bored out of my mind this week. I only had three calls with Katrina, and my email inbox is going through the longest dry spell it's ever had. It might catch up to the dry spell my vagina has been experiencing as well. In fact, I kept refreshing it, making sure I hadn't missed something.

And I hadn't. Katrina and my team are proving to be the well-oiled machine I know they are which means I was bored this week. There, I said it.

And if it weren't for the painting, I might have actually gone a teensy bit insane.

"What do you do for fun then, Goose?"

Glaring at him from his use of the nickname he coined for me, I reply, "Uh, I work, Dallas."

"Your front yard is the ocean. You're in a town that has plenty to explore. Did you at least make it down to the boardwalk?" he asks.

"Uh, no."

Shaking his head, he tsks. "That's unacceptable, Goose. All work and no play is just going to make you cranky. And you can't see everything Carrington Cove has to offer if you stay tucked away in that house."

"I'm not cranky," I argue, ready for a fight. At least when he riles me up, it makes me forget that he almost kissed me.

Is that what he's doing? Trying to move past that moment because he thought it would be a mistake too?

He smirks at me. "That's debatable. Well, tell me how the painting went at least."

"It went well…I mean, as well as painting can go. I finished the downstairs bathroom, the master, and moved on to one of the other bedrooms. They're empty, so it went pretty fast. But I swear, no matter what you do, the paint gets everywhere."

"Like in your hair?" he asks, glancing to my hair that is still in my bun from work today. Suddenly, I'm reminded of his comment from the other day. *"You never wear it down."*

"Yes."

"I can see that."

"What?"

I watch him slide my drink across the counter and then reach up to play with my hair, pulling a few strands of my bangs forward. "You still have some paint in your hair, Willow."

Oh God. Bury me alive in this moment, please.

"What?" I whisper as he carefully scratches his short nails against my hair, flecks of gray paint falling to the bar like imaginary tears of my mortification.

Dallas chuckles as he slides his eyes to my face and then back to what he's doing. "Don't worry. It wasn't that noticeable since your hair is light anyway. But I saw it the moment you sat down when the light overhead caught it."

"You were going to let me sit here like that all night?" I ask as he pulls his hand away.

His brow furrows. "No. I did just remove it for you, didn't I?"

Conflicted about his intent, I decide to focus on my drink instead, pulling the glass toward me and taking a large gulp. "Well, thanks, I guess."

He leans over the bar, supporting his body on his forearms, his voice low as he says, "I know that was your attempt at manners, but the sarcasm under there was detectable." He chuckles, wipes the paint from the bar, and walks away, leaving me embarrassed and no clearer about the status between the two of us.

From the moment we met, we've been frank with one another.

But now that frankness is laced with flirtation and something else—intrigue, maybe? The more we interact, the more I feel like Dallas is just as curious about me as I am about him—and the sexual tension is racing toward the point of erupting.

"Was Dallas playing with your hair?" Astrid comes up behind me, whispering in my ear as I spin on my stool to face her.

"No," I huff. "He was getting paint out of my hair."

Astrid snorts. "Oh God."

Slapping my hand to my forehead, I say, "I know. It was mortifying."

"But he touched you," she argues. "And believe me, Dallas doesn't touch women. Hell, I can't remember the last time I've seen him pay attention to any woman. It's been years."

"I don't want his attention."

Liar, liar, pants on fire.

"Oh, Willow," she tsks before patting me on the head. "Just keep telling yourself that." And then she's off, checking on her customers once more.

"You play darts?" A gravelly voice from my left has me spinning on my stool once more.

"Excuse me?"

"You play darts?" he asks again, completely serious. The man is older than dirt, dressed in a blue checkered flannel and dark blue ball cap with a Marine's Veteran logo on it that looks eerily familiar, but his eyes and smile are sincere.

"Uh, not really."

"Well, we need another player, and you look like you might be able to throw a few."

"I do?"

"Yeah. There's a fire in you, sweetheart, and a death glare. I'm sure you could narrow your eyes on the target real fast and hit the bullseye."

"You think so?" I smirk, fighting with the pull I'm having toward this old man and genuinely enjoying his determination and conversation.

"I'm rarely wrong. And better yet, if you can't, I'll buy your drinks tonight."

I twirl the toothpick that still has one olive around in my glass. "That's a hard bargain to pass up."

"Then you'll play?" His entire forehead crinkles as he waits for my answer.

I've never played darts a day in my life, even during the handful of times I've gone out to bars, and that was back in college. Frankly, I can't remember the last time I spent a Friday night in a bar having fun. But I'm here, I'm two drinks in, and it's not like I have anything better to do.

When in Carrington Cove, right?

"I've never played, so this is your warning if I suck."

"Like I said, I have a gut feeling about you. Let's go." He takes my hand, pulling me up from my chair and leading me over to the corner of the bar where the dartboards are set up. Two of his friends are waiting for him, nursing beers.

"I got our fourth," he states proudly, putting his arm around me. If a strange man did that any other time, I'd be kneeing him in the junk, but I can tell he means no harm. "Little lady, this here is Thompson and Baron, and I'm Harold, by the way."

"Willow, and it's nice to meet you gentlemen." I notice they're all wearing the same hats with the same logo on the front. "I tried to tell Harold here that I've never played, but he wouldn't take no for an answer."

"That's 'cause you're a pretty little thing, Willow, and Harold is a dirty old man."

"Shut your pie hole," Harold scolds his friend, Thompson, I think it is. "Willow, I am an utter gentleman, I assure you."

"Sure," the one who must be Baron adds.

"Well, how about we play some darts and we'll see who the real man is after all?" I challenge, and they all smile in my direction.

I watch Baron collect the darts for our two teams, writing our names on the scoreboard. But as I turn around to take another sip of my drink, I catch Dallas watching me from behind the bar, his scowl apparent even though there's a considerable distance between us. And my entire body hearts up from his stare, like he's keeping an eye on these men, making sure I'm okay.

When I turn around, I try to focus on the game and even do pretty well for my first time, all the while battling this feeling of contentment that makes the evening go by in a blur.

Before I know it, I'm three martinis deep and Harold and I have won two rounds of darts.

"Never played before, my ass," Thompson grumbles as Harold and I celebrate our win with a hug.

"Beginner's luck, I swear." I hold up three fingers like a boy scout, giggling just as I feel an ominous presence come up behind me.

"Can I get you gentlemen a refill?" Dallas's voice sends a shiver down my spine, followed by a trail of heat that could be the alcohol, but I'm beginning to doubt that since it happens every time he's near.

"I think we're done, Dallas. Goldilocks here hustled us," Baron whines jokingly.

"Is that so?"

I hold my hands up defensively. "I swear, I've never played before. They don't believe me."

"I believe you," he says, staring down into my eyes.

And that makes my hands drop. "Why?"

"Something tells me you're not the type to play darts on a Friday night in a bar...am I right?"

As if he just took a pair of scissors to a balloon, Dallas bursts the bubble I've been swimming in for the past hour, reading me like an open book and I hate that he's right.

"Well, she's a natural," Harold interjects, breaking the moment and squashing my inner turmoil for the moment.

"Good to know. You guys have a good night and I'll see you at the center sometime this week," he says, ushering me away like he's my bodyguard.

"I wasn't done playing."

"Yes, you are," he murmurs in my ear. "Come on. Let me get you a glass of water."

Sulking, I huff but don't argue as I follow him back to the bar where Astrid is grinning from ear to ear as she watches us.

Taking a seat on an empty stool, I roll my eyes and she hides her laugh. Dallas slides me a glass of water. "Thanks."

"Looks like you were having fun," Astrid says, standing across from me with her hands on her hips.

"I was." My answer is so easy, and that makes me feel unsettled because it's been so long since it felt natural to admit something like that.

I shouldn't feel guilty for having fun. And part of me does, but part of me doesn't. Part of me...*really* enjoyed myself tonight. "Then the 'big bad bar owner' had to come break it up."

Astrid smiles and Dallas just glares in my direction. "Those old men were leaving anyway."

"Still..."

"Harold, Baron, and Thompson are the sweetest." Astrid leans forward on the bar. I notice the restaurant has emptied out a bit, so I glance at the clock and realize it's after ten already.

"They were very nice." And it felt good to have genuine company for the evening. Most of my evenings at home are spent alone. Hell, I don't even have a pet to go home to after work. And I thought that's the life that suited me, but after a few weeks here, I'm discovering new possibilities.

"Are you ready to go?" Astrid stands up straight again. "I'm almost off and I can give you a ride home."

"I'm fine."

"No, you're not," Dallas interjects. "You've had three martinis. You're not driving."

"You're not my keeper," I fire back at him, aiming my lingering frustration on the man that has caused it.

"No, but I am the owner of this place and I have a responsibility. I can't let anyone take a risk like that. Let Astrid drive you home, and you can come get your car tomorrow."

"But..."

"It will be fine here, Willow. Nothing happens here in Carrington Cove."

Yeah, nothing but inheriting a house you didn't want, becoming addicted to delicious blueberry muffins, and salivating over the broody bar owner that is everywhere I go.

With a harsh exhale, I relent. I already planned to get a ride from Tommy—of Tommy's Taxi and Tours—anyway. But I hate that it feels more like Dallas just trying to boss me around and exude his authority.

It'd be okay if he bossed you around in bed though, right?

"Yeah, I think I'm done for the night." My brain is obviously being affected by the alcohol as images of Dallas handcuffing me to my bed flash behind my eyelids.

Jesus, get me out of here before I surrender to him in front of all these people.

"Perfect. Let me finish up a few things and then we'll get going." Astrid strides away, leaving me alone with Dallas once more.

"How are the geese?" he asks, which confuses me at first. Then my mind catches up.

"Oh, well, I think they're starting to like the scarecrow. They ventured up on the deck again yesterday."

"You might need more repellent."

"Or a scarecrow with *your* face on it like I suggested in the first place. You seem to be keen on scaring people away. I'd still be playing darts and having fun if it weren't for you."

Dallas comes around the bar, standing so close to me that I have to crane my neck back to look up at him from my seat. But then he lowers his voice, dips his head down, and grates out, "I'm just looking out for you."

"I didn't ask you to do that. I'm a big girl, and I can handle myself just fine. And honestly, Dallas...those men are old and just looking to play darts. You can't possibly be jealous? Can you?" I tease as a hiccup leaves my lips.

His eyes get even more narrow. "I'm not jealous."

"Could have fooled me."

We stare at each other as I continue to wonder why he had a problem with me hanging out with those men.

Was it because I was having fun? Was it because I was hanging out with men old enough to be my grandfather?

Or was it because I am in his bar, his town, and the house that he wants, and he doesn't want me here?

"I'm ready," Astrid says behind me, breaking our stare and the whiplash I'm experiencing every time I'm around this man.

Just the other day I thought he was going to kiss me. And then tonight, he looks like he's about to kidnap me and lock me up in his basement.

"Yeah. Me too." I stand up so my chest brushes against Dallas's, who quickly steps back, suddenly aware that there are people all around us potentially watching our exchange.

"Get her home safe, Astrid." He turns away from me, not bothering to glance in my direction again as he pushes through the door that leads to the kitchen and disappears.

"Oh boy…" Astrid clicks her tongue once we leave the restaurant and arrive at her car. After situating ourselves, she pulls out of the parking lot and heads for my house. "Did you say something to rile him up?"

"Nope. I played darts with three old men. Apparently that was enough of an offense."

Astrid laughs. "God, I can't wait until this blows up."

"Nothing is going to blow up."

"Uh, yes it is. There's a storm brewing, Willow. And you'd better be prepared because I have a feeling you've never dealt with a man like Dallas before."

Why do her words give me a thrill like it's a challenge rather than a warning? A warning I shouldn't ignore but, truthfully, deep down I hope to meet head-on.

Chapter Eleven

Dallas

"God, you're a life saver." Parker rushes into the restaurant just after twelve, pulling his glasses from his nose and placing them on the bar next to him as he takes a seat right in front of the burger and fries I just finished making for him.

"Is the office that crazy?"

He takes a giant bite out of the burger, moaning as his eyes close. "When is it not?" he mumbles around his food.

"This is why I don't have a pet." I shake my head as I wipe down the bar in front of me. "Too much responsibility."

He finishes chewing and then drains half of his Coke. "Not to mention you don't have a place for one since you live in the apartment above this place."

"That too."

"Penn said he's working on your house, though." The lift of the corner of his mouth tells me all that I need to know—my dickhead brother told my other dickhead brother about my current predicament involving Willow.

"It's not my house…yet," I add, even though my initial desire to take it from her is dwindling by the day.

"I have to say, it's quite ironic that the owner leaves it to a woman that just so happens to get under your skin."

My head spins toward him. "She doesn't get under my skin." But if I knew who the damn original owner was, I'd definitely bombard them for more information about where the heck she came from.

"That's not what Penn said." Parker pops a fry into his mouth.

I slam the towel down onto the bar this time, scrubbing furiously at the same spot. "Penn doesn't know what he's talking about. In fact, the last time Willow and I spoke was rather pleasant."

"Oh, she has a name."

I glare at him for a second. "Most people do."

Parker squints at me. "And *pleasant*? Where hell did that word come from?" Then he shakes his head and takes another bite from his burger, mumbling around his food. "Nope, I think Penn's right. This woman has you rattled. Your vocabulary is even changing."

"Fuck. You."

"Seems I walked in on a good conversation." Grady Reynolds, Astrid's brother, takes a seat right next to Parker.

"And if you still want your lunch, you'll stay out of it," I reply, grabbing his burger that's already waiting for him under the heat lamps in the kitchen window.

Every Thursday, Parker and Grady come by for lunch before the restaurant opens to the public. I know what it's like to own your own business and need a break from time to time. That's why I hired Brian, my other manager, a few years ago, so I could get a break now and again and not burn myself out. And when my father fell ill, I was even more grateful that I had time to step up for my family when I had to.

Parker doesn't own the vet's office outright, but he practically runs the place by himself. The owner, Richard O'Neil, is semi-retired, only working three days a week while my brother serves the town and their pets at all hours. But from what it sounds like lately, he needs some help and another doctor.

Grady moved back to Carrington Cove shortly before Brandon, Astrid's husband, died almost four years ago. Before that, he was the classic small-town celebrity, leaving our coastal town for California to play professional baseball. Everyone kept tabs on him and cheered him on throughout his days as one of the top pitchers in the MLB. But when an injury ended his career, he reluctantly came back home to start the next phase of his life. No one will come right out and tell him, but he's been a bit of a grump ever since he moved back.

Luckily for him, the owner of the auto repair garage he worked at as a teenager was looking to sell at the time, so he took over an already established shop and clientele to pursue another passion of his. His former celebrity status obviously helps his business, but he's also made a name for himself with custom engine work and reliable service. And all of the single ladies in town just love to ask him to help with their car troubles.

"I need food, so you're on your own, Parker," Grady grumbles as he picks up his burger with both hands and nearly devours half of it in one bite.

The guy is intimidatingly large, that I'll admit.

I wonder if that's another reason why Penn doesn't want to pursue his feelings for Astrid? Is he afraid of Grady?

"It's okay. Penn seems to be keeping me in the loop and I'm sure he'll tell you soon enough." Parker motions to me for a refill of his Coke.

Grady wipes his mouth with a napkin. "Oh, if you're referring to the smoking hot blonde who inherited the Bayshore House, he's already told me." He smiles over at me before taking another bite of his burger.

"Jesus Christ." I pinch the bridge of my nose and move over to the soda machine, refilling Parker's glass before sliding it back to him. Then, I head for the ice machine, filling the bucket before refilling the steel bar well. "Good to know Penn's spreading my business around."

"How are you going to convince her to sell you the house, man?" Grady asks as I grab a box of lemons, slicing them on a cutting board and placing them into smaller steel bins.

I watch my hands, making sure not to slice my fingers off, but also so I can avoid their eyes on me. "I don't know. We didn't get off on the right foot, as you know. I'm not sure that there's much else I can do except try to smooth things over and hope she changes her mind about me."

But lately, every time we're near each other, all I want to do is trace every inch of her body with my tongue and make her shut her sarcastic mouth with my own.

I'm fucking losing it.

"Yeah, but there is one thing you could use that I'm sure could persuade her." His eyes drop down to my crotch and then back up to mine just as I look up.

Perplexed, I say, "Please tell me you're joking, or that you hit your head before you came in here."

Parker nearly chokes on his food. "Oh shit."

Grady shrugs, smugly smiling as he chews. "I'm just saying. Give a girl some good dick, and there's a lot more she might be open to."

Parker tilts his head from side to side, as though considering. "The man has a point."

I jut my chin at him. "That's rich coming from you, Mr. I'm-swearing-off-women-forever."

Parker points a finger at me. "You know exactly why I made that call, but you're not me. And if I didn't know any better," he continues, narrowing his eyes at me, "I'd say you're not keen to the idea because you actually *like* this woman. At least, that's what people were saying when you were watching her play darts here the other night."

Jesus, am I that transparent? Apparently the whole town can tell that I can't keep my eyes off Willow. Making her the talk of the town certainly won't convince her to sell me the house.

Maybe I need to keep my distance now more than ever.

Yeah, good luck with that, Dallas.

Grady clears his throat, his face laced with confusion. "What? I thought you just wanted her house. If you like this chick, then trying to convince her with your dick is the last thing you should do."

I slice the lemon in front of me, barely missing my own finger with the knife. Slamming the knife down on the cutting board, I say, "You two are such a great help. Thanks for the unsolicited advice."

"Seriously though, man," Grady says. "Don't go there if what Parker said is true. It's only going to make things more complicated."

"You make that sound so easy. She and Astrid are becoming friends, Penn's doing the work on her house, and I swear, every time I go out in town, I see her or feel like she's there."

Grady pinches his nose. "Then you're fucked. You might as well kiss that house goodbye because you can't have both."

"I don't want her," I lie, trying to be convincing even though I don't believe my own god damn words. "But I'm not going to be shady and use her or my dick to get the house either."

Parker chuckles. "Still the noble brother, I see."

"I don't know about noble. Just maybe his conscience has matured a bit," Grady declares just as I throw a slice of lemon at his head.

"What do you know about maturing, ass wipe?"

"More than you, the guy who just threw fruit at me."

Parker eats his last fry, tosses his napkin on his empty plate, and shoves the plate to the side. "Hey, since I'm here, I've been meaning to ask you if we're all going to the veterans' dinner together? Are we meeting at Mom's and one of us can drive, or…"

"I don't know yet." I turn to Grady, grateful for the change in conversation. "You coming too?"

He nods. "You know I'll be there. Gotta support your pop, and Astrid. Each year I wonder if she'll make it through the night, but she seems to be in a good place lately, so…" He shrugs, not finishing his thought.

"I think it might be better if we all show up together," Parker suggests.

"Yeah, maybe. But I know Hazel had mentioned driving mom separately just in case Mom wants to leave early."

Parker nods. "That could work too."

The sound of Grady's stool screeching across the floor rings out in the quiet restaurant as he stands. "Well, let me know what you decide. I might hitch a ride with you boys if that's okay—so I can drink and not worry about driving."

"Sounds good. I'll text you."

Parker stands as well. "Thanks again for lunch. I've got to get back to the craziness. Why must dogs eat the most random shit?"

"I don't know," I reply. "That's one of life's greatest mysteries."

Grady laughs. "Sure. And so is who is going to win the Carrington Cove Games this year."

Every fall, the town hosts a weekend-long competition among teams formed in the community, fighting for bragging rights and the Cove Cup. Each team is sponsored by a local business, and the winning team's sponsor gets to showcase the cup proudly for the following year. Tourism booms during that weekend, bringing in out-of-towners that spectate and cheer on each team while spending their hard-earned money at the same time.

It's one of our biggest weekends of the year, and it's a tradition that I missed when I was deployed. But last year, Catch & Release's team came in second, and I've been dying to get our shot at winning first place again.

"It's going to be me this year, buddy," I tell Grady as the competitive spirit grows in the room.

"Don't count your chickens before they hatch, Dallas. You know I almost took you out last year."

"Key word being *almost*."

Parker slaps Grady on the back and turns him toward the door. "Okay, we'll have time for more shit talking later. Right now, we all need to get back to work."

"That's right! Go back to your losing team at the vets' office," I call after my brother as he flips me the bird, making me laugh out loud.

Grady glares at me once more before they leave, and then I spend the next thirty minutes finishing my prep work, all the while thinking about how I'm going to repay Penn for sharing my personal business with Parker and Grady.

But thinking about Penn leads me to think about Willow, wondering what she's up to. Our last few interactions have been so hot and cold, I swear, I can't figure out where the hell we stand with each other. One minute, she looks like she's plotting my murder, and the next she's thanking me for doing something for her—building her a chair, buying that fucking scarecrow, or bringing her a box of old painting supplies.

Part of me wants to go over there and check on her after the other night and offer to help with something around the house like Penn suggested. But I'm not sure if that would make things better or worse with her.

I don't know what else to do. At this point, I can essentially kiss my chance of getting her to sell the house to me goodbye, especially because my dick wants much more than that from her. He wants to know her on every intimate level she'll show me.

She has layers. I can see slivers of them exposed each time we speak.

She's strong, but fragile. She's fierce, but funny. She's stubborn, but knows when to accept defeat, even though she doesn't want to.

And there's something she's keeping close to the vest, a part of her I feel like she doesn't let anyone ever see.

But God, do I want to be the one who does.

Chapter Twelve

Willow

"Are you sure I don't look overdressed?" I slide my palms down over my navy blue dress again, nerves running all through my body.

"You look amazing, Willow. Seriously. Stop questioning it. In fact, I think this is the first time I've seen you with your hair down and it looks fantastic," Astrid assures me as she sizes me up once more with her eyes in approval.

It's the night of the veterans' dinner in Carrington Cove, and I'm definitely regretting the decision to attend right now. Dressed in a body-hugging navy dress with a lace overlay that offers just the right amount of cleavage, I'm standing in Astrid's living room, trying to come up with an excuse to get me out of this.

It's been a few weeks since our beach day, but we've hung out several times since then and she still loves teasing me about Dallas. She's honestly the closest friend I've made in ages, comparable to Shauna only, or Katrina, my assistant.

I smooth my hand down the half of my hair I left down, feeling even more self-conscience about it now. My bun is a piece of the armor that helps me play the part of a successful businesswoman, a fact that it took me a long time not to be ashamed of.

But tonight isn't about business.

Tonight is about community and friendship, which is something I have very little experience with and I feel is pressing down on me with each passing second as we wait to leave.

And tonight, I'll see Dallas for the first time since our little tryst at his bar last week.

And he likes it when my hair is down.

The doorbell ringing behind me pulls me from my thoughts.

"That must be my mom." Astrid steps around me, her short red dress sparkling as she moves. Her dark brown hair is down as well in soft curls, falling just below her shoulders. I've never seen her this dressed up and she looks stunning, not that she isn't beautiful any other day. I overheard a young man in the grocery store the other day describe her as a MILF, and I definitely agree—Astrid is a knockout in that girl-next-door kind of way.

"Hi, baby." Her mother enters the room, kissing Astrid on the cheek and then turns to me with wide eyes. "Oh, you must be Willow."

"Yes. It's nice to meet you..."

"Melissa," she finishes for me, reaching out to shake my hand. "Astrid has told me a lot about you, but it's great to finally meet you."

"Likewise."

"She also told me that you own the Bayshore house now, huh?"

"Yes, the house is mine, although it's proving to be a lot of work and I'm not sure what I was thinking taking that on."

Melissa smiles at me. "I think it's great that you're choosing to bring some life back into that place. It's been vacant for such a long time."

"Well, Willow has faced a few challenges since she got here, but it's nothing she can't handle," Astrid adds, forcing me to smile at her sentiment.

"I'm not going to let a few geese stand in my way," I add, which makes them both laugh.

"That's fantastic." Melissa rubs her palms together. "So where are my grandkids?"

"Lilly is playing in her room, and Bentley is playing video games in the living room. I told him he only gets one hour and he's already been on there for about fifteen minutes," Astrid answers.

"Sounds good."

"There's pizza in the freezer that you can pop in the oven when you guys get hungry, and ice cream sandwiches for dessert."

Astrid's mom waves her hand at her daughter as if she's a pest. "In case you've forgotten, I raised you and your brother. I've got it handled, and if not, we'll figure it out. You two go have fun. Enjoy talking with other adults and have a few drinks. And if you have too much, catch a ride home and I can take you back in the morning to get your car."

"I'm sure we won't get too crazy," Astrid assures her. "It's just the veterans' dinner, Mom."

"I know," she says softly, walking up to Astrid, framing her face with her hands. "But I also know that the night can be depressing if you let it. Try not to focus on the bad, okay? Remember your husband, but also remember that you still have a beautiful life even though he's not here."

The light catches on the moisture building in Astrid's eyes. "Mom, you're going to make me ruin my makeup."

"You look beautiful." Her mother releases her and then turns to me. "Make sure she has a good time all right, Willow?"

I give her a small smile. "I'll try."

Great, more added pressure for the evening.

We say our goodbyes to the kids and then walk out to my car. I offered to drive since Astrid has been so gracious to me with… everything.

"So what exactly can I expect tonight?" I ask as we cruise along a few of the main roads in town to get to the center, streetlights streaking through the windows as we pass by.

"Well, the first hour is mostly a cocktail hour. People mingle, catch up, and have a few drinks. Then they'll serve dinner and Mr. Hansen, the head of the center, will make his speech and introduce the officer who will recognize the veterans of the evening, including the men and women we've lost this year. That part can get pretty emotional." I swallow down the lump in my throat and hear her clear hers. "And then they'll present a slideshow, showcasing all of the events from the past year, highlighting those that helped raise money for the center and what they have planned for the year ahead."

I take a deep breath, feeling a little more at ease now knowing what to expect. "Okay. That sounds manageable."

"Are you really that nervous?"

"I am, Astrid. This is…" I struggle with how to explain this to her in a way she'll understand and instead chuckle through my nerves. "It's a lot for someone like me."

"What do you mean?"

"It's hard to explain."

"Well, *I'm* glad you're here. I'm nervous too, but knowing you'll be there with me makes me feel better." She reaches across the center console and grasps my hand. "I'm grateful for our friendship. It's hard to make friends the older you get, especially in a small town, and part of me feels like you were meant to be here." I see her shrug from the corner of my eye. "I know that may sound corny, but I've learned not to let things go unsaid and I want you to know that's how I feel."

And that human contact, that simple gesture along with her words—they weave a path around my heart and settle right in the center.

I have a friend.

And for the first time in a long time, I actually want to be there for someone else just like she's been there for me.

I cast my eyes over at her for a second. "It means a lot to me too, Astrid."

Her smile puts me at ease. "Plus, Dallas will be there tonight, so you'll know at least one other person," she teases, and suddenly the nerves are back.

"Uh...that's not helping, Astrid," I deadpan.

"On the contrary, Willow." She bounces her eyebrows at me. "I think Dallas could help you in more ways than one."

***

Walking into the room steals the oxygen from my lungs as I take in my surroundings.

Round tables are stationed throughout the room covered in white tablecloths with centerpieces full of white and red roses. Navy blue lights shine up from the floor, making the walls appear blue, highlighting the patriotic theme of the night. Soft music plays from the sound system and more people than I can count are standing around in small groups, chatting with drinks in their hands.

"Here we are," Astrid says to me, weaving her arm through the crook of mine. "Just breathe and stay around here. I'm going to go get us two glasses of champagne."

"Yeah. Champagne sounds nice." I watch her walk away and then survey the room, attempting to see if I know anyone while I listen to my heartbeat in my ears.

It almost feels like the entire town is here tonight. But based off what Astrid has told me about the camaraderie here, I wouldn't be surprised if that were true.

Large poster boards displaying pictures are set up around the edge of the room on gold easels, so I walk toward one to admire the faces staring back at me. Groups of Marines and local veterans stand proudly shoulder to shoulder, dressed in their respective uniforms, or gathered together at local events with stoic expressions on their faces.

"Here you go." Astrid comes up behind me and hands me a glass of champagne, pulling my attention from the photos.

"Thank you. I don't know what I was expecting, but this is quite the event."

"They seem to have upped their game this year." She looks around the room. "It gets better every year, but they definitely put in extra effort tonight. Probably to honor Mr. Sheppard."

Sheppard?

It can't be.

But before I can give this revelation more thought, I'm pulled back to the room full of people around us.

"Astrid Cooper, dear. You look lovely." A woman approaches us, and I immediately recognize her from the chair fiasco at the hardware store. She pulls Astrid in for a hug while my heart continues to hammer.

"Hello, Mrs. Hansen. How are you?"

"Doing well, dear. How are you?"

"Oh, just grateful to have a night away from the kids." They share a laugh.

"I remember those days well. Enjoy the time for yourself." She looks around Astrid and finds me, her eyes going wide. "Willow? Is that you?" Her eyes bounce up and down my body as she assesses me, but the same kindness in her voice she had speaking with Astrid is now laced with curiosity.

"Yes. Hello, Mrs. Hansen. It's nice to see you again."

"Likewise, Willow. I must say, it's a surprise to see you here."

Great. Even other people are picking up on my hermit tendencies. "Yes, well, I thought this event was worth venturing out of the house for."

"Hmm. And how is that chair working out for you?" she asks, referring to our encounter from almost a month ago now.

Reigning in my desire to be snarky, I reply as sweetly as possible, "Perfectly. Thank you. Well, thanks to Dallas, really."

"Glad to hear. I hope you're finding Carrington Cove to be welcoming to you."

"For the most part it has."

"Except for the asshole you met at Catch & Release your first night here, huh?"

I spin around to find Dallas standing behind us, clearly eavesdropping on our conversation with a pleased smirk on his face. But it's what he's dressed in that's taking my breath away.

I feel like Rachel in that episode of *Friends* where Ross comes into Central Perk, dressed in a Navy Sailor's uniform, fulfilling one of her fantasies.

Except Dallas is wearing his Marine dress blues, and I didn't know that a man dressed in uniform was one of *my* fantasies until now.

I've seen many men in a suit, but none of them even compared to the fine male specimen standing in front of me. And the worst part is, he's not even trying—he just does so effortlessly.

He's wearing that uniform like it was designed just for his body.

It makes me both hate him and want him even more.

It's bad enough that Dallas is the type of man that is good-looking in a rugged way—a *manly* way—the type of man that makes blue jeans and a simple black shirt look like a coat of armor or the newest version of male lingerie. His aviators seem custom-made to highlight the sharp lines of his face, and when he takes them off to reveal his eyes can hold you captive with a searing power that makes you feel frozen in place.

But now I know he can make a uniform look better than a five-piece suit.

And that beard.

I never thought a beard was something I would be attracted too, but Dallas wears his trim beard like he is the spokesperson for facial hair.

And I'm becoming desperate to feel it burn the inside of my thighs.

His presence is overwhelming—strong, proud, intense, and yet comforting, like being in his vicinity means you don't have to look over your shoulder at every turn. Although, in a town like Carrington Cove, I assume there's not much to be wary of, unlike D.C.

And that's when I realize he makes me *feel* protected—and that's a more serious problem than the throbbing between my legs.

As I come back to reality and remember that I have a voice, Mrs. Hansen chimes in. "Oh, that can't be right. I expect better from you, Dallas."

"Yes ma'am. And I assure you I'm working on making it up to her."

Flabbergasted, I continue to stare up at him as Astrid clears her throat. "Well, Mrs. Hansen, it was so nice to see you, but I'm going to take Willow around to mingle a bit. We'll catch up with you later."

"Oh, yes, dear. Have a good evening. I'm going to go find my husband before his speech." She pats Astrid on the arm before walking away, and I finally feel like I can breathe again, even if for just a second.

"Hello, Willow," Dallas says, pulling my attention back to him.

I clear my throat and straighten my spine. "Hello, Dallas."

As I stand there, I watch his eyes eat me up appreciatively, and I swear I can feel the livewire of electricity move across my skin with his eyes. "You look…"

"Dallas!" A short brunette waves her hand in the air, marching across the room toward us and interrupting his thought. "Where the hell have you been?"

Irritation washes over him, but he brushes it off quickly. "I just got here, Hazel. Calm down."

"Can you please just come over to our table? Mom looks like she's getting overwhelmed, and I think it would make her feel better if we were all there."

His eyes bounce between me and the woman whom I now know is his sister—a detail I know thanks to Astrid's intel, though the uncanny resemblance between them would give it away regardless. "Yeah, I'll be right there." Hazel rolls her eyes before walking away, but thankfully, Astrid chimes in.

"Go, Dallas. We'll catch up with you later. I'll make sure to come by and say hello to your mom. I haven't seen her in a while."

Every feature of Dallas's face finally softens. "She'd like that, Astrid. I'll see you both later then, I guess."

"We'll be here."

"Glad you're here, Willow." With a curt nod but a lingering stare, he walks away, leaving us standing there as I study his purposeful strides and the way his body is enhanced by every line of his suit.

"You okay there, girl?" Astrid asks, stepping directly in front of me so I have no choice but to focus on her.

"Uh." I swallow roughly and nod. "Yeah."

"I think you have a little drool coming out of the side of your mouth." She reaches toward me as if to wipe it off.

"What? No I don't!" I reply, reaching up to wipe the corner of my lips and finding nothing there.

Astrid just laughs at me. "Jesus, Willow. Could you be any more transparent?"

Sighing, I tip back the rest of my champagne and then search the room. "I think I need to walk around a bit. Get some fresh air."

Astrid narrows her eyes at me. "Yeah. Okay. Just don't go too far, and let me know if you need anything. I'm going to go say hello to a few people and I'll meet you at our table for dinner."

I nod. "Sounds good."

Astrid leaves me to my own devices, so I decide that another glass of champagne is necessary. I head toward the bar, secure my drink, and then continue to walk around the room, surveying the remaining posterboards displaying pictures.

There are so many stories, memories and lives lived and lost on the faces of these men and women. But there's also a sense of family, like everyone in this room is connected through this common organization, through the oath and purpose their loved ones took on by signing up to serve their country.

I wonder if that's how my parents felt—like they were part of this too, connected to the men and women they went to write about. I wonder if they ever thought they'd sacrifice their lives without agreeing to yield a weapon. And I wonder where I would be right now if they were still here.

Not in Carrington Cove, that's for sure.

I turn back to face the room full of people, catching several sets of eyes directed toward me. Dolly from the inn smiles and waves at me from across the room, but her face is the only friendly face I recognize in a crowd of strangers.

I've been in this town for a little over a month, and yet I still don't know many people here, which is glaringly obvious by the judgmental stares I'm receiving right now, accompanied by muttered observations.

With a deep breath of courage, I attempt to make the most of this evening and decide that this is as good of an opportunity as any to put myself out there.

I head for Dolly first, catching her up to speed on the developments with the house and sarcastically thanking her for my coffee and muffin addiction. She introduces me to Greg and Jenny, the owners of the Sunrise Bakery, whom I then proceed to gush to about the blueberry muffins—which, come to find out, is actually Astrid's recipe, and I can't believe she never told me. I'm going to give her shit for that later. Then they lead me to Judy, who created the scarecrow that Dallas got me, which she instantly picks up on the moment she sees me. My conversation with Judy leads me to Harold, Baron, and Thompson, the men I played darts with last week, who are apparently still bitter after their loss.

I'm having such a good time talking with these people that I feel slightly disappointed when it's interrupted by the call for dinner being served.

"Hey. You doing okay?" Astrid asks as we settle into our seats.

"Yeah, actually. I'm having a good time." My eyes nearly sting with tears as those words leave my mouth.

What is happening to me?

Surprise paints her features. "See? I told you. Tonight is going to be good for you."

We wait for our turn for the buffet, filling our plates with two different kinds of pasta, salad, and freshly baked bread. I fight the urge to moan out loud at the taste of the food because it's that delicious. But a few of the people we're seated with divulge that it's from a local Italian restaurant that catered the event for free.

For a moment I feel like I'm living someone else's life, until my phone buzzes with email after email coming through. Part of me wants to answer, but the other part of me knows that if it were urgent, Katrina would call me.

So, I decide to turn it off completely, which is something I haven't done in years.

But I don't want any distractions tonight.

My mind and heart are invested in this room full of people.

Mr. Hansen calls everyone's attention to the stage, beginning the festivities and presentations for the night. He gives a brief history of the center, and then passes the microphone to the Marine acting as the emcee for the ceremony.

"Good evening, ladies and gentlemen!" His deep voice echoes through the sound system, pulling everyone's attention to the stage. "I'm First Sergeant Hank Lyle of the United States Marines, and it is an honor to be gathered with you all tonight." The crowd drops their utensils and rings out in applause. "I'd like to welcome you all to the thirty-third annual veterans' dinner at the Carrington Cove Center, and thank you for attending this celebration this evening."

He continues with his speech, going into the history of the Marines, how many local men and women have served, and how this center has expanded since it was founded over thirty years ago. Then he moves into discussing the Marines that lost their lives this year, starting with active duty.

Emotion clouds the room as family after family gathers on stage, receiving a plaque from the center in honor of their loved ones. A few of the men were so young, less than three years into their service when they died in battle. One woman died while saving the life of a civilian off-duty.

And then the crowd grows quiet as Sergeant Lyle clears his throat and speaks about the last recipient.

"I know that the last person we're here to honor tonight is no stranger to most of you in this room. If you have been around this center in the last thirty years, then you know the man we're about to talk about was a pivotal player in the services we offer to our Marines. Michael Sheppard dedicated time and energy into the healing process that many men and women require and need after serving in active duty, both on and off the battlefield. He paved the way for us to offer counseling services and co-sponsors for those that faced problems with addiction. He spent more time in this building than he probably did in his own home." The audience chuckles and murmurs in agreement. "And though that man probably experienced some of the most gruesome and traumatic events during his service, he managed to come home and find a way to turn that experience into something good. Unfortunately, this year, he lost his battle with cancer and joined our Lord and Savior on the other side." He pauses to give everyone a moment. "It's a shame that a man can survive a war only to lose the battle for his life at home." The crowd grows eerily silent as goosebumps cover my skin.

He's talking about the man who left me his house.

"It is with great honor that I recognize Sergeant Michael Sheppard tonight and his family for the service he not only gave to his country, but to this center. The entire crowd moves to their feet, and I follow their lead, clapping while my heart beats erratically and a sense of awareness creeps up my spine. "I would like to call Sergeant Sheppard's son, Staff Sergeant Dallas Sheppard, up to the stage along with his family as we honor his memory."

And time stands still before reality hits me, slamming into my chest like a freight train and stealing the oxygen from my lungs.

Oh my God, it can't be.

All eyes shift in the room as Dallas, his three siblings, and his mother all rise from their seats and gather on the stage as Sergeant Lyle presents them with a plaque honoring their dad.

This has to be a dream.

No. A nightmare.

Michael Sheppard is Dallas's dad?

His father is the mystery man who left me the Bayshore house, his dream house?

What the actual fuck?

All the noise and chatter around me fade away as the only thing I am aware of is the sound of my pulse in my ears. I feel my legs wobble beneath me as I stand in place, feigning a smile and compassion while I'm panicking on the inside.

Astrid looks over at me with tears in her eyes until she notices the change in my demeanor. "Hey. Are you okay?"

"Yeah," I manage to croak out. "It just got really hot in here." I fan my face frantically. "I think—I think I'm going to go outside for some fresh air."

Perplexed but with no reason to question me, she just nods. "Okay. Let me know if I can get you anything."

I put on my best smile. "I'll be fine."

And then I walk away as fast as my feet will carry me without drawing attention to myself. Overwhelmed by thoughts that stir up unresolved feelings and a million questions, I find the nearest exit and barrel through it, grateful for the railing that I find in front of me as I reach for the cold metal and take a deep breath, fighting for oxygen.

Moonlight glows out against black water beneath me, the small lake off the back of the property providing a pristine backdrop for the evening, an endless abyss that looks oddly comforting right now, given the developments in the last few minutes.

I have no idea how long I've been out here until a voice behind me pulls me from my thoughts.

"Didn't realize I'd have company out here."

I spin around to see Dallas shutting the same door I just walked through behind him before joining me at the railing.

All I can think about is the name he shares with the man who was somehow connected to my parents.

Not the concern in his eyes as he approaches me.

Not the way he overwhelms me and makes my body heat up.

No.

It's the fact that this man has no idea how connected we are and how much more fucked up this entire situation between us just became.

"Are you okay?" he asks, checking me out from head to toe as if there may be something physically wrong with me. And then he reaches up and cups the side of my face with one of his hands, the singe from the contact of his skin against mine making my heart lunge forward and my body almost do the same.

I've been dying for this man to touch me again, and the sincerity of his caress is borderline overwhelming. Dallas's eyes stare down into mine, searching for answers that I can't give him, and some that I just don't want to.

Luckily, he can't see my inner turmoil or the invisible scars I carry.

The longer his hand remains on my face, the longer the world seems to be frozen around us.

"I'm fine. Just needed some air." The smile I give him is one I've practiced before so I know it's convincing enough, and with as much strength as I can, I remove myself from his grasp, turning away from him slightly and fighting to control the shaking of my hands.

"It can get pretty warm in there with all of those people." He reaches up and pulls on the collar of his shirt while avoiding my gaze. "And I forgot how hot this uniform can get."

Focus on the conversation, not what you just found out, Willow. Don't blurt out something stupid and make this situation even worse.

"What are *you* doing out here?"

"I guess I just needed some air too." He walks forward now, grabbing onto the railing and looking out over the water, blowing out a harsh breath. I look over at him briefly, but long enough to capture the shadows in the lines of his face, the way he looks so powerful and commanding in the darkness with his suit of armor on, but the light is catching the pain etched into the lines around his eyes.

"I'm sorry about your dad." Inside I slap myself in the forehead, berating myself for bringing him up, even though I know the sentiment is appropriate given the evening.

"Thank you. It was a rough year watching him whittle away. At least he's not in pain anymore."

"Yeah," I say, feeling my pulse increase with each passing second.

I need to get out of here. I feel the words on the tip of my tongue, bound to come out if I stay here for one more second. But I'll be damned if I taint this night for him or his family—*for us*.

I know I could share my own struggles with the loss of my parents.

I know I could apologize again for the fact that his dad isn't here.

But all I can focus on is *who* his dad is and how this man has played a pivotal role in why my parents aren't alive and why I'm in Carrington Cove to begin with.

We're finally starting to get along. My feelings toward him are shifting.

But now?

Now everything is one big clusterfuck and I need to process it.

This information about his dad changes everything.

"So—" he starts, but I cut him off.

"I'm sorry, Dallas. I need to go." I twist away from him, walking as quickly as my heels will allow and leaving him confused, I'm sure.

"Willow!" he calls after me.

But I don't turn back around. I walk back through the door I came out of earlier and hunt down Astrid as quickly as I can.

"Astrid?"

She spins around from her conversation with a few other women to find me practically hyperventilating. "Willow? What's wrong?"

"I'm—I'm just not feeling very well. I hate to do this, but I need to leave." I twist to the side, glancing toward the stage where Dallas's family is seated at their table, their mother wiping tears from under her eyes, and my heart crumbles once more.

"Oh. Okay. Do you want me to come with you?" She moves to reach for her purse from the table, but I stop her.

"No. I'm fine. Please stay. I just need to know that you'll be able to get home."

"Yeah, I'm sure Penn could give me a ride."

"Okay. Perfect. Thank you. Again, I'm so sorry." I grab my purse, trying to hide the tremor in my hands as I do.

"It's okay. I hope you feel better." She rubs my arm before I turn to walk away.

With a tight-lipped smile, I head for the front entrance, feeling Dallas's stare on me as he comes back inside, but I don't dare look in his direction. I just keep moving forward—out of the crowd, out to my car, and back toward my house—Dallas's dream house that his father gave to me.

Once I'm settled inside, the walls that were starting to feel like a home now feel like they're closing in on me, hiding secrets under the drywall and in every nail holding the place together.

Just when my heart was beginning to open up to the possibilities and people here in Carrington Cove, yet another revelation has stirred emotions that I don't want to deal with.

However, nothing could have prepared me for the visitor I received later that night, another person tangled in this web I'd been drawn into that made the plot thicken even more.

Chapter Thirteen

Dallas

"Dude, I think that counter is clean."

"Huh?" When I turn to the side, I see Penn staring at me with a shit-eating grin on his face.

"You've been wiping that same spot on the counter for about five minutes now."

"Fuck." I toss the towel in the bucket nearby and let out a heavy sigh.

"I take it you've got something on your mind?"

"More like someone." Penn's smirk grows wider, and I roll my eyes. "Yeah, I know. And you have every right to give me shit, but I'm really not in the mood."

"I'm never in the mood when you give me shit," he retorts.

"Noted," I grumble.

"So what did Willow do now?"

Crossing my arms over my chest, I lean my hip against the counter. The restaurant is empty since we haven't opened yet on this Sunday morning, but there are several employees around getting things ready for when I do open the doors. "She ran away from me last night."

"Why?"

"Obviously, I don't know, hence why I'm over here staring off into space, idiot."

"No need for name calling," he teases. "When was this?"

"After we went up on stage to receive Dad's award." A heaviness that won't let up has been resting in my chest all day after the veterans' dinner last night. Being surrounded by the people that my dad gave so much of his time to fills me with pride, but also remorse. I almost felt like everyone in that room had a stronger relationship with him than I did because I didn't listen to his wishes when it came to the decisions I made for my life.

Despite how he felt about my service, I always admired how he steadfastly showed up for other veterans as much as he could.

My father volunteered at the Carrington Cove Center up until he physically couldn't anymore. He spoke to men who were just getting out, or who were honorably discharged, like he was. He connected veterans with counseling services, doctors to prescribe medication and help with PTSD.

He took care of his fellow Marines.

But he always had a chip on his shoulder about me being one of them.

And then there's Willow—stubborn, independent, and fucking gorgeous, *Willow*. God, this woman is making my brain malfunction.

Pretending to hate her was easier when I didn't feel reciprocation in this attraction. But after trying to smooth things over, it's only made ignoring this pull I feel toward her even more difficult.

When she showed up at the soccer game and I inconspicuously glanced in her direction, watching her cheer on the boys, it made my chest ache. Her smile was captivating and she was more relaxed than I'd ever seen her, except for the moments during the game that caused her to bite her nails, of course. But she looked like she belonged there, talking to Astrid, becoming a part of our community.

And when she thanked me for the scarecrow, I got the intense urge to kiss her, to press my lips against hers and figure out what sounds she would make when I swept my tongue into her mouth.

Then I dropped off the painting supplies a few days later, and fuck—that was the pivotal moment for me. Her hair was down, she was wearing that flimsy excuse for a robe, and the outline of her nipples through the silk tested every ounce of restraint I possessed in my body. With one flick of my fingers, I could have yanked the string loose that held the robe together and had her naked and exposed to me, completely vulnerable and mine for the taking.

Montages of me pulling those pebbled nipples into my mouth along with everything else I want to do to that woman have been playing in my brain for the past two weeks, and it's taken all I have to keep my distance from her. Because I know I'll give in at this point. It's only a matter of time.

Willpower is a fickle thing when there's a woman involved, and it turns out, Willow is my weakness.

And then when she came into the bar and let loose, playing darts with Harold, Baron, and Thompson—looking so settled, like she was relaxed and carefree and having fun for probably the first time in her life, a fact that was only confirmed through our conversation that night.

But it was all I could do not to stomp over to her, crush my mouth to hers in front of everyone, and then take her upstairs to fuck the animosity out of her.

So instead, I acted like an overprotective, possessive asshole, and put us back in our original roles.

But then at the dinner, something in me shifted. I admitted how tired I am of fighting her and before she ran away, I was going to ask her if she wouldn't mind spending some time *together* intentionally—like on a date.

I was a Marine and I know my willpower is strong. But this woman is in an entire league of her own when it comes to resisting temptation. And seeing her last night, dressed up in that skintight dress that accentuated her curves had me fighting to hold myself back from stealing her away and showing her exactly how crazy she's making me.

Willow is headstrong and tenacious with a body that was made to be worshipped. I've never wanted to smack a woman's ass more than I do hers, just to see my red handprint across her milky skin. And at the same time, I want to hold her, learn everything about her, and find out exactly what makes her tick.

I want to be the one to show her how much fun she's missing from her life.

She's the most complex puzzle I've ever come across, and I'm dying to figure out how her pieces fit together.

"Well, the night was emotionally heavy. Maybe it just took a toll on her," Penn continues, pulling me back to our conversation.

"Yeah, maybe. It definitely affected me." I stare off into space again.

"You know, I get what you're feeling, that internal battle about doing what's right or just going after what you want."

"You don't say?" I reply sarcastically.

He flips me off. "My circumstances are different, and you know that. Look, I'm just gonna tell you what I think. I think there's obvious sexual tension between the two of you, so fucking go for it. If nothing else, you'll have a way to let off some steam for the few weeks she's still here, and then you can go your separate ways. Or...maybe there's more there. But the longer this childish repartee goes on between the two of you, the more time you're wasting that could be spent exploring what's there."

Frustrated, I run a hand through my hair. "Yes, I want to fuck the woman, all right? I fucking admit it. But I feel like it would just make the situation more complicated, Penn. And I want that house, okay? That's why all of this started in the first place."

But do you want her more, Dallas?

He turns away from me, stacking glasses. "I guess you have to weigh the risks then."

"Is that what you did with Astrid?"

His head snaps in my direction. "Yes. And not that it's any of your business, but I took my shot, okay? And she turned me down."

"What? When?" I push myself off the counter, but he instantly retreats.

Shaking his head, he sighs and then walks off. "Doesn't matter. Worry about you and Willow, Dallas. I'm going to go grab some stuff from the back, and then I'm leaving early. There's a storm coming in tomorrow, and I need to make sure Astrid has supplies, and that her and the kids are safe."

Watching my brother walk away, I wonder if he'll ever get out of his own way so he can be happy. And when the hell did Astrid turn him down? I sure as fuck never knew about this.

Dark clouds hover over the water in the distance, an indicator of the storm Penn mentioned. Reaching for the remote, I turn on the television over the bar and flip to the news, hoping to get more information on this weather that is brewing off the coast. Strong winds, lots of rain, and hurricane warnings will be in effect for the next two days.

And that's when it hits me—*Willow.*

I wonder if she knows how to prepare or what to expect.

"Time to open the doors, boss?" Caroline, one of the waitresses asks me as she heads for the front door with the keys in her hand, a few patrons already waiting to come inside.

"Oh, yeah. Let 'em in."

Brushing off my concerns about the tenacious blonde that is taking up way too much of my headspace, I settle in the behind the bar, prepared for a long day ahead, hoping the distraction will help time pass while forcing me to figure out what to do about Willow later.

***

"Jesus." Shielding my eyes from the rain pelting my face, I slam my truck door shut and head across the gravel to the front of the Bayshore house the next night , hoping to God Willow is safe inside—because if she's out in this, there's no telling where she might be or if she's in trouble.

Even driving over here I knew I was taking a risk, but I couldn't stand the thought of her here alone and probably scared, and ill-prepared for the magnitude of this storm.

It's ingrained in me to help people. That's all this is—my long history of being a Marine coming out on instinct.

Whatever you need to tell yourself, Dallas.

Climbing the front steps, I brace myself for wind and rain that's hitting me, turning my back to the elements as I pound on the front door.

"Willow? Are you home?" The sound of the whipping wind makes it difficult to hear anything, so I slam my fist into the door again, over and over. "Willow!"

Her face pops up in the window to the right of the door, eyes wide, mouth agape, her hair cascading around her face, looking so fucking gorgeous. The sight ignites something within me, and I know it's impossible for me to stay away any longer.

That's why I'm here, isn't it?

"Dallas? What on earth are you doing here?" she shouts through the glass.

"I—I wanted to make sure you were okay. That you're prepared for this." Blinking away the water that's collecting on my eyelashes, I see the conflict in her eyes.

"I—I'm fine. You should go!" she shouts over the lashing wind and rain.

"What?" I wipe my face with the sleeve of my jacket, which doesn't do much since my sleeve is soaked too. "Do you have a flashlight? Candles? Water? Some pre-packaged food?" I hold up the plastic bag of supplies I brought with me just in case, all stuff I grabbed from my place and the store yesterday, anticipating this visit even though I was trying to talk myself out of it.

"Of course not! I've never done this before! I've never had to, but that doesn't mean I can't figure it out." She shakes her head at me. "I've been doing many things on my own for years and will be just fine without your help!"

This stubborn fucking woman.

I could leave and let her stay on her soapbox. But now that I'm here, I'll be damned if something happens to her when I could have prevented it.

"And did you think you'd just drive down the road right now to gather those things in this storm? Because newsflash, that'd be stupider than you're being right now by not letting me in."

"Excuse me?"

"You heard me, Goose. Now let me in before I get taken away in this wind!"

She bites her bottom lip in contemplation as anger flares in her eyes, but I can't stand out here any longer, waiting for her to make a decision.

"Christ, woman. I don't even know why I'm here!" I spin around in a circle, clutching my hands in my hair. But then, before I can talk myself out of it, I spin back to face her and dig my heels in, determined not to back down. "But fuck it. I am."

So the next move I make is one I know she won't be happy about, but I don't give a rat's ass. Her safety is top priority right now, despite my better judgment. I just hope she doesn't fight me too much.

Or maybe I hope that she does so I can shut her up with my mouth.

Chapter Fourteen

Willow

Before I can respond, he tears open the door that I stupidly had unlocked, pushing me aside prior to slamming it shut and locking it like I should have.

"What the hell are you doing, Dallas? This is breaking and entering!" I shriek as his broad frame towers over me, drenched from head to toe.

He narrows his gaze at me before closing the distance between us, worry and frustration wafting off him. "I'm making sure you're safe, Willow. Because if something were to happen to you, and I fucking walked away, I would never forgive myself." He points a finger at his chest. "I've lost too many people in my life because of shitty circumstances and instances where there was nothing I could do. But this? This I can protect you from."

Rearing back, I'm caught off guard by the command in his voice and the clear worry in his eyes. But something tells me that pushing him away would only make him react more, so instead, I relent, even though my stomach is in knots just being in the same room as him again.

"Okay. Fine."

His jaw clenches like he was ready for a fight. "Wow. What a relief to see you can be reasonable."

"I'm fucking terrified right now. And even though you're the last person I wanted to see, I guess it's better than being left alone in this chaos."

He huffs, wiping water from his face. And at that moment, I take the opportunity to really take him in.

His dark hair is plastered to his forehead, drenched from the rain, dripping water all over his face and the floor. His signature black shirt and jeans are soaked as well, and his boots are squeaking as he takes steps toward the counter to drop off the bag of supplies he brought with him.

He came over with supplies.

For me.

He wanted to make sure I was safe.

This is exactly why resisting him has been such a feat. But after what I learned Saturday night, my reasons for staying away have multiplied exponentially. I guess the weather had other plans to make avoiding him even more difficult, though.

"Could you throw these in the dryer while we still have power, please?" he asks, yanking his jacket and shirt over his head in one smooth motion before I can respond.

And holy hell.

The man standing before me is rippled with muscle and sinew that I want nothing more than to paint with my tongue. His tan skin is glistening from his rain-soaked clothes, and then he turns to me, arching a brow as I stand there, shell-shocked, his hand outstretched with his clothes, waiting for me to speak. But all I can do is stare at the water droplets cascading down his chest, rolling over his nipple that I have an alarmingly strong urge to bite.

"Willow?"

"What?" I blink, clear my throat, and then rip the clothes from his hand. "Sure. Fine," I say as I walk away, trying to keep my dignity intact.

"You can come back and stare a bit more, if you want. I won't judge."

His self-induced laughter makes my blood boil again as I go down the short hallway off the kitchen to the laundry room, tossing his clothes in the dryer and turning it on, huffing out my frustration in solitude for a moment.

"Jackass," I mutter to myself.

"I heard that." Or, so I thought.

As if he appeared out of thin air, I spin to find Dallas blocking the doorway, watching me intently as I jump.

"Ugh. Are you just going to follow me around all night?"

"No. But I do need your help loading batteries into the flashlights, setting up candles, and putting away the food."

"Sure. Just give me a minute, okay?"

He rolls his eyes and leaves the doorway, somehow making it easier for me to breathe again. "I'll meet you in the kitchen."

I walk back out to the main part of the house, trying not to stare too hard at his back, but when he turns to face me again with the packages of batteries, that's when I notice a detail about him I must have been too blind with rage and lust to detect sooner.

An anchor tattoo rests right over his left pec, etched in black and blue ink. There's an inscription on a banner across the symbol, but I can't quite make it out.

My eyes instantly veer over to the refrigerator magnet that Penn gave me my first week here, and somehow, the connection makes me smile.

"Are you going to help me or just continue to stare at me?"

Flicking my eyes up at him, I tear the package of batteries from his hands and take residence on the other side of the kitchen counter just as a loud crack of thunder booms above us, making me jump. "Jesus!"

Dallas looks outside before our phones start blaring with a high wind warning. "We should hurry. And then we need to go in your downstairs closet and take shelter."

"Why?"

"In case windows shatter or anything falls on the house. You're safer in an enclosed space."

"What the hell have I gotten myself into?" I whisper to myself.

We keep filling the three flashlights, small electric candles, and then I look at the food Dallas brought with him.

"I have some leftover sandwich stuff from the restaurant, so we need to eat those right away. Otherwise, I brought chips, beef jerky, protein bars, some apples and bananas, and of course, candy and bottled water."

"Why candy?"

His eyes narrow on me beneath his dark lashes. "I have a sweet tooth, and maybe some sugar will sweeten you up too."

I roll my eyes at him. "Ha. Very funny."

Another loud crack booms overhead. "Shit. I hate this." I can see my hands trembling in front of me as I grab the bag of food and take it to the closet.

"I'm right behind you. Do you have any extra blankets or pillows? Or even towels?"

"They're all in there. I don't have much, but we'll make do."

He juts his head in that direction. "Go inside. I'll be right there."

The entire house creaks from the wind as I scurry along the floor, reaching the closet and ducking inside the small door to go under the staircase. I set the food to the side on one of the shelves and then turn and find the blankets, unfolding them, as well as grabbing two spare pillows and covering them in cases, making the floor more comfortable. I'm lost in the task as Dallas steps in behind me, getting a full access view of me bending over in front of him.

Peering up at him between my legs, I say, "It's not polite to stare."

"I'm only returning the favor," he says with a smirk before I stand up and spin to face him. But I must have misjudged how much blood went to my head because I topple over, headed to smack my face on the shelving to my left.

However, Dallas catches me before I make contact. "Fuck. Are you okay?"

Holding my upper arms, he keeps me steady as I stare up at him, getting lost in his stormy brown eyes.

"Yes, I—I'm okay. Thanks."

He releases me hesitantly and I blow out a breath, turning around again to gather myself while cursing this storm and where it's landed me.

This is bad.

But he smells so good.

Jesus, shut up, Willow!

I take a seat at the head of the seating area I made and grab the food from the shelf, gesturing for him to take a seat right next to me.

"Uh, I'm still wet." He points down to his jeans.

"Oh. Well, I don't have anything that would fit you, so…"

He chuckles, and the sound instantly calms me a bit. His rare laugh is something I didn't know I needed in this moment. "I didn't think so."

"You could grab a towel from the bathroom next door if you want."

"Yeah, I think I will. I'll be right back."

Waiting for him to return, I sigh as I open the containers of food. The sandwiches are packed with turkey, bacon, lettuce, tomato, and mayo—a perfect club sandwich that I remember eating the other night and devouring, along with fries and onion rings.

"I knew I made the right call bringing the club."

Staring up at him as his voice alerts me to his return, I watch him run the towel through his hair, taking the moisture out of it before tossing it aside and placing the other one right next to me, situating it under himself as he sits.

"That was..." I look over at him, finally at a loss for words. "Thank you."

"I don't want to fight with you anymore, Willow," he says in a low voice, just above a whisper.

"You don't?" I sound comically shocked, his unexpected admission throwing me off.

"That's what I was trying to tell you Saturday night before you ran off." His words make the air around us shift.

Oh.

Oh.

Regret fills me as I look into his eyes and see the heated intensity I've noticed before.

Before Saturday, I was ready to stop fighting him too. I was ready to give into this attraction and physical need I feel every time he's near.

But then I discovered that explosive secret, the unlit stick of dynamite that will inevitably blow up both of our lives, especially after my unexpected visitor the other night.

Now I'm torn. Should I light the fuse while I can still try to contain the flames? Or do I foolishly explore this fire between us, hoping to stamp it out before anyone gets burned?

"I'm sorry." Staring down at my lap again, I pick up a piece of the sandwich and begin eating, trying to keep my mouth busy so I don't say something else I'll regret since that seems to be the norm around him.

Why is it that this man makes me feel unsteady, unsure of who I am and how I've been for so many years?

Maybe I was never sure of who I was in the first place.

"And I'm sorry." He blows out a breath before reaching for a piece of the sandwich as well. "You make me a little irrational, but I meant what I said in the park. I'm trying to get you to see that I'm more than just the asshole who wants your house."

I finish chewing and then reach for a bottle of water, twisting off the top as the storm picks up outside, rattling the walls. "My life would be so much simpler if I didn't inherit this house, Dallas, *believe* me. If I hadn't…"

"Then you wouldn't be here," he finishes for me, causing me to freeze and slowly gaze up at him again. "You would have never come to Carrington Cove, Willow. We wouldn't be at each other's throats, or in this closet together right now. And yeah, if you weren't here, it would be easier to get what I want, but it seems that has changed."

"What's changed?"

"What I want," he answers resolutely.

He takes my sandwich and his, places them back in the box, and pushes it out of the way before sliding closer to me, making my pulse pick up speed as I wonder what he's going to do next.

"This is a bad idea," I mutter, my skin practically vibrating from his proximity.

"How so?" He trails one finger up my forearm, making my breath hitch. A smatter of goosebumps breaks out all over my skin, but my eyes are firmly locked on his, waiting to see what happens next.

"I just…it's complicated, Dallas…this thing between us." I pull my arm away from his touch and wave my hand back and forth in the miniscule space between our bodies.

I swear I see his eyes darken. "It doesn't have to be. Why don't we just go by what we want and how we feel and forget all the rest for now?"

His solution sounds so simple, and yet it's almost as if I can see the future—the feelings that will undoubtedly develop and the torment they'll cause when he finds out the truth.

Feelings are messy, pesky little bastards.

It's why I avoid mine.

Doesn't take a rocket scientist to see that, Willow.

But then his fingertips brush the hair from my face, his thumb pulls down my bottom lip and glides down the column of my throat, and as his hand drifts over my collarbone and down my arm to grip my waist, I feel my entire body surrender to him, and my mind is too slow to protest.

I want him.

I shouldn't.

But I do.

And I'm so very tired of fighting it.

"Fuck it." Before my mind can catch up and talk me out of it, I grip the back of his head and pull him toward me, smashing our lips together, the growl that travels up his throat spurring me on.

It feels as if this kiss erases everything—the bickering, the arguments, the jokes and low blows, and even the eminent truth hovering over us like the storm.

But its promise is also raging like the storm outside—wild passion, intense pressure, and rapid release of the torment we've both been under since I got here.

Dallas wastes no time taking control of the kiss, stroking his tongue against mine, burying his hands in my hair, crushing me to his chest and refusing to let me go. It's like he's claiming me with this one kiss, and I want him to own every part of me until there's nothing left.

I surrender willingly, practically climbing up his body, wrapping my arms around his neck, meeting his lips and tongue for every stroke, feeling like I can't taste enough of him.

Dallas groans as I straddle his lap and rub my pussy along his crotch, run my fingers through his damp tresses, and claw at his shoulders.

We continue to maul each other for who knows how long before he finally releases my lips and stares into my eyes, each of us fighting for air.

"Willow..." Thunder cracks again and a loud crash echoes outside, making me jump in his lap. "It's okay. I've got you." He wraps his arms around me, holding me to his bare chest as I rest my forehead on his shoulder and catch my breath, both from the kiss and the scare.

"I'm glad you're here. I'm sorry I was stubborn about letting you in, but now I'm *really* glad that you're here, Dallas," I mumble against his shoulder.

I feel his lips hit my temple. "Me too, Goose."

I outwardly smile at the nickname for the first time. "So, what happens now?" I lift my head to find him staring at me, his stormy eyes from before warmer now somehow, brighter and almost ethereal.

"We wait out the storm. Finish our dinner. Kiss some more." He reaches up and toys with my bottom lip again with his thumb. "Definitely more kissing."

I can't help it—I giggle at his words, burying my face in his neck.

"Don't get shy on me now, Willow. I'm pretty sure you're the one that kissed me first."

"I did not," I say, popping my head back up.

"Oh, yes you did, Goose." I glare at him as he tucks my hair behind my ear. "But that's okay. If you hadn't made the first move, I would have."

Locking my eyes on his, I say with trepidation, "This changes everything, Dallas."

"*You* changed everything the night you walked into my bar, Willow. I was just too stupid to admit it."

Thunder booms above us, rattling the windows and making me flinch, even though I'm still in his arms.

His hand draws smooth circles on my back. "Relax, Goose."

Please don't let me go.

"The worst of the storm is hitting now, according to the weather report. It should calm down around three in the morning."

Feeling my pulse in my ears, I say, "Then I need you to distract me."

He lifts my chin so our eyes connect. "Distract you?"

"I'm sure you can think of something," I say suggestively as tension builds between us again, that sweet sexual tension that has been there since the night we met.

The corner of his mouth lifts. "Yeah, I think I have something in mind." Before I can say a word, he continues, "Lie back." Keeping my eyes on his, I follow his command, climbing out of his lap and crawling backward until I feel the wall behind me. Dallas situates a pillow behind my head and grabs both of my legs, yanking me down so my back is flat.

"Jesus!"

"Don't worry. You'll be talking to God soon, but I need you to remember that I'm the one who's about to make you scream." I roll my eyes but don't have much time to think when Dallas starts peeling my leggings down. "Now's the time to back out if you don't want this, Willow."

I swallow down the lump in my throat and nod. "I want this."

God, do I want this.

Ever since I laid eyes on this man, I've been fantasizing about what his mouth would feel like on me, how his touch would ignite my body.

That was before you found out who his dad was, though.

I shove my subconscious out of the way and decide to deal with that another time. I'm pretty sure that fallout is inevitable, so why not enjoy the ride on the way down, right?

"Thank fuck." He tosses my leggings to the side and then drops his head to my pussy, situating himself between my legs while inhaling my scent. "When's the last time you've been truly worshipped, Willow?" he mumbles against my inner thigh.

I swallow hard as my pulse races. "Never," I admit embarrassingly.

"Well then, I have one hell of an impression to make on you so no other man gets the opportunity."

Holy shit.

Smirking up at me, he drags his finger through my slit over the silk of my thong, the silk that is soaked with my arousal from just being near this man for the past half hour.

And then he peels the fabric to the side, baring me to him. Licking his lips, he kisses the inside of my right thigh, then the left, getting closer and closer to where I'm exposed but not touching the part of me where I need him.

"Dallas," I groan as he chuckles darkly between my thighs.

"Patience, Willow."

"I don't have any," I groan in agony.

"Well, you're going to find some real quick if you don't want me to stop."

He hooks his thumb under the string on my hips, pulling my thong from my body, tossing it on top of my leggings, and then he ever so gently drags the tip of his tongue through my slit as I let out an embarrassing moan.

"Fuck, this pussy is perfect."

I push myself up on my elbows and watch the man gently tease me with his tongue, drawing light circles around my clit while his eyes are locked on mine.

"Don't stop." I clutch onto the hair on the top of his head, relishing in the feeling of his mouth. "More…"

"More what?" he mumbles against me.

"More pressure."

He grins. "That's not what I meant." He stops his movements completely, drawing his head away.

"What are you doing?"

With an arch of his brow, he says, "You're forgetting the magic word, Willow."

I glare at him, biting my cheek to keep from screaming. "You and your manners."

"I told you. Manners go a long way."

"How about *now*, Dallas?" I say through clenched teeth, desperation laced in every word.

My body is practically vibrating with need and this man insists on trying to give me a lecture right now?

The smile drops from his face. "Your commands might work in other aspects of your life, Willow, but when I'm the one touching your pussy, I'm in control." *Why is the way he's talking to me right now making me even hotter?* "Now, do you want to come?"

Tipping my head back, I groan in frustration. "Yes!"

"Then how do you ask?"

Against all of my willpower, I grate through my teeth, "*Please*."

"Good girl. Now cover my face with your cum."

That's when the feminism leaves my body, my desire for control snaps, and I nearly launch from the floor as Dallas feasts on my pussy like a man starved, working my bundle of nerves with his tongue like he's on a top-secret mission and I'm the one with all of the answers that he needs.

I dig my hand in his thick, black hair, watching him eat me, squirming under his command. "Oh, God…yes…"

"God can't help you right now, Willow. You wanted this, remember?" he murmurs between licks.

I shamelessly begin to ride his face. "Yes. Shit." I bite my bottom lip. "Right there…"

He slides a finger inside me and I nearly come apart, his touch so precise as he curls his finger, stroking that magical spot that no other man has ever reached.

"Squeeze my fingers, Willow," he mumbles against me as he slides another finger in, continuing with that same curling motion. "Clench that pussy." I do as he says, tightening around his fingers as he works me higher and higher. "Fuck, that's it." He watches his fingers slide in and out of me, the sight beyond erotic. "God, I can't wait for you to squeeze my cock."

Dallas puts his tongue back on my clit, taking me higher and higher, playing my body like an expert. His movements are calculated, smooth, and sharp at the same time, like he's trying to learn my body—like he's worshipping me just as he said he would.

He reaches up to my chest with his free hand, caressing my breast, pinching my nipple through my bra before dragging his hand down my stomach, teasing my skin with his fingers before he moves back to my chest.

And then he drags his thumb down my bottom lip, making eye contact while his mouth stays on my pussy, so I suck his thumb into my mouth, moaning as I feel my orgasm bloom.

"Dallas...I'm almost there..." I breathe out shamelessly when he takes his hand back, squeezing my hip now, keeping me in place while feeling like I'm about to break out of my skin.

"Come for me, Willow. Fall apart for me, sweetheart."

And those words are all it takes as with one final stroke, my orgasm detonates, sending me catapulting off a cliff. I moan and suck in air as I convulse, my animalistic sounds echoing off the walls of the small closet until the final wave subsides and I collapse back onto the pillow, out of breath.

"Oh my God," I breathe out, eyes still closed, legs open, still exposed but too spent to care.

Dallas kisses the inside of my thigh, sucks my arousal from his fingers, and then grabs a blanket, pulling it over me. I vaguely recall the sound of a zipper and then peek to see him taking off his pants, throwing them in the same pile as my leggings.

When he catches me staring, he says, "Don't worry. We're not going there tonight, but I can't sleep in wet jeans."

"Dallas, that was..."

He crawls over to me, propping himself up on his elbow, peering down at me as I take in his entire physique.

The man looks like he's photoshopped.

And then I see the bulge in his briefs.

Yeah, there's no way that's gonna fit inside me.

But he's so hard that it looks painful.

I reach out to touch him, wanting to return the favor, desperately wanting to make him feel as good as he made me feel just now, but he stops my hand before I make contact.

"Not tonight." He shakes his head slowly.

"But..."

"Tonight was about you." He taps his finger to my nose.

My brows draw together. "That doesn't seem fair."

"Trust me, I'm excellent. I have your scent in my beard and your taste on my tongue. I'm plenty satisfied for right now. They'll be time for you to repay me later." I roll my eyes but he leans forward and kisses me, my taste lingering on his lips too. "Now, let's try to get some sleep."

"I'm not sure I'll be able to," I retort as a yawn escapes my lips. It seems like that orgasm did its job of helping me relax, but the sound of the wind whipping outside and the imminent threat of destruction to my house is sure to keep me up all night.

"I think you'll be just fine." He reaches out to brush my hair from my face as I close my eyes, and that's the last thing I remember until we wake up hours later, the aftermath of our hook-up more evident in the light of day.

Chapter Fifteen

Dallas

A soft snore escapes her lips as I fight back my laughter. Willow passed out shortly after I ate her pussy like she was my last fucking meal, and barely stirred all night. But my sleep was scarce as the storm passed over us, even though it was mostly my brain keeping me up. I managed to doze off for a few hours, but honestly, knowing the woman sleeping next to me was Willow made it hard for me to fall asleep and afraid of what dreams might come alive if I did.

Last night was...*affirming*. That attraction and electricity that I've been feeling for the past month combusted the second our lips touched.

And even though I know this will make our circumstances more complicated, right now, I really just don't give a fuck.

Willow stirs beside me, slowly opening her eyes to find me watching her. "It's not polite to stare," she murmurs, her voice groggy.

"Well, you were snoring and woke me up."

Her eyes widen. "I was not!"

"Sorry to break it to you, Willow." I tap her on the nose. "You snore."

She pulls the covers over her head. "Ugh, that's embarrassing."

I whip them right back off. "I don't know, I found it kind of sexy, Goose." I lean down to kiss her lips, and she pushes me away.

"I think you can stop calling me that now."

"Never." I grin down at her.

Willow blinks, our eyes still locked on one another. "You slept here."

"Was I not supposed to?"

"No. I just..." She takes a deep breath. "What happens now, Dallas?"

"Well, I need coffee and probably some breakfast..."

Her lips part and her eyebrows draw together. "I meant...with us. I still plan on selling this house, you know..."

The reality of our situation slams right back into me. But last night, that was the last thing I was thinking about.

I was just worried about *her*—her safety, her fear, her being here all alone.

"Last night wasn't about that, Willow. And you know it."

"I mean, I wasn't really sure what your motives were..."

I cup the side of her face. "I was worried about *you*, and I wanted *you*. That's why I came here. And tomorrow, I'm gonna take *you* on a date."

Her brows pop up. "Is that so?"

"Yes."

"What if I wanted to say no?"

"You don't."

Her face falls. "This is complicated..." she trails off, biting her bottom lip.

"You know, at first, I thought so too. But honestly, it's not." Cupping the side of her face, I wait for her eyes to meet mine again. "I've felt drawn to you since the second I saw you, and for once, I'm tired of overthinking shit. If you're only here for a limited amount of time, I think we owe it to ourselves to enjoy each other's company."

A no strings attached agreement sounds easy, but the truth is, there are several strings tethering us together. But all I know is, for the first time in a long time, I want to be around a woman for more than just one night. So, consequences be damned, I'm going to listen to my gut—and maybe my dick a little bit too.

"Well, I definitely enjoyed last night, crazy storm aside."

I lean down and press a soft kiss to her lips. "I did too."

"Do storms like that happen often here?"

"During the summer and fall, yes. Don't you get weather up in D.C.?"

"Yeah, but not like that."

"The best part about those storms is the calm after."

"What do you mean?"

I launch from the ground, pulling her up with me. But as she stands, I realize she's still naked from the waist down.

"Shit," Willow curses, grabbing the blanket from the ground to cover herself.

"No need to be shy, babe. My tongue was all over the sweet pussy of yours last night."

"Dallas..." Her cheeks turn pink.

I reach for my jeans that are still damp. "I'll let you get dressed. Meet me in the kitchen."

As I leave the closet under the stairs, reminding my dick that now's not the time to get excited, rays of sunshine cut through the remaining clouds, bathing the inside of the house in an iridescent light. The windows are still intact, but I see shingles from the roof scattered on the ground outside. Good thing Penn hasn't replaced it yet, although I'm curious if there are any leaks after all that rain.

I head toward the kitchen, searching for coffee and start a fresh pot just as Willow comes around the corner.

Her hair is wild, but down around her face the way I love it, her skin glows in the sunlight, and she actually looks the most unsure that I've seen her since she walked into my bar that first night.

Our eyes meet and then she turns her head toward the window, gasping as she stares at the ocean.

"Wow..."

The coffee pot beeps, so I pour two cups for us. "How do you take your coffee?"

"Just a little bit of cream, please."

I fix her cup and then carry them both over to the front door. "Come on. Let's go outside."

Willow opens the door for us, and then I hand her the cup of coffee I made for her as we lean against the railing on the front porch, watching the ocean glimmer in the distance.

"It's so quiet," she murmurs.

"I know." I cast my eyes to the right. "After the rain, the waves calm down, almost like they've exhausted all their energy in battle."

"I can't imagine growing up here." She takes a sip of her coffee, looking out to her left.

"I'll tell you this—when I was on deployment, the thing I missed the most about home was the ocean. Every time I was away, I felt like a part of me was missing, a peace that was grounded in me only when I was here."

Willow turns to face me. "How long were you in the service?"

"Twelve years."

"And your dad?"

Her question catches me off guard. But she was there the night of the veterans' dinner, so she knows about my family history now. "Ten years."

"So you beat your old man, huh?" She bumps her shoulder into mine, but my body instantly grows tense.

"Yeah. He wasn't happy about it either."

I don't need to get into the shitty relationship I had with my father right now. That's not exactly how I like to start my mornings.

"Did Penn or Parker serve?"

I huff out a laugh before bringing my coffee cup to my lips. "Ha. No, not after they saw what I went through."

"What do you mean?"

"Do you have any siblings?" I cut her off, avoiding her question for the time being. The last thing I want to do is sully our morning with the topic of my father.

She shakes her head. "No. I don't."

"You sound sad about that." Leaning against the railing, I face her head-on now. She mimics my stance, holding her mug in front of her, staring down at the liquid steaming from her cup.

"I can't be sad about something that I never had." She shrugs.

"Yes, you can," I counter.

Her eyes lift to mine and she straightens her spine. "Well, I don't want to be. I have the life that I was handed, and I've chosen to make the best out of it."

I feel like there's more to her explanation, but I'll let it slide for now.

We stay in a standoff, neither of us speaking first. I feel like walls were just erected right in front of me, but I'm partially to blame.

I don't want to dull the afterglow of our night by talking about heavy shit this early in the morning. But part of me does want to tell her, to open up to someone other than my siblings or my mom. And lord knows, she's dealing with her own emotions right now.

"Your life full of work and no fun, right?"

The corner of her mouth tips up as she huffs out a laugh. "Right." She sighs, looking back out at the water. "God, I wish I had a blueberry muffin from the Sunshine Bakery right now."

"Sorry to disagree with you, but I think the apple cinnamon ones are better."

Her mouth drops open as she twists to face me again. "You take that back!"

"Have you tried the apple cinnamon ones?"

"Well, no...but I have no desire to. The blueberry ones stole my heart and I refuse to cheat on them."

I push off the railing and head for the front door. "Then you can't form an opinion otherwise until you do."

She follows me into the house and into the kitchen where I drain the last of my coffee and put the mug in the sink.

"Why do you insist on arguing with me about everything?"

I close the distance between us and pull her into my chest. "Be honest...you wouldn't want me if I didn't, now would you?"

I practically see the cogs spinning in her head as she studies me. "You're infuriating."

"Infuriating and hot, right?"

Her lips curl in a smirk that I desperately want to kiss off her face. "More like full of yourself."

"Don't worry, Willow. One of these days, you're going to be full of me too."

***

"Mrs. Hansen saw you leaving the Bayshore house this morning. Anything you want to tell me?"

I glare at Penn over my shoulder, taking a break from the accounting I'm catching up on at my desk. "Nothing you need to know."

"Just want to make sure you're thinking straight."

I drop my pen and lean back in my chair, staring up at my brother.

When I left Willow this morning, which was the last thing I wanted to do, I drove back to the restaurant and decided to find any and everything to distract me until our date tomorrow night. But it turns out that even crunching numbers can't make me forget the way her lips felt against mine and the sweet taste of her pussy.

Fuck. I'm gonna be hard for the next twenty-four hours, I just know it.

"I went over there last night to make sure she was prepared for the storm, okay? She was scared, so I stayed to comfort her."

"With your dick?" Penn's chest bounces up and down with silent laughter.

"Not that it's any of your business, but some stuff did happen. And tomorrow, I'm taking her out."

His arms and smile drop as the truth hits him too. "Damn. You're really going for it then?"

"Yeah." I shrug, staring up at my brother. "I can't stay away from her, Penn, and I'm tired of fucking trying."

He nods, like he's accepting the circumstances just as much as I've had to in the past few days.

And this is what I've arrived at: she may own the house that I've always dreamed of owning myself, but the pull I feel toward her is stronger than that old desire.

There will be other houses.

But there's only one Willow.

And if she's here temporarily, then I owe it to myself to explore this connection that we have.

My gut tells me she belongs here, like something brought her here that is bigger than us both, and rarely in life do you get a feeling like that, so why not listen to it?

This could monumentally blow up in my face.

But after last night, I realize that I don't fucking care.

I've made choices and sacrifices throughout my life that have paid off, and some that still haunt my dreams.

But not going after Willow?

I'm fairly certain that regret could turn into a nightmare I'd have to face for the rest of my life.

"So what happens now?" Penn asks, pulling me back to our conversation.

"Now I show her exactly what Carrington Cove and I can offer her."

"And the house?"

I shrug. "What will be, will be."

"Then I hope it's worth it."

Something tells me that she is.

***

"That thing has seat belts, right?" Willow stares at my Mustang as I guide her with my hand on her lower back, down the gravel alongside her house toward my car.

I drove over to her house to pick her up for our date, and when she opened the door, my jaw nearly hit the floor.

She had on a light blue sundress with white polka dots, thin straps draped over her shoulders exposing her creamy skin, and a hem that hit just above her knees. It was the most casual thing I've seen her wear yet, but that wasn't what stopped me in my tracks.

Her hair was down on purpose.

All. Of. It.

Silk waves of gold hung around her face, her blonde hair glistening in the sunlight, and her lips were painted the same red she wore the first night she stepped foot in my restaurant.

I felt like a fucking sap trying to form words in my head for how strongly she took my breath away.

The only word I could come up with was…*wow*.

And now that I have her next to me and the whole evening ahead of us, I can't wait to bury my hands in her hair later while I bury my tongue in her mouth.

"Yes, there are seat belts."

"I know it sounds like a stupid question, but I've never been in an old car like this before."

I reach for the handle on her door, opening it so she can slide inside. But I stop her with my free hand before she does. "The term you're looking for is classic, Willow. She's a *classic*."

Her brows rise. "*She*?"

"Yes, Goose. *She* is my pride and joy, so all I ask is that you show some respect."

Her eyes narrow as she says, "Then stop calling me Goose. Otherwise, your car is just plain *old*, Dallas."

I smack her ass gently right before she sits down. "Watch it, babe."

Her jaw hangs open as I shut her door and round the front of the car. Once I situate myself inside, she turns to me and says, "Did you just smack my ass?"

"Yeah, I did. And there's more where that came from. I have a feeling that sass of yours has never been challenged, but that's about to change tonight."

"And what if I'm not on board with that?"

I twist in my seat, resting my forearm over the back of her headrest, leaning forward slightly so there's very little space between us. "Let me ask you something." She purses her lips but waits for me to continue. "When I slapped your ass did your body warm up? Did heat flash under your skin and travel down between your legs?" She swallows but doesn't answer. So I lean in closer and whisper, "If I slipped my hand under your dress right now, would your panties be wet?"

"Dallas..."

"I think you and I both know the answer to that question, don't we, Willow?"

She lets out a growl that makes my lips curl up, pleased that I've read her correctly, and so fucking excited to show her just how fun giving up control can be.

Hell, she's already let her hair down for the evening—time to let it fly in the wind.

Before she can tell me off, I lean over all the way, gently place my lips on hers, and remind her of our connection. And when I break the kiss too soon, she groans in frustration.

Now you might understand how frustrated you've made me since the moment we met, Willow.

"So, are you ready for me to show you a night out in Carrington Cove?"

Huffing out her defeat, she tilts her head at me and says, "Fine."

Laughing, I check over my shoulder to back out onto the road. "You sound so excited about it."

"Honestly, I'm nervous, Dallas." She huffs and then slaps her palm to her forehead. "Jesus, I can't believe I just admitted that."

I cast a glance at her before focusing back on the road, heading up the coast to a spot I want to show her. "How come?"

She fiddles with her fingers in her lap. "I, uh...haven't been on a date in a long time."

"How long?"

She winces and then turns to me and says, "Since college."

I nearly run a red light, slamming on the brakes before I do. "Shit. I'm sorry." Gripping the steering wheel, I continue, "But seriously? That long? How old are you?"

"Thirty-four, and don't you know it's not polite to ask a woman her age?"

Huffing out a laugh, I say, "I wasn't trying to insinuate that you're old. Just needed a frame of reference."

"I've just been really busy." She shrugs, looking out her window as the light turns green, avoiding my eyes now. "The last thing I was thinking about was my love life."

"I get that." I don't want to give her a complex, but part of me wonders if there's another reason she hasn't dated. I know I had my reasons for keeping women at arm's length, which is why when I felt myself being pulled into her orbit, I had to fight to stop resisting it. "My time in the service kept me from wanting to grow attached to anyone, and then when I returned home, I dove headfirst into making my business thrive."

"Well, so did I."

"You own your own business? I thought you were in advertising."

Her spine straightens and then she says, "I own my own advertising firm back in D.C., Dallas. Marshall Advertising."

"Holy shit. That's impressive, Willow."

Damn. I can only imagine what a ballbuster this woman is. That explains a lot more about how she carries herself and the fact that she's always working.

"Thank you."

"So while you've been down here..."

"I've been managing things remotely. Honestly, I was apprehensive about it since I'm very hands-on in my business, but the break has been kind of nice." She stares out the window, sighing.

No wonder she's so eager to get back to D.C.

Fuck. Maybe this is more complicated than I thought.

Not sure of what to say after her admission, but knowing one thing she needs is some fun in her life, I tell her, "Let's roll the windows down."

"What?"

"See that handle down there?" I point to the handle on her door since this car is so "old" you have to manually roll down the windows.

"Yeah?" "Turn it toward you." I do the same to my side as a gust of ocean breeze flows through both sides of the car.

"Oh my God!" Willow shouts over the sound of the wind, her hair blowing wildly all around her face. "You have no idea how much time I spent on my hair, Dallas!"

"Doesn't matter to me." I smirk over at her as her grin builds. "I like you a little messy."

Her smile drops as she stares at me. "You have no idea how messy my life is."

"Willow, there's nothing you could tell me that would make me want you any less."

"You don't know that for sure."

I reach over and cup her face, feeling something take shape deep in my gut. "Yeah, Goose. I do."

***

"This spot is incredible."

Willow and I are standing on the edge of the pier that extends into the ocean a few miles up the coast, staring off over the water. There's a reason I brought her up here, but we have a little while to wait until I can let her in on that.

"It is."

"This place—the scenery, the people, the way it makes you feel like you're in your own little slice of heaven…" She sighs. "It's beautiful."

But my eyes never look anywhere but her as I say, "Yeah. It is."

And then she turns to face me, realizes I was staring at her, and the space between us grows louder somehow, like we're waiting to see who's going to make the next move.

"I didn't realize there was a pier up the coast from town." She looks around us, breaking the moment. "And those crab cakes?"

"Best you've ever had, huh?"

"Yet another food item I'm addicted to here."

Franny's Crab Shack is a Carrington Cove restaurant that survives on tourism much like my own, but word of mouth keeps her business thriving when the locals can't manage to visit. Franny opened this place when I was in middle school, and to date, she still serves up the best seafood, and crab cakes particularly, that I've ever had in my life.

"I know the feeling. This place gets overlooked sometimes because you can't see it from the highway when you're driving down the coast, but the locals make sure to point tourists in this direction, especially because of the businesses out here."

"It's amazing."

"Best date you've ever been on?"

She smirks over at me. "Well, with very little to compare it to, I'd say yes."

I shrug. "Doesn't matter how many others there were. This is the only one that matters, as far as I'm concerned."

She turns to face me. "So cocky."

I mimic her stance, leaning against the wooden railing. "No. Confident, Goose."

"What was it like growing up here?" She rests her back against the railing this time, watching the people on the pier mill around us.

"Everything you would expect in a small town."

"Well, that idea is foreign to me, so please, explain."

Pinching her waist, she squeals and then glares at me. "Watch that sass."

"You love it."

Yeah, I kinda do.

"Well, I was born here, along with all four of my siblings. Dad served in the Marines until I was four, and we stayed here even after his honorable discharge. My parents lived in the same house my entire life, though Penn and I have done some updates to it in the past five years. Mom was a teacher at the elementary school for thirty years. She retired two years ago, but still likes to volunteer there every once in a while. Our life was always here, and I guess the four of us never saw a reason to leave." I look out over the water.

"There's a comfort in knowing you have somewhere in the world that grounds you, a place that's familiar and feels like its own little world separate from everything else. I remember hearing about things that would happen in big cities, crime or fights between people, and I'd think, those things would never happen in Carrington Cove. I had the kind of childhood you'd see in old movies. Hell, Penn and I would ride our bikes all over town when we were young and only had to come home when the streetlights came on. Everyone helps one another, and everyone knows you by name, which was both a blessing and a curse, especially when I was up to no good as a kid."

"You? A troublemaker?" she teases.

"Only as a teen. My dad and I butted heads a lot, so I did some shit I'm not super proud of."

"Like what?"

Sighing, I tilt my head at her. "Drink underage, sneak out to parties, and I stole my dad's car once."

"Yikes. Now I'm not so sure I should be hanging out with a guy like you."

I pinch her waist again. "Hey, I cleaned my act up, and I have the Marines to thank for that."

"Why did you join?" she asks, growing serious again. "I mean, I can't imagine what a sacrifice that was, but I'm also curious why you made that decision."

There's an underlying tone to her voice that has me wondering if there's another reason she's asking. "Honestly, I think it went back to September eleventh. I was only twelve when it happened, but the tone of the world after that day is one I won't soon forget, nor the way my father reacted. He'd been out of the service for years, but he was devastated, wanted to reenlist but my mother begged him not to."

"Why not?" she asks, trepidation in her voice.

"Because his time overseas messed him up pretty bad. My siblings and I all knew it, but he and mom never talked about it. Hazel probably remembers that time less since she's nine years younger than me, but it became a big issue between him and me the older that I got. I wanted to serve, and he didn't support that idea."

Willow stares down at her hands, fiddling with the hem of her dress. "I'm sorry."

"It is what it is. However, you can probably gather that my dad didn't want me to follow in his footsteps because of it, and I didn't listen." I understand his concern, but I still don't understand why my father couldn't be proud of his son wanting to serve his country like he did.

"He loved the Marines, though. I mean, I was there at the veterans' dinner. I heard the way people spoke about him."

Talking about my dad is the last thing I wanted to do on our date, but I also don't want to shut down our conversation.

"Haven't you ever heard someone talk about your parents, and you've thought, that's not how they are when no one's watching?"

Willow's face falls and she grows silent.

Fuck. Did I say something wrong?

"Willow?"

"My parents died when I was two, Dallas, so I never really knew them."

Her admission makes me freeze. "Fuck." I reach out to her, pulling her into my chest and she lets me. "I'm sorry."

"It's not your fault," she mumbles against my chest.

"I know, but…"

She pushes off me way too soon, smoothing her hair from her face. "It's fine. In fact, I think we should change the subject because the night just got way too depressing."

I huff out a laugh, tucking her hair behind her ear. "Yeah, but at the same time, I feel like I just got to know you on a level you don't allow many people to. Am I right?"

Her brown eyes lock onto mine. "Yeah, you are."

I take her hand and place it over my wildly beating heart. "Then I'm honored."

Fuck. What is this woman doing to me?

"You should be," she fires back, making me laugh.

How is that one moment our conversation can be so heavy, and the next, I can't hold back my smile? How can the desire to lift those burdens from her shoulders overwhelm me so soon after meeting her?

I don't know her—not deeply, at least. But at the same time, I feel like I do, like she's meant to fucking be here.

It's a magnetic force that I can't explain, but one I'm listening to nonetheless.

"You know what would make me even more honored tonight?" I squeeze her hand that is still on my chest.

"What's that?"

"You being my plus-one on the Ferris wheel."

Willow peers up at the metal structure towering over the pier behind us, a centerpiece that catches your eye instantly. "You want me to go on that thing?"

"Yup. Believe me, the view from the top is worth the trip here as well."

Her head drops down as her eyes meet mine. "Uh, I'm not getting on that, Dallas."

I grab her by the hand and pull her toward the back of the line that's already forming. When the sun sets in the distance, people gravitate toward the ride to catch the spectacular view. If we don't get in line now, we won't make it on in time to see the sky light up in yellows, oranges, and pinks.

"Yes, you are, Goose."

"No, please." She resists my pull, but when we find our place in line, I spin her into my chest, so her back hits my front.

"Don't tell me that the badass businesswoman is afraid of heights?"

"That's exactly what I'm about to tell you." I can feel her shaking in my arms.

Leaning down so my mouth lines up with her ear, I whisper, "You don't have to be afraid, Willow." She lets out a breath. "I've got you and I won't let anything happen to you. I promise."

I've uttered those words a few times in my life, but saying them to her does something to my heart.

It makes me want to uphold that promise in a different way.

I'm not trying to save her life.

No. I'm trying to get her to see a life that she could *live* if she stayed—and somehow, the stakes seem higher because a different part of my heart is on the line this time.

"Okay," she whispers back, and that's good enough for me.

When we get to the front of the line, I help her into our seat and secure the safety bar across our laps.

"I cannot believe you got me on this thing," she mutters.

I drag her closer to me, wrapping my arm around her shoulder. "Trust me. It will be worth it."

The seat jolts and we begin to propel up into the sky.

"Oh my God! This is how I'm going to die, isn't it?" Her knuckles turn white as she grips the lap bar. It never fails to amaze me how strong this woman appears on the outside, but how human she truly is.

And I'm honored that she allows me to see that.

I glance over at Willow, chuckling until I notice that her eyes are closed. "Don't shut your eyes, Goose. You'll miss the view."

When her eyes pop open, the gasp that leaves her lips is everything I wanted from her in this moment. "Oh my God, Dallas."

"This is how Carrington Cove is meant to be seen."

Down the coast in front of us, lights start to pop on, illuminating the town in orbs of bright white and yellow. The sun has cast the sky in a hue of pink that grows to dark blue above us as the sun dips below the horizon, letting night take over. But our town still stands out against the backdrop, like a photograph you might see in a magazine.

"I've never seen anything like this in my entire life."

"And you won't see anything else that will ever compare."

I've seen this view many times before, but with this woman by my side, it feels different. Monumental.

Purposeful.

After a few moments of silence, she turns to me, her eyes meeting mine. "Thank you for tonight, Dallas."

"Thank you for trusting me to come up here."

Our seat jolts to a stop, swinging slightly as another couple gets off below, leaving us frozen in time at the top of the ride.

"Sometimes I still can't believe that I'm here in the first place." Willow stares back at the view.

"All because of a house, huh?"

Her head dips down. "Yeah."

"Are you happy with the progress so far?" I ask, trying to distract her, but also curious about where her head is at.

"I am. Penn has done a great job. I know you didn't look around the other night, but it's such a stark difference from what was in there before. He wants to start on the floors next week."

"Sounds like things are moving along then." I gently trace her bare shoulder with my fingers.

"They are. I think he'll be done in about a month." Her phone buzzes in her purse, interrupting our conversation.

And it's probably a good thing because the thought of her leaving is making me tense all over again.

A month? Things are definitely moving quicker than Penn thought they would.

She silences the call and slips her phone back in her bag. "Sorry."

"No worries. You can answer that if you need to." I drop my eyes to her lap.

"No. I don't want to ruin this moment." She looks back up at me.

Reaching out to cup her face with my other hand, I say, "I don't think anything could." I lean in, waiting for her to meet me halfway, and she does. Her lips touch mine just as the ride jolts back into motion, but our mouths don't part.

Willow dives into the kiss just as much as I do, gently moving her lips over mine, teasing me with her tongue as the Ferris wheel continues to spin.

I pull her closer to me, lunging deeper into her mouth, burying my hands in her hair like I envisioned doing the second I saw her tonight, showing her that what's happening between us is just as thrilling as the view we shared.

When we part, we're both breathing heavily, resting our foreheads on each other's.

"God, why do you have to be so good at that?" she mumbles.

"There are other talents I possess too, Willow. Ones you haven't even experienced yet."

She leans back, staring directly into my eyes. "Care to share them with me sometime?"

"Just tell me when and I'm yours."

"How about right now?"

My heart skips a beat, but my dick jumps at the idea. "Uh, we're kind of strapped into a giant metal wheel at the moment."

Her laughter rings out as she tips her head back. But then she moves closer to me again, pressing her lips to mine before dragging my bottom lip between her teeth. "Maybe I need to be more clear."

My dick hardens painfully, but I manage to rasp out. "That might help."

She licks her bottom lip, eyes glittering in the remaining sunlight in the sky. "Take me home, Dallas, and give me another experience I won't soon forget."

***

I've never been in a car accident before, but something tells me I'm tempting fate as I speed back to Willows' house. And the fact that she's been touching my cock, teasing me through my pants for the past five minutes, isn't helping.

"Fuck, Willow. Are you trying to make me crash?" I ask as she nibbles on my ear lobe from her spot next to me on the bench seat.

"You'd better not. Otherwise, our night might end up in a hospital instead of with you buried inside of me."

"Jesus." I grip the steering wheel harder as her lips move to my neck, licking and teasing my skin there, her palm continuing to rub my length.

Her phone buzzes in her purse again, making her groan. And even though she moves away from me to check it, part of me is relieved since it allows me to focus on getting us back to her place in one piece.

"This must be important. It's my assistant and she's been calling me all night."

"Then answer it. I don't mind," I assure her.

"I just didn't want work to affect our date."

Grasping her hand, I bring it to my lips and press them to her skin. "It's not. I own a business too, remember? I get it."

Her soft smile hints that she appreciates my understanding, and then she hits a few buttons on the phone before bringing it to her ear. "Katrina. What is it?" I can faintly hear another voice on the line while Willow listens to what her assistant is saying. "He has a lot of nerve making that threat. Does he not remember the one hundred fifty million dollars we helped him make last quarter?"

One hundred fifty million?

Jesus, just how successful is her company?

"Well, tell Fletcher that if he wants to continue to dominate the tech field, he needs to be patient. Remind him that we haven't let him down yet, nor will we in the future. But good ideas take time." Another break in the conversation. "Yes, I'll touch base with you tomorrow and I'll be on the call to reassure him myself." I hit the blinker to turn onto Bayshore Drive. "It's okay. Just call him back and promise him I will speak with him tomorrow. Thanks, Katrina."

Willow ends the call and then breathes out heavily.

"Everything okay?" I ask as I pull into the spot behind her house.

"Yeah, just one of my biggest clients being impatient. We're designing a new advertising campaign for his company, but it's taking longer than normal, and he's getting antsy. He's talking about looking for a different firm."

"Sounds stressful."

She finally turns to me and says, "It is, but we've proven ourselves to him. If he wants to walk, I can't stop him. But I also know that he'd probably feel better if he heard from me directly." She looks out the front window at the house. "This would be easier if I were there."

"Working remotely makes this kind of thing difficult, doesn't it?"

"Yes and no. I could have called him this week and touched base with him about everything, but I trust my team, and I'm trying to take a step back. I was waiting to contact him instead of trying to ease his nerves before it got to this point." She looks back at me now. "Part of my coming down here was to help remind myself that I don't have to work twenty-four seven. Now it's coming back to bite me."

I reach for her hand again. "Look, there's nothing you can do tonight. It sounds like your assistant is handling it, and you'll talk to him tomorrow. But you are right—you shouldn't work twenty-four seven. You have to make time for fun, Goose."

"Like the kind of fun we had tonight?"

"You talk like that fun is over."

The corner of her mouth lifts. "You're right. It's not over yet."

A groan escapes my lips as I cup the side of her face and lean closer to her. "No, Willow. It most certainly is not." I bring her lips to mine again. "Now, you might be the boss in the boardroom, but I'm your boss in the bedroom. Got it?"

She licks her lips and says, "Yes, sir."

Groaning in appreciation, my dick presses against the seam of my jeans as I climb out of the car and go around to open her door for her, leading her up to the front porch. Luckily, the geese are nowhere to be found. But when my eyes land on the scarecrow in the sand, I can't help but chuckle at how far we've come since then.

"What are you laughing about?" she asks as I shut the door behind us, flipping the lock.

"Just remembering the first time I saw you on that porch, fighting off geese."

She puts her purse on the counter and turns to me. "Those birds were out for blood, I'm telling you."

My feet carry me over to her so I can wrap my arms around her waist. "Good thing I was here that day then, huh?"

"Oh, you mean when you were begging me to let you inside so they didn't eat you too?"

I tip her chin up with my fingers. "I was a desperate man in many ways that day."

"And now?" Her eyes bounce back and forth between mine. "Now what kind of man are you?"

"The kind who's going to own every inch of your body, baby. And the whole street will know because you'll be screaming for God to help you."

We lunge for each other at the same time, Willow jumping up into my arms, securing her legs around my waist. Our kisses are frantic, carnal, full of energy, need, and want.

With our mouths still connected, I head for the stairs, moving slowly to keep my balance but also because Willow moves her mouth to my neck once more, biting my skin and clawing at my back with her nails.

"Fuck."

"Hurry, Dallas."

When I step into her room, the moonlight has cast the entire space in an ethereal glow, showcasing its brightness through the open window, highlighting the waves of the ocean in the distance.

I cradle Willow's head and then let us both fall to her bed, covering her with my body as my hands roam her curves. Her dress is hiked up around her waist, giving me access to her silky thighs and her bare ass that I squeeze with my hand.

"Please." She rubs herself along my length covered by my jeans, seeking out friction, and I'm sure she can feel what's she's doing to me.

My dick has been hard since the moment she opened her door earlier, and his patience is wearing thin.

Pushing myself off her, I stare down at her gorgeous form splayed out on the bed as I undo the buttons on my shirt, one by one.

"Listen to those manners." I shake my head at her slowly. "Such a good fucking girl. You're learning."

She licks her lips and then reaches up to push one of the straps of her dress down before moving to the other. With her other hand, she slides the zipper down along the side of her dress, and then slowly peels the fabric down her torso, exposing her bare chest, soft stomach, and scantily covered pussy to me before tossing the dress to the side.

"You weren't wearing a bra all night?"

"Nope." She pops the p. "Is that a problem?"

As I stare at her chest, I'm about to admonish her for not telling me until now. But then her rosy, pink nipples harden right before my eyes, and suddenly, I don't give a fuck as long as I have those breasts in my mouth right this second.

I shove my shirt off, tossing it in the same direction as her dress, and then pounce on top of her again, taking one of her nipples into my mouth.

"Yes," Willow moans as she buries her hands in my hair, panting while I nibble on her, licking and sucking voraciously. She rubs herself against my chest, squirming and moaning while I move to the other breast, cradling both in my hands.

"Your tits are perfect, Willow. So fucking perfect the way they fit in my hands."

I squeeze her breasts together and then flick my tongue back and forth between her nipples as she watches, pausing to suck on one before moving to the other.

"Dallas...I need more."

"I know, baby. And you'll get it when I'm ready to give it to you."

She tips her head back and groans. "Damn you."

"Get used to it, Willow. I'm about to show you who's the boss in this bedroom, like I said."

She glares at me as I stand up and unbutton my jeans, shoving them down while she crawls down the bed toward me. I take a seat on the edge of the bed, and then move her between my legs, so her back is to my chest. I want to explore her body as she squirms in my arms, feel her writhe and clench my fingers with her pussy again. As I reach up to caress her breasts once again, her head falls back on my shoulder and she pants.

"You're such a tease." She lets out a sigh of contentment as my hands work over her body, skimming her skin lightly, roaming and learning what turns her on.

"Makes the pleasure that much better." I nibble on her earlobe. "And for some reason, watching you squirm just makes me even harder."

She pushes her ass into my crotch. "I know. I can feel you."

"Just wait until I'm buried inside of you, Willow," I whisper in her ear as one of my hands descends down her stomach, disappearing underneath the white silk of her thong, teasing her slit and finding her dripping with arousal.

"I can't wait."

Gently, I move my finger in slow circles over her clit, holding her to my chest with my other hand as I watch her breasts rise and fall with each of her labored breaths. "You can and you will until I say it's time."

My finger dips lower, testing her wetness and moving it around, exploring her pussy that I can't wait to get another taste of later. And when I slide my finger inside of her, she lets out a moan that's fucking music to my ears.

I don't know how I was thinking I could stay away from this woman. She waltzed into my town with a suit of armor on, but in the past six weeks, I've realized she's delicate, vibrant, hilarious, and so fucking sexy—even sexier when she's about to come.

I move my hand back to her clit, circling her nub with two fingers now, building her up higher and higher. Her nails dig into my forearms as she braces herself for her release.

"Come for me, Willow. Drench my hand."

"Dallas!" she cries, pushing back against me, riding my hand while her orgasm takes over her body. Pleasure consumes her, pushing us closer together as her body writhes and tightens through her release. And when she's spent, she relaxes while I pepper her neck and cheeks with kisses.

"Good girl."

She heaves out a breath. "The way you touch me..."

"I know what you need, sweetheart." She nods against my shoulder, pressing a kiss to my jaw. "You've just got to trust me to give it to you."

She spins in my arms, facing me now, and runs her hands up my thighs. "I do, but now...I want to return the favor."

When she drops to her knees in front of me, I nearly choke—not because I don't know what to say, but because the sight of her there, looking up at me, trusting me, being in this moment with me—it has far more of an impact on me than I expected.

Her hands dig under the elastic band of my briefs, pulling them down as I lift up from the mattress to help her. When I kick them off, her eyes focus on my cock bobbing up and down, hard as steel, precum leaking from the tip.

"Willow..."

She locks her eyes on mine as she lowers her head, opens her mouth, and takes me down her throat in one smooth movement that nearly steals the breath from my lungs.

Tilting my head back, I groan. "Fuck."

She hums in agreement, and then begins to suck me in and out of those perfect lips, her red lipstick smearing all over my cock.

I think red just became my new favorite color.

"Jesus, baby. Slow down."

She shakes her head, wraps both hands around my length, and twists them in opposite directions slowly while she sucks on the head.

I'm seeing fucking stars, aren't I?

My head grows dizzy, I feel that tingle at the base of my spine, and if I don't stop her soon, I'm gonna blow my load before we get to the main event. Stamina has never been a weakness of mine, but Willow is quickly testing that, and that means all of my preconceived strengths are quickly changing.

No matter how incredible Willow's mouth feels, though, I know without a shadow of a doubt that her pussy will be my undoing, so I reluctantly pull my dick from her mouth and watch her bite her bottom lip coyly as she stares up at me. "Why'd you stop me?"

"Because I was about to come down your throat. And I want to be balls deep in your pussy when that happens." I reach out and wipe her red lipstick from her face even though most of it is gone now and help her up from the floor. I go to help her lie on her back, but she bends down to my jeans, takes my wallet from the pocket, and tosses it at me before I can.

"I assume you need this then?"

"I do." Taking the condom out, I toss my wallet back to the floor and then tear open the foil, covering myself as I lean back and Willow begins to crawl over me. "Fine, you can be on top first, Goose. Don't matter to me. I'll still own you."

"I'm counting on it."

I position myself at her entrance and watch as she slowly sheathes me with her warmth, clenching my dick like a velvet glove, and taking me to heaven in a matter of seconds.

She looks down between her legs as she keeps working me in deeper.

"Go slow, baby. There's no rush." I grip her hips, helping her move. "Adjust to me. Let me in."

When she finally takes me in all the way, she stares down at me, her blonde hair hanging around her face like a curtain. "Dallas…"

"Fuck, baby. You feel so fucking good, so tight and hot," I say as Willow lifts her hips and I thrust up into her, setting a pace as we begin to rock against each other.

I squeeze her waist, using her hips to help guide her as she moves up and down my cock, our heavy breathing filling the room.

"That's it, baby. Use me." I bury my hands in her hair and pull her lips to mine as she speeds up, griding her pelvis against mine, the sound of our skin slapping in the background, our words hitting my ears like the perfect soundtrack.

"Dallas…oh God…"

"Keep riding me, baby."

"It feels so good."

"Hell yeah, it does. Fuck…"

"Shit. Right there…"

"Are you gonna come, Willow?"

"Yes," she moans as she falls apart, clenching my dick so hard that I struggle not to follow her over the edge. But I keep my composure, letting her ride out her release until she takes a moment to compose herself and collapses onto my chest.

"God damn it, you're so fucking sexy when you come. Hell, I need to taste you." I roll us over, slip out of her, and then drop my head down to her pussy to lap up her release.

"Fuck. Dallas, I can't." She tries to shove me away, but I pin her hands down on her stomach.

"Yes, you can because this wetness right here? It was my cock that made this happen," I mumble against her flesh, feeling like a man possessed.

And I am.

I've fallen under Willow Marshall's spell, and I don't care what the consequences are.

I've never felt like this about someone before.

And it's not just the sex, even though that is fucking blowing my mind to a monumental degree.

It's her quick wit, her beauty, the hurt in her eyes that's lurking beneath the surface.

It's her headstrong stubbornness, her independence, but also her ability to let me take control when I know she wants to fight me on it.

I feel like she's the part of my life that I've been missing.

But is it too soon to know that? Or even think it?

And I wonder if she feels it too.

As I lap at her clit, I release her hands and watch as she reaches up to pinch her nipples, sighing and moaning every time my tongue flicks her sensitive nub. My body reminds me to focus on the task at hand, worrying about feelings and conversations that need to happen later, so I dive back into making this woman feel incredible and making sure she knows she's doing the same for me.

"Fuck, I could eat this pussy every day."

"I might just let you," she teases as I push back up on my knees, line my cock up to her core, and slide home.

I take one of her legs, drape it over my shoulder, and then lean forward to change the angle as I thrust, folding over her so I can meet her lips with my mouth. "Your cum is addictive, Willow. And you take me so fucking well, like your pussy needs my cock."

"More, Dallas." She cups my face and kisses me, moaning in approval and nodding each time I thrust—I'm trying to get as deep inside this woman as I can.

"Do you feel this?" I reach down and drag my hand between her breasts, feeling her heart hammer beneath my fingers, and then take her hand and place it on my chest in the same spot. "Do you feel what you do to me?"

"I do." She throws her head back. "God, keep fucking me. Please, please, please!"

"Shit, you're gonna make me come," I grate out, grabbing her hips for leverage now, afraid I can't hold back much longer, speeding up my thrusts as her words spur me on.

"Yes, please."

"Fuck. I love hearing you say please."

As I hover over her, pounding her pussy harder and deeper, she lines her lips up to my ear and whispers, "*Please* come inside me and fill me up."

And that's when I lose it.

I come on a groan that bounces off the walls, stilling inside of her as my dick fills up the condom, feeling like my soul has left my body. I grip her hips so hard I'm sure to leave bruises, but my orgasm keeps going, powerful and intense. And then I collapse on the woman who officially just ruined me for all others when the last drop has left my body.

Willow drags her nails up and down my back. "Dallas…"

Breathing heavily, I manage to croak out, "Yeah, baby?"

"Who knew manners were your kink?"

I lose it, laughing out loud as I roll off her, watching her come apart as well, clutching her hands to her chest.

"I sure as fuck didn't."

She turns her face to me and says, "I don't know why that was so hot, but it just spurred you on."

My hand meets her cheek, and I say, "It wasn't just the words, Willow. It was you."

Chapter Sixteen

Willow

"I didn't wake you, did I?" Clutching my phone to my ear, I grab my cup of coffee and quietly shut the front door behind me. I lean against the railing on my front porch, staring out at the ocean as I pull my robe tighter to my body.

"I have a newborn, Willow. I've been up for two hours already."

"Aw. How is my sweet little nephew?" Shauna had her baby boy two weeks ago after going a week past her due date, and I promised her once the house was done, I'd be flying straight out to visit. I offered to be there for the birth, but she assured me that between Forrest's family and her own, she'd have too many people to worry about, and wanted our visit to be just about us spending time together.

"He's perfect. Doesn't understand the concept of sleep yet, but we're getting there."

"I'm sorry I haven't called in a while—"

"Nonsense," she says, cutting me off, "I've been busy, Willow, and I knew you'd call when you needed me. So, to what do I owe the honor of this phone call?"

Sighing, I stare down into my cup of coffee. "Shauna, I think I've done something bad…"

"Oh God. What?"

"But it felt sooooo good," I whine.

Her laughter fills the line. "Quoting Taylor Swift? I like where this is going already." She grows quiet, and then says, "You slept with the restaurant owner, didn't you?"

"I did. But that's not the problem."

"First of all, having sex with whomever you want isn't even a problem to begin with. You're a grown ass woman and deserve to get off when and with whom you see fit."

"Thanks for the pep talk."

"No problem. Now, what's the issue you're concocting in your head?"

"I'm not just speculating, Shauna. This is serious."

I hear the baby cry in the background. Shauna tells her husband to bring her their son, Hudson, so he can eat. I wait for her to get situated and then she replies, "Sorry. Mom duty calls."

"You don't have to apologize to me."

"I'm just a human milk factory now." She chuckles, sighing in contentment. "Anyway, please continue."

"Well, remember that the man that left me this house said he knew my parents?"

"Yes."

"Well, it turns out that man was Dallas's dad."

"And Dallas is?"

"The restaurant owner, Shauna!" I hiss, lowering my voice instantly because I don't want to wake up the man in question. I left him sleeping alone in my bed when I opened my eyes far earlier than I wanted to, especially because he kept me up until almost two in the morning, giving me some of the best sex I've ever had. It's been years since I've stayed up that late, but I guess when you're sleeping with someone whose business doesn't close until midnight, late nights are par for the course.

"Please tell me you're joking."

"I wish I were. Believe me. He came over earlier this week to keep me calm during a crazy storm that blew through, and then some stuff happened that night, which led to him asking me out."

"Holy crap."

"And last night he took me out and we ended up back at my house."

"And he has no idea about the connection?"

"No. The worst part is, he wants this house, Shauna, and his dad owned it the entire time, saving it for me." I yank on my hair. "What am I supposed to do about all this?"

Shauna blows out a breath. "This is a lot. But why is it a problem if you're just gonna leave and sell it to him anyway?"

"I...I don't know if I want to sell anymore."

There. I said it—the thought that's been on my mind for the past week.

"Are you serious?" she asks through a whisper.

I set my coffee cup on the railing and brush my hair behind my ear. "Being here for the past six weeks has made me realize that my life has been so lonely. And I don't know what it is about this town—"

"Small towns will suck you in and never let you go, Willow. Hence why I'm back in Newberry Springs," she cuts me off, saying out loud what I've been afraid of.

"My mind is a mess, Shauna. And now my heart is involved too, even though that's the last thing I wanted."

"You can't avoid feelings, Willow. You can try, and lord knows that you have for years, but eventually they'll catch up to you. Trust me on that."

"But this isn't just my *feelings*, Shauna. This is my life. My business is in D.C., my apartment is there. But down here, I feel…"

"Like someone new?"

"Like me," I whisper, afraid to say it louder because it scares me how true those words are.

For most of my adult life, I feel like I've had to be strong because that's what people expected of me, especially once they heard my story—the two-year-old girl who lost both of her parents, had no other family to speak of so was taken in by their best friends, and still managed to turn into a successful businesswoman, building a multimillion-dollar advertising business from the ground up.

I wasn't allowed to fall apart, to be angry about the fact that I was robbed of a life I could have had if my parents hadn't died. I was still so fortunate, grew up in a loving home, never went without, and experienced financial success on a level that most people only dream of.

But I always felt like some part of me was missing—real roots, a foundation—a place where I belong. Sometimes I feel like the life I'm living isn't the one I was supposed to have.

"That's a good thing, Willow."

"It is, but it's also complicated. This man, Shauna…" I groan out loud. "He's stubborn and cocky, but he sees *me,* he's thoughtful even when I've given him plenty of reasons not to be, and he makes me feel safe. He listens, doesn't shy away from the fact that I'm successful, and the way he touches my body…" I shudder at the memory. "In fact, he overheard me on a call last night and told me the way I handled the situation was a turn on."

"Sounds like he doesn't mind a woman in control."

"That's the thing...in bed though? He's the one in control, and it's so fucking hot."

Shauna laughs. "Sounds about right."

"What do I do? I'm completely out of my depth here."

"Honestly, Willow, it depends on what you want for the long term. Do you see a future with this guy? If this is just a vacation fling, then there's no reason to bring up the past and rattle his life with unspoken secrets if you plan on leaving. But if you want to stay, is it for you or him?"

"I don't know. Part of me gave into him because I thought this would be temporary, but after last night..."

"You want more."

"I think I might." Biting my lip, I lift my coffee cup and take another sip. "Oh, shit. I can't believe I forgot to tell you the worst part."

"Jesus, there's more?"

"The night I found out about the connection between Dallas and his dad was the night of the veterans' dinner."

"I remember you telling me about that."

"Yeah. Well, later that night after I left in a hurry, I had a visitor. And you're never going to believe who it was..."

"There you are."

I spin around so fast, I nearly fall over as Dallas walks out the front door, shirtless and in nothing but his boxer briefs. The muscles of his torso glisten in the sunlight, highlighting the scar on his ribs I noticed last night, sending a flood of heat right between my legs.

We had sex three times last night, but apparently that wasn't enough for my greedy vagina, and she's ready for round four.

"Hey. I didn't want to wake you so I came out here to make a call," I say, still awestruck by the mouthwatering specimen of a man standing in front of me.

He runs a hand through his messy hair—his *sex* hair—and damn him, it makes him look even more appealing. "I appreciate that. Is there more coffee, though?"

"Yeah. Let me end this call and I'll be right in."

He takes a few steps toward me, tilting my chin up before gently pressing his lips to mine. "Take your time, Goose."

I wait for him to go back in the house before remembering that I'm on the phone with Shauna.

"Hello? Earth to Willow. Are you still there?" her voice calls out to me.

"Uh, yeah. I'm here." I clear my throat and continue, "Look, I've got to go."

"You're going to leave me hanging like that? Who showed up at the house? And why did he call you Goose?"

I lower my voice and turn my back to the house again. "I can't have this conversation with Dallas around, okay?"

"Willow, you need to decide what you want to do."

"I know..."

"And honestly, I say go for it."

"I don't know if I can."

"You can do whatever you want, Willow. It's your life. The question is, do you have the guts to make a choice for yourself? One that isn't tied to your job or what you think people expect from you?"

"Get right to the point, why don't you?" I reply sarcastically, even though I know she's right.

"That's what I'm here for. But I will tell you this, coming from my own experience—secrets will come out eventually, so the most important thing is that he hears the truth from you and not someone else. Trust me. If you want to explore this relationship with him further, you need to be prepared to tell him everything."

"What if he can't look past it?"

Shauna sighs audibly. "That's just a chance you're going to have to take, but trust me, you can't have a relationship built on half-truths."

I close my eyes. "Okay."

"In the meantime, enjoy the sex, and keep me posted."

Chuckling, I say, "I will. And you'd better keep sending me pictures of my nephew."

"I have about five hundred I could send to you right now."

"I expect them all within the hour."

She laughs, making me feel slightly better. "I love you, Willow. You'll figure this out. I know you will."

"Thank you. Talk to you soon."

As I end the call, Dallas comes back outside, holding his own cup of coffee. "Everything okay?"

I turn to face him again, admiring how attractive he is, remembering how his body felt on top of mine, and the fact that those darkened eyes were focused on me last night. And then I think about how he makes me feel beyond physically—like I'm worth his attention, like he wants me here, like what I have to say is important. I've shared more of myself with this man than any man before him, that's for sure.

Doesn't that tell you something, Willow?

"Yeah. I was just talking to my best friend, Shauna. She lives in Texas."

"And what were you two talking about?" He crowds me against the railing, pushing his hips into mine. I feel him grow hard the second we touch.

"You."

He smirks before taking a sip of his coffee. "What about me?"

"How horrible the sex was and I wasn't sure how to break things off with you this morning."

He narrows his eyes at me. "You may be able to pull off a bullshit statement like that with someone else, Willow, but I know for certain that you couldn't have faked all eight of the orgasms I gave you last night. So, care to try again?"

I swallow hard as my body screams for him to make the total nine. "You counted?"

"No need to, babe." He taps his temple. "The sight of you coming undone each and every time will be seared into my brain for all eternity."

With one hand still holding my coffee and phone, I wrap the other around his neck, drawing his face closer to mine. "I've always strived to leave a lasting impression on people."

"Oh, you're leaving one on me for sure, Willow." The taste of coffee on his lips melds with my own as he kisses me softly, giving me just the tip of his tongue. When he draws back, he says, "I guess the question is, what do you want to do about it?"

That's what I've been debating since before he took me out last night, and what I was trying to explain to Shauna.

But I think she's right. Until I know exactly what I want to do, there's no use in stirring up the past and baring truths that may never need to be revealed, especially since my visitor the cautioned me with the same sentiment.

For the time being, why can't I just enjoy this man, this town, and my time here? Because ultimately, when I look back on my adventure in Carrington Cove, I want to do so with fond memories, not a list of regrets—although at this point, I feel like that might just be impossible.

"I think you should take me back to bed before I have to do some work," I answer honestly and my libido jumps at the idea as well.

His grin is borderline lethal. "Good answer."

***

"Hey, stranger." Astrid bumps her shoulder against mine just as I find my footing next to her. Cheers erupt from the sideline of the field across from us as the other team scores a goal. "Damn it."

"What's the score?"

"Three to one now. We're losing."

I cast a glance over to Penn and Dallas, their heads stuck together talking strategy. "There's still time left, right?"

"Yeah, we just started the third quarter." Astrid blows out a breath and then turns to face me. "So, where have you been? I feel like I haven't seen you since the veterans' dinner."

It's true, but everything that has happened since that night has taken me by surprise and even now, I'm not sure where it's leading me.

Only time will tell, I guess.

"Work and stuff with the house have kept me busy."

She eyes me curiously. "And has Dallas been keeping you busy too?"

I fight to hide my smile but fail miserably. "Maybe."

She shoves my shoulder again. "I knew it. You dropped me for a man."

I reach for her hand and she lets me take it. "I did not drop you."

"I know, I'm just giving you crap," she says with a wink.

"Good. It's just been a crazy week, and now..." My eyes find Dallas again as he finishes talking to a player on the field. Our eyes meet and then he tips his chin up at me, flashing me his panty-melting smirk before focusing back on the game.

"Now you're dating my boss and can't remember your own name?"

"Huh?" I ask, my eyes still locked on Dallas's before dropping down to his ass.

Astrid waves a hand in front of my face. "Hello? Is anyone home over there?"

Blinking, I focus back on her. "Sorry. What did you say?"

"Jesus, should I go ahead and mark my calendar for the wedding?" she teases.

"God, no. Look, I have no idea what is happening between us, but whatever it is, it's fun and good…*really* good." I bounce my eyebrows at her.

"Lucky." She sighs. "It's been years since I've had a *good* time, if you catch my drift."

I wrap my arm around her. "That's understandable, Astrid."

"I know, but hey, I'm happy for you." And then something dawns on her. "What does this mean about the house then? Are you still planning on leaving?"

"I—" My response is cut off as Bentley kicks the ball into the goal, scoring for his team.

"Yes! Great shot, Bentley!" Astrid screams, clapping and jumping up and down beside me.

"Heck yeah!" Dallas clenches his fist in front of him, running up the sideline to high five Bentley as he runs past us. But before he heads back to his post, he comes over to me, places a quick kiss on my lips, and squeezes my hip. "Hey, Goose."

Astrid and I both watch him walk back to Penn, whose knowing smile indicates he's privy to the developments between Dallas and me as well.

"Um, that didn't look casual, Willow," she mumbles in my ear. "In fact, I'm pretty sure he just called you Goose. That's quite the nickname. Care to explain?"

Rolling my eyes, I cross my arms over my chest. "It's nothing."

She stands in front of me as the ref blows the whistle and the game starts back up. "It's okay to like him, Willow. Hell, I saw the sparks fly between the two of you the moment you stepped foot in Catch & Release."

"We're just two single adults having fun." *Yeah, keep telling yourself that, Willow.*

"Doesn't look like just fun to me." She arches a brow and I do the same, telling her with my eyes to end the conversation.

"I think it's time we turn the discussion to you. What's new? Anything exciting?"

She yells something at the boys on the field and then looks back at me. "Actually, yes. Greg and Jenny, the owners of the Sunshine Bakery, are looking to retire. And I think I might try to buy the store."

"Oh my God, that's incredible! You'd be amazing at running that place, Astrid."

She laughs me off. "Thanks, but it's not the business side I'm worried about. It's qualifying for the loan. We live off the death benefit from when Brandon died, plus my tips from the restaurant and my part-time paychecks from the bakery, which aren't much."

Without any hesitation, I say, "I'll invest in you."

Astrid nearly falls over as she spins to face me. "What?"

Shrugging like it's no big deal, I say, "Let me be your investor. You can pay me back on whatever timeline works for you. Let me help you, Astrid." Money is no object, but that's not why I want to do this.

"I can't ask you to do that."

"You're not asking, I'm offering." I grab her hands. "You're the only one who made an effort to be my friend here, and even if I don't plan on staying, I believe in you, and you deserve this. You deserve something of your own."

God, it's like speaking to myself all those years ago, taking the leap of faith to start Marshall Advertising.

She worries her bottom lip between her teeth. "I can't."

"You can, and you will. Let me know when you want to go to the bank, and I'll be there."

"Willow…" Her eyes brim with tears until she throws herself at me, wrapping me in her arms. I reciprocate her hug. "Thank you."

Feelings—so many feelings rush through me—contentment, gratitude, and purpose.

If I hadn't come to Carrington Cove, I never would have met this woman. I never would have gotten the chance to know someone that is a true survivor. I know Shauna says that *I* am, but I haven't endured the same loss that Astrid has.

She deserves this—a chance to stand on her own two feet, to show her children how to be independent, and to have something of her own, a business that can change her life.

Just like she's changed mine.

The thought of leaving her nearly knocks me back as we release each other.

If I leave Carrington Cove, I'm not just leaving Dallas, I'm leaving her too.

"Let me talk to Greg and Jenny this week, and I'll get back to you." She wipes away tears from under her eyes just as the ref blows the whistle, signaling something happened on the field.

"I'm not going anywhere anytime soon."

She grabs my hand again and squeezes it. "I wish you wouldn't go anywhere at all."

After the game is over and I've said my goodbyes to Astrid and her kids, Dallas finds me waiting for him under a tree, shading myself from the sun.

"This was a nice surprise," he says in greeting.

I take his aviators off so I can see his eyes. "Good job today, Coach."

He leans down and plants his lips on mine. For a moment, I worry about people seeing us, but then his tongue touches mine, and my reservations fade away. "If you want, I can show you some of my moves from my other playbook."

"Don't you have a restaurant to run?" I ask as he presses his erection into me.

"I could play hooky…for you."

No man has ever offered to skip work to spend time with me.

Dallas isn't like the other men that have momentarily popped in and out of your life, Willow.

"I can't ask you to do that. Plus, it's a Saturday night. You know the place will be crazy." His lips dance all over my neck before he groans.

"You're right. What if I come over after?"

"I'll be asleep. Someone kept me up the past two nights and I'm exhausted."

"You should file a formal complaint with his manager." He nibbles on my earlobe before moving his teeth to my collarbone.

"I would, but he's the boss."

Dallas lifts his head to meet my eyes. "Yes, he is. And you like it that way."

A shiver runs down my spine. "Yeah, I kind of do."

He kisses me once more, rendering me speechless. "So, what about tomorrow night? I want to hear you scream my name again, and soon." His fingers tighten on my hips.

"Penn is coming by the house tonight and tomorrow, but I'm free at night."

"Then come to the restaurant. I close earlier on Sundays. I can feed you and then maybe you can stay with me this time?" The lack of confidence in his voice has me fighting back a grin.

Was he nervous to ask me that?

"I think that might work."

A triumphant smile graces his lips. "Then it's settled. I'll see you tomorrow night."

***

After a long day of painting and sanding cupboards, Penn comes up to me, wiping sweat from his brow. We both look like a mess, but the house is coming along nicely.

After the game on Saturday, he followed me home and helped me take the doors off the kitchen cupboards, preparing them for paint, and all day today we've been working around each other, trying to knock out the first coat on the doors and the frame of the cupboards in the kitchen before he starts on the hardwood floors this week.

"The cupboards are turning out great." He eyes the slabs of wood lying on the floor I've covered with sheets.

"Thanks. I really like the navy blue. I think it was the right color choice."

"I agree. And once the white marble countertops get here, the color contrast will be perfect for the house."

"I think so too." Pushing my hair out of my face, I stare up at him. "Any word on the roofing materials?"

"They should be delivered this coming weekend, so I can get that done next week. Dallas will probably come over and help me."

It was only a matter of time before one of us brought him up. "Oh, good."

Penn chuckles. "That's all you have to say?"

"Was I supposed to say something else?"

He crosses his arms over his chest, staring at me intently. "I don't know. How about you tell me what's going on with my brother?"

"What has he said to you?" I mimic his stance.

"Nope. I asked you first."

Sighing, I drop my hands and busy myself with cleaning up my mess for the day. The paint needs to dry before I can do my second coat, and I can't look at Penn or he might see right through me. "Nothing is going on. We're adults. We're having fun." I sneak a peek at him as his brow furrows. "What?"

"What about the house?"

I turn my back to him. "What about it?"

"You know what, Willow. He wants it, still does. But now?"

I spin back to face him. "He's the one that pursued me, Penn. And for once, I gave into the moment. Do I regret it? No. But…"

Penn shakes his head. "It makes this complicated."

"You have no idea," I mutter under my breath as I stare out the front window at the ocean.

"If you're going to leave, you have to sell this house to him, Willow. At least give him that."

My eyes snap to his. "I haven't decided anything yet, okay? And don't you think Dallas would be pissed if he knew you were talking to me about this?"

"I don't give a shit about what my brother thinks, but I am going to look out for him."

"What's that supposed to mean?"

Penn drops his arms now, his expression softening. "He's different now, Willow, and it started when you walked into town. My brother has been through some shit. Hell, my entire family has. But since we were kids, he's wanted this house, and when he finally gets the chance, you show up. Dallas doesn't let people in. Trust me, I know. I've watched him keep blinders on for years, until you made him drop them." He runs a hand through his hair. "I guess I'm just asking you not to hurt him."

Swallowing down the lump in my throat that formed from his admission, I say, "What makes you think I'm the one that will hurt him?"

"Because I see the way he looks at you, and I know that look all too well."

I tilt my head at him. "You mean the same way you look at Astrid?"

Penn freezes. "That's irrelevant."

"No it's not. It's very much the same."

"Regardless," he says, his jaw clenched, "this is about you and Dallas, which brings me to my next point." He waves his hand out to the side. "I'm starting on these floors on Tuesday, and it would be a lot easier to knock them out if you weren't here."

"Are you kicking me out of my house?"

Penn chuckles. "Kind of, but I happen to have a brother that I'm sure wouldn't mind you staying with him." He winks over his shoulder as he heads toward the kitchen.

"Did you already speak to him about this?" I call after him.

"Nope. I thought it'd be better coming from you." When he comes back to the living room, he says, "And I'd probably say something soon, you know, before you change your mind and chicken out."

"I wouldn't chicken out."

Penn bobs his head from side to side. "I guess that's debatable, huh?"

"God, you're just as infuriating as your brother."

"Nah, he's still got me beat, but at least I gave you the courtesy of asking before he thinks I'd offer for you to stay at my place."

"Do you have a death wish?"

Penn laughs. "Nope, and the fact you know what his reaction would be tells me all I need to know about how you feel about him too."

***

I walk into Catch & Release just after eight o'clock, freshly showered and dressed in clothes that don't have paint all over them.

Astrid flags me down as soon as our eyes meet. "What are you doing in here?"

"She's here to eat," Dallas answers for me as I take a seat at the bar.

Astrid casts him a knowing glance. "Are you sure that's the only thing she's here for?"

"Don't you have tables to take care of?" he fires back, ignoring her question.

"I see how it is. You two are playing it close to the vest." She mimics zipping her lips. "I understand." Grabbing a tray full of drinks, she hoists it up on her shoulder and then saunters off.

After she's out of earshot, I turn to Dallas. "Sorry about her, but she does know about us. I hope that's okay."

Dallas leans over the bar, bringing his head closer to mine and planting a swift kiss to my lips. "I don't care who knows about us, Willow, but Astrid likes to give me shit just as much as Penn. It's what we do." He shrugs before standing tall again.

My shoulders drop with relief. "I can tell. Speaking of Penn," I say, getting to the point of why I'm here. "He wants to start on the floors on Tuesday and says I should vacate the house. Says it will be easier if I'm not there."

"Okay..." His brow furrows as he waits for me to continue.

"I think I'm going to head back to D.C. for a few days."

Dallas's shoulders tense up. "Oh."

We stare at each other for a few moments before I finally clear my throat. "I've been gone for weeks, and honestly, I should really check in on my company." Toying with the coaster in front of me, I focus on the distraction instead of meeting his eyes.

Dallas pushes himself off the bar and reaches for a towel, wiping off the bar. "Makes sense."

"I'll be back by Thursday, Friday at the latest..."

Our eyes finally meet. "It's okay, Willow. I get it. Your life is up there. The choice is logical." One of his employees calls him over, halting our conversation. Dallas holds a finger up to him, and then says to me before he leaves, "I've got to get back to work. We can talk more about this after we close."

"Okay," I mumble as he walks away, just as Astrid comes back behind the bar.

"Everything all right?"

I groan, dropping my head in my hands. "I have no idea what I'm doing."

And after seeing Dallas's reaction to my leaving, I seriously wonder if I'm making the right decision about a lot of things. I know Penn suggested I stay with Dallas, but that would only make it that much harder to leave when my time here is over. Besides the floors, the only things left are the roof and a fresh coat of paint on the exterior, a decision we came to before he left today. If I'm going to put a new roof on the place, might as well spruce up the rest of the house, right?

With only those projects left, the timeline for renovations ended up being shorter than we anticipated, which means my time here in this magical town is coming to an end soon.

Going back to D.C. is inevitable, and even though every moment I spend here makes me fantasize about a life in Carrington Cove—with Dallas, Astrid, and those muffins—it's just not possible.

My business is six hours away.

My life has been there for the past ten years.

I still don't know what to think about my surprise visitor.

And I'm keeping a secret from this man that could destroy him.

I can't be responsible for doing that to another person.

"What's going on?" Astrid asks, pulling me from my inner turmoil.

"I have to go back home for a few days."

"Okay…" She glances over at where Dallas is standing, smiling and talking to a few customers, and then it hits her. "Oh."

"Yeah."

"Well, you'll be back, right?"

I lean back in the chair. "Yes, but not for much longer."

Astrid takes a deep breath. "I hate to ask this, but does your offer to invest in the bakery still stand even though you're leaving?"

"Of course, Astrid. I wouldn't go back on that promise," I assure her.

She sighs in relief. "Okay. Well, Greg and Jenny agreed to sell to me, and the bank said I wouldn't qualify for the loan on my own. So, maybe when you get back this week we can meet up at the bank? You know, before the chaos of the Carrington Cove Games starts?"

"Oh, crap. That's this coming weekend, huh?"

"Yes. And you can't miss that." She tilts her head at me. "Don't worry about Dallas, Willow. He's a big boy and I'm pretty sure he knew the score before he started whatever it is y'all have going on."

"I know, but it still doesn't make me feel great. I guess part of me feels like I'm leading him on."

She tips her shoulder up, smiling. "Well, is there any chance that you might consider staying? And I'm not just asking for my own selfish reasons."

"I—"

But I don't get a chance to answer before another server comes over and places a club sandwich in front of me, along with a dirty martini with three olives.

"Oh, uh…I didn't order this."

The server tips her head in Dallas's direction. "Dallas ordered it for you."

Our eyes meet and in that moment, I try to answer Astrid's question for the hundredth time.

Do I want to stay in Carrington Cove?

Yes.

But can I stay without dire consequences?

Part of me already knows the answer to that too.

Astrid leaves me to tend to her customers. I keep my seat at the bar, finishing my meal and drink as the night winds down. Sunday nights aren't as busy as a Friday or Saturday, which is why Dallas closes the restaurant at nine.

When the last customer leaves, he locks the door and stands there for a minute with his back to me. He hasn't said a word to me since I told him my plans, and I'm dying to know where his head is at.

Timidly, I ask him, "Everything okay?"

He turns to face me, and there's a determination in his eyes. "Yes and no."

"Care to elaborate?"

His legs carry him over to me, his strides purposeful and deliberate. His shoulders are pressed back, his dark eyes locked on mine, and when he finally stands before me, he frames my face in his hands and crushes his lips to mine.

The kiss takes me by surprise, but it only takes me a second to fall right into step with him, sliding my tongue against his, pressing my breasts to his chest, trying to get as close to him as possible.

I never want to get this close to anyone.

"Fuck, I missed this mouth," Dallas mumbles against my lips, dragging my bottom lip between his teeth before licking the sting away and pulling me closer to him again.

"I'm right here."

"Yes, you are. For tonight, you're still here and my goal is to remind you of what will be waiting for you when you return."

Goosebumps scatter all over my skin. "That sounds promising."

"Oh, I always keep my promises, Willow." The gravel of his voice makes heat pool between my legs. "Now strip."

"What?"

"You heard me, Goose. Get naked so I can play." He smacks my ass and walks away from me, going behind the bar as I stand there bewildered. When he casts a glance at me over his shoulder, he says, "I mean it, Willow. We're running out of time."

Yes, we are.

My hesitation only lasts for one more second before I begin to unbutton my blouse and drape it across the back of the barstool. I pop the button on my shorts, and then shimmy those down my legs as well.

Dallas wipes the bar clean in front of me as he watches me lose my clothes. "Everything, Willow. I want you naked."

Drawing in a long breath because I feel like I'm forgetting how to breathe in this moment, I reach behind me and pop the clasp on my bra, pulling it down my arms and adding it to the pile of my clothes as my nipples pebble when the cool air in the room hits my skin. And then I slide my thong down my legs and kick my shoes off, waiting for his next instruction.

Dallas's jaw clenches as he taps the bar with his fingers. "Hop on."

"You want me to get up there?"

"Now, Willow."

Normally, I'd fight back, but the power behind his voice has my vagina driving instead of my brain, and I attempt to gracefully use one of the stools to climb on top of the bar where I just ate my dinner, along with numerous other people. Then, I slowly lie back, attempting to make myself look as sexy as possible because I have a feeling the sight of me climbing up here was not in the least.

"Do you have any idea how hard it was for me to get through work tonight, knowing that you're leaving?" His words are harsh and laced with hurt.

Shaking, I try not to tremble too hard. "I wouldn't know, seeing as you ignored me all night."

He pinches my nipple, making me squirm. "Don't sass me right now."

"But that's what we do," I counter as Dallas trails his fingers up the inside of my thigh, stopping before he reaches where I ache for him.

"Not right now. Tonight, I'm going to make sure you feel me between your legs for days. I want you thinking of me and my cock, of what my hands feel like on your skin." He swipes a finger through my slit. "What my fingers and tongue feel like on your pussy, and how my fingerprints mark you." He pushes my legs open, bending my knees, and then drags his tongue through my slit, making my back arch off the bar. "And then I want you to promise me that I get to do this to you again when you return."

"Dallas…"

"Promise me," he commands.

On a shaky breath, I say, "I promise."

"Good girl. Now, hold on, baby."

"But Dallas," I retort, wanting to get more words out of him, something that tells me we haven't made a mistake by crossing this line.

"I'm busy," he growls before he lifts one of my legs over his shoulder, spins me ninety degrees so he has the perfect access to me over the bar, and then devours me, exploring my pussy with his mouth as the cool air from the vent above us blows on my naked body.

And then I forget what I was going to say.

All I do is feel him everywhere.

My body takes over my mind, letting me experience every sensation that Dallas elicits as he moves his hands over my breasts, pinching my nipples, biting the inside of my thighs, and bringing noises out of me that I've never made before.

"This is *my* pussy, Willow," he mumbles against my clit before sucking it back between his lips. "I've gone two days without tasting it and now you're making me go even longer."

"I—I have to work."

"I understand"—he licks me from bottom to top—"but I don't have to like it."

Burying my hands in his hair, I admit, "I don't like it either."

"At least we're on the same page about something." Dallas runs his tongue over every inch of me, sucking my clit between his lips, pushing two fingers inside of me, slowly rubbing them in and out, caressing every inch of my core. He eats me slowly, purposefully, and intensely until my orgasm starts to bloom.

I can feel myself getting closer to the precipice, but then he abruptly stops touching me.

"Dallas..."

He stands up, wipes his mouth with the back of his hand, but his beard still glistens with my arousal. Cradling my head and my hip, he spins me back so my entire body can lie on the bar again, and then he reaches beneath the counter and grabs a bottle of tequila.

"Are we drinking?" I ask, my body still vibrating with my release that's just out of reach.

He holds the bottle above my stomach, pulling the cork from the top. "I am." Gently, he tips the bottle, and a small amount of alcohol fills my belly button, overflowing down my hips on either side.

"Holy shit," I gasp while watching his every move.

Pleased with the amount, he puts the bottle down and then grabs one wedge of lime, placing it between my breasts before he leans down and swirls his tongue over each one. Then he takes a pinch of salt from the container on the bar and dusts it over both of my nipples.

I'm about to be a human shot glass.

"Do you know why I chose tequila for this, Willow?" he asks as his eyes bounce up and down my body, admiring his work.

Trying not to pant in desperation, I reply, "Why?"

"Because tequila can mess you up if you let it, or it can lend you the courage to do things you wouldn't otherwise." He grips my chin in his hand and turns my head so I can see him when he says, "And that's how you make me feel."

Before I can reply, he lets my chin go, drops his head to my stomach, and sucks the tequila from my belly button, licking the remaining trails of it from my skin. He drags his tongue up my stomach to my nipples, cleaning the salt from the pebbled peaks, and then takes the wedge of lime between his lips, sucking the juice from it.

I watch him with fascination, growing more desperate as the seconds tick by, but Dallas spits the lime out on the floor and then smashes his lips to mine. Swiftly lifting me and cradling me in his arms, he turns away from the bar and heads toward a door in the back.

He opens the door to reveal a small staircase, holding me to his chest as he climbs higher and higher to another door, turning the knob and entering a small apartment before setting me down gently on my feet.

I push his shirt over his head, dragging my nails down his chest and stomach as he tosses it to the side. Then he cups my face in his hands and brings his lips back to mine.

No other man has ever had control over me like this before.

And I'm not sure that another man ever will.

Dallas pops the button on his jeans, shoving them down, along with his briefs, before stepping out of them and kicking them to the side, stroking his cock as he stares at me. "Stay right here."

"Where are you going?" I ask as he walks away from me down a small hallway, but he doesn't respond.

When he comes back, he's holding a strip of condoms, and my body grows warmer and wetter watching his muscular form stalk toward me. He takes one off and tosses the rest on the dining room table before leading me over to one of the cushioned chairs at the table.

I watch him sit down, his cock standing proudly as he covers himself with the rubber, and then motions for me to join him. "Ride me, Willow."

You don't have to tell me twice.

I straddle his thighs as he drags his crown through my wetness, and when he lines himself up, I slowly sink down on him, joining us together as we both moan in unison.

"Fuck."

"God, Dallas."

Wrapping my arms around his neck, I sink down further until he fills me completely. Our bodies are pressed together so tightly that his chest hair is rubbing against my nipples, creating the most glorious friction as I start to bob up and down on his cock.

"That's it, Willow. Take me deep, beautiful."

I lock eyes with his and swivel my hips, hitting that spot deep within me that makes an orgasm start to resurface.

"This is what you'll be missing when you're gone." He buries his fist in my hair, yanking my head back, exposing my neck to him. "And I'll be missing this pussy."

"Yes…"

"But that's not all I'll miss, Willow." He drags his tongue along the column of my throat before wrapping his other hand around my waist. "I'll miss the feel of you next to me, the sound of your voice, the way you let me in like no one else."

He releases my hair and allows me to dip my head back down so our eyes meet. "You make me feel like I can," I admit.

Smoothing away my hair from my face while I continue to move, he says, "I want you to feel that way, Willow, because you make me feel shit I've been avoiding for a long time."

Dallas grips my hips and pushes me to ride him faster as I whisper back the truth, "You make me feel shit too."

But those are the last words we speak as I move quicker and higher, chasing my release as Dallas grows more desperate. He pulls my nipple into his mouth, squeezing my breasts as he lavishes my nipples with his tongue. He moves one hand between us to find my clit, stroking the nub with just enough pressure that I feel my orgasm rush forward. And then I shatter a few thrusts later. Dallas roars out my name and joins me at the end.

"Fuck, Willow." His large hands splay out on my back while I bury my face in his neck.

"I'm coming back, Dallas," I murmur against him, feeling like I just ran a physical and emotional marathon.

"I know." I feel his grip on me tighten. "But I still don't want to let you go."

Chapter Seventeen

Dallas

The sound of the door jostling startles me from staring off into space for the hundredth time today. It's been two days since Willow went back to D.C., and you'd think she broke up with me and flew halfway across the world with the way it's hit me.

But that's the thing—we aren't in a relationship, and she's only six hours away, but her life is up there and soon, she'll be back there permanently.

I knew the reality when I gave in to my attraction toward her. I just never imagined that being without her would hit me this hard.

My pillowcases and sheets still smell like her—warm vanilla and citrus that grabbed hold of my lungs and refused to let go.

I found a piece of her blonde hair on my shirt the other day, and all I could think about is what she looked like on our date with her hair down around her face, and that cherry red lipstick that revealed the siren she truly is.

And when I ran by her house this morning just to check on things and the geese started chasing me in the sand, all I could do was fucking laugh.

Everything reminds me of her in some way, and there's only one logical conclusion I can arrive at—I'm fucked up over this woman.

"Did you see a ghost?" Parker asks as he strides up to the bar, Grady on his heels. It's Thursday so the boys are stopping by for lunch, like usual.

"No, just lost in thought." I turn around, grab the burgers from under the warming lamps, and set them in front of the guys, placing a stack of napkins and a bottle of ketchup on the bar in front of them. "What do you want to drink?"

"The usual," they say in unison before taking bites of their burgers.

I fill up two glasses with Coke and ice, and set them down next to their plates. "There you go."

"Fuck, I needed this today." Grady wipes ketchup from the corner of his mouth. "Mrs. Hansen's car is giving me trouble, and I haven't figured out what the hell the problem is yet. It's been three hours."

"Well, it's a dinosaur, so that's probably why," Parker mumbles around the bite he just took.

"Be careful about calling cars dinosaurs," I say, thinking back to when Willow called my Mustang old.

Fuck. I can't go five minutes without thinking about her.

"I agree." Grady takes a sip of his Coke. "I wish cars were still made that way. All this new technology is a pain in my ass. Did you know I have to take an entire fender off some cars now to change a fucking battery?"

"That's ridiculous," I grumble, only slightly interested in the conversation because the longer I stand here at the bar, the more the mental image of Willow lying on the wooden surface the other night steals my attention.

Fuck, she looked good splayed out on my bar.

Tasted fucking amazing too.

"No, what's ridiculous is that Dallas has been moping around town for the past two days ever since Willow left, and he's pretending that no one has noticed," Parker declares, pulling my attention back to him.

Irritation taps against my temples. "I'm not moping."

"The fuck you aren't," Grady counters. "You look like someone took your favorite toy away."

Well? He's not wrong.

"Willow isn't a toy, asshole." And that's the truth. Of course, I've enjoyed playing with her in the bedroom, but what's going on between us is far more than just casual, regardless of what she thinks and what I convinced myself I was capable of.

"So it's for real then?" Parker questions.

I throw my hands out to the sides. "I don't have a fucking answer for you, okay? You know as much as I do. She needed to leave the house for Penn to finish the floors, which he's doing today, so she decided to go back to D.C. to check on her business."

Parker pops a fry into his mouth. "And what is it that she does?"

"She owns an advertising firm. A fucking successful one."

Yeah, I might have Googled her last night when I couldn't stop thinking about her and was wondering what she was up to.

Marshall Advertising earned $565 million dollars last year in revenue, which is more money than most will ever see in their lifetime.

As soon as I saw that number, my stomach dropped.

No wonder Willow is in a rush to go back to her life.

And how the fuck was I thinking I had anything to offer her if she decided to stay in Carrington Cove.

My restaurant does well, but not *that* well.

I live in an apartment above my restaurant that is fine for a single guy like me, but not somewhere I would want to start a life with someone.

And as far as money goes, the chunk that I do have was enough for a down payment on the Bayshore house, the house that Willow could sell to me if she leaves, and that's it.

But that means she'd be gone too.

I swear, sometimes I hate the fucking internet.

"Like how successful are we talking?" Grady asks as he leans back in his chair.

"Fucking millions."

Both of their sets of eyes nearly pop out of their sockets. "Shit."

"Yeah, so needless to say, she won't be staying."

Grady arches a brow at me. "But you want her to?"

I set the rag I was holding down on the bar. "Look, we don't have to get all touchy feely during lunch, all right? I'm dealing with it."

Parker scoffs. "Sure, whatever you say. Just make sure you get your head in the game for Saturday."

Crossing my arms over my chest, I lean against the bar. "Don't you worry about me. I'd worry more about Barb from your office slowing you down."

"I've given her light roles to play this time. She might think she can still do the wheelbarrow race, but I think we all know that's not true after she snapped her wrist last year."

Saturday marks the first day of the Carrington Cove Games, and it's probably the only thing that has given me even an ounce of distraction since Willow left. Although, she should be back before then, and I hope she makes it because I want her to be a part of my team.

My crew at Catch & Release is ready. We've been practicing for the wheelbarrow race, tug of war, and each year, there's a surprise competition that no one knows details about until the day of. Each team faces off in a tournament-style competition, racking up points based on how they place.

My competitive spirit is alive and well, and I'm ready to bring home the Cove Cup.

Part of that wouldn't be so you can impress Willow, would it?

What are we now? Sixteen? Trying to win over the girl with our athleticism?

Heck, at this point, it couldn't hurt.

"Doesn't matter. Penn and I are gonna wipe the floor with y'all."

Speaking of the devil, Penn walks through the door with a bandana tied around his head, his shirt soaked in sweat, and his jeans and boots covered in dust. "You got another burger back there?"

"I can whip you up something really quick." I move to fill a glass of water for him first, setting it in front of him.

"Thanks." He heaves out a sigh before taking a seat on the stool next to Grady. "Jesus, what a job."

Parker peaks his head around Grady so he can look at Penn. "Finish the floors?"

"Yes. Finally." Penn grabs the water and drains the entire thing. "Now it's just the roof and paint. I talked to Thompson Painting to help with that since if I did it by myself, it would take a week and I don't have time for that. But are you still up for helping me with the roof?" he asks me.

"Yeah, I told you I would."

"Good. Then we're starting next week after the games are over."

"That's if neither of you gets hurt," Grady interjects.

"Look who's talking, old man." Penn smirks back at him.

"I'm only one year older than you."

"Yeah, but you're all in your thirties, which means you could throw your back out just throwing away a piece of trash," Parker says.

Grady flexes his giant arms, and out of all of us, he's definitely the one packing the most muscle. "Not gonna happen."

"Don't get cocky, old friend. Haven't you heard the saying, 'the bigger they are, the harder they fall?'" Penn taps the bar with his finger.

Grady, Parker, and Penn continue their trash talking while I head for the kitchen to make Penn something to eat.

But he's right.

The bigger anything is, the harder it falls.

A tree.

A wall.

And a former Marine.

Because as much as I don't want to admit it, I think I fell head over heels for Willow a long time ago. I just didn't want to admit it.

***

The restaurant is packed for a Thursday, a common effect of the games approaching this weekend. Tourists have been flocking in all week, and the residents are all placing bets on which team is going to win.

I'm in the middle of running food out to a table when a blonde by the front door catches my attention.

But it's not just any blonde.

It's Willow.

As soon as I make sure the customers have everything they need, I head toward her and she starts making her way toward me. When we meet in the middle of the crowded restaurant, I don't say one word to her before smashing my lips to hers.

Fucking finally.

I pull her into my chest, bury my hand in her hair that's falling in waves around her face, and show her just how much I missed her over the past two days.

Our tongues tangle as cheers ring out around us, customers clapping and telling us to get a room.

And that's exactly what I intend to do as soon as this place shuts down for the night.

Perks of having a room right upstairs.

"Well, hello to you too," she murmurs when we part, resting her forehead on mine.

"Hey, Goose."

"That was quite the greeting."

"There's more where that came from. Just wait." I give her one more soft kiss and then lead her by the hand toward the bar.

"Hey, Willow!" Baron calls out to her from the table where he's seated..

"Willow, you look gorgeous, honey!" Dolly says as we walk past her table.

"Thanks, Dolly."

"Good to see you've found someone to keep you busy in town." She waggles her eyebrows as Willow's cheeks turn pink.

When we get behind the bar, she's practically burying her head in my chest. "I feel like everyone is looking at me."

I cast my eyes over the restaurant, confirming that we are definitely the topic of discussion as my customers glance in this direction.

So that's when I reach down and grasp her chin softly, forcing it back up. "They are. They're taken back by the beautiful woman that just walked into my restaurant, the woman that doesn't look frigid with a chip on her shoulder like the first night you walked in here."

Willow continues to stare up at me. "You aren't wearing shoes that cost more than their mortgages anymore. Your hair is down instead of pulled back in that bun that must give you a fucking headache, and you're smiling easily. You look human. Beautiful. Like you're one of us." Her eyes move back and forth between mine. "You look *happy*, Willow."

I can see her fight the curl of her lips, like she wants to smile but won't let herself. "I don't know about happy…but I am definitely optimistic for a change."

Hell. I'll take what I can get. "Optimistic is a far cry from frigid."

"Did you think I was a bitch?" she asks, her voice just a whisper now.

"At first, I wasn't sure what to think of you." I drag my finger down the side of her face. "But now? Now I just can't *stop* thinking about you, in multiple ways if you catch my drift."

Her arms move around my neck. "Perhaps you can share those thoughts with me sometime."

"I'll do you one better. I'll show you just what I'm thinking later."

"Yes, please," she whispers before kissing me again.

"Fuck. You know what those manners do to me, Willow." I press my hips into hers so she can feel what she's been doing to me since the moment I met her.

"I do. So I'm ready to beg later if that's what you want."

"Hell yeah, I do."

Giggling, she takes a step back. "I do want to go check on the house first and drop off my stuff."

Disappointment rolls through me that she doesn't plan on staying. "Aren't you hungry?"

"I picked up some food on the way down here." She pushes my hair back with her hand. "Don't worry. I promise I'll be back."

"Okay. I'll be here."

She starts to back away from me. "I'm counting on it."

***

I'm finishing up balancing the register when I hear a knock on the back door. It's way past closing, and the only people that use that door are my employees. For a moment I wonder if someone forgot something or needs some kind of help, but when I exit my office and walk back to answer it, I realize the person standing on the other side is exactly the surprise visitor that I was waiting on.

"Hey, Goose."

Willow stands there in the same white tank top and jean shorts from earlier, looking like a delectable treat, her hair down around her face still and her smile bright and wide. "Hey."

"Fuck. Get in here." I pull her inside by her arm, slam the door behind her, and then press her up against it, covering her mouth with mine.

"You act like we didn't see each other a few hours ago," she mumbles against my lips as my hands cup her ass and pull her closer to me. "I take it you're happy to see me again?"

I thrust my hips into her stomach. "I don't know. You tell me."

Her eyes bounce all over my face as she drags her nails through my beard. "Well, if it's any consolation, I'm happy to see you too. Thankfully alone this time."

Our mouths meet once more as I push her against the door, showing her how much I've thought of her for the past two days and ready to make good on my promise.

She tastes like chocolate and bad decisions, warmth and sin, and her body in this outfit is the perfect kind of trouble that I want to get wrapped up in.

Unfortunately, she detaches her mouth from mine. "Not that I'm not enjoying our reunion, but I'm really thirsty and need to pee."

"I'll meet you behind the bar then."

Willow heads out toward the bathrooms while I adjust my dick in my jeans and make my way to the bar. But when I get out to the front of the restaurant, I notice that one of the tables has chairs that weren't put up. Walking over there, I flip the chairs over and rest the seats on the tabletop, making the floors clear and easier to be mopped in the morning.

When I turn around, I find Willow standing behind my bar with a coy smile on her mouth and a sparkle in her eyes.

"You look good standing there," I say, watching her every movement.

"Do I now?" She purses her lips and spins a glass in her hand, attempting to be fancy as she moves to fill a drink. But then she almost drops it on the floor, saving it at just the last second. "Um, just pretend you didn't see that."

Chuckling, I reply, "No can do, Goose. That image is now tattooed on my brain among the others."

She rolls her eyes, but then smirks in my direction again. "That's fine. Let me give you another one to add to the collection then, shall we?"

Slowly, she drags her tank top up her torso, extracting it from her body, leaving her standing there in a simple white bra that looks so good against her tan skin. Next, she unbuttons her shorts and shoves them down, shimmying her hips as she does so, and then stands tall again, licking her lips seductively.

And I'm instantly hard again, contemplating just how fucking lucky I am to be here with her, and not questioning how we got here.

Because all I see in front of me is not a practically naked woman whom I'm about to devour.

No.

I see a woman rooted in place.

She looks happy.

She looks like she belongs there.

She looks like she's mine.

And I show her how much I like that idea all night long.

***

"I wasn't sure if you were going to make it." My mother treads across the sand to where I'm standing with my team, waiting for the first game to begin. The Carrington Cove Games are about to be underway and we couldn't have asked for better weather.

The sun is shining, the ocean breeze is light but strong enough to ward off the heat, and the crowd of spectators is growing by the minute.

"You know I wouldn't miss the games." She pats me on the shoulder before pulling me in for a hug.

"I know. It's just the first one since Dad died, and…"

She straightens her spine. "I can't be afraid to live because of the emotions that are going to pop up, Dallas. Your father may not be here, but I still am."

I pull her closer and kiss her temple. "Yes you are, Mom."

As I go to release her, Willow approaches us from behind, her voice causing me to spin around. "Sorry I'm late." But before she gets close to me, she freezes. "Oh. Um, hi."

My mother clears her throat. "Hello there."

My eyes bounce back and forth between them, and if I didn't know any better, I'd say that Willow is nervous about meeting my mother. I didn't exactly tell Willow that she'd be here, but I knew this meeting was inevitable.

This is a small town after all.

"Willow, this is my mother, Katherine. Mom, this is Willow, the woman…"

"Who inherited the Bayshore house," my mother finishes for me. "I know."

"You two have met?" I ask, staring at them both.

"Not officially," my mother answers. "But you know how people talk, Dallas, and a name like Willow isn't one you hear very often."

Willow tucks her hair behind her ear even though most of it is pulled back in her signature low bun. "It's nice to meet you, Mrs. Sheppard."

"Please, honey. Call me Katherine."

"If you insist." Willow turns to me now. "Anything you need me to do?"

"Actually there is." I reach down to the bag by my feet and pull out the shirt I brought just for her. "You can put this on." Holding up the navy blue t-shirt with the Catch & Release logo on it, I study her face for her reaction.

Her eyes bounce between me and my mom. "You want me to be on your team?"

I cup the side of her face. "Yeah, Goose. I do."

My mother clears her throat. "I'll give you two a minute."

I watch her walk away and then pull Willow into my chest. "What do you say? Wanna help me bring home the cup?"

She gnaws on her bottom lip. "I'm honored, Dallas. I am, but I'm not a resident of Carrington Cove..."

"Yes, you are, Willow," I cut her off. "You can fight it all you want, but you own a house here now, which makes you one of us. And the best way to experience the Carrington Cove Games is to participate."

Her smile slowly takes over her face. "Okay, but I'm warning you. I have the athletic ability of a giraffe that's just been born, so don't get upset if my lack of physical prowess prevents us from winning."

I give her a quick kiss. "Don't worry. Something tells me you're stronger than you think."

Chapter Eighteen

Willow

Dallas walks off to go check on his team, giving me a chance to compose myself.

I had every intention of just watching him compete from the sidelines, but it looks like I just got roped into playing myself—and part of me feels emotional about the idea.

"You own a house here, Willow, which makes you one of us."

As I was driving back into town last night, my hands wouldn't stop shaking with the anticipation of returning to this small town, of seeing Dallas, and taking the next steps to change my life.

I want this—the house, the town, the friendships, and the man.

Being back in D.C. for only two days told me everything I needed to know. That place isn't my home. My business may be there, but I can change that if I need to. The only family I have there is Mandy, my godmother, whom I haven't spoken to in months.

I came to the realization that there really isn't anything holding me back except for myself, which is still an obstacle, but I'm ready to face it.

I haven't figured out all the details yet, but after the house is done, I plan to have a conversation with Dallas and figure out where his head is at because he's a huge reason why I want to move, of course. His actions tell me he wants me, and every time we're together, my body craves him even more.

But it's not just the sex.

He sees me, knows how to calm me in a way I've never experienced before. I feel protected when I'm in his arms, and this desire to share my life with him, even the mundane details, overwhelms me each time we're together. But the most nerve-wracking part of it all is that he makes me feel like I belong here.

I've never had that feeling in my life—but *he's* given it to me.

And I'm taking that as a sign.

I haven't told Shauna yet, or Mandy, or Katrina, but I don't want to broach the subject until I know that everything is going to work out, and that won't be possible until I talk to one other person, someone I wasn't anticipating seeing again so soon.

Dallas jogs back over to me as the rest of the restaurant crew follows him over, Astrid and Penn included. "All right, we're all set. We're going against Carrington Cove Animal Hospital first, so this should be a sure thing."

Penn rubs his hands together. "I love kicking Parker's ass first thing in the morning. It's going to be a great day."

Astrid shoves him playfully. "You're such a bully."

He wraps his arm around her shoulder, pulling her close. "It's my duty as his older brother, right, Dallas?"

Dallas nods in agreement. "Sorry, Astrid. It's true. I do it to Penn every chance I get. Parker is a better man for taking a regular beating from both of us. He'll be fine."

"You three have issues," Astrid replies while shaking her head.

I roll my eyes. "I'd hate to see what the family dinner will be like after today."

Dallas drops his lips to my ear. "Why don't you join us and find out?"

With wide eyes, I twist to face him. "What?"

Before he can respond, a whistle blows, signaling the start of the competition. But my mind is reeling with what he just said.

He wants me to have dinner with his family? Did I hear that right?

Suddenly, the desire to throw up grows as I follow the crew over to the setup in the sand for the human wheelbarrow race.

Everyone pairs off as partners, Dallas choosing me.

"Are you sure you want to be my partner?" I ask him, growing more nervous by the minute.

"I'm sure, Willow. Now, do you want to be the wheelbarrow, or do you want to be the one pushing?"

"Uh, my upper body strength isn't exactly something to brag about."

Dallas chuckles. "Well, let's see if you can support my legs then." He gets down on the sand, putting himself in a push-up position as I grab his feet from the ground.

Dear lord, he is not a small man.

"I'm gonna start to crawl," he says, slowly moving his arms out in front of him. I rest his feet on my shoulders, holding his ankles steady as he moves.

"This isn't too bad."

"Yeah, I think we can handle this. Let go of my feet." I do as he says and then he stands up, brushing the sand from his body. "We've got this, babe."

"I'm glad you have confidence in us."

He pulls me into his arms. "I do." His lips meet mine. "I'm holding onto that faith enough for the both of us."

Somehow, I feel like he's talking about more than just the games, but I don't have time to contemplate it.

We all line up, Penn and Astrid ahead of us, volunteering to go first, and when the whistle blows, the games begin.

***

"Oh my God!" I scream, letting the rope go from my hands so I can jump up and down to celebrate our win in Tug of War. Grady, Astrid's older brother, starts cursing from the other side, chastising his team after their loss. But the Catch & Release crew is hollering and hugging one another in celebration.

"Hell yeah!" Dallas scoops me up in his arms, covering my lips with his own, kissing me deeply. "You did great, Goose!"

"I don't know that I did that much."

"Hey, this was a team effort, and we couldn't have done it without you."

Shit, I can't start crying again.

After we won the human wheelbarrow race, I shed a few tears. Astrid pulled me aside and asked me what was wrong, but it felt silly to tell her that I was emotional because I'd never won a wheelbarrow race before, let alone been on a team besides within my company. So I told her that I got sand in my eyes, and I think she bought it.

But honestly, I'm not sure that she did.

I continue to hold onto Dallas, my arms wrapped around his neck as he spins me around. When he sets me on the ground, he releases me and then I find Astrid.

"We did it!" She turns and screams to her brother, "Sorry, big bro! Sucks to suck!"

My jaw falls open. "You were just giving Dallas and Penn shit earlier about ganging up on Parker, but here you are, rubbing our win in your brother's face."

She winks. "It's all part of the games, Willow. Besides, my brother's ego can stand to be taken down a peg or two."

Dallas's mom comes waltzing over, making the hair on the back of my neck stand up again.

I know I need to talk to her, but now is not the time or the place.

"Congratulations, Dallas!" She hugs her eldest son as I stand back and admire the love he has for her. Every time he speaks about his mother, you can tell he holds a soft spot for the woman, but it's a totally different experience to see it in front of me.

"Thanks, Mom."

"Your sons are about to be legends, Mom." Penn comes up to her next, scooping her up in his arms.

"Put me down, Penn!"

"Never!" He runs around the sand with her, finally depositing her back on her feet, the two of them bursting out in laughter.

"One more game, babe. And then we can go home and celebrate," Dallas whispers in my ear from behind, wrapping his arms around me.

And for the next hour until the final game, I choose to focus on fantasizing about the *celebration*.

***

"I don't think I'm going to be much help on this last one."

Astrid stands next to me, rubbing my shoulder. "You don't know that. They could ask us anything."

The final game, which is always a surprise the day of, happens to be a scavenger hunt consisting of questions relating to Carrington Cove. Everyone on the team has to hand in their cell phones so no one has access to Google, and each item you have to collect must be brought before the judges in person.

"I know, but I don't know the town like you do."

"You know bits and pieces. Trust me, you will be able to contribute, and be prepared to. If Dallas doesn't win this game, he might punch a hole through the wall of the restaurant."

"Why are men so damn competitive?"

Astrid shrugs. "Too much testosterone?" We share a laugh. "But honestly, I like to win too, so I can't blame them."

"This is pretty exciting. I can see why people love this tradition." My eyes cast over the scene around us, people milling about on the edge of the beach, sitting in their chairs, waiting for the final game to start. A few local businesses have set up booths on the boardwalk to sell food, hats and umbrellas to ward off the sun, and foam fingers and t-shirts to commemorate the event.

"It's part of who we are," Astrid says. "But next year, I'll have my own team, and I'm so grateful to you for that."

I squeeze her hand. "You deserve it."

Friday morning, I went to the bank with Astrid to co-sign the loan for the bakery. As of next month, Astrid will be the full-time owner of the Sunshine Bakery, and I can't wait to see what she does with the place.

"I seriously can't thank you enough, Willow. You've changed my life."

"You've changed mine too," I whisper as Dallas comes over to where we're standing.

"Everything okay?" he asks, watching me blink away tears.

"Yeah, Willow just got something in her eye again," Astrid answers for me, winking at me discretely.

"Well, get it out because we have a cup to win." Dallas grabs my hand, leading me over to the table where the judges sit, waiting for the paper to start the scavenger hunt. And as soon as we and the team from Franny's Crab Shack all gather around, the final game begins.

After gathering a hammer from Hansen's Hardware Store, a coffee from Keely's Caffeine Kick, and a tourist guide from Cove Real Estate, we're scurrying along the boardwalk back toward the beach for the final clue.

Most of us split up as we had to search for each object, but I see Penn and Astrid heading in our direction, as well as a few of the other employees from the restaurant.

"Did you get the bingo chips from Baron, Harold, and Thompson?" Dallas calls out to Penn as he gets closer.

Penn holds up the yellow and red markers. "Sure did. That journey to the Veteran's Center was no joke though."

No one is allowed to drive for this final game, which means running and walking in this heat.

"We're almost done, though." Dallas intercepts the chips from Penn and hands them to Timothy MacDonald, who is one of the judges for today.

"Nicely done, Dallas." Timothy checks off something on his paper and then hands us the final clue, but not before turning to me and asking, "How's the house treating you, Willow?"

"Oh. Uh, good. We're almost done with the renovations."

Timothy nods. "Nice to see that you've made progress. Let Pam over at Cove Real Estate know when you're ready to sell."

"Pam can wait," Dallas tells Timothy before tearing open the envelope with the final clue. "Now, if you don't mind, Timothy, we have a cup to win."

Dallas spins toward the rest of the team, all standing around in a circle, waiting to hear the clue. "A symbol of hope, steadfastness, calm, and composure. Carrington Cove is full of them."

"Jesus, could that be a more generic clue?" Penn grumbles.

"Carrington Cove is full of them?" Astrid taps her chin. "Geese?"

"Uh, pretty sure geese aren't a sign of hope," Dallas fires back.

But then a lightbulb clicks on in my brain thanks to a late-night Google session pertaining to the man standing in front of me.

"An anchor..." I declare, not as confident as I should be, but I look up at Dallas as I speak.

"Shit, that's it!" Brian, the other manager of Dallas's restaurant, agrees.

"Are you sure, Willow?" Astrid asks.

"Yes." With my eyes locked on Dallas, I say, "And that's why all Dallas has to do is take off his shirt and we win."

His smirk builds slowly, but he knows where my mind is. And even though this is not the time, my body heats up from head to toe as I think about all the times I've explored his body and his tattoo.

"Damn, Goose. You just won us the cup."

Franny's Crab Shack team starts racing down the boardwalk toward the judges table with a wooden anchor in their hands.

"Hurry up and strip, Dallas!" Penn shouts, cutting through our moment and making the rest of the team laugh.

Dallas shakes off our stare and mumbles, "Fuck. Okay." He reaches behind his back, rips off his shirt, and points to his chest. "Right here, Tim. An anchor. That's the final answer."

Timothy eyes the judge sitting next to him. "Can we accept that?"

She shrugs before looking at Dallas's torso appreciatively. "I don't see why not." And then she smirks. "Definitely the best thing I've seen all day."

Timothy shakes his head and then stands, holding a megaphone to his mouth. "We have a winner! Catch & Release are the new Carrington Cove Games Champions!"

Applause and screaming echo around us as Dallas scoops me up in his arms, bouncing me up and down. "Hell yeah!"

Celebration continues all around us, people running over from the boardwalk to join in on the fun. But when Dallas sets me down on my feet and frames my face with both of his hands, he whispers to me, "Fuck, Willow." His lips meet mine in a blistering kiss that steals my breath before he whispers, "You were the teammate I needed today, baby. We won. And now it's time to celebrate."

And in that second, my heart agrees with this unfamiliar feeling in my chest.

Oh my God.

I'm in love with Dallas Sheppard.

***

"Fuck. Right there."

Dallas grinds his hips into mine from behind, leaning over my back so he can line his lips up to my ear. "Jesus, Willow. Clench that pussy, babe. Fucking milk me."

I reach behind him and pull him closer by his ass, sending him forward yet again. "Don't stop."

Dallas is so deep in my pussy right now that he's reaching depths I don't even think I've discovered myself. His cock continues to stroke me expertly, building up my release quickly. The way this man fucks me should be illegal. I didn't know it could feel this good, be this intense, like some sort of religious experience.

Our bodies are slick with sweat, blood is rushing through my veins, and every inch of my skin is alive with electricity. The stroke of his hands on my body sends pulses of energy and lust straight to my clit. I feel like I'm coming undone from the inside out.

This is the second time we've had sex since we went upstairs to his apartment after the games. Dallas took everyone back to the restaurant and made food and drinks to celebrate their win, putting the Cove Cup on the shelf behind the bar so everyone can see it when they walk in.

But now, as I feel Dallas start to lose it behind me, I focus on going over the edge with him, eager to relax and rest after a long but amazing day.

"Fuck, I'm gonna come, baby." He reaches under us, finding my clit and circling it gently. "God, I want to paint your skin with my cum. I've been thinking about what you'd look like, covered in me, marked and owned…" His fingers put the perfect amount of pressure on me. "How does that sound to you?"

"Do it." The second those words left his lips, my gut reaction was that I want that too. I want this man to own me, and giving myself over to him is more liberating than I imagined.

"Shit," he groans. "Come with me then, Willow. Fall apart for me." He lets out a growl as I scream and shatter simultaneously. When the final tremors race through my body, Dallas pulls out of me, rips the condom off, and releases his cum all over my back, groaning out loud.

I turn back to watch him stroke himself, cursing as he stares at my back, covering me in his release.

God, I want to be his in every way.

When he's spent, he stills, his chest rising and falling rapidly, his abs contracting with each breath. Then he moves one of his hands to my back and rubs his cum into my skin, admiring his work. "Fucking beautiful."

I sigh as he falls to the bed beside me, our bodies plopping down on the comforter below us.

"So good," I mumble into the sheets.

"Incredible, Goose." Dallas pulls me over to him so he can kiss me. "I'll be right back."

I watch his naked back side as he walks over to his bathroom to dispose of the condom, and then returns with two wash cloths to clean me up. He starts on my back, but not before smearing his cum into my skin again, grinning as he does so. But when he's finished, he nudges my hip. "Roll over, sweetheart." I do as he says, watching him gently clean between my legs with a second washcloth and then he tosses them in a clothes hamper beside the bed before lying back down with me. "You okay?"

I rest my head on his chest, tracing over his tattoo with my finger. "Better than okay. Today was…"

"Incredible."

"Yeah, it was." Sighing, I continue, "I've never been a part of something like that, Dallas. It's crazy to me that there are places on Earth like this that feel like their own little worlds…"

A world I desperately want to be a part of more and more.

"Not even while growing up? You didn't participate in relay races or carnival games?"

I shake my head. "No. My godparents weren't keen on stuff like that, and sports were never my thing. I was more interested in studying."

Dallas chuckles, making my head bounce with his laughter. "I can see that."

"Are you saying you think I'm a nerd?"

His eyes meet mine again as he shifts to his side to face me. "Maybe, but in a sexy way. You're intelligent and witty, Willow. And a strong, successful businesswoman. So all of that studying obviously paid off, right?"

I run my finger through his chest hair and back to his tattoo, studying his body. "It did." My finger finds the scar on his ribs, the one I've seen many times now but have never asked about, wondering if now might be appropriate.

"Just ask, Willow."

"What?"

"You wanna know where that scar came from, don't you?" His voice is gravelly, deep and almost darker than just a moment ago.

"I mean..."

"I was shot." He takes my fingers and digs them into the warped skin. "Right through my ribs. Collapsed my lung, but I was lucky. There were people that were far worse off than I was that day."

"I can't imagine what that's like," I whisper, envisioning Dallas lying in the dirt, bleeding from his side and hating every second of the image taking over my mind. "Not knowing if you're going to live or die."

"Situations like that never leave you, Goose. They come to me in my dreams a lot, so I never truly escape them."

"I wasn't sure if you dream," I tease him. "You're usually so still when you sleep."

He drags down my bottom lip with his thumb. "I haven't had those dreams since you and I have been together, actually."

Oh God.

How much more can my heart take today?

Dallas stares at me, his dark lashes blinking every few seconds. For a moment, I just let him look, let him see me.

I don't know if I could live without his eyes on me for the rest of my life.

"I bet your parents are so fucking proud of you, Goose."

The mention of them startles me, especially because that was the last thing I imagined coming out of his mouth right now. "Wh—why do you say that?"

"I can just see it in your eyes when you talk about your childhood." A tremor of sadness races through me. "That question of what your life would be like if they were still here, if days like today would have been the standard." He runs his fingers through the ends of my hair. "And I want you to know that they'd be so proud of the woman you are."

I hold back my tears, but the truth still spills out. "I think about them every day."

"I get that." Dallas stares up at the ceiling now, lying on his back again. "I think about my dad all the time too, even though I feel like I let him down at times."

"He's proud of you too, Dallas."

I can't say that with firsthand knowledge, but how could any father not be proud of this man?

"I hope so." He strokes his hand up and down my arm as I get comfortable on his chest once more. "I hate that I didn't get to clear some things up with him before he passed. That regret…" He sighs. "It haunts me."

That's what secrets do, too.

"I understand that feeling."

"How did you know about the anchor meaning today?" he asks, looking back down at me and changing the subject, which I'm grateful for because the mention of Mr. Sheppard just feels like a ticking time bomb waiting to go off.

My eyes flick back up to his. "I googled it after I saw your tattoo."

The corner of his mouth lifts. "Really? Why?"

"I was curious about why someone might tattoo something like that on their body."

"Why didn't you just ask me?"

I shrug, focusing back on his chest. "I don't know. It seemed like a really personal question back then."

"Willow, my mouth was all over your pussy within an hour of you seeing my tattoo. I think we got personal pretty quickly, babe."

I can feel my cheeks heat up. "Okay, then why the anchor, Dallas?"

He looks down at his chest where my hand is, resting his over the top of mine. "Well, as you know, the anchor is a symbol of our town, and this place has always been my home. But mostly, it was about the symbol of stability." He sighs. "I've never felt like I've been on stable ground most of my life—with my dad, and with my time in the service. It wasn't until I came home permanently that I started to feel like it was time to build a life I was proud of, and I wanted that here. I was tired of drifting, not being certain about where I was going and what I wanted. So, like a ship does, I decided to drop an anchor down. I got this shortly after I bought the restaurant to commemorate that choice."

That yearning for stability? God, do I feel that need too.

I smile up at him. "I love that. And do you feel like you've found something stable now?"

His eyes bounce back and forth between mine. "I think I'm headed in that direction."

I run my nails through his beard. "You have an amazing life here, Dallas."

"You could too, Willow," he says, his voice low. But before I can respond, he clears his throat and pulls me closer to him by my hip. "I meant what I said earlier about having dinner with my family. I want you there."

My heart starts beating faster. "Dallas, I..."

"I know you're leaving, but my mom was asking about you after the games, and I'd like you to meet Parker and Hazel. Plus, my mother's cooking is top-notch."

His mom was asking about me?

And he still thinks that I want to leave?

My stomach instantly drops.

"I've never had dinner with a man's family before, Dallas."

His brow pinches together. "Never?"

"No."

"Then it's settled. Next Sunday, after Penn and I finish replacing your roof this week, you're coming with me to family dinner. It will be the perfect way to celebrate."

God, he makes it sound like that's a good thing when we both know once the house is done, decisions have to be made—decisions it feels like we're both avoiding discussing. And my reasons for avoiding them are going to slap me right in the face when I eat a meal with his family.

"Are you sure?" My heart feels like it's about to jump out of my chest.

He tucks a strand of my hair behind my ear. "I've never been more sure of anything in my life."

Chapter Nineteen

Willow

"How's it coming along?" I shade my eyes from the sun and peer up at the roof of the house, where Dallas and Penn are standing shirtless in blue jeans with tool belts around their waists.

Damn. What a sight.

"It's going," Dallas calls back to me. "We're going to finish this section and then come down for a break."

"You guys hungry? I can make some lunch."

"That'd be great, Goose. Thanks."

Fighting back my smile, I make my way into the house and straight for the kitchen to whip up sandwiches for the three of us.

This is the second day they've been working on the roof, and the two of them are hell-bent on finishing it today so the painters can come tomorrow and they won't be in their way. Which means, after tomorrow, the house will be done.

Between that realization and the impending dinner with Dallas's family on Sunday, I've been anxious all week.

I know what I want and I'm pretty sure that Dallas feels the same, but the truth is, I have no idea how he's going to react to the connection with his dad. My worst fear is that he won't be able to look past the fact that I kept something like this from him, even though I was asked to.

And facing that person again in a few days is another reason why I'm restless and having trouble sleeping. Thank God Dallas likes to fuck me almost every night, stealing energy from my body long enough for me to at least get a few hours of rest. But then by two in the morning, I'm awake and ruminating on the impending changes of my life.

As I pull six slices of bread from the loaf, a knock on the front door startles me. I make my way over to the door and am immediately thrown off guard when I open it.

"Oh. Hi, Pam." The realtor from Cove Real Estate is standing there, along with a couple that I don't recognize. But the woman has the most beautiful long red hair I've ever seen, and the man with her is tall and holding her like she's his most prized possession.

"Hello, Willow. I hope this isn't a bad time."

"Um, not really. I was just making lunch for me and the boys." I point above me to the roof.

"I heard them hammering away out there. The improvements look amazing." Pam steps inside the house, the couple trailing her closely. "In fact, McKenzie and Dylan here are looking for a vacation home in Carrington Cove, and I know you haven't officially listed the house yet, but I thought they should see it. I mean, heck, we could eliminate listing this place altogether if they fall in love with it, right?"

Oh my God. She brought these people here to look at the house?

"Well...I, uh..."

Pam waves McKenzie and her husband toward the living room. "Take a look around, you two."

"Uh, Pam…" I try to get her attention, but she's too busy talking about the breathtaking views, refinished hardwood floors, and new bathroom remodels. "How did you know about everything I've had done?"

Pam turns to me now. "Penn told me. I ran into him at the hardware store, and he mentioned that the house will be done this week, so…"

"Uh, sorry to interrupt." Dallas and Penn both stand in the front doorway, still shirtless, as all eyes in the living room turn to them.

"Not at all! You two must be hot and hungry. Just ignore us." Pam leads the couple up the stairs to check out the bedrooms, leaving me, Dallas, and Penn alone.

"What is she doing here?" Dallas asks, reaching for his shirt off the back of one of the dining room chairs. Penn follows his lead. You can hear Pam showing the master bedroom as we speak.

Thank God I made the bed this morning.

"Apparently, she's showing the house to this couple that is looking to buy a place out here." I turn to Penn. "She said you told her I was looking to sell."

Penn flicks his eyes between me and Dallas. "Well, aren't you?"

"She hasn't decided yet," Dallas answers for me.

Oh God. Is he still hoping I will sell it to him?

Have I read this entire relationship wrong?

"This home is beautiful!" McKenzie exclaims as the three of them come back from upstairs, interrupting our conversation. "The view from the upstairs balcony is reason enough to make an offer. I could see myself writing a lot from up there."

"You're an author?" I ask.

She smiles proudly. "Yup. A romance author, and this house could be the setting for so many perfect stories, especially with that view."

"I know. It's one of my favorite parts of the place."

Dallas pulls me into his arms, spinning me to face her. "Mine too," he says. I can feel my cheeks flush when I think of what he did to me out on that balcony this morning.

"How did you come about owning the house?" McKenzie asks, watching us. I can feel myself tense in Dallas's arms, but he squeezes me tighter.

"Oh, I inherited it."

Her eyebrows rise. "Wow. What a nice gift."

"Yeah. It's pretty beautiful." I look around the first floor, knowing that I can't leave this place like I thought I'd want to two months ago.

"It's going to be even more stunning when it's done." Dallas plants a kiss on my cheek, releases me, and then nods at McKenzie and her husband. "We'll wait outside." Penn follows him back out front.

My eyes trail him as the two of them engage in conversation about the house as Dallas points to the eaves.

But all I can hear in the back of my mind is that I'm not being honest with him about everything, and now this sudden visit isn't making me feel any more confident about our future.

"And why are you selling?"

"Huh?" I spin back to face her. "Sorry. I was distracted."

McKenzie chuckles, and then licks her lips, fighting a knowing grin. "Oh, never mind. We'd better keep looking, babe." She taps her husband's shoulder.

Dylan turns to her from the kitchen where he was scoping out the storage in the cabinets. "What? Why?"

"This place isn't really for sale." She looks at me, arching her brow. "And I just got a book idea, so I need to grab my notebook and jot it down before I forget."

"Is that true, Willow?" Pam asks me, stepping closer to me now.

"Honestly, Pam, I haven't made up my mind, but I know I wouldn't feel comfortable accepting an offer without knowing one hundred percent that's what I want."

Pam grins and then clutches her clipboard to her chest. "Well, that's a shame because I know this place would sell easily, but I can't blame you. Carrington Cove will suck you in and bury itself in your heart." Her eyes dart out the front window for a moment and then back to me. "And so will handsome restaurant owners."

I lower my eyes to the floor, not needing her to read me even more.

"Sorry to waste your time, you two," she says to Dylan and McKenzie as they head for the front door.

"Not a waste of time at all. Like I said, I just got an idea for a book. You never know where inspiration will strike." Then she turns back to me and says, "I hope you figure out what you want, Willow. And when you do, trust your gut and your heart. The two together will very rarely steer you wrong."

***

"It's been a while. I was beginning to think you were avoiding me." Shauna stares through the screen on our video call, holding Hudson to her chest.

"No, it's just been a busy few weeks. But right now, I really need your words of encouragement."

"Why? What's happening?"

"I'm having dinner with Dallas's family tonight."

Her eyes nearly pop out of their sockets. "Holy shit."

"Yeah. I'm freaking out, Shauna."

"Why? You're good with people, Willow."

"I'm good with *clients*, not people that are related to the man I'm sleeping with. I've never met a boyfriend's parents before. You know that."

It's sad to admit as a thirty-four-year-old woman, but it's the truth. Work has been my focus for the past ten years, not love.

"Does that mean Dallas is your boyfriend?" She nearly leaps off her couch. "Dear God, Willow. What the heck has been happening down there and why haven't you told me any of this?"

"Because I'm falling for this man and it's scaring the shit out of me," I admit on a whisper, clutching my robe around my chest. My hair and makeup are done, I'm just waiting to get dressed before Dallas picks me up.

"Jesus, Willow," Shauna breathes, patting Hudson on the back. "This is huge."

"I know, and I want a life with him, but…"

"He still doesn't know about his dad," she finishes for me.

"Or his mom."

"What? Something happened with his mom?"

"That's what I wanted to tell you the last time we talked. She was my unexpected visitor the night of the veterans' dinner!"

God, it feels good to finally get that off my chest.

She blinks at me several times. "And you didn't think to call me back and try again? Holy shit!"

"Shauna, my life has been crazy these past few weeks, okay? I'm sorry, but now I'm at a crossroads and I need your advice."

She nods. "You're right. I can yell at you about that later."

"Thank you."

"So why did his mother visit you?"

"She knew about the house, about Dallas's dad leaving it to me. She knew the entire time. And she asked me not to tell him myself because she wants to be the one to do that."

"This is some daytime soap opera shit."

"No, this is my life and my future hanging on by a thin string. I'm pretty sure I'm in love with him, Shauna, but I'm afraid once he finds out, he's going to be so angry with me."

"Oh my God." She looks like she's about to cry. "You're in love? Willow, that's…"

I stare out the sliding glass door at the ocean. "I know, Shauna. But his mom…"

"That's not on you, though. His mother *asked* you not to say anything, right? All you were doing was following her wishes."

"I'm just not sure that will be enough for him to understand why I kept this from him."

I stare at the letter next to me on the bedspread, reading over the words his father wrote to me all those months ago. And right now, I'm cursing them even more because, even though Michael Sheppard brought Dallas and me together, he may also be the reason we fall apart.

"And Dallas doesn't know any of this yet?"

"No. I'm hoping tonight that I'll get a moment to speak with his mom alone. I can't talk to Dallas about my decision to stay until he knows the truth."

"And what about your company, Willow? Are you going to sell it? Continue to work remotely? I feel like there are a lot of other decisions you need to make too."

Sighing, I stare at the letter again. "I have a few options but can't make that call until I talk to Dallas." Tears start to build in my eyes. "I can't believe this is my life right now, Shauna. This was just supposed to be an adventure, remember? I wasn't supposed to fall in love, to find somewhere that actually feels like home for the first time in my life."

"But the fact that you did tells you that this is where you are supposed to be, Willow. I just hope it all works out the way you want it to."

"Me too, Shauna. Me too."

***

"You look gorgeous, Goose." Dallas stands just inside my threshold, beaming from ear to ear.

"Are you sure I'm not overdressed?" I opted for a high-waisted, wide leg pair of black linen pants and a tan high neck tank top. It's not the most formal outfit I could wear, but it isn't exactly casual.

"You look perfect. In fact, I can't wait to strip you out of those clothes later."

I roll my eyes at him. "You would say that."

"Don't want you to ever forget how much I want you." He grabs my hand and yanks me toward him.

"I appreciate that. And just so you know, the feeling is mutual."

"You ready for this?" he asks as his eyes move all over my face.

"No."

He chuckles. "Don't worry. The whole family is going to love you, and you've met most of them anyway."

He leads me out to the Mustang and we head for his mother's house, which is more inland than my house.

When we arrive at the home with light blue siding, white trim, and a brown roof, I picture a younger version of Dallas running around the sprawling yard, tumbling in the grass, and riding his bike up and down the street, and it instantly makes me smile.

"What are you smiling about?" he asks as he helps me from my seat.

"I just love this yard. It looks like an amazing place to grow up."

"It was." He closes my door behind me, placing his hand on the small of my back as we walk up the sidewalk and to the front door. "And the plants and flowers can all be attributed to my mother. She has quite the green thumb."

"You can tell she takes pride in the yard."

"Get her talking about it, and she won't let you leave," he jokes as we walk right inside, finding all his siblings standing in the kitchen.

"It's about time. I can't believe you'd show up late to family dinner," Penn chides Dallas as he winks at me.

"It was Willow's fault. She took forever to get ready."

My jaw drops and I swat his arm. "You liar! I was not late."

Parker, whom I recognize from the veterans' dinner and Carrington Cove Games, steps up to us. "He's just giving you shit, Willow. In this family, you should take that as a compliment." He sticks out his hand to me. "It's nice to meet you officially. I'm Parker."

I glare over my shoulder at Dallas, who's still grinning. "Likewise. You're the vet, right?"

"Yup. Do you have any pets?"

"I don't, but maybe someday soon."

"Well, when you do, I'll make sure to give you the family discount."

Family.

My eyes instantly start to mist over.

If things work out between Dallas and me, these people could be my family.

It would be the first time in my life that I'd belong to one of *my* choosing.

I clear my throat, warding off the emotion threatening to spill over. "Can I get something to drink, please?" I say to Dallas, avoiding his eyes.

"Sure, babe. Water? Wine?"

Wanting to keep my head clear, I opt for water. He kisses my temple before heading toward the kitchen, and then his sister strides up to me next. "Hey, I'm Hazel."

"I saw you at the veterans' dinner, but we didn't get a chance to speak. It's nice to meet you," I say as we shake hands.

"Yeah, sorry about that. I was on Mom duty that night."

"Oh, don't act like I need to be babysat." Katherine walks into the kitchen now, commanding the attention of all her children. The love and admiration they have for her is evident in the way each of their faces softens.

I wonder if I would have had a good relationship with my mother if she were still alive?

When our eyes meet, she walks over to me and grabs my hands. "It's so good to see you again, Willow. Thank you for coming over."

"Thank you for having me. Your home is lovely." There are so many pictures and unique touches that you can tell this house has been lived in for a long time.

"I've heard the same about yours." There's a twinkle in her eyes when she mentions the Bayshore house. The last time she was there, the inside and outside looked vastly different. "Penn's been taking care of you?"

"He has."

Dallas inserts himself in the conversation. "What about me? Have I not been taking care of you, Goose?" The smirk on his lips is suggestive, and Hazel picks up on it, of course.

"Really, Dallas? I thought you were supposed to be the mature one since you're the oldest."

Katherine laughs. "Hazel, honey, men never fully grow up. The sooner you learn that lesson, the better." She moves deeper into the kitchen, washing her hands at the sink as the smell of whatever is cooking in the oven hits my nose.

"Hey, Dallas. I wanted to get your opinion on the tree that needs trimming out back. Come with me, yeah?" Penn stands from his chair, motioning toward the backyard.

"Sure." Dallas turns to me and says, "You'll be okay if I'm gone a minute?"

"Yes, she'll be fine," Katherine answers for me. "In fact, all boys outside. Now. I'll let you know when dinner is ready."

Parker pops the top on his beer as he follows Penn and Dallas to the back door. "It's just like when we were kids. Some things never change, I guess."

All three boys hustle outside, leaving me alone with Hazel and the matriarch of the family.

"Hazel, honey. Can you go outside and make sure those boys aren't talking about rearranging my yard, please? You know how Penn gets when he gets an idea in his mind."

Hazel rolls her eyes, grabbing her glass of wine and moving toward the door. "Sure, but you and I both know none of them listen to me."

"That's not true. Now go on. Willow can help me with the last-minute touches on dinner."

Hazel grumbles as she heads outside, leaving me and Katherine alone.

Finally.

"Take a deep breath, Willow," she tells me, like she could sense that I was holding mine in.

I inhale and release just as quickly. "I'm sorry. This is just..."

"Nerve-wracking. I know." She reaches out for my hand across the counter before darting her eyes to the window that gives a view of the backyard. "But you haven't said anything to him, have you?"

"No, but I have a feeling he's not going to be so thrilled with me when he finds out."

"Well, that depends on what you've decided to do."

"I want to stay here," I tell her. "I'm falling for your son, but this is so complicated, Katherine."

She hangs her head. "I know, but I signed on for this, Willow. Michael and I knew Dallas would be angry, but my husband was adamant that the house was yours."

"I just don't get it. Why me?"

She straightens her spine. "My husband was not in a good place after he came back home, after your parents..." She clears her throat. "The guilt he was living with was so heavy I thought I was going to lose him to it. Then, one day, he came up with a way to give you something in an attempt to make amends, even though he knew it would never bring your parents back. It was all he had to give, a piece of our town that he felt could make a difference in your life."

"But I never thought I'd fall for your son..."

"Neither did we, honey." Her face softens and a smile forms on her lips. "But I'd say that's a pretty amazing thing to come out of all this, wouldn't you?" I shrug, not sure how to answer that because part of me thinks it's true, and the other part is so frustrated by the circumstances. "You've made my son smile again, Willow—find his light. He's different with you, more of the boy he was before he left for the Marines, my son who wanted to help people, who loved to laugh and enjoy life, not the one who fought with his dad in a circle about the path he chose for his life or the man who witnessed death and destruction that no one should ever have to see."

"If my parents never died, this mess wouldn't have happened." The emotion I've been shoving down starts to bubble up. "I wouldn't be here…"

Katherine comes around the counter to wrap her arms around me as I let a few tears free. "Oh, honey. It was an accident, a horrible accident that impacted us all."

"My entire life changed because of that day, and now so has Dallas's."

With her hand, she gently grabs my chin and turns my face toward hers. "Honey, you can sit here, blaming everyone else for how your life has turned out…or, you can start living your story the way you want it written. Those are your options and I have a feeling you know which one makes sense." My bottom lip trembles as her hand moves to my shoulder.

"I'm just so angry, for how everything has played out and put me in this position now. I'm so mad at them for leaving me—"

"A parent's love is unwavering, Willow," she says, cutting me off. "No matter what you think, your mother and father loved you. No one could have known what was going to happen. And it's okay to be angry, but know that your parents were human, just like you and me. And sometimes, that means we have to make the best choice for ourselves despite the potential consequences. We don't know how our decisions will eventually impact those we care about. And it's unfair really, because as parents, we think we're supposed to have all the answers. But we don't, because we're still learning about life right alongside our children." She brushes away a tear from my cheek. "And

Dallas not knowing his father left that house to you, that's something that we had to live with, and I will have to deal with the consequences of."

At that moment, the back door creaks open. Dallas stares between us as I whip around to look at him, but turn back around just as quickly, trying to hide the fact that I've been crying.

"What's going on? Are you making her cry already, Mom? Jesus, I was gone for ten minutes…"

Katherine places her hands on her hips. "Why on earth would I be doing that?"

"Well, she was fine before I walked outside."

"We were just talking about my parents," I interject, batting away the last remaining tears. "She asked about them, and it made me emotional."

Dallas's face grows worried as he stalks toward me, wrapping his arm around my waist, rubbing his thumb beneath my eye to swipe away the reaming moisture there. "I'm sorry. The last thing I wanted tonight was for you to feel sad."

"It's okay. I'll be fine." I flash him my most convincing smile. "I've dealt with this my entire life. Just sometimes, it catches me off guard, especially when I'm around someone else's family." *It just reminds me of what I will never have.*

Katherine reaches for my hand. "You'll always be welcome here, Willow."

I turn to her, pausing before saying, "Thank you."

The timer on the oven goes off, signaling that dinner is ready.

"Dallas, wrangle up your siblings to do your jobs. It's time to eat."

Dallas kisses my temple before going back outside. "I'll be right back."

When he leaves, I turn back to Katherine. "Can you please talk to him, Katherine?"

She inhales deeply. "I'll talk to him tomorrow, if that's okay. I just don't want to ruin tonight—your first family dinner."

Hoping it's not also my last, I nod in agreement.

***

"So, Dallas had to call Mom to come pick him up from school because he shit his pants." Penn holds his stomach while he howls with laughter, and I'm wiping tears from my eyes.

At least these tears are from laughing and not emotional turmoil.

"Yeah, yeah, yeah. Laugh it up, everyone. Don't forget I have blackmail on all of you, too." Dallas points a finger at each of his siblings, moving around the table.

"Sorry, but that's pretty bad, Dallas." I place my hand on his shoulder, my chest still bouncing with laughter.

"It's a cautionary tale—don't eat Taco Bell before a rivalry game." He shrugs like it's no big deal, and I love that he can just let the embarrassment roll off of him like that. "At least I didn't wear women's underwear during one of the games." He directs his gaze over to Penn, whose laughing immediately stops.

"Fucker."

"Hey, watch your language." Katherine points her fork across the table at Penn. "And sorry, son, but you started this battle. Dallas just seems intent on finishing it."

I turn to Penn, arching a brow in his direction. "Women's underwear? Maybe you aren't as manly as I thought."

He glares at me, clenching his teeth. "It was a dare, and I was not about to back down."

"And he had a rash on his balls for a week afterward."

Hazel gags dramatically. "Gross. I did not need to know that."

Katherine chimes in now. "Yeah, neither did I."

"Well, I think this is the perfect way to end the evening," Parker declares before standing from the table, adjusting his pants and pulling his shirt in place. "I have an early morning anyway."

"You mean you want to leave before Dallas and I share dirt on *you*," Penn says.

Parker points a finger at Penn. "Precisely."

"Yeah, I think we're going to call it a night too." Dallas stands from the table, grabbing my hand to help me up.

The past two hours have been nothing short of incredible. This family is one of a kind, so welcoming, and funny. The conversation never stopped, only whenever someone mentioned Mr. Sheppard, and it was obvious that he's truly missed.

I wish I could have met him myself, heard from his own lips about my parents and who they were in their last moments.

Dallas and I say our goodbyes, Katherine wraps me in a long hug, and then we settle into the Mustang, headed back to my house.

"So, how do you feel?" Dallas asks me, reaching for my hand as he drives.

"Like my heart is about to burst out of my chest."

He clears his throat. "I'm glad, because there's something I want to talk to you about when we get home."

Home.

"Okay..."

"It's nothing bad. In fact, I think it could be really good, Willow." He adjusts himself in the seat, bringing my hand to his lips, kissing the back of it. "But I don't want to have this conversation while I'm driving."

"All right. There's also something I want to talk to you about."

He casts his gaze over to me quickly. "Yeah?"

"Yeah. It's a good thing too."

The rest of the drive we spend in silence, anxious to pull in behind the house and make our way inside.

As soon as I close the front door behind us and twist the lock, Dallas pulls me to the kitchen, lifting me up on the countertop so we're more at eye level.

He stares at me, his eyes dancing appreciatively over my face and body, his hands following the path of his sight. My heart hammers wildly, waiting for him to speak, but I give him time because what I have to say may depend on what he says first.

Is this what love feels like? The fear of losing someone and the joy of your future with them flowing through you simultaneously? The crazy thoughts that you could be staring into the eyes of your entire future, but also that this person has the power to shatter your heart in a matter of seconds?

I hope we're both on the same page.

"Willow..." He takes a deep breath and blows it out. "The night you came into my bar, I was taken aback by your presence. I couldn't understand how someone like you would ever fit in here, and honestly, I hoped you'd leave as quickly as you came in." I huff out a laugh as he plays with my bottom lip. "And when I found out you inherited this house and wouldn't sell it to me, I *really* wanted you to leave."

"Oh, I remember. I swore that day I would sell it to anyone *but* you just to spite you."

"I wouldn't put it past you, Goose." He looks down at my lips and then right back to my eyes. "But then, every time we interacted, it was clear that there was a reason I couldn't get you out of my head, and the more you pushed me away, the harder I wanted to push back." He tilts his head. "The night of the storm, I knew I was done fighting my attraction to you, and that night changed everything."

"It did."

"And now, the house is done." He looks around, admiring the transformation. "You did good, Goose. I couldn't have done better myself if it were my decision. But now, you have another decision to make, and I want you to know something before you do."

I swallow hard, waiting for him to continue.

"I want you to stay, Willow." His words cover me like a warm blanket, soothing my fears. I let out the breath I was holding as he brings both of my hands to his lips. "I want you to move your life down here so we can be together. I know it's not ideal, and there's a lot to figure out, but—"

"I want that too," I blurt out, shocking him for only a second before his lips spread into a smile that might just be the end of me.

His eyes move back and forth so rapidly that it almost makes me dizzy, but then he finally breathes out, "Fuck. Really?"

I nod rapidly. I know I was going to wait to have this conversation with him, but I can't wait. Katherine is going to speak to him about the tough stuff, but right now, his words are conveying everything that I'm feeling. "Yes. That's what I wanted to tell you. I want to stay too. I don't want to sell this house. This town, you...you've changed my life and I..."

I don't get a chance to continue before he slants his mouth over mine, shutting me up with his kiss.

He swallows my moans, lashes his tongue against mine and owns me with this kiss, cocooning me in his arms as the very last shred of my defenses melts away.

He's owned me for a while now, if I'm being honest, and that's what I want moving forward—to feel this way with him forever.

"Fuck, Willow. I need you, baby. I don't think I'll ever stop needing you."

"Yes," I mumble against his lips. "Take me upstairs. Please."

"God, I'll never grow tired of hearing that word fall from your lips—for me."

Dallas lifts me so I can wrap my legs around his waist and heads for the stairs, keeping our mouths fused as he climbs higher and higher toward my bedroom.

Perhaps one day, it will be *our* bedroom.

When we reach the bed, he tosses me down and then hovers over me, just as the sound of paper crinkling beneath us causes us both to pause.

Oh God.

No.

Dallas pulls the paper out from under me, eyes quickly scanning it and I see the change in his expression when he recognizes a name I'd hoped I had a few more hours to figure out how to explain.

"Willow? What is this?"

I push myself up, crawling across the bed to him, but he steps back as his eyes move across the paper alarmingly fast.

"Willow!" His voice echoes in the room now. "What the fuck is this?"

My heart is hammering so hard that my entire body is shaking from the impact. "It's a letter."

"I can see that." He begins to squeeze the paper tighter. "The question is, why do you have a letter from *my* dad?"

He finally meets my eyes, and all I can see is confusion and hurt in his.

"Dallas...I can explain."

"I sure as fuck hope so." He keeps reading and then whispers, "What the fuck?" Then suddenly, as though the paper burned him, he tosses it back onto the bed. He clenches his hands into fists as his chest heaves with short, labored breaths. His eyes are black with fury now. "Start talking, Willow. Now."

I swallow down the lump in my throat and finally tell him the truth. "Your dad is the one who left me this house, Dallas."

His head rears back as though I've slapped him. "What?" His response comes out in a whisper, laced with disbelief.

"I wanted to tell you, but your mom..."

And then his eyes light up with rage as he takes a step closer. "My *mom*? She fucking knew about this too?" He gestures sharply back down to the paper.

"Yes, but she asked me not to tell you!" I hate to put the blame on Katherine, but the reality is, we wouldn't be in this situation right now if she had told just Dallas in the beginning.

But it's not entirely her fault either. I should have figured out a way to explain this to Dallas, especially after we started to fall for one another.

"So let me get this straight. You both knew about this but didn't think I deserved to know?" The veins in his neck are popping, and he transforms from the teddy bear I was just about to snuggle all night to a slightly smaller version of the Hulk.

"I was going to tell you! But she asked me to let her talk to you first. She was going to tell you tomorrow. She didn't want to ruin our first night with your family."

He runs a hand through his hair, his brows drawn together, his breaths growing more shallow. "I can't fucking believe this."

I hop off the bed and reach for him, but he backs away. "Please, Dallas. We can work through this…"

"No. This changes everything, Willow."

The threat of tears builds again. "It doesn't have to."

"How can you say that? The woman I want to start a life with inherited the house I've always wanted from *my deceased father*, who, it turns out, was keeping this secret from me. And then I find out that you and my mother knew about it but decided to keep me in the dark too. And the irony of it is, I didn't even care about the house anymore…because you were more important." He shakes his head, his eyes full of anguish, as he turns and walks out of the room, leaving me frozen until I snap out of my shock.

"Dallas, wait!" I chase after him, trembling so much I nearly trip down the stairs.

"I can't even look at you right now, Willow," he says flatly as he reaches the front door.

I choke back a sob. "But I meant what I said. I want a life with you. We can work past this…"

He glares at me over his shoulder as he opens the door. "That's nice, Willow, but I'm not sure I can trust a word that comes out of your mouth. Turns out you're just as good an actress as you are a CEO. Who would have thought?"

As the door slams shut, I sink to the floor and let the tears fall, sobbing and crumbling because there's nothing more I can do.

And I hate that it all came about like this.

Chapter Twenty

Dallas

Willow,

I can only imagine what must be going through your head right now, receiving a letter from a man that you've never met. But the truth is, I feel like I've known you your entire life, and I regret that we will never meet, although that's probably for the best.

My name is Staff Sergeant Michael Sheppard of the United States Marine Corps, and I knew your parents. In fact, I was with them the day they died. Correction: I'm the person responsible for their deaths.

I hate that I even have to write those words, let alone be the one to admit this to you, but please know that your parents loved you. In fact, moments before they died, they were bragging about their daughter and how full of life she was—the little girl with pigtails holding a stuffed duck in the picture your mother was clutching in her hands. I only hope that's still true about the woman you've grown into, minus the stuffed animal, that is.

I want you to know how sorry I am, how much I have suffered with guilt over taking your parents away from you. As a father myself, I can't imagine my children having to grow up without me or my wife, let alone both of us.

But hopefully, after you've read this letter and you visit my attorney, you'll understand that this is my way of trying to make up for my mistakes. This is the only way I could think of to do that, so please at least hear what my attorney has to say.

I hope life has treated you well. I hope you've found love and joy in other ways. And I hope you can find it in your heart to forgive me one day for the love that my actions stole from you.

When you read this letter, I will have left this earth as well. If I see your parents, I hope to stand beside them and watch you live your life to the fullest from the other side, if that place even exists.

But most importantly, I hope you find peace and love in my hometown of Carrington Cove—because that town is what saved me.

Best wishes,

Michael Sheppard

***

"Mother fucker!" I slam the heels of my hands against the steering wheel as I speed away from Willow's house—the house *my father* gave to her.

I swear to God, this better be a dream.

More like a fucking nightmare, Dallas.

I have no idea where I'm headed, but what I do know is that I couldn't be near her for one more second.

She fucking knew.

I wonder when she found out.

Has she known this entire time?

These are all questions I could have asked her if I'd kept my cool, but I couldn't bear to look at her any longer, betrayal clouding my sight and fury racing through my veins.

It's not as if my father and I had the best relationship to begin with, but now this? He's freaking messing with my life from the grave?

How can I not feel like he just fucked up my life completely? Stole yet another choice from me and tainted it with his actions?

There's only one person who can answer these questions, though, so that's where I'm headed—back to my mom's house, hoping to God she can help me make sense of this.

Otherwise, I'm not sure either one of us will recover.

***

When I pound on her door, I wonder if she's already asleep. It's after nine and my mother is usually in bed by eight. But when she opens the door in her robe and sees me, her shoulders drop and she hangs her head.

"She told you."

"She didn't have to. I found the letter from Dad."

Shaking her head, she opens the door wider so that I can enter. But standing in my parents' house feels so fucking wrong right now.

My parents.

My own fucking parents kept this from me.

For years, they've heard me talk about wanting that house, my plans for the future, wanting that place for my own when I was done in the Marines.

And now the woman I'm in love with owns it because of them, and they all kept it from me.

All of them.

I need a fucking drink.

I head for the kitchen, straight to the liquor cabinet where a bottle of Jack Daniels sits, untouched for months. My dad was the one that drank this shit, so I guess it makes sense that I should drown my fury with his drink of choice.

Bottoms up, Dad. I bet you're laughing right now.

"Dallas, come sit."

"I need a minute, Mom. In case you weren't aware, my entire world was just flipped upside down and you're partially to blame for that." I take a swig from the bottle, wiping my mouth with the back of my hand when I'm through. My eyes move around the house, looking at these walls with suspicion of what other secrets they could hold, what other lies have been concocted in the place I called home, in the family I should have been able to trust.

My mother pulls her robe tighter around her body as she moves into the kitchen, standing on the opposite side of the island. "I know that you're hurting and that we have a lot to talk about, but you're in *my* house right now, and you'll damn sure show me some respect while you're here. Do you understand?"

Sighing, I hang my head in shame. "You're right. Sorry, Mom. I just…" The sting of tears threatens to build, but I grab the bottle instead and tip it back once again.

"Come sit. Bring the bottle if you want, but we need to talk." Grabbing my emotional support drink, I follow my mother to the couch, taking a seat on the opposite side from her, avoiding her eyes.

"Look at me, Dallas," she commands. It takes me a minute to do so, but when our eyes meet, I see the hurt in hers as well.

Fuck. This is going to suck, isn't it?

"How long?" I ask her, not wanting to waste any more time getting down to the truth. Perhaps the rage coursing through me will subside faster if I get some fucking answers.

"How long did I know about the house?" I nod. "Since you were five."

"Jesus Christ. That fucking long?"

"That's when your father set up the trust for Willow, honey."

I shake my head, taking another swig from the bottle. "All this fucking time."

"We never meant to hurt you, Dallas."

I shoot my eyes back over to my mother. "Why leave her the house?"

"I thought you read the letter?"

"I did, but I want to know everything."

Sighing, my mother settles into the couch deeper. "Your father came back from Iraq honorably discharged, but we never told you kids what happened because"—she chokes back a sob—"I didn't want you to live with the image of what your father survived...what never allowed him to be the same again."

I lean back, swallowing down the lump in my throat. "What happened?"

"He was in a Humvee with Willow's parents, Dallas. They were journalists, overseas to report on the war. They stopped for a civilian who was flagging them down, and your father stepped out of the vehicle to approach him. Within seconds, there was an explosion. The Humvee was destroyed by an IUD."

Holy shit.

"It took me two years to get your father to speak about it."

I think back to all the shit I saw in Afghanistan, stuff that still haunts my dreams, dreams I haven't had since the night of the storm with Willow. "That's why he never wanted me to join, huh?"

She nods. "Yes, because the guilt that he lived with after that almost killed him."

My brow pinches together. "What do you mean?"

She shakes her head, staring off across the room. "I found him with a gun in his hands one day, Dallas. He wanted to kill himself, said he couldn't live with the guilt." My eyes start to burn. "You and Penn were little, and I was pregnant with Parker. I couldn't lose my husband, so I begged him to get help. He started going to the Veteran's Center, doing talk therapy, taking medication. Those were some dark years, getting him healthy again. And when you were five, he decided that part of his way of making things right would be to leave the Bayshore house to Willow. It was all he had to give her. He knew it wouldn't bring her parents back, but he had so many memories growing up there with his grandparents that he wanted to give her that joy too."

That house belonged to his grandparents?

Shaking my head, I say, "I can't believe you never told me this."

"I knew I would have to eventually, especially after he died."

"Why didn't he tell me?"

"You know that he had his feelings about you joining the Marines, and that it had already strained your relationship. He didn't want to strain it more, so I agreed to be the one to tell you. That was a sacrifice I took on and I'd do it again."

I stare at the fireplace, the mantel decorated with family pictures and my father's medals, the smile on his face hiding years of trauma he had to work through.

Guilt.

He was responsible for Willow's parents dying.

I know what that guilt feels like.

I wish I could have told him that.

"But he never supported me, he always criticized my decision to serve." I point to the side of the room. "He would help at the Veteran's Center and help other Marines, but he couldn't help his own son!" My voice booms through the room as my mother's tears glisten in her eyes.

"Do you know how many times I said the same thing to him, Dallas? How much we fought about that very thing?" She sniffles and wipes her nose against the sleeve of her robe. "Your father became a different person, but he never wanted to share that part of himself with you, and he regretted it. I know he did."

"I do too, Mom." I pound my fist against my chest. "I do too because I should have told him how he made me feel!"

"What good would it have done?" she whispers. "The best thing you did was serve your country and show your father the strength you have inside of you, Dallas. I know you must have seen your own horrors overseas, but you kept yourself together when you came home. You bought a business and you give back to your community just as much as your father did. He was proud of you, even if he never said it." One tear slips down her cheek. "I know he was."

I let my mother's words settle in my mind.

I hate feeling this sense of regret, of letting words unspoken affect my life still to this day. I guess the question is, do I want them to affect my future, too?

And can Willow still be a part of that future?

"Willow said that you told her not to say anything to me about this," I finally say, breaking the silence.

She nods. "That's right."

"So when did she find out?"

"The night of the veterans' dinner. I went over to her house after the dinner and introduced myself. I ditched your sister and told her I wasn't feeling well because I had to speak with Willow as soon as I could." Sounds about right, my mom escaping my sister's watch. "Willow told me she put two and two together when she saw you go up on stage to accept your dad's award. *I* am the one who asked her not to say anything, so please don't hold that against her."

"It hurts that she kept something from me, but the person who's really to blame for all of this is Dad."

"Your dad didn't do this to punish you. He did this out of guilt for how he affected Willow's life. This is way bigger than you and how you think your father felt about you, Dallas."

"Oh, I *know* how Dad felt about me. He made that clear when I left for bootcamp, and every deployment after that."

"Can't you see that he wanted more for you?" She leans forward, locking her eyes onto mine. "Do you know what it was like watching him blame himself for years, fight through demons and struggle with just surviving? There was a point where I thought I would lose him, that he contemplated taking his own life, Dallas. Did you hear me? Don't you get that?" My stomach drops from the way her voice shakes. "We almost divorced when Penn was two." She inhales and then continues. "Being a spouse to a Marine is sometimes just as hard as being one yourself. He didn't want that struggle for you—because he *loved* you, Dallas. He didn't want you to have to sacrifice a part of yourself out of obligation. He wanted to protect you from the horrors he experienced, despite the honor it was to watch you serve."

It's those words that make me break.

I reach up and pinch the bridge of my nose as I fight back sobs.

The couch dips beside me as my mother scoots closer and holds me to her chest, letting the emotions overtake both of us.

My father didn't want me to live a haunted life like he did.

"He could have said that to me, you know?" I manage to croak out.

"Your father wasn't the best at communicating, so maybe he tried in his own way, but please don't hold this against him. He only did what he thought was best, and I had to support his decision about the house because it helped me get part of my husband back." And then she forces me to look at her, tears clouding both of our eyes. "So please don't hold this against me too."

I lunge for her harder, soaking up her hug, holding onto the woman who has always supported me, and now I realize just how much she gave of herself to support my father too.

Talk about strength and love that is indescribable.

She squeezes me tighter. "I love you, Dallas. And I'm so, so sorry."

"I love you too, Mom."

"Please don't let this ruin what you have with Willow." She releases her hold on me as we both wipe our faces. "I saw the two of you together tonight, how she fit in here so seamlessly. She's the one, honey."

Nodding, I declare solidly, "I know she is."

"I've never seen you like that with a woman before." *Because they've never been like her.* "And as upset as you might be with your father, in a way, he actually brought you the love of your life." Tilting her head, she says softly, "How can you be mad about that?"

Repeating those words over again makes me feel like a weight has just been lifted off my chest.

My mother is right.

My dad brought me Willow.

He may not have been there for me in other ways, but even though he's gone, he's still trying to lead me down the path he thinks is best—one that leads to the woman I'm head over heels in love with—my future, my life—*the one I belong to.*

I don't want Willow to be a ghost that haunts me, catching me off guard everywhere I turn with memories of how she waltzed into my life in her Louboutin's and lit a match under my ass, one that had me admitting how lonely I'd been.

No.

I'm not going to settle for her ghost. I need her to know how I feel, and hopefully from there, we can figure out the rest.

"Now I know you're probably itching to talk to her, but you've been drinking and there's no way I'm letting you drive." She holds her palm out. "Keys."

"You could drive me over there…" I slap my keys into her hands, pushing my bottom lip out for good measure.

Looks like the alcohol has done its job.

"You need to be sober when you apologize to that woman, and I think our talk tonight gave you enough information to absorb. Give her some space tonight, and then fight like hell for your girl tomorrow."

"I can't let her get away, Mom."

"Don't Dallas. Please. For all of our sakes." She cups the side of my face with her hand, but then her eyes go wide. "Oh my God. I almost forgot." She launches from the couch, practically racing down the hallway toward her room, returning just a few short seconds later. "You need to give her this the next time you see her."

The old polaroid picture she hands me is faded and singed on the corners, but the little girl standing in the center, holding a duck is still crystal clear.

"Is that..."

"That's Willow, Dallas. Her parents had that picture with them the day they died. I know she'd want it."

All I can do is nod slowly. "Yeah, Mom. I think you're right, yet again."

***

The next morning, I wake up with a stiff back from passing out on the couch in my mother's living room, smelling like alcohol and feeling the effects of it as my head pounds. But the first thing that pops into my head when my eyes open is Willow.

I have to make things right.

But before I get very far, an envelope addressed to me sits next to my keys on the counter. My mother is nowhere in sight, so I slide my finger under the seal and extract the folded piece of paper, nearly falling over when I see the writing on the inside.

Dallas,

Son, if you're reading this, then you now know about the Bayshore house.

I can only hope that your mother was able to explain the situation to you more eloquently than I ever could. Please don't be mad at her. This was my decision, and as my wife, she supported it because your mother is the kind of woman who loves with all of her heart. She loved me even when I felt like I didn't deserve it, and she loves you and your siblings with everything she has.

That house belonged to my grandparents. Much of my childhood was spent there, running across the sand, enjoying summers in Carrington

Cove. It's why when I had a family of my own, I knew this was where I wanted to raise them.

I just never knew how difficult being a father would be sometimes.

I wish I had the courage to say these words to your face, but after spending years in heated arguments with you, the last thing I wanted was to get in one last one before I took my last breath. So, I hope you'll accept this letter from me instead... because the last thing I ever wanted was for you to live with regrets like I have.

I should have told you this years ago, should have understood your decision and supported it instead of fighting with you about it. And even though you may never believe me, I want you to know: I. Am. So. Proud. Of. You.

My son. My firstborn.

You signed up to sacrifice your life for peace, freedom, and your country.

You followed your dreams even when I didn't want to risk losing you.

And when you returned home, you did the work to live as normal a life after your service as you could.

I'm proud of you.

I love you.

And I hope you can trust that even though our relationship was futile at times, I have never been more honored to be your father.

If Willow doesn't want the house, ask her if she'll sell it to you. But selfishly, I hope she keeps it. I hope she falls in love with Carrington Cove. I hope the people here can help her heal like they helped you and me.

And I hope you'll help her see that.

I love you, Dallas.

Love,

Dad

By the time my eyes find the last word, I can barely see through my tears.

My mother knew I'd need to process this alone, I'm glad because I feel like I'm about to break in two.

My ass finds the couch again as I reread his words, my father giving me what I needed from him when he was alive. But I guess I should be grateful that his words are at least reaching me after his death.

I stare off into space for so long—numb, angry, remorseful, and shocked, that I have no idea how much time has passed. But as I read through the letter once more, my brain flips back on when I see Willow's name again.

I need to talk to her. I need to make things right.

So, I find my keys on the counter again and head back to the restaurant so I can shower because I smell like ass and feel pretty shitty too. I practically run back to my car once I'm clean and speed to her house, hoping to God she won't shut the door in my face.

This woman had no part in our complicated connection. I know that now.

She was just this innocent little girl that lost her parents and inherited a house as a peace offering.

My mother was right. I have no basis for placing blame on her, and if it weren't for this crazy situation she never would have crashed into my life.

I just hope she'll let me tell her that.

When I pull up to the house, her car isn't there.

Maybe she went to the bakery for muffins? Or out to run an errand?

I wait on the porch for two hours before I finally decide to text her. I wanted to surprise her, but at this point, I want to make sure she knows I'm trying to make this right.

> **Me**: Hey. I'm at your house. Where are you? I want to talk. There's so much I need to say.

My phone is silent for about fifteen minutes before I finally get a reply.

> **Willow**: I'm halfway to D.C. Stopped to charge my car.

No. Shit. I'm too late.

> **Me**: Fuck. Turn around, Willow. Please. I'm so sorry, baby.

> **Willow**: I can't. I need to go home for a while. I have a lot to think about.

> **Me:** I'm so fucking sorry, Willow. I can make this right, I know it. I talked to my mom. She told me everything. Please don't leave like this.

> **Willow**: I'm sorry too.

> **Me**: When will you be back?

> **Willow:** I don't know.

> **Me**: Please come back to me.

But I don't get a reply, and that's when I wonder... *Have I lost her forever?*

Chapter Twenty-One

Willow

"Willow? What are you doing here?" Katrina walks into my office at seven in the morning, shocked that I'm not in Carrington Cove. But it might also be my lack of makeup, my puffy eyes, and my athleisure outfit that cause her shock.

"I need to work." I start shuffling papers around my desk, looking for a file that I'm sure was here when I left. But Katrina's hands come down on mine, stopping my search.

"Willow. Are you okay?"

"I'm fine." My bottom lip trembles but I reach up and pull it away from my face to keep it from moving more. "Totally fine," I say in garbled words.

"Not to sound insensitive, but you sound like Ross from *Friends* right now when he's had too many margaritas."

I release my lip and focus back on my computer. "No margaritas for me. I've just been driving for the last six hours." My fingers start to dance over the keys on my keyboard, even though the damn computer isn't on.

"You left Carrington Cove at one in the morning?"

"Yup. My company needs me. This is where I'm meant to be, not down there." My bottom lip trembles again. "Not there."

Katrina sits on the edge of my desk as my body threatens to break down again, but I'm surprised that I still have tears left to cry. I've been having periodic cry fests all night as I drove, stopping along my trip a few times to cry and charge my car so that I didn't crash or end up alone on the side of the road. If it weren't the time when normal people would be sleeping, I would have called Shauna, but I didn't want to wake her if Hudson was resting.

"Turns out you're just as good an actress as you are a CEO. Who would have thought?"

The words Dallas spoke to me before he left echo in my mind for the thousandth time, along with his texts, but I shove them down and turn my computer on instead. "I just need to work. That will make everything better."

Katrina stands, wary as she stares at me. "Okay…if you say so. I'll be right outside if you need anything, all right?"

"I'm fine," I repeat, mostly to myself, watching her leave before focusing back on my computer, eager to find something to distract myself from the turmoil in my life right now.

Let's just hope this works.

***

"Willow?" A hand meets my shoulder, startling me awake.

I shoot up from my desk, a paper glued to my cheek by my drool, only to find Katrina standing right at my side.

"How long have I been asleep?"

"About two hours." She pulls the paper from my face and sets it to the side of my desk. "You should go home."

"I don't have a home," I reply, feeling the effects of last night hitting me again.

"You don't have your apartment here anymore?"

Sighing, I stand from my desk and grab my purse. "No, I do. I just…"

"I don't know what happened down there, Willow, but it's nice to have you back." Katrina smiles politely, but it doesn't meet her eyes.

"It's good to be back," I lie before leaving my office and heading out to my car, driving to some place besides my apartment so I don't have to be alone again because that's the last thing I want right now.

***

"Mandy?" I call out as I walk through the front door. The house is quiet, but then the sound of a cupboard shutting in the kitchen has my feet moving in that direction.

"Willow?" Mandy walks around the corner, clutching two cups of coffee. The woman who is the closest thing I have to a mother smiles in greeting, extending a cup that I gladly intercept from her hand. "How are you doing?"

"That is a loaded question," I reply with a sigh as I follow her to the couch, depositing my purse on the floor before taking a seat in the cushioned chair across from her. My lack of sleep is catching up to me, and even though I really should try to rest, I called her as soon as I left the office. She might be able to help me work through everything I'm feeling because she's one of the only people in my life who actually knew my parents.

She knows how much their deaths have affected me.

My next call is Shauna, but I need sleep before I talk to her.

Mandy moves her long, light brown hair that's streaked with grays behind her shoulders and then settles in. "Well, let's hear all the details then. You didn't sound like yourself on the phone."

"Believe me. I don't feel like myself at all right now."

Mandy was my mother's friend from college who ended up being my guardian along with her husband, Jason, when my parent's died. I was nine when I finally asked why I looked nothing like them, and that was years after they divorced, but that's when my entire world felt like it truly came crashing down.

Growing up without your parents is something I wouldn't wish on anyone. But knowing they chose to put themselves in a dangerous situation that ended up costing them their lives is a detail I still can't seem to get over, even thirty-two years later, and especially after these past few months.

Two journalists seeking the thrill of televised war, my parents ventured overseas to chase fame and a story, and left me back home with their friends, who ultimately ended up raising me upon their untimely deaths.

Mandy and Jason didn't tell me all the details right away surrounding how they died. But when I got older, they gave me the brutal truth.

I don't really keep in contact with Jason anymore, but Mandy and I have remained close. In fact, she feels more like an older sister to me than a mom most of the time. No one in my life has ever seemed to fill that gap, this hole of not knowing where I came from or all of the memories I lost with my parents being gone. And the older I got, the more comfortable that hole became, until the letter from Mr. Sheppard showed up.

"I got a letter about two months ago from a man that knew my parents," I start, filling her in on what led me to Carrington Cove. When I tell her about the details of the letter and who it was from, I watch the goosebumps pebble on her skin.

"Holy shit."

"Yeah. Tell me about it."

Her mouth is hanging open for a few seconds before she finally clears her throat. "I...I honestly had no idea about any of this, Willow," she says, pleading with her eyes for me to believe her.

"I figured. You've always been pretty honest with me." I shrug, focusing my sight on the cup of coffee in my hands.

She nods, bracing herself for me to continue. "So you went down there..."

"Yes. I had to meet with his attorney that sent the letter, and that meeting left me with an even bigger surprise."

"What did he say?"

"The man left me a house."

Her eyebrows shoot up. "A house?"

"Yup." I take a long drink of my coffee. "It's old, and needed a lot of work, so I've been working remotely down there for the past two months, overseeing the renovations. The house was finished this week, but..."

She narrows her eyes at me. "But what?"

I shake my head, thinking back to the conversation with Dallas last night, how close I was to having a future I wanted with someone. Finally. "There's something about that place, Mandy. It's right on the beach. It has vacation home written all over it. Even just standing on the front porch and looking out over the ocean...I don't know..."

"Are you thinking about keeping it?"

"This week I decided I would." I meet her eyes. "Because I also met someone down there."

"Oh."

Smiling even though thinking about Dallas makes my heart ache, I say, "His name is Dallas. He's a former Marine who now owns a restaurant and bar. He's stubborn and bossy, strong and funny, and..."

"You want to be with him."

My lips start to tremble again. "I did."

Her brow furrows. "*Did?* What happened?"

"His dad is the man who left me the house. The house Dallas has wanted for *years* but had no idea it belonged to his father. Last night he found out his mother and I had been keeping the truth from him."

"Oh my." She takes a sip of her coffee. "I take it things didn't end well then..."

"No, they didn't."

Mandy studies me from across the living room. "You know, Willow. I get why you are the way you are—"

"And what way is that?"

She smiles softly. "Closed off. A workhorse. Impenetrable."

"Okay..." I bite, feeling defensive almost instantly.

"You are that way because it allows you to maintain control. You're the one who gets to make the decisions about what you do, where you go, who you see. But this is one decision that was made for you, and I can tell it's rattling your resolve."

I huff out a laugh. "That's putting it mildly."

"When's the last time you took a vacation, or any time off work for that matter? When's the last time you felt like this about a place? When's the last time you let yourself fall in love?"

"Never," I admit in a whisper.

"Exactly. And just those few months away have seemed to lighten your aura."

I cock a brow at her. "Is this something new you're into that you didn't tell me about?"

She laughs. "No. I'm just saying your energy is different. I can tell you're conflicted, but it's almost as if it's not just irritation that has you in knots. It's the fact that you want to be there with him, but don't *want* to want that."

Damn. She hit the nail on the head.

"All of me wants that, Mandy. But it's just so inconvenient with work and he was so angry with me…"

"Most things that change our lives are inconvenient," she counters. "But like you said, you want that life for yourself, so you'll figure out a way to make it happen. When people care about you, they get upset with you sometimes."

"But Dallas walked away and now I'm not sure where we stand."

Just those few words have tears building in my eyes. And I don't ever allow myself to cry in front of people, even Mandy. But I guess that's changed, too, because I've never cried this much in my life.

He walked away. The second things got hard, he abandoned me.

Just like my parents did.

This is why it's easier to be alone.

"Oh, honey." She stands from the couch and walks over to me, scooting onto the cushion as I adjust myself to make room for her. "It's okay," she says as I lean my head on her shoulder, resisting the urge to let the emotions I've been holding under the surface break through.

"Maybe it's time to let go of some of the anger, Willow. Maybe this is all part of your journey to healing. To learning how to let people in."

"I was doing fine, Mandy. Life was exactly as it should be, and then I got that stupid letter and it drudged up all of these thoughts, regrets, doubts, insecurities..." I swipe a tear from my cheek.

"It made you feel."

I nod, not stable enough to respond as I choke back a sob. "I don't cry, Mandy. That's not me. Emotions are a sign of weakness." *At least that's what I've always told myself.*

"No, they're not. They're a sign of strength, Willow. And I think it's time you let some of yours out." She holds me as I shudder in her arms, giving me time to gather myself before she speaks again. "You know, I never wanted kids, Willow," she whispers, and her admission has my head popping up.

I wipe under my eyes and nose. "What?" It comes out as a whisper.

She smiles, brushing my hair behind my ear. "I didn't want children. I felt like that wasn't what I wanted my life to be about. Women shouldn't have to have children to feel validated. It's a societal norm that women have been told they *should* want, but I didn't. And Jason and I had plans for our life. But then your parents died and suddenly I was thrown into this role that I resented."

I swallow hard as her words ring out loud, wondering if this is her way of dropping another bomb on me all at once so it doesn't feel like I'm being hit over and over again—like ripping off a Band-Aid instead.

Am I the reason they divorced? Because they didn't want me?

I don't think I could take knowing that on top of everything else right now.

"But the second I signed the papers as your guardian, I realized that this was the role I was *meant* to have—to be here for *you*—this little girl who had part of her world ripped from her far too young. Your presence opened up this entirely different side of me, and I could never regret having *you* in my life."

"Mandy—"

She lifts her hand, gesturing for me to wait. "So the reason I'm telling you this is because I feel like this is a similar experience for you. It's not ideal. I know it's stirring up all kinds of shit for you. But maybe this is one of those forks in the road that will change the entire direction of your life if you let it." She brushes a tear from my cheek. "Open yourself up to the possibilities. Prepare for the worst, but hope for the best. Go back to him and try to work it out, and see if you can finally find a place where you belong and people who make you feel that way too."

"Thank you," I whisper.

"I'm always here. But you and I both know you already know what you want. And I have a selfish desire to visit the coast. Knowing you're there may just make the trip worth it."

"The house isn't a mess anymore, thank God."

"A little mess never stopped me. Some of the biggest messes turn out to be the most beautiful masterpieces when they're complete."

God, I hope she's right.

***

"Um...that looks like the inside of your apartment, Willow."

I'm sitting in my bed, holding the phone up on my knees so we can see each other. "It is."

Shauna sighs, resting her chin in her hand. "I take it things didn't go well with Dallas then?"

"He saw the letter from his dad, Shauna. I left it on the bed when we were talking and forgot to put it away."

"Oh, Willow. I'm so sorry." Concern is etched into every line of her face.

"It's okay. I came home and have been here for a few days now, trying to find the courage to go back and make some decisions."

"Are you thinking about selling the house now?"

"I think I might."

That's where my head has been for the past forty-eight hours. After talking to Mandy, I've been working from the office during the day and sitting on my couch at night, wondering if trying to reconcile is even worth it. If things got that ugly during our first fight, do we really belong together? Dallas and I might think we want the same things, but there's no guarantee.

"Why would you do that? Don't you want to try to work things out with Dallas?"

"He said some horrible things, Shauna. If the man really feels that way about me, I'm not sure I can forgive him."

His texts say that he's remorseful, but I'm still hurt. Ever since I left Carrington Cove, he's texted me every day—pictures of the sunrise from the house, pictures of him eating blueberry muffins from the Sunshine Bakery, and the latest, a picture of the gaggle of geese hanging out in front of my house.

They're waiting for you to return. Come back to me, Willow.

She adjusts Hudson in her arms. "Willow, I hate to break this to you, but that's going to happen. Hell, Forrest and I have said all kinds of shit to each other that we both wish we could take back. It's part of being in a relationship—making mistakes, learning to communicate, and saying sorry… a lot."

"I just don't know how we move past this."

"You won't know until you talk. Look at Forrest and me, hun. We survived and there were plenty of hard discussions that got us to this point. Nothing in life is guaranteed, but we can't let it stop us from living." I stare off into space. "Do you love him?"

"I do," I say without hesitation. "I've never felt about anyone the way I feel about him." And that's the truth.

"Do you see a future with him?"

"I thought I did. He's changed my life, Shauna."

"Then don't you think that's worth fighting for?"

"Yes."

"Then stop wallowing, put your big girl panties on, and get your man. Welcome to being in an adult relationship. You're going to fight, you're going to disagree. That doesn't mean you just walk away."

Laughing, I push my hair out of my face and voice the concerns that scare me the most. "What if he doesn't want me anymore? What if he's changed his mind and realizes that I'm too much for his small-town life?"

"First of all, I doubt it. And secondly, you'll never know unless you ask."

"I'm scared," I admit, looking at my best friend through the phone.

"As you should be. Anything worthwhile is scary. But trust me from my own experience, going after what you want is worth it."

"Okay," I breathe out. "I'll go back, but if it doesn't work out, then I'm moving to Texas. I'll be your live-in best friend."

Shauna taps her chin with her finger. "Live-in childcare? I think Forrest could get on board with that."

"I love you, Shauna."

"I love you too, Willow. Now go get your man."

***

I took one more day at home to go back into Marshall Advertising and speak with my board of directors, letting them know about my impending plans should things go the way I want with Dallas. They were all extremely supportive and respected my decision. And as much as my company means to me, my time in Carrington Cove has shown me that there's more to life than work.

And that's my new focus for my future.

As I drive back into town, I roll down the windows of my car, letting the ocean breeze whip through my hair. The smell of the salty water, the view of the lights—it all makes me look back on each trip I've taken to and from here and how each time, this view has become more familiar and meaningful.

But this return holds the most weight because the next steps of my new life depend on how this trip goes.

When I pull into the back of the Bayshore house, I shut the car off and stare at the structure, the place that led me here in the first place, knowing that regardless of what happens, I will never regret coming down here at the direction of that letter.

This town, this house, and the people here have helped me see what really matters, and those things will be my focus moving forward in my life, despite where I end up.

I head up the gravel walkway on the side of the house, ready to step up on the porch, but the gaggle of geese that have been M.I.A. for weeks are waiting for me tonight of all nights, stalking toward me like a gang that is out for blood.

Just fucking lovely.

"Get out of here!" I shout, holding my purse by the handle, swinging it back and forth, ready to use it as a weapon, if necessary. These birds are messing with a woman who's on the brink of a mental breakdown and huge life shift, so they have no idea what I'm capable of right now.

"HONK!" The leader turns his head to the side so our eyes meet, stopping in his path.

"Honk right back, asshole. You wanna fight?" He flaps his wings like he's riling himself up and for a moment, I debate doing it right back to him. But I refrain. "Fine then. It's your funeral."

"Are you planning bird murder?" Dallas's voice scares the shit out of me as I turn to my right and see his face behind the window, a small crack in the opening allowing me to hear him.

Distracted, I turn to him and drop my purse to my side. "What the hell are you doing in my house?"

"Do you want to wait outside while I answer that?"

The geese start honking again as I twist my head back and forth between them and the man I haven't seen in nearly a week—the one I desperately need to talk to. "Not particularly."

He moves from the window, opens the front door, and pops open an umbrella, blocking the geese from the porch with just enough space that I can squeeze by, ducking inside the house. Dallas shuts the door behind me and then puts the umbrella away, setting it to the side before standing tall and holding my gaze with his own.

"How did you get in here?" I finally ask, breaking the silence even though I feel frozen in place.

"No *thank you* for helping you inside?" he asks, a teasing lilt to his lips.

I set my purse on the floor by the door and plant my hands on my hips, staring at the man that has made me feel alive for the first time in my life, his mere proximity overwhelming me after five long days away. My body remembers our connection, but my heart is still nervous about whatever he has to say. "You're really going to start with the manners right now?"

"Seemed appropriate. And to answer your question, I've been here for days, waiting for you to come back." I watch his Adam's apple bob up and down as he swallows roughly. "Penn gave me his key."

I guess I shouldn't expect anything less from those two.

We stand there, staring at each other, and just remembering how it feels to be in his arms has my resolve dwindling fast. But then my eyes shift, and that's when I see what he's done with the house, everything so bright I'm surprised I didn't notice before.

Electric candles fill every empty surface, flickering softly as the sun sets over the ocean, casting the house in a twilight glow. Everything is bathed in a soft, golden light that takes my breath away.

On the kitchen counter sits a basket of blueberry muffins and next to it is a framed picture of us from the Carrington Cove Games, me staring up at him after we won, smiles plastered on both of our faces.

And that's when I surrender.

"Willow..." he starts, but I drop my hands and rush over to him, wrapping my arms around his neck as he intercepts me, the warmth of him cocooning me and letting me know that it's safe to fall apart. The moment his arms band around me and squeeze, my entire body relaxes and my resolve breaks. "Fuck, I'm sorry, baby."

"Me too. I'm so sorry, Dallas." My body shudders as I leap into his arms. He carries us over to the couch, sitting down with me still clinging to him.

God, it feels so right being back in his arms.

How could I ever think I could live without him?

"You have nothing to be sorry for, Goose. You didn't do anything wrong." His lips press against my temple, holding me to him so tightly as though he's afraid I might disappear.

"But I lied to you."

"My mother asked you to, baby. And you listened. I can't fault you for that."

I lean back so I can see his eyes, wiping furiously under my own. "And I hated that she did, but..."

"She told me everything, Willow, every detail I needed to know about my dad and why he left this house to you." He brushes my hair from my face, studying every inch of me before sighing out loud. "I get it now. Your parents, the way they died...I can't blame him for wanting to make things right in the only way he could think of."

His understanding gives me pause, especially at the mention of my parents. For days, I've been ruminating on every circumstance that led me here, and the one emotion I still haven't come to terms with is my anger—so I let it out.

"But *I'm* mad, Dallas," I say through clenched teeth. "I'm so fucking mad—at my parents for choosing their jobs over me and leaving me to survive without them my entire life, for the hundreds of moments throughout my childhood that I missed out on or were ruined because my parents weren't here, at your dad for leaving me this stupid house that I went and fell in love with, and for the fact that he hid it from you, preventing you from fulfilling your dream."

"Willow—" he starts, but I cut him off.

"But most of all, I'm fucking mad that coming here made me feel all of this," I say, tapping the center of my chest. "Every emotion that I've been burying my entire life because I knew what confronting them would mean—it would be like a thousand shards of glass piercing my chest, my eyes burning with tears until I had none left, and agony overtaking me for wanting a life beyond the secluded one I'd built." Tears start falling down my face, the tears you cry from anger and frustration, not necessarily sadness—but there certainly is anguish in there too. "I'm mad that I want this life now, but it's all been tainted by lies, secrets, and heartache."

Dallas tilts his head at me, cupping my face in his hands. "I want you here, Willow. For days, all I've been dying to tell you is that…that I want you to stay with me, and I'm a fucking idiot for the things I said to you. I'm. So. Fucking. Sorry." A deep breath makes his chest rise. "But I *need* you. I don't want to live without you. My father brought you to me, and I'd be a fucking fool to let you go."

I shake my head at him, sniffling and wiping away my tears. "How can you be sure? How can you trust that the truth behind our connection won't haunt us later?" I turn my head away from him for a moment. "I don't blame you for being upset, but I know that this is a lot to take in. Trust me, that's what I've been trying to process for the past five days…"

He cuts me off, gripping my chin firmly and forcing me to face him again. "No. You listen to me, Willow Marshall, and you listen good." Planting both of his hands on the sides of my face, he forces me to look at him and nowhere else. "You had your chance to talk and now it's mine."

Our eyes lock and my heart rate spikes.

This is it.

This is either the end or the beginning.

"I know you're pissed right now, baby. Hell, I'm fucking mad still too. But ultimately, I realized that none of what happened in the past matters anymore. We can't change it. We can only move forward. And I want to do that with you." A soft smile forms on his lips as he says, "I want to be your fucking anchor, Willow." He takes my hand and places it on his chest, right over his tattoo, making my pulse fire faster. "I want to keep you here, in the same place as me, and build a life with you. I want to hold you and protect you from any storm that comes our way."

A smile starts to spread across my face. "And I want to fight off all the geese that try to attack us." Laughter escapes my lips. "I want to wake up next to you every morning in this house, staring at the ocean, knowing each day we have together is better than the last" He leans his forehead on mine, breathing me in. And I take the same moment to take a breath of relief as well. "I'm in *love* with you, Willow. Every fucking part of you. And no matter how we met, or what brought you here, I can't deny that. You are the piece of my life that was missing."

The tension in my shoulders dissipates, the tightness in my chest starts to loosen, and my stomach does a little flip as I whisper, "I love you too."

Our mouths meet and then I feel like I can finally breathe again. When our tongues touch, my entire body comes alive.

This is where you belong, Willow.

Here.

With this man.

"God, I love you," he mumbles against my lips again, encasing me in his arms.

"I'm sorry, Dallas. I'm so sorry…"

"Stop fucking apologizing."

"I just don't want this to be a sore spot in our future." I rub our noses together. "Please promise me that we move forward from here. No living in the past…"

He stands, keeping me locked on his waist and in his arms, taking me into the kitchen. He places me gently on the counter and then grabs the framed picture from two weeks ago, holding it up so I can see it clearly.

"This is the moment I knew I couldn't live without you." His eyes flick to the picture and then back to mine. "We were a team that day, Willow, and that's what I want from here on out—to be someone you can count on no matter what."

"This will forever be one of my favorite days, Dallas." I trail my finger along the silver frame.

"Mine too, baby. And I swear, I'll never leave you like that again."

I stare back at him. "Please don't. I don't think my heart could take it a second time."

"I promise."

"I've never felt like I belonged somewhere before. Do you get that?" He nods. "But that day, I did."

Dallas sets the frame on the counter and holds my face in his hands again. "Carrington Cove *is* your home now, Willow, and you belong here with me."

Chapter Twenty-Two

Willow

"I just need you to be patient with me." My fingers run across Dallas's chest as we lie in bed, staring out the sliding glass door as the sun rises over the ocean. Last night we spent hours reconnecting, declaring our love for one another with our bodies, and now a new day begins in this new life that I've chosen for myself—*my choice*. No one else's. "I've never done the relationship thing, and I know I'm going to mess it up."

"We're in the same boat, Goose. Don't worry." He presses his lips to my temple, cradling me in his arms. "We'll figure out what works for us. First promise though...no running away from talking about tough shit again."

"I like the sound of that."

Dallas stares down at me, his head propped up on his pillow. "I do too. This is it for me, Willow. No one else will ever come between us, okay? I won't let anything dull that fiery spirit of yours, and I promise to love you for who you are because that's who I fell in love with, scars and all."

I trace the scar on his ribs. "Mine run deep, Dallas. I don't know if they will ever heal."

"They will, but not in the way you think." He stares down at where my fingers touch his skin. "They dull, become less noticeable, but still hold a story. It's just easier to accept them as time goes on, like they're an extension of you. Scars are fascinating, Willow. And I love yours. They brought you to me."

"I love you." Our lips meet and the contentment that rushes through me tells me that I'm right where I'm supposed to be. This man knows me better than almost anyone else, and he brought me *home*. I fight off a yawn as I say, "But there's still a lot of things to figure out."

"Such as?"

"Well, what are we going to tell your brothers and sister?"

He closes his eyes. "I haven't thought that far ahead. After I spoke to my mom, my only thought was getting you back. I know we need to talk to them. They deserve to know about Dad and how he's connected to you, but it was honestly the last thing on my mind the past few days."

"I don't want them to hate me for lying to you and them," I whisper.

"They won't. They all had very different relationships with him. And I know Mom will help explain things as well."

"And your mom...is she okay with..." I gesture between us. "This?"

He narrows his eyes at me. "I think you already know the answer to that question, Willow."

Huffing out a laugh, I reply, "I mean, she knows how I feel about you, why it was so hard for me to keep this to myself. But after the two of you talked, I wasn't sure…"

Dallas presses a finger to my lips. "I told her you're the one, and I made myself pretty clear on that."

I swallow down the lump in my throat. "Oh."

I heard Dallas say that this was it for him, but that reassurance, hearing him call me *the one*—it just makes it all so much more real, even after last night.

Part of me was afraid I would wake up this morning and it would have all been a dream, that this adventure of mine was all a figment of my imagination.

But it's very real.

And my mind and heart are finally accepting it.

"Oh? I thought I made myself clear…" He pulls me against his chest. "It's you and me, Goose. I'm all in." He drags his nose along my neck before our lips meet softly. "You own me. I'm stuck in your orbit and have no desire to leave. Whatever galaxy you exist in is the one I belong in, too."

"That was very poetic of you."

The corner of his mouth lifts. "I have my moments. I may not have much experience with relationships, but with you?" He brushes my hair from my face. "It just comes easy."

Running my hand up his chest, I say, "Care to make any rules for our relationship then, since neither of us know what we're doing?"

"I like that idea." Dallas taps his chin with his finger, staring up at the ceiling. Then he drops his gaze to mine again, and says, "Rule number one: always use your manners."

I giggle. "Especially during sex."

Dallas growls, burying his head in my neck. "Hell yeah."

As his lips dance over my skin, I add, "Rule number two: always have blueberry muffins ready for my breakfast on the weekends." I've decided to cut down on my muffin intake since my pants started to get a bit snug last week, but I figure a weekend treat is still acceptable.

Damn those little pillows of heaven.

"I can do that." I feel Dallas grow hard against my leg and then he starts shifting. "Rule number three: always have your pussy ready for *my* breakfast on *any* given day." He dips below the blanket, shuffling down the mattress while pressing me on my back, and finds me wet and ready as he drags his tongue through my slit.

Moaning, I arch my back and say, "I think rule number three is my favorite."

"Mine too, Willow," he mumbles against me. "Mine too."

***

"Why do I get the feeling you're about to tell us someone died?" Penn stares across the living room at me and Dallas, sitting in the giant cushioned chair together, me perched on his lap.

"It's not that, but we do have something we need to talk to you guys about." Dallas looks at Katherine, who nods in approval.

It's Sunday night, which means family dinner night in the Sheppard house.

But this family dinner is going to be a little more serious than the last.

After Dallas and I reconciled, we had dinner with his mom, who apologized profusely for the heartache she caused us both. It was that night that Dallas also gave me the picture of me as a little girl that my parents had with them the day that they died.

I bawled like a baby for almost an hour.

And then he showed me and his mother the letter his father left. Katherine and I cried for another thirty minutes.

But the three of us agreed that the rest of the family should know about all the circumstances around what led me here, and so that's why we're gathered in the living room right now, having just enjoyed Katherine's homemade chili and cornbread before sullying the evening with heavy emotions.

"Do you wanna start, Goose?" Dallas asks as I bite my thumbnail. He pulls my hand from my mouth and raises his brows at me.

"Yeah, I guess."

Hazel nearly jumps out of her chair. "Oh my God! Are you pregnant, Willow?"

My head spins toward her in a flash. "What? No!"

"She's not pregnant, Hazelnut." Dallas looks at me for confirmation. I shake my head. "Nope. Not pregnant." Although as of last night, we agreed not to use condoms anymore, so the possibility is definitely there if my pill fails.

But we both know the risks and we're okay with that.

"I want you guys to know what led me to Carrington Cove. It wasn't just some random inheritance in which I got the Bayshore house." I turn to Dallas and take a deep breath. "I was left the house by your father."

You could hear a pin drop in that room for several minutes before the questions started to pour out. And after about an hour of questions and plenty of tears, the entire Sheppard family knew our story.

"This is fucking wild," Parker declares, draining the rest of his beer before standing from the couch, pacing for a minute before heading to the kitchen for another.

Hazel dabs a tissue under her eyes, staring at us from the couch still. "I know it's sad, but I think it's so romantic that dad led you here, Willow."

Dallas grins at his sister as he pulls me closer. "You'll have to forgive Hazel. She's a hopeless romantic."

"I am, all right? I admit it. This is like romance book worthy." Hazel launches herself from the couch and heads down the hall. "Ugh. I need to blow my nose again."

Penn stands from the couch and hovers over us, trepidation in his gaze. "So this is real?"

"It is." Dallas stands and looks him dead in the eye. "I went after what I want, and I got it."

"Then I'm happy for you." He looks to me and says, "Both of you." Penn pulls his older brother in for a hug, slapping his back before releasing him and turning to me once more. "So, you're not selling the house?"

Rising from the chair, I meet his gaze with a smile on my lips. "Nope. I'm here to stay."

"Good, because it didn't feel right the thought of you leaving."

Dallas's eyes meet mine almost instantly. "I couldn't have said it better myself, brother."

***

One Month Later

"I'm glad we came to an agreement." I stare at the computer screen, watching Thomas Fletcher, one of my biggest clients, smile from ear to ear.

"Me too, Willow. I miss seeing you around here, but Natalie and the team did me proud. This campaign is a winner. The sales have already been outstanding."

"I told you they would. You know I'm always here if you need my input, though."

"I appreciate that, but I must say, it's nice to see you with your hair down. You look…" He pauses while he searches for the correct word. "Content."

I glance above the computer, finding Dallas grinning at me, bouncing his eyebrows as he cooks us breakfast.

I am content, feeling more fulfilled and grounded than I have in my entire life.

And yes, my hair is down, because that's the way my live-in boyfriend likes it.

Dallas moved in shortly after we spoke with his family about their dad. It just made sense for him to stay with me in a space that was big enough for us both. The apartment above the restaurant is still there for those late nights if he needs it, but more often than not, he sneaks into our bed in the wee hours of the morning and wakes me up with his tongue between my legs.

Rule number three is definitely our favorite.

And now the man who wanted my house to begin with is finally living in it—*with me*.

"Well, that's what living by the beach will do for you, Thomas. Make you relax a bit. That and the right person to help you see what's truly important in life." My eyes meet Dallas's again, a hint of reverence in his gaze.

"Glad to hear it. We'll talk soon."

"Looking forward to it." I log off the call and then lean back in my chair, watching the muscles in Dallas's back clench and ripple as he moves, finishing our breakfast. "Well, that went well."

"And now you're done for the day?" He slides two eggs onto a plate and then butters two slices of toast.

"Yes, I am."

"Good, because we have a busy one ahead of us."

When I left D.C., I made an arrangement with the board of my company that allowed me to feel more comfortable with moving here permanently. The thought of leaving entirely wasn't what I wanted. I built the company myself, and still wanted ownership, but I was ready for far less responsibility. So, I stepped down as acting CEO, and let Natalie, my VP of marketing, step up. She was ecstatic about the opportunity, and I've been mentoring her as needed, as well as communicating with clients who have been with me since the beginning, like Thomas Fletcher.

I still have a say in certain campaigns. I still log on to calls and check my emails every day. But I have a much better work-life balance than I did before, one that is more conducive to living in a small town and dedicating time to the new man in my life—the only man I know I'll ever need. There are days where old habits try to sneak their way back in, but Dallas comforts me and encourages me to look out at the ocean to remember that change is good.

Like the waves lapping at the shore, change is unpredictable and sometimes scary, but it can wash away old scars and shape us into something new.

"Are you ready for today?" I reach for my cup of coffee, sipping on the now lukewarm liquid.

Dallas nods as he finishes plating our food. "It's gonna be a good game."

Bentley's soccer team made it to the championship match, and the final game is at eleven. After we eat, we have a few errands to run before heading over to the field.

My, how different my life looks after just a few months.

"You'd better eat up, Coach." I point to Dallas's plate as he brings both of our meals over to the table, taking a seat right next to me.

"Don't worry about me, Goose. The person you should be worrying about is Astrid."

I stab my eggs and bring a hefty bite to my mouth. "Oh, I know. She's been crazy lately with the bakery renovations and then during the games, she practically bites her fingernails off."

"She just gets invested like most parents. It's fun to see the boys win."

"I agree. And I enjoy watching you coach more than anything." I bounce my eyebrows at him this time.

"It's the backward hat and aviators, huh, Goose?"

"God, yes," I admit on a sigh. "It does it for me every time."

***

"Astrid, if you don't stop, you're not going to have a single fingernail left." I pull her hand from her mouth, holding it with my own instead.

"God, I hate this. Bentley wants this so much." She's practically vibrating with nerves as she stands next to me, so I stroke her arm, trying to offer her an ounce of comfort. We stare out at the field, watching the teams fight tooth and nail, each pass and missed goal amping up the anxiety on the sidelines.

"I know, hun. But losing is part of life too. He'll be fine either way." I'm really just speculating right now.

I never played sports. The only time I ever competed in anything was during the Carrington Cove Games and we won, so I honestly don't know what it's like to lose.

And to be an eleven-year-old and lose?

God, I hope he just wins so I don't have to experience that aftermath.

Astrid shakes her hands out at her sides, releasing mine from her grasp. "I'm just so on edge."

I watch her dance around, her eyes wild and her limbs jittery. "You are, more so than usual. Are you okay, girl?"

Her eyes dart over to mine quickly before returning right back to the field. "I'm—I'm fine."

"Uh, I don't believe you." I step in front of her, snapping my fingers in her face, which forces her eyes to meet mine. "Astrid Marie, what are you not telling me?"

"That's not my middle name."

"I don't care. There's something else going on here, and you'd better spill. We don't keep secrets from each other, remember?"

After the whole thing with Dallas, I confessed the story of what led me here to Astrid. We cried together, and I told her how sorry I was for keeping the whole tale from her. She was very understanding, but we promised not to keep secrets from each other anymore, which eventually led to her telling me how she really feels about Penn.

As if anyone with two eyes in this town didn't already know.

Astrid chews on her bottom lip. "Willow..."

"Do you need an attorney? Did you do something illegal?" My pulse starts to climb as I wait for her answer.

"What? No!"

"Then what is it?"

She looks around before leaning over and whispering, "I had sex with Penn."

"What?" I shout, drawing attention to us as Astrid's eyes widen. "Oh my God, I'm so sorry," I whisper now, even though the damage has been done.

"Jesus, Willow. Now everyone is going to know." She buries her head in her hands.

I pull her hands away and force her to look at me, lowering my voice and leaning in closer to her. "No, they won't. All they heard me say was 'what.'" We both blow out a breath at the same time. "Now, tell me how this happened. And more importantly," I say, arching a brow at her, "was it good?"

Astrid groans, closing her eyes and sighing. "It was incredible. So hot. There was frosting involved." She opens her eyes and chews on her bottom lip.

"Frosting?" *Damn. I didn't think Penn or Astrid had it in them.*

"Yes. It happened at the bakery. But it can't happen again." She shakes her head furiously as our team scores a goal. "Never again."

We pause our conversation to celebrate.

As soon as the game starts back up, I turn my head toward her once more. "Why not? I thought that's what you wanted?"

"I can't, Willow. It's Penn…he's my friend. *Was* my friend?" Her brow furrows. "How do you stay friends with a man after you sleep with him?"

"Brandon has been gone for four years, Astrid. And it *is* Penn. He wouldn't let this come between you two."

"I know, but…" She takes a deep breath and says, "There's something that Penn doesn't know. And when he finds out, it's going to ruin our friendship."

My mouth falls open as a whistle rings out on the field. But I don't turn to see what happened, because it turns out Astrid *has* been keeping secrets, and I feel like this is a big one.

THE END

***

Not ready to say goodbye to Dallas and Willow? Download a special bonus epilogue here and get a glimpse at their future!

***

If you or someone you know is suffering with PTSD, please contact Headstrong Project or Wounded Warrior Project for more information.
And to all of those who have served or are family to those that serve, I thank you for your service.

***

Curious about Penn and Astrid's story? Don't worry. You can find out what happens in *Someone You Deserve*, coming Fall of 2024!

Curious about Shauna and her husband Forrest? Their story can be read in *Everything But You*, book 3 in my Newberry Springs series. (But it can totally be read as a standalone.)

And the couple that wanted to buy Willow's house, McKenzie and Dylan?

They have a story, too, in *McKenzie's Turn to Fall*.

Also By Harlow James

The Ladies Who Brunch (rom-coms with a ton of spice)
Never Say Never (Charlotte and Damien)
No One Else (Amelia and Ethan)
Now's The Time (Penelope and Maddox)
Not As Planned (Noelle and Grant)
Nice Guys Still Finish (Jeffrey and Ariel)

***

The Newberry Springs (Gibson Brothers) Series
Everything to Lose (Wyatt & Kelsea)
Everything He Couldn't (Walker & Evelyn)
Everything But You (Forrest & Shauna)

***

The California Billionaires Series (rom coms with heart and heat)

My Unexpected Serenity (Wes and Shayla)

My Unexpected Vow (Hayes and Waverly)

My Unexpected Family (Silas and Chloe)

***

The Emerson Falls Series (smalltown romance with a found family friend group)

Tangled (Kane & Olivia)

Enticed (Cooper & Clara)

Captivated (Cash and Piper)

Revived (Luke and Rachel)

Devoted (Brooks and Jess)

***

Lost and Found in Copper Ridge

A holiday romance in which two people book a stay in a cabin for the same amount of time thanks to a serendipitous $5 bill.

Guilty as Charged

An intense opposites attract standalone that will melt your kindle. He's an ex-con construction worker. She's a lawyer looking for passion.

McKenzie's Turn to Fall

A holiday romance where a romance author falls for her neighborhood butcher.

Acknowledgements

The excitement I feel from finally having this book out in the world is unreal.

This story—it's been in my mind for years. A letter leads a woman to a town she has no idea existed. She inherits a house, fights with a grumpy bar owner, and then she falls in love. Add in wild geese and a blueberry muffin obsession, and you have the perfect recipe for a smalltown romance I wish could be real.

I started writing this story in the Fall of 2021. I got about halfway through and I was struggling with it, and then I got the idea for Never Say Never, and followed my heart and gut to write The Ladies Who Brunch series. I don't regret that decision at all, but I knew this story would get it's time when it was right, and now here we are.

By the time you read this book, the second and third books in the series will have already been written. I've been living in Carrington Cove for months now and I can't wait to share everything I have planned for these characters and this town. AND this series will have the first simultaneous audio releases from me, and I'm so grateful to be able to to do this moving forward!

To my husband: Thank you for believing in me and cheering me on every step of the way. Thank you for traveling with me, investing in my success, and being my person, my best friend, and the man that inspires all of my book boyfriends. I love you.

To my beta readers: Keely, Emily, Kelly, and Carolina: you four are the best voices I have in my corner. Each of you gives me the advice, feedback, and support that I need in your own way. I'm so grateful to have the four of you in my corner still after all this time. I love you all and appreciate you more than you'll ever know.

And to my readers: thank you for supporting me, whether you've been here since the beginning, or you're brand new. I LOVE this hobby turned business of mine. It's an amazing feeling to be able to create art for someone to enjoy and forming a relationship from that. I never take my readers for granted and know that there would be no Harlow James without you.

So thank you for supporting a wife and mom who found a hobby that she loves.

Connect with Harlow James

Follow me on Amazon

Follow me on Instagram

Follow me on Facebook

Join my Facebook Group: https://www.facebook.com/groups/494991441142710/

Follow me on Goodreads

Follow me on Book Bub

Subscribe to my Newsletter for Updates on New Releases and Give-aways

Website

Printed in Great Britain
by Amazon